ULTIMATUM: MARRIAGE
BY
ANN MAJOR

AND

FOR THE SAKE OF
THE SECRET CHILD
BY
YVONNE LINDSAY

How ironic that the spot his bride had chosen for their wedding had once been the most popular dueling ground in New Orleans.

Too bad the twenty-first century was more civilized. If Jake could have called his bride's father out and shot him, he would have.

Jake wanted to hate Alicia for complicating his life, but reason told him he was equally to blame. He didn't want to marry her, but with every word that the priest uttered binding him to Alicia Butler, his desire for her grew until it felt like a crushing weight. Indeed, ever since he'd agreed to the marriage, thoughts of Alicia in his bed had consumed him.

They say a little piece of paper doesn't matter; that it changes nothing.

They don't know anything. He felt trapped. Doomed. At the same time his body raged to have her again.

Dear Reader,

I believe that love is the most powerful positive force in the world and that if we open our hearts, it will find us and change our lives for the better. Not that I think we always get to choose who we love or when we fall in love, but isn't that what makes it so interesting?

After Alicia's wealthy father is accused of embezzlement on a grand scale and arrested, she is devastated. Just when she thinks she's lost everything and has nowhere to turn, she discovers she's pregnant by Jake Claiborne, the man who slept with her and then reported her dad to the feds.

Although she'd rather never see Jake again, she knocks on his door and tells him they're going to have a baby.

Having lost her own mother young, Alicia has always longed to be part of a loving family. Naturally, she wants this for her baby as well. At first she sees no possibility of realizing her dream in her temporary marriage of convenience to Jake, but slowly, miraculously, she finds ways to build on what they feel for one another until she does.

Enjoy,

Ann Major

ULTIMATUM: MARRIAGE

BY
ANN MAJOR

All the characters in this book have no existence outside the imagination of
the author, and have no relation whatsoever to anyone bearing the same name
or names. They are not even distantly inspired by any individual known or
unknown to the author, and all the incidents are pure invention.

Published in Great Britain 2011
by Mills & Boon, an imprint of Harlequin (UK) Limited,
Eton House, 18-24 Paradise Road, Richmond, Surrey TW9 1SR

© Ann Major 2010

ISBN: 978 0 263 88319 0

51-1011

Harlequin (UK) policy is to use papers that are natural, renewable and
recyclable products and made from wood grown in sustainable forests. The
logging and manufacturing processes conform to the legal environmental
regulations of the country of origin.

Printed and bound in Spain
by Blackprint CPI, Barcelona

Ann Major lives in Texas with her husband of many years and is the mother of three grown children. She has a master's degree from Texas A&M at Kingsville, Texas, and is a former English teacher. She is a founding board member of the Romance Writers of America and a frequent speaker at writers' groups.

Ann loves to write; she considers her ability to do so a gift. Her hobbies include hiking in the mountains, sailing, ocean kayaking, traveling and playing the piano. But most of all she enjoys her family. Visit her website at www.annmajor.com.

This book is dedicated to my talented editor,
Krista Stroever.

One

"Sorry, Claiborne. The decision's been made. You're off the project. A lot of people don't like all the notoriety and publicity you've been getting lately because of your association with Mitchell Butler and his daughter, Alicia."

Jake knew better than to defend himself by saying he was a victim of Butler, too.

"I'm just the messenger," the caller said.

Jake clenched the phone but said nothing more. He wouldn't beg.

Not that he hadn't tried to defend himself to the press earlier in the week after they'd set up base camps outside his home and office. All he'd accomplished was to give the reporters words to twist in such a way as to make him look like he was guilty of having been a partner to Butler's embezzlement scheme.

A final click was followed by a dial tone.

For a second Jake thought about Mitchell Butler and his beautiful daughter. Had she aided and abetted her father?

Jake Claiborne felt his headache build as he replaced the telephone. Not that he hadn't been expecting such a call.

He wouldn't think about *her.* Or the night he'd spent in her arms. Or how cool and aloof she'd been ever since. Not that he could blame her. Hell, he and Hayes Daniels, his twin brother's CEO, had turned Mitchell into the feds the day after Jake had made love to her.

No doubt she was as guilty as her father. To think or feel anything about such a witch was a recipe for more disaster. No, the thing to do was to move on.

For a long moment he stared down at the miniature New Orleans he'd built. The structures, which were composed of cardboard, plastic and painted foam, looked vivid and exciting on his table against the window. When his icy-blue gaze swept to the model of the brazenly dramatic stadium that until five minutes ago he and his team had still dreamed of building, the hammer in his right temple pounded even more viciously.

Don't think about her.

Mitchell Butler had been rich and powerful and admired—until six weeks ago. Now his shipyard was bankrupt and his plans for a merger with Claiborne Energy defunct. His pampered daughter had been fired from her job as editor of the *Louisiana Observer.* Millions were missing from Butler's offshore bank in the Caymans and from Houses for Hurricane Victims. Or was it billions? The figures quoted by the media seemed to grow exponentially.

Mitchell was broke and so were his investors. Butler,

who was the most despised man in Louisiana, was responsible for ruining a lot of people besides Jake.

Tempted to smash the little buildings to the floor, Jake made a fist. He needed a few moments to himself to get his mind off the Butlers and regain his control.

Leaning against his desk and relaxing his hand, he stood there for a long moment, wondering how he'd tell his employees the bad news.

Better to face them now. Better to get it over with.

He jammed his hands into the pockets of his faded jeans and strode out of his private office into that of his secretary.

"Vanessa. Have everybody assemble in the boardroom. Say, in five minutes. And hold my calls."

Vanessa, who had twenty years on him and a will of iron hardened by a bitter marital experience, continued to tap steadily on her keyboard. She was a formidable worker, A single mother, she'd raised her three boys on her own.

Jake stepped closer to her desk and whispered, "It's not my fault your ex cheated on you and got that other woman pregnant."

Frowning, she pulled her gaze from her computer screen and looked up at him.

"Just checking to see if you even knew I was here or heard a word I said," he said.

"Five minutes. Boardroom. Everybody assemble. Hold calls." She poked her pencil into her bun, whirled, got on the intercom and barked out the order.

Ten minutes later, his headache much worse, Jake stood before sixty of his employees.

"I have some bad news," he said, stiffening when they whitened. He disliked disappointing those who counted on him almost as much as he hated failing.

"We can't get the funding we need to build the stadium. Jones won't even pay for our latest revisions to the designs...so I'm afraid I have no choice but to..."

He was about to mention he would be calling quite a few people into his office to discuss their termination when Vanessa whirled toward him looking as dark as those first ominous storm bands on the horizon that signaled a hurricane. She slapped a phone into his palm.

She was frowning so coldly he knew better than to ask what could possibly be more important than his informing his employees that because of Mitchell Butler he was going to have to let quite a few of them go.

"Your house alarm system went off. Your service says it's broken glass and that a perimeter has been breached."

"So? Tell them to send the police."

Vanessa's thin, painted eyebrows arched. "I did. Officer Thomas, who's on the phone, is there now. He says a Miss Alicia Butler's at your house demanding to see you and that she has her cat and a suitcase with her. What is this about?"

"I don't know."

But what was she doing there? She wouldn't return his calls and now she was at his house with her cat? Had she been trying to break in? Why? His pulse accelerated. With rage, he tried to tell himself.

"Claiborne speaking," he growled impatiently into the receiver.

"Mr. Claiborne. Officer Thomas. Sorry to bother you. You've got a yard full of reporters along with some angry hecklers."

"I know." They'd been there ever since a lead story in the newspaper had all but accused him of helping

Mitchell Butler embezzle funds from Houses for
Hurricane Victims, a charity Jake had created and
foolishly put Mitchell in charge of.

"A Miss Alicia Butler and her cat were on your
veranda when I arrived, sir," the officer explained.
"Apparently, some of her father's investors followed her
from her apartment, and the crowd got pretty stirred up.
Someone threw a brick through your front window and
ran off. I've got Miss Butler and her cat in my patrol
car. She's pretty shaken up, and her cat won't stop
howling."

Although Jake rented his home, it was a large, modern
house in a top-end neighborhood. Unfortunately, he lived
next to his landlady, Jan Grant, who was both nosy and
highly opinionated. Jan had already complained about
rude reporters disrupting her mornings. The last thing
he needed was for her to get upset about the arrival of
the police and evict him.

"Officer, I'm sorry about all the excitement. Give me
a minute. I was in the middle of something when you
called."

Rubbing his brow, he tried to think what he should
do. He wanted to deal with the layoffs now. But…Alicia,
who'd been hounded in the papers and on television
because of her father's problems, was in big trouble.
She'd come to him for a reason. Why?

Ever since Mitchell had been federally indicted and
put under house arrest, she'd been pestered by the federal
government, the press and her father's investors. She'd
looked thin and vulnerable in the pictures he'd seen of
her on television.

Against his will he remembered a night that should
never have happened and a delectable, silken, female
body writhing beneath his…a body that had been in tune

with his like no other. Prim and proper Alicia Butler had driven him past the brink of sanity. He wished he could erase all memories of her, but despite what he'd learned about her father since that evening, he hadn't been able to.

Indeed, he'd thought about Alicia and how sweet she'd seemed and what they had done that night too often. Hell, they'd barely managed to get inside his house and lock his door before they'd stripped and made love.

Aware that his employees were watching him and hanging on his every word, he realized he had to get his mind off sex with Alicia and act quickly.

"You said she has her cat with her? And a suitcase?"

Alarm bells that had more to do with memories of Alicia's sensuality than her cat and suitcase had his temple throbbing harder than ever.

She hadn't come to see him on a whim.

"The girl seems unwell."

"Whatever...do you mean?" Jake asked, suddenly more concerned than he should have been.

"Her voice is so soft I can barely hear her."

Jake's eyes burned as he remembered the honeyed tones of Alicia's cultured voice whispering his name as he'd made love to her. Why did every detail about their night together stand out?

The faces of his employees blurred.

"I'll come home immediately and take care of this," he said.

Sounding relieved, the officer said a quick goodbye.

Jake handed the phone to Vanessa.

"I didn't realize you were personally involved with

Alicia Butler," Vanessa hissed as soon as she had him all to herself in his office.

Her accusing tone set him on edge. The last thing he desired was the third degree from his secretary. Without looking at her, he grabbed his keys out of a drawer and slung his jacket over one shoulder.

"I'm not," he lied.

"Then what is she doing on your doorstep?"

"I can't let you know until I find out, now, can I?"

"I don't like the sound of this. If there are reporters and cops along with Alicia at your house, there'll be more bad publicity. The Butlers are thieves. You'll be tarred with the same brush. We're barely surviving this downturn as it is."

"You think I don't know that? I'm already taking the rap for what Mitchell did. Look, why don't you concentrate on taking care of things here while I go to see what she wants, okay?"

"You're right, of course. This whole thing just has me upset."

When he reached the parking garage, his gut twisted as he thought about all the people he'd have to fire later because of Alicia Butler and her father.

Damn her.

When Jake braked sharply in his drive, six reporters stampeded across the wet grass toward him. There had been only one this morning. No sooner did he open his door than they shoved raised microphones at his face.

The curtain next door on Jan Grant's front window was pulled aside and he made out the stout bulk of his landlady, who wasn't about to miss anything.

A snicker from the closest reporter. "What was Alicia Butler doing on your doorstep?"

Instead of dignifying the man with an answer, Jake focused on the slim figure hunched in the back of the single patrol car parked in front of his home beyond the reporters' dripping black umbrellas. Then he looked at the broken window beside his front door.

He knew he should hate Alicia, but he couldn't forget the beating she'd taken from the press for the past few weeks. Ever since that article about how he'd appointed Mitchell Butler treasurer of Houses for Hurricane Victims, and about how all the funds had vanished, he'd really been able to relate to what she must have been going through.

She looked too crushed and defenseless cowering in the back of that car, so utterly unlike the tall, elegant woman he'd bedded or the defiant woman who'd told him to go to hell the next morning. He couldn't hate her. Fool that he was, his chest constricted with sympathy.

A cop, who was probably Officer Thomas, pointed needlessly toward his car. "She's over there."

"Thanks."

Jake loped past the reporters, his Italian loafers sinking into the ooze of his soaked lawn as he made his way toward the patrol car.

"Alicia?" he muttered in a harsh tone as he rapped his knuckles on the glass window.

She rolled the window down a few inches and his gaze roved the length of her willowy body, taking in her white, translucent skin. Mascara ran beneath her long-lashed, almond-shaped, brown eyes. Wet, dark ropes of her hair stuck to her neck. Despite her thinness and her pallor, she affected him every bit as intensely as she had their one night together.

Opening the door, he took her hand, which felt icy, and helped her out.

She wore a white, gauzy dress that clung. When his gaze lingered on the raindrops moistening her full lips, he remembered with an almost visceral ache exactly how soft that mouth had been against his and exactly how sweet she'd tasted.

His lips thinned as other memories of the intimacies they'd shared assaulted him. With all her problems, why was she here?

"Thank you for coming so fast," she said.

"How did you get here?" he asked.

"Taxi."

"Well, you were reckless to come in a public taxi and let your horde follow you."

"I—I didn't think. Sorry I embarrassed you."

"You could have called me. We could have met somewhere discreet."

"Sorry. I hate all this as much as you do."

The officer had been right about her looking ill. The brown eyes that had sparkled with fire each and every time he'd kissed her or licked her *that* night were dull and glazed with pain.

"Meow!"

Frowning, Jake looked across his yard and saw Officer Thomas talking to the reporters. Jake's selfish agenda would be best served if he told the officer to see about her. But an unhealthy mixture of curiosity, sympathy and some self-destructive emotion that was better left unanalyzed overpowered him.

Fool that he was, instead of signaling for the policeman, he grabbed her hand and pointed her in the direction of the sidewalk that led to his front door. Then he leaned inside the car and picked up Alicia's suitcase and her cat carrier. Hissing, the animal lunged at the walls of his cage. Ignoring the beast, Jake strode up the walk after Alicia. Pulling out his keys, he unlocked his door, then thrust it open so violently it banged the wood paneling of his interior wall.

He stood to one side so that she could enter. Reluctant to follow him, she remained frozen, her skirt dripping, her eyes staring at him, so he said, "In case you didn't notice, I'm inviting you inside."

"I noticed," she whispered in a sexy croak that unnerved him.

"So, ladies first."

A bolt of lightning was followed by a crash of thunder. Then several flashbulbs went off in their faces.

Yowling, Gus hurled himself against the side of the cage, rocking it even harder.

"Your cat says he thinks going inside would be a very good idea," Jake said.

"He has issues about water, not to mention thunder."

"Well, if you came over here to grant interviews on my porch, enjoy. But Gus and I have had enough of our five minutes of fame. We'd prefer to go inside and open a can of tuna."

Once he had set her cat and her bag down inside his ultramodern foyer, which was now covered in glass shards, he ran his hand along the slick, polished surface of his paneled wall until he found the light switch. Flipping it on, he looked back outside. She was still glaring at him.

"Your foyer is not exactly neutral territory," she whispered.

"Don't remind me."

Suddenly he was remembering how they'd torn off their clothes the last time they'd stepped across his threshold. He hadn't bothered to turn on any lights. Once naked, they'd launched themselves at each other. Heat engulfed him as he remembered how they'd sunk to the floor, and he'd straddled her on top of the Kilim carpet on which he now stood. He'd thought her adorable and sexy as hell.

More flashbulbs captured her ashen face.

The worried little crease between her dark brows deepened and she went even whiter. When he reached for her anxiously, she sprang away from him and jumped across the threshold.

Damn it, he'd only wanted to soothe her. Hell, maybe it was a good thing she'd stopped him.

She plastered herself against his mahogany wall as far away from him as possible, her delectable breasts heaving beneath that thin white dress that clung closely.

The memory of what he'd done to those pink-tipped breasts made him feel much too warm. With a start he realized he'd awakened every night since aching for her sweetness and sexiness.

Annoyed that she was so afraid of him and he so jittery around her, Jake slammed his door. Once it was bolted against the goggle-eyed reporters and their flashbulbs, she began to shiver.

"You're freezing," he said, stating the obvious in a harsh tone to conceal his concern.

"S-sorry. A-air-c-conditioning." Struggling for control, she sucked in a breath. "I'm dripping all over your fancy floor, too."

"It's stone. It won't melt. But wait here. I'll turn the AC off and get you some towels."

Thankful for an excuse to leave her and get a grip on himself, he strode down the hall before she could object and quickly adjusted the thermostat. Ducking into his guest bath, he grabbed some fluffy white towels. When he returned, he ripped off his jacket and wrapped it around her shoulders and placed the thick towels in her hands.

Although their fingers touched briefly, it was long enough for him to register that her soft skin felt like ice.

With a breathless sound she cringed away from him.

"Thank you," she whispered as she wrapped a towel around her head and began to pat her hair dry. "I'm s-sorry to be so much trouble."

"No trouble." He tore his gaze from her stricken face.

How could he actually want to help her? Whatever was wrong was no business of his. There were at least a dozen reasons why he should hate her, most of them names of people his charity couldn't build houses for and employees he would soon be forced to fire. But she looked too much like a drowned waif for him to even consider chastising her in any way at this point. The feds and reporters hounding her seemed to have that job well in hand.

Steeling himself against the impulse to hold her close until his body warmth made her stop shaking, his voice was rougher when he spoke. "You'll feel better when we get you out of those wet clothes and dry you off."

"We?" She blushed at his suggestion. His own heart began to thud as he realized how that comment had sounded. With an effort he forced himself to look anywhere but at her softly alluring breasts.

Had she deliberately dressed in that filmy, see-through number so he'd want to stare at them? Impotent rage that she could arouse him so easily swept over him.

"What I meant to say is there's a bathroom down the hall. You probably remember showering in it."

When she reddened, he wished he hadn't reminded them both they'd showered together.

"I'll bring you a robe and more fresh towels," he said, his tone more clipped.

Glad for the excuse to leave her again, he went back down the hall. But he was soon much too aware of her heels clicking rapidly on the flagstones behind him.

When she stepped inside the bath, the beige marble walls seemed to close in, trapping him. Staring down at her, he recalled again how they'd laughingly showered after making love all over his house. He'd washed her hair, dried her off, taken her back to bed where he'd held her close for hours.

He backed out of the bathroom on the pretense of finding her more towels and his robe. For his own sanity he knew he should figure out what she wanted and then get rid of her as soon as possible. But as he grabbed the robe off a hook in his master bath, he knew he wasn't going to do anything so sensible.

She'd fascinated him from the first moment he'd seen her in that tight gold sheath on his brother's arm at his grandfather's eightieth birthday party. When Cici had asked him to look after Alicia so she could dance with Logan, he'd jumped at the chance. Then Logan had disappeared with Cici, and he'd offered to drive the stranded Alicia home.

Over a late-night coffee he'd found her even sweeter than she was gorgeous—not at all like her calculating father. A writer and an editor, she hadn't been the shallow rich girl he'd expected. She'd been intelligent and insightful. When he'd kissed her after she'd laughed at one of his jokes, they'd both gone up in flames.

The morning after they'd made love, Logan's CEO, Hayes Daniels, had presented him with irrefutable proof that her father was a criminal. When Jake and his CPA had checked the books and bank statements for Houses for Hurricane Victims, they'd discovered alarming discrepancies. Jake had gone with Hayes to turn Mitchell in to the feds.

Since her father was a crook, a crook he'd blown the whistle on, Jake should rid himself of her immediately. But she looked so lost.

Even after he'd discovered her father had robbed Houses for Hurricane Victims, she'd consumed his thoughts. He'd called her repeatedly. Not that she'd answered. No doubt she blamed him for her father's downfall.

How could he still find her attractive? But he did.

From their first tentative kiss, when her velvet-tipped fingers had singed his flesh through his cotton shirt and her lips had been so soft and hot as they'd parted for his tongue, his groin had tightened with unbearable need.

That a single kiss could have given such a contagion of pleasure should have been a warning. Instead, he'd staked his claim by arching her body against his.

He still wanted her. Which meant he should make her leave before he did something really stupid.

Two

After sweeping up the glass in the foyer and opening a can of tuna in the kitchen, Jake was unlocking the cat crate to let the beast out when he heard a crash from the bathroom.

Ears flat, the cat raced out of the kitchen so fast he collided with a china flowerpot and knocked it over.

Ignoring the cat and the dirt spilling from the shattered pot, Jake ran down the hall to check on Alicia.

"Alicia?"

When she didn't answer, panic slammed him.

"Alicia? Alicia! Are you all right?"

No answer.

When he pounded on the door with his fists and there was no response, he tried the doorknob, which turned. He shoved it and the door flew open, thick vapors enveloping him. "Alicia?"

Blindly he made his way through the steamy mists to the glassed-in shower-tub and slid the door open.

Through the steam he saw her lying in a crumpled heap, warm water streaming over her naked thighs. Shutting off the faucet, he leaned down and picked her up. Grabbing the towels and robe she'd placed on a stool, he clutched the unconscious woman and carried her down the hall into his den. She wasn't heavy, so he bore her easily.

He was careful not to a glance at her nude body more than necessary. Still, his gaze did linger on the heart-shaped birthmark on her left breast that he'd once tongued so ardently the night he'd made love to her. Settling her onto his couch, he couldn't have cared less how the water might stain the expensive leather. He was too worried about her.

He lifted her wrist and felt a pulse. He smiled when it was steady and strong. Maybe she'd knelt down for something she'd dropped and had stood up too fast.

"Alicia! Wake up!"

She mumbled something he didn't understand and then turned her face away from him.

Had she hit her head? Did she have a concussion?

"Daddy!" she whispered. "Daddy! Where are you? Why can't you ever, just this once, stay home?"

Was she delirious? Thinking to inspect her scalp for injuries, Jake slid his fingers through her hair. Parting the thick waves with his blunt fingers, he discovered a lump.

"Open your eyes!" he commanded.

Much to his surprise, the long, feminine lashes fluttered. Her plump, sexy lips quivered.

Brown irises slowly filled with light as she struggled

to focus. "Jake…it's you? What's wrong? Why are you shouting at me?"

She reached out and took his big hand, sending a sexual shock of awareness through him. "Where am I?"

"My living room."

"What am I doing here?"

That was the question upper most on his mind, but he couldn't ask her until he was sure she was all right.

Slowly, as she continued to stare at him, her expression changed.

"Where are my clothes?" Her voice rose. "What did you to me?"

"Not a damn thing that I shouldn't have, so calm down. You fell in the shower. I heard a crash, rushed inside, turned the water off, carried you here, dried you, put you into my robe and checked your pulse. And now that you're conscious and yourself again, I think we should call your doctor."

"No need for that! I'm fine," she said huffily. "Or at least I would be if…" She stopped, clearly troubled by some new thought.

"Did you faint? Or trip?"

She stared at him. Her eyes were huge, wary. "Everything just went black. I guess I fainted."

"Like I said, you should see a doctor."

"I will. But not right now. I'm very hungry. I…I haven't eaten much for a couple of days."

He'd read in some newspaper that reporters stalked her every time she left her apartment, even to go to the grocery store. Had she been starving herself as a result? Again, he fought the impulse to feel sorry for her.

"Could I possibly trouble you for a cracker…or two…

and maybe some tea?" she asked, her tone formal and polite now.

She and her father had made a mess of his life. He should forget she looked defenseless and sexy and make himself call the cops and ask them to send Officer Thomas back. Jake could ask him to drive her to a soup kitchen or a hospital—anywhere.

This whole thing was beginning to feel much too complicated. But instead of doing anything remotely sensible, he nodded.

"Why did you come here?" he demanded.

She rubbed the back of her head and winced. "Jake, before we get into that, I—I'm, I really am seeing bright spots. I...I...I really do need that cracker first."

"You threatening to faint on me again?"

"I don't feel so good. Really, I don't. That's a fact... not a threat."

"One stale cracker coming right up," he whispered gently. "You stay put on the couch while I make a tray. The last thing either of us need is for you to faint again."

As Jake's footsteps receded, Alicia sat up on his couch and squeezed her eyes shut.

Oh, God, how could she tell him, him of all people, the man who'd turned her father in to the feds and blown his life and her to bits, that she might be pregnant with his baby?

She'd tested positive on four home pregnancy tests. *Four.*

Pressing her fingers to her temple, she counted her thudding heartbeats until the bright spots faded.

It wasn't as if she hadn't rehearsed a little speech—several speeches.

*Jake, every morning I wake up clammy with nausea.
Just for the record, my period's three weeks late…. I
know that because I always note the event by writing a
little p—in red—on my kitchen calendar on the exact
date of the month. And I'm never late!*

She knew what he'd say—that it wasn't possible, that
he'd used a condom. Several condoms.

She sucked in a tight breath as too many embar-
rassingly intimate memories flickered. Sex had never
been her favorite sport. She was too shy and repressed.
Sex was something a woman like her never even
considered with a virtual stranger. But she'd forgotten
all her aversions and hang-ups with Jake. She'd given
herself to him, a man she'd barely known, with such
uncharacteristic abandon she blushed every time she
thought about how many times and where they'd done
it.

And then the next morning he and Hayes Daniels had
turned her father in to the feds. Shivering, she must have
sat there on his couch twisting that strand of hair for a
full five minutes. Even in his thick robe, she felt chilled
to the bone. Well, at least the awful morning sickness
had passed.

He'd think she was crazy for not waiting to tell him
until she was sure. But—because of him—she hadn't
had a choice. The feds, or rather that officious little agent
with the wire-rimmed glasses atop his bulbous nose,
had shown up without warning and had kicked her out
of her apartment, explaining again why the feds had the
right to seize all her father's properties, which included
her apartment and furniture.

She wouldn't have come here if she'd had anywhere
else to go. Before she'd left the apartment, she'd tried her
father's cell phone. He had caller ID, so if his phone was

near, he'd know she was calling. But he hadn't answered. Had he seen her name and punched the word *ignore?*

Sometimes she thought that that little button on his phone was a metaphor for the way he'd always treated her. Everything else in his life had always come before her. Jake, on the other hand, had come home as soon as he'd known she was here. Not that she liked him… or anything; not after what he'd done. Still, he'd shown up the minute he'd heard she was in trouble. And he'd invited her inside.

Clutching his robe and knotting the sash tightly, Alicia rose and tiptoed down the hall to his kitchen. One foot into the kitchen, she stiffened at the sight of the kitchen table where Jake had made love to her so heatedly he'd sent silverware and plates crashing to the floor.

Desperate to shift her attention away from the embarrassing memory that had her pulse thudding she stared at Gus's empty carrier, which lay on its side. Broken bits of a pot she vaguely remembered having admired in the hall earlier littered the counter.

"Where's poor Gus?"

"Poor Gus, my eye. When I let him out of his carrier, he practically tore the place apart. Broke a pot that doesn't belong to me."

"You better not have hurt him."

"He made a clean break. I was too worried about you to chase him."

"Oh."

"I cut some cheese and peeled a banana to go along with the apple that I also peeled for you. Sorry to disappoint, but I don't have any stale crackers."

She bit her lip to keep from grinning.

Watching her guardedly, he set a plate on the table.

She grabbed a piece of apple and began to munch noisily as she admired his handiwork. He'd done rather a good job with the food actually.

Some of her anxiety drained away. It was suddenly too easy to remember why she'd fallen for Jake that night and gotten herself into this mess. Her father had confided to her that he was in terrible trouble, so she'd been worried even before Logan had disappeared with Cici at the party.

Then Jake had appeared, insisting he'd take care of her. He'd been so warm and attentive, and soon they'd been able to talk about anything. In no time she'd found herself having fun just drinking coffee with him and laughing at his stories about his adventures in the wild. Unfortunately, she'd confided her concerns about her father.

Jake place a fork, knife and napkin on the table and sat down across from her. His chocolate-dark hair fell across his brow and temple. He was so close, and he looked so sexy as he watched too intently.

She set her apple sliver down and avoided his gaze. But his having taken trouble with the plate pleased her—too much. Why did she always read more into small kindnesses than she should?

It was a plate of food, that was all. He'd fed Gus, hadn't he? He didn't like Gus, did he?

"Eat," Jake said gently. "A single bite won't do you much good."

She thought about the baby that they might be having together and blushed. How to tell him?

"How can I, with you watching me?"

No sooner did he stand up than his phone rang.

"Sorry," he said. "It's my secretary. I left things in a mess. I'd better take this."

He stepped into the hall and pulled the door shut.

After that Alicia could only catch bits and pieces of his conversation.

"Yes, I'm coming back—

"How can you think I could have forgotten them—

"No, she hasn't told me why, not that this is any of your business—

"Damn it. That's what I'm trying to determine—

"Pregnant? I suggest you get your mind out of the gutter and focus on your work instead of my personal affairs—which, by the way, are none of your business...."

Pregnant.

The woman was an oracle.

Her appetite gone in the space of a heartbeat, Alicia knew she had to tell him the truth, and fast.

Thankfully, he was much too annoyed at his secretary to even glance at her as he strode back in.

"You've barely touched your food. Why?" he demanded, his voice colder as he set his phone down.

"Bad news, huh?"

"I have a life. Not that you probably give a damn what I was doing before the cops called me about you."

"Try me."

"I was just about to fire a lot of hardworking people, people who really need their jobs."

"And your secretary thinks it's all my fault."

So many people blamed her for what her father had supposedly done. Some believed he'd stashed a fortune in a secret, offshore account in her name.

Her father said he was innocent and she wanted to believe him. Not that it was easy when everybody else thought he was guilty. And what did it matter whether he was innocent or not when her own bank accounts here in New Orleans and her credit cards were frozen? When two days ago Sam, her editor in chief, had caved in to mounting pressure to fire her from the editorial/writer job that she'd dearly loved. She had no money, no job, no reputation and no future. And four home pregnancy tests had been positive.

His anger crackled between them. "People distrust me now. Whatever I think about who's to blame, I need to get back to the office. So, what do you say we cut to the chase? Why are you here?"

"You have an incredibly smart secretary."

"What the hell does she have to do with anything?"

"I think I'm pregnant."

He looked so dumbstruck, she truly felt sorry for him.

"What? No way!"

Three

His legs spread apart, Jake towered over Alicia as she silently hunched lower at his kitchen table. "Would you kindly repeat that."

"You heard me."

"Did you say you think…you're pregnant. You don't know? Why would you come here before you were sure?"

His glowering made her squirm uneasily. "I took four pregnancy tests, and they were all positive. I can't eat. And I fainted, didn't I? I've been nauseated the last two mornings. My period's late. I could go on with the symptoms. Did I tell you I really like pickles right now? What do you think all that adds up to?"

A sledgehammer was pounding in his brain.

"Plus, because of you the feds kicked me out of my apartment, and I have nowhere to stay."

"Have you had your condition confirmed by a doctor?" he asked.

She grabbed another sliver of apple. Shaking her head, she bit into it. "Not yet, but the way things have been going, I'd bet my miserable life that we're probably pregnant."

"We…"

"*We!*"

"Okay, but you could still be wrong about…*us*." He looked sick to be using the plural pronoun.

"Right…. Four pregnancy tests can definitely be wrong on planet Earth. Anything in our magical realm is possible," she said dully.

"Could be a bad batch."

Shaking her head at him, she decided to try the white cheese he'd put out. In between bouts of nausea, she had a voracious appetite. What she really wanted was a dill pickle. Not that she was about to ask for one.

His face was hard and set as he watched her. "And you're sure that if you are…"

Beneath his critical gaze, she lost her craving as a strange panic welled up inside her. She'd told him she couldn't eat with him staring at her like that, but his mood was so bitter she thought maybe now wasn't a good time to nag, so she laid the piece of cheese back on the platter.

"What? What is it? Why are you scowling at me like that?" she said. "What have I done now?"

He took a deep, worried breath.

"*What?*" she demanded.

"Sorry I have to ask this. Are you absolutely sure that…if you're right…about *you* being pregnant…that I'm…that I'm the father?"

Vertigo made his granite countertops whirl round and round. His darkly handsome face blurred sickeningly.

"You moralistic jerk!" Fury consuming her, she sprang out of the chair and lunged at him. "Am I sure? Damn right I'm sure!"

He caught her wrist in midair and used it to swing her against the long length of his muscular body. Her full breasts slid against his ripped torso. In an effort to catch herself, she grabbed his lean waist. Then she fought to launch herself free of him. He used the leverage to pull her closer.

"Calm down. I just had to be sure."

"I'm totally positive," she yelled, kicking at him even as she pushed at his chest. "I told you that you're the only man I've....I've slept with...in months."

His eyes had taken on the polar chill of blue ice chips. "What about my brother?"

Fury suffused her.

"Your father said you were going to marry him," Jake persisted.

"My father made that up. Logan and I dated, but our relationship didn't work on any level other than friendship. Not that my lack of a sex life is any of your business!"

"Maybe I disagree. After all, you claim I'm the father of your child."

"If I'm pregnant, so are you! Not that I would choose you!"

"Nor I you!"

"Believe me, I...I wish it was somebody else's! Somebody I met in a bar would be nicer! So let me go!"

"Are you going to try to hit me again if I do?"

"After what you just said, you deserve a bullet…you know where. But no, since I'm a lady."

"You could have fooled me." Releasing her, he watched her warily.

She backed a few steps away from him and rubbed her wrist.

"Okay," he said. "I'm sorry to upset you, but I had to know. I used condoms, if you'll remember. Lots of them. I took precautions."

"Oh, yeah, well, you didn't take enough!"

He stared at her for a long moment. "I'm sorry," he repeated. "If what you say is true, and you're pregnant, and it's mine, I'll accept full responsibility for the child…and for you…despite who you are…which means our next step should be to see a doctor."

"If what I say is true? *If?* You still don't believe me?" Her eyes narrowed and her pulse sped up. "Well, it's true! *Despite who you are!* I hate this…."

"So the hell do I, but it looks like we're stuck with each other, at least until we get some sound medical advice."

"I'm afraid a doctor will only confirm the worst!"

"Obviously, you believe that," he said. "But I won't believe it until I hear him say it."

"Dr. Preston's a she. When she does, then what?"

"We'll handle it," he muttered.

"Well, if you think you can make me stop this pregnancy…"

His black brows slashed together. It was his turn to hiss in a breath and gape at her. "You don't know me at all if you think I'd destroy my child."

His outrage was so intense, she knotted her hands and stood up taller.

"How could I know what you feel on the subject or

on any subject, when for all practical purposes we're strangers?" she whispered.

"Strangers, *cher?* You wish. I wish. Unfortunately, that's the last thing we are. I'd say we're intimately connected."

"I shouldn't have come. Look, I'll figure out how to do this on my own. I have a friend in London who's offered... Never mind! Forget I ever came here."

"As if I could."

She turned away from him and stared at his backyard, which looked overgrown and badly in need of pruning. She did so love working with plants. Oh, how could she think of gardening at a time like this?

Jake was silent and still for a long moment, but she imagined his eyes boring into her back. Then his breath sped up, and he spanned the distance that separated them.

"I don't want you to go," he said, planting his hands on her shoulders. "You were right to come here. We'll figure this out...together."

Before she knew what he was about, he'd pulled her tightly against him. Some part of her wanted to twist out of his grasp, but another wanted to relax into his hard warmth and strength, so she let him pull her closer. The times when someone had held her and comforted her in life had been so rare since her mother's death, and that night with him had been wonderful.

Then the next day her father's empire had crashed very publicly, and her father had told her that Jake had been one of the main whistle-blowers who'd brought him down.

"I am to blame for what happened that night," Jake muttered against her throat, his voice deepening with needs that at first she did not understand. "I wanted

you and you wanted me, too. I didn't realize what your
father had done until the next day."

"No."

She shut her eyes, but it was impossible to ignore how
wonderful she felt in his arms. Only gradually did she
grow aware that he had become aroused.

"Stop this!" she whispered, trying to pull away.

"God help me, I still want you," he whispered,
snugging her even closer. "You feel the same. Kiss
me."

His husky tone and his hot, male body molded so
tightly against her with such ardent need triggered…
something.

She knew she should fight him, but instead she
twisted around, ever so slightly, just enough so that she
could tilt her mouth up to his.

He claimed her lips, hesitantly at first, but soon took
all she was willing to give as greedily as he had the night
he'd made love to her. He kissed her long and hard, his
tongue plunging between her lips. She gasped as an
answering desire began to course through her blood.

The sash of his robe came loose, and he yanked the
edges of the robe aside, cupping her breasts, tracing his
thumbs across her nipples, which were tight and hard.
Ripping his shirt out of his slacks, he pulled it up, so
that when he dragged her even closer, her breasts were
mashed against his bare chest.

Contact with the coarse hair of his torso made her
nipples peak and her blood burn.

"Oh, no." She felt crazy with unwanted needs. Against
her will, she arched her body so that her legs and thighs
fitted his. His skin grew so hot she felt as if she was
being consumed in a roaring furnace.

He was right about her wanting him. Limp with

desire, she felt meltingly alive caught in his hard, strong arms. His mouth was on hers again and it was as if their bodies spoke a language all their own. Everything about him was sensually delicious and made her feel starved for more.

Despite his part in bringing her father down, she'd remembered his kisses and lovemaking longingly, and every night she'd dreamed of him and had awakened in the dead of the night, her body aching for his mouth and hands to caress her like this again, even though she denied it.

"I want you," he said softly. "Despite everything, I want you on my kitchen table. On my foyer floor. In my bed. On my couch. In my shower. I want to repeat everything we did before. I want to do it again and again and more…until I'm too weak to stand and you have to feed me by hand in bed to revive me. And when I do revive, I'll want you all over again."

"God help me, I want all that, too," she admitted shakily.

In that moment she actually believed she would never want to die anywhere else but in his arms.

Then he kissed her again, nibbling her lower lip at first. Gradually his kiss lengthened and grew hard. He fused his mouth to hers endlessly, his tongue mating with hers until she felt she was burning up like a star. She could hardly breathe when he pulled away at last.

"You are beautiful," he said gently. "Unforgettable." His hand slid over her body until his fingers closed over her plump breast. "Easy to talk to. And fun. I've thought about these breasts, their softness and the tightness of your nipples many many times these past few weeks. In fact I couldn't stop thinking about you or them, no matter how diligently I tried."

"Which means you don't really like me…if you don't even want to think about me," she said, struggling to regain her senses. "All you feel is lust."

Part of her wished he'd deny it.

"Call it whatever you like, it's very powerful," he said.

"Let me go," she whispered. "Please…. This will only make an impossible situation worse."

"But I want you," he insisted.

"We have more serious things to think about. Plans to make. We're already in over our heads as it is."

"Have you ever had a habit you couldn't break?"

"Is that what I am to you—a bad habit?"

Pulling her closer even as she fought to resist him again, he gripped her arms hard. But just as he brought his mouth down to hers and she thought she would soon be lost on a wild, dark tide, he froze.

For a long moment he stood as immobile as a statue. He stared down at her as if he were struggling as hard as she was for control. Then he cursed low under his breath and pushed free of her.

Feeling hurt and rejected, which made zero sense, she jerked the edges of the robe together and spun away.

Hot color flared in his cheeks, too; a savage muscle was jumping along his jawline. His devouring gaze flamed with a fierce blue light.

"Sorry," he finally muttered in an edgy, unapologetic tone. Then he rubbed his jaw where the muscle twitched. "I don't know what…happened. I…I just lost control there for a second. Sorry."

He looked down at the floor and raked a hand through his mussed dark hair. Then he clumsily jammed the edges of his shirt into his waistband. "If I can't trust myself around you, even knowing what you are, I've got to get the hell out of here."

One minute he'd been out to prove she desired him; in the next he was running as scared as she was. And all because he'd lost his precious control.

She clenched her teeth and then unclenched them. "But we have to decide what to do."

He took a deep breath. "First we have to find out if we have a problem or not. You need to call your doctor, make an appointment as fast as possible."

"I need a place to stay tonight. Because of you, the feds took my apartment, all my furniture…and my car. I have no friends left in Louisiana." She paused. When he didn't say no immediately, she said, "I'd need a litter box and litter for Gus."

"Okay. Of course, you can stay here if you like. But if you do, I'm moving out."

"Where?"

"I don't know."

"You mean I'll be here alone?"

"Just for tonight. Trust me. You're better off with me gone. I don't know what just happened between us or why. But I'll be fine once I get off to myself, do some thinking and get a grip. I don't like feeling trapped in this situation with you."

"And you think I like it?"

"I'm not a mind reader, so I can only take your word for how you feel."

She envied the way he could compartmentalize, the way his deep voice sounded almost cool and contained now when her heart was still racing.

Trying to copy him, she took a deep breath and tried to push down her emotions. It was probably better that they spend the night apart.

"Okay then," she said. "Sounds like a plan."

"I'll give you my cell number. Call me after you make that appointment with your doctor." He pulled a set of car keys out of his pocket. "I want to know when and where it is."

"You're leaving now?"

"I've got to get back to my office. Like I told you before—because of you, *cher,* I've got a lot of nice people to fire."

"I'm sorry about that." She truly was.

He hesitated. "Just so you know where I'll be… Tonight I think I'll drive out to Belle Rose and spend the night in a friend's houseboat in the swamp. I need to be by myself—to think."

She arched her brows. Poor guy. If it hadn't been for his part in her father's downfall, she might have felt sorry for him.

He'd been having a bad day even before she'd showed up on his doorstep and announced they might be pregnant. And what had he done—he'd given up his house for the night, so she'd have a safe place to stay.

Four

When the sagging roofline of Bos's houseboat loomed out of the steamy gloom of shadowy dwarf palmettos, bald cypress trees and water tupelo, Jake cut the motor and sprang toward the bow. He'd hoped he'd experience at least a slight lifting of his mood once he was out of the city and had returned to his boyhood refuge. Despite the familiar roar of bull alligators, locusts and frogs, he felt like a stranger in a foreign land. His leaden heart kept him alienated from all that should have been familiar and dear.

Images of a big-eyed, pale Alicia in the patrol car, the dull stares of his employees after he'd let them go, Cici's and Logan's radiant smiles at their wedding bombarded him in a never-ending loop. The thick heat of the swamp pressed too close, making him feel trapped by business and personal problems—and most of it was the Butlers' fault.

The air was dank with the stench of rot and mold. He would have preferred to be rock climbing in Utah or Alaska rather than hanging out in the swamp. Still, this was the wild and life was always simpler in the wild. He kept a cabin south of Denali National Park in Alaska that he visited every summer. Too bad he didn't have time to go there now. It was the one place that was far enough away from his real life so that he could count on solitude there clearing his mind.

Grabbing the bowline, he spread his legs so that he stood in the middle of the eight-foot aluminum flatboat as it drifted silently through the mirror-black swamp water toward the houseboat.

A night to himself even in this wild place wasn't long enough to sort it all out, but it was a start. If Alicia was pregnant, he couldn't abandon his kid—even if she was Mitchell Butler's daughter.

He thought about the families still living in three-room trailers to whom he'd promised homes before the funds to build them had vanished—because of her father.

Wrapping the line around a rusting cleat, Jake made sure the flatboat was snug against the used tires Bos had nailed as crude fenders along the side of the houseboat. Then he ran his gaze over the shabby structure.

The houseboat had two tiny bedrooms, a kitchen, no bath. Surprisingly, the place didn't look any worse for wear. It must've been a good ten years since he was last here. Bos had been ill of late, but when Jake had visited him a month ago, he'd told him he'd managed to do what was necessary to maintain it.

"Not that I get out to the houseboat much these days," Bos had said. "You're welcome to it—just like always, anytime. The fishin's still pretty good even if the water in the swamp gets saltier every year."

Bos was another man who felt the need to get away from civilization upon occasion.

With a frown Jake set his gear down beside Bos's stacked crab traps. After opening the door to the cabin, he pitched his backpack inside.

This fish camp was located between the Claibornes' ancestral mansion, Belle Rose, and Bos's less developed properties to the south of Belle Rose. Pierre, Jake's grandfather, had never approved of Jake hanging out at Bos's camp in the swamp when Jake had been a kid. The truth was, his grandfather had detested Bos with an irrational passion. The old man had considered Bos, who'd run a bar and fought cocks, a bad influence, so most of the time Jake had chosen to sneak off, willingly risking the consequences of Grand-père's rage later.

A rebel from birth, Jake had been as fascinated by Bos's bad reputation as his grandfather had been repelled by it. Not that Bos was really such a bad sort once you got to know him. Bos had adopted his orphaned niece Cici, hadn't he? He'd understood what it was like not to feel you fit into your family, and he'd taken Jake hunting and fishing and crabbing without even so much as asking a single prying question about his need to escape his domineering grandfather and cocky older twin.

Bos had encouraged him to learn to fend for himself in the wild, so as soon as he'd been old enough, Jake had explored the endless marshes and bayous on his own, hunting doves and ducks and swimming off forested islands.

Back then Noonoon, his nanny, used to fuss at him, saying she couldn't keep a glass jar in the house because

Jake was always borrowing them to house his crabs and frogs and minnows and turtles.

Jake smiled briefly at the memory of Noonoon's dark face until concern about Alicia alone in his house intruded.

She was fine, he told himself. She was a big girl. He'd showed her how to set the alarm. Hell, he'd even sent Vanessa over to his house to make sure Alicia had everything she needed.

Alicia was fine.

Why couldn't he forget how pale and shaken she'd looked in that patrol car?

His stomach growled, reminding him that he hadn't brought any groceries.

Forget her.

He was hungry. If he was going to eat, he had to shoot something or catch something.

Whatever she'd expected when she'd come to Jake's house, it wasn't kindness and concern.

"If you don't need anything else, I really do have to get home to my boys." Vanessa's voice was crisp and hurried and yet there was a maternal compassion in her dark brown eyes that reminded Alicia of her own mother.

Alicia caught herself. This woman was a stranger. She had a life and didn't have much time to deal even briefly with her boss's personal crisis. Mothering her sons was her top priority.

"I'll be fine," Alicia whispered. "Thanks for sending that man over to board up the window."

"You could spend the night with me and my boys if you're afraid to stay in such a big house all by yourself."

"What a sweet offer, but really, I'll be fine," Alicia said. "It's just the night."

"I'd enjoy some adult companionship," Vanessa coaxed.

Alicia shook her head.

"Okay, then. He told me to tell you to set the alarm. And if you get lonely—call."

Nodding at the older woman, who Jake had paid to take care of her, Alicia held on to the two sacks of groceries as Vanessa shut the front door and then locked it firmly behind her.

Clutching the grocery sacks to her breasts, Alicia walked back to the kitchen. Mechanically she removed the lunch meat and cereal boxes, a loaf of bread and a bottle of milk and set them on the counter. It was nice of Jake to send food.

The last rays of the setting sun gilded the edges between the shades and the windowsill. Soon it would be dark outside. She had the rest of the evening to think about her problem. At least Jake had listened and said he would assume his share of the responsibility. He hadn't thrown her out.

She wished he was here, and that confused her. She'd felt so wonderful when he'd held her and kissed her. That perplexed her, too. How could she feel this powerful connection to a man who'd made love to her and then had turned her father in to the feds?

Maybe it was being in this house, where they'd talked and laughed and made love. They had so much fun together that first night.

Don't think about it!

Okay, enough! I have things to do. I'll make supper, clean the dishes, get ready for bed, hunt for Gus, watch some TV, set my alarm.

Is it really so important to set an alarm when my doctor's appointment tomorrow isn't until noon?

Just do it.

She called to Gus, who for once came running. Slathering mayonnaise on two pieces of bread, she made herself a turkey sandwich. When she sat down at the table, Gus hunkered over his bowl and ate his tuna.

Her thoughts turned to Jake and what she'd said to him before he'd left.

"But why do you have to go away?" she'd whispered. "I feel guilty running you out of your own house."

"Don't. It's what I do sometimes—when I need to think."

"Think about what?"

"About what the hell we're going to do if you're pregnant."

"What are you saying?" she'd asked.

He'd stopped slinging fishing gear into his backpack and had walked over to her. Cupping her chin with blunt, tanned fingertips so that she was forced to stare up into his blue eyes, he hadn't spoken until he was sure he had her full attention.

"If there's a baby, I want it," he said softly. "Do you understand me?"

But he didn't want her. She'd nodded and after a long moment he'd freed her chin.

"Okay then," he said.

"I could lock myself into the downstairs bedroom and not come out until morning. You wouldn't even know I was here."

He'd turned and smiled at her. "Trust me. It wouldn't be the same. I need to be completely alone."

"But I wouldn't bother you."

"The hell you say. Every fiber in my being would know you're nearby. You bother me by existing."

"Oh."

She must have looked hurt because his expression had gentled.

"But not always in the worst possible way."

Not always in the worst possible way. Was that a compliment?

Before he'd left, he'd locked his office and his bedroom upstairs. She'd stiffened at those final clicks as the bolts shot home and he'd withdrawn his key.

When she'd been a little girl, she used to follow her father everywhere when he'd packed for a trip. She'd lingered, watching him lock all the doors that kept her out of entire wings of their houses and apartments too.

The servants, of course, had had keys so they could clean. But his only daughter had had no access.

All her father's homes had been furnished with valuable antiques and art collections worthy of museums. He'd said he didn't trust the servants to keep her from sitting on the chairs and spilling drinks or food on the furniture or tainting one of his precious sculptures or paintings with oily fingerprints.

How different her mother had been. Their homes had previously been filled with sunlight and flowers and friends. She'd always had time to sit on the floor and play with her daughter or read to her or chat.

After Alicia finished her sandwich, she sat in silence sipping her milk. Finally, she rose and washed the dishes.

Feeling too restless and lonely to shower and get ready for bed, she began to pace, calling to Gus, who had disappeared again.

Climbing the floating stairs, she lingered outside Jake's locked bedroom and remembered the night he'd carried her inside and kicked the door shut. The walls of his bedroom were either floor-to-ceiling bookshelves or tall windows with views of his large backyard and pool.

They'd made love on his bed and then on the thick woven rug by his bed. Then they'd lain in bed talking. When she'd noticed that only books filled his shelves, she'd asked him why he didn't have a single photograph of his friends or family.

"I left home when I was very young. I traveled light. This house is rented, like all the houses I've lived in. So—no pictures."

"You've never built yourself a house?"

"Maybe someday."

"My father didn't like photographs either. He wouldn't even let me have a picture of my mother in my room. He said photographs depressed him because they reminded him of things that were dead and over. He said he wanted to live entirely in the present."

Jake's face had hardened at the mention of her father, but he'd stroked her mouth with a fingertip and had said nothing. Had he known then he would team up with Hayes Daniels the next day and accuse her father? Or had Hayes approached him?

After Jake had blown the whistle on her father, Jake had called her; maybe to explain his side. Or maybe to hear her side.

Not that she'd taken his calls.

Still, how many times had she nearly picked up the phone because she'd ached to hear his voice and had wondered why he was calling?

Part of her wanted to hate him for what he'd done

to her father, but he wasn't her father's only accuser. Serious amounts of money had gone missing. Someone was responsible. Naturally she didn't want to believe it was her father.

Turning, wishing she could empty her mind of all her confusion concerning Jake and her father, Alicia walked back downstairs.

Her footsteps were hollow taps echoing through the house, which felt too empty without Jake.

At the bottom of the stairs she shut her eyes. More than anything she wished he was here.

What was going on?

Never had she felt more mixed up by the impossible, mysterious longings in her heart.

Five

"I told you I was pregnant, didn't I?" Alicia said gloomily. "You should have been prepared."

"*Should have been* is definitely the operative figure of speech here." Jake gripped her elbow and hurriedly propelled her out of the doctor's office building into the parking lot.

It was nearly one o'clock and the heat was searing. Cars whizzed past them on the busy street.

"I didn't realize how much I hoped you were wrong about this," he said, moving to the street side of the walkway to shield her from the traffic.

With an effort, she tried to ignore the sting of his words. She'd hated the way he'd barely looked at her or the doctor, the way he'd barely said a word during the office visit. The instant the doctor had confirmed Alicia's fears, Jake's tanned face had hardened into a stony mask. No matter how the doctor had attempted to get him to open up, he'd rebuffed her every question. The only sign of life in Jake's set face now was the fiery turbulence in his grim blue eyes that hinted at the inner battle raging inside him.

"You certainly put on a happy face in the doctor's office," Jake muttered. "I couldn't believe all the questions you asked the doctor, like this is a normal pregnancy and we are a normal, happy couple."

"I'm not exactly happy," she whispered, warier of him because of his dark mood. "But I wish I was. Just as I wish you could be, too. Any child deserves parents who want him—even ours."

"Hell."

"I can't help it if I want our child to be wanted and have a normal, loving childhood. Any mother would."

"Even a mother who despises the father of her baby?"

But she didn't despise him. She'd liked having him with her at the doctor's office.

"Do you want me to lie to you and your doctor about how I feel?" he continued. "Where will we be if we lie to each other about everything?"

"Where will we be if we concentrate on nothing but how much we hate each other all the time? How can we build on that?"

"What the hell could we possibly build?"

"A positive world for our child."

"I'd say we're off to a damn poor start then."

"Which means we have nowhere to go but up," she said in a whimsical voice that thankfully was too low for him to hear.

"What?"

Unable to deal with his hostile attitude, she said in a louder tone, "Thank you for at least meeting me here.

I really do appreciate it. I was sick again this morning. I wasn't so sure there for a while I'd ever be able to get out of the house."

Her gentle, polite approach calmed him, if only a little.

"I'm sorry you were sick again. It was my idea for you to see a doctor first thing, remember? The least I could do is show up."

"Believe me, some men wouldn't have bothered." *Like her father.*

Jake opened her door of his large, black SUV for her, and she got in. "Fasten your seat belt," he ordered. He waited to make sure she did so before walking around to get in too. Why was his concern about even that small detail such a comfort?

She hated that his doing so registered on such a profound level with her. She was so eager for happiness she grabbed anything positive.

Once he was behind the huge wheel, the woodsy scent of pine, cypress and smoke enveloped her. Strangely, despite the heat, it didn't make her feel the slightest bit sick as some scents did. In fact, he smelled so good, she couldn't resist glancing at him out of the corners of her eyes.

He was so tall and broad shouldered. A lock of dark hair fell across his brow. Why did he have to be so attractive even when he wasn't trying, like now? When he wanted no involvement with her? Dark stubble shadowed his hard jaw and chin and made him look incredibly masculine. He hadn't had time to shower or shave or even to change out of his jeans before their appointment. Shadows ringed his eyes.

He'd obviously been in such a hurry to pick her up

and rush her to the doctor's office, he hadn't bothered about himself at all.

"You look tired," she said, feeling too much unwanted sympathy for him. Yet, even exhausted, he was so virile and utterly male that some feminine, idiotic part of her wanted to swoon over him, despite knowing he probably considered her his enemy.

"Couldn't sleep," he muttered as he leaned forward and started the SUV. He turned on the AC. "Lumpy, stinky mattress. Hot night, too. Couldn't stop thinking about stuff." He shot her an accusing glance and she wondered if concern for her had kept him from sleeping.

He adjusted the air-conditioning. "Is the air okay?"

She nodded.

"What about you? I mean besides the morning sickness." He turned away and pretended to watch the traffic. "You okay? You don't look so perky yourself."

"Couldn't sleep either." Not that she was about to admit to him that she'd tossed and turned because she'd been longing for him all night—because his nearness made her feel safe and secure in ways she'd never known in her whole life. Which was ridiculous, considering the situation.

When his dark head swiveled in her direction, she shyly turned. Under his scowling gaze, her lungs froze.

Suddenly she couldn't breathe. Why did being so close to him in his big vehicle make her so nervous? Why didn't he just drive them home so they weren't trapped in such a small space together with emotions they couldn't deal with? At least on the way she'd have scenery to distract her from him. Now she felt as overwhelmed by him as she had that first night.

"I...I still can't believe this has happened," she said in a low quiet tone.

"I felt like that at first, I mean when Dr. Preston confirmed your fears, but the reality is sinking in pretty fast. You and I are going to have a baby—whether we want it or not. The question is what are going to do to resolve this situation?"

"I haven't thought that far ahead."

"Oh, I bet you have." His deep voice darkened. "You came running to me first thing in need of money, didn't you?"

"No! That's not it. I—I don't want my baby to be illegitimate, that's all."

His dark head jerked toward hers, his blue eyes piercing her. *"That's all?* Surely you're not talking about—marriage?"

She bit her lips and swallowed.

"About you and me...being together...in some sort of permanent arrangement. It's not like this is a hundred years ago and your father's going to follow me down the aisle with a shotgun between my shoulder blades," he said. "Hard to do that under house arrest."

Could she help it if she saw things so simplistically? Every time a teacher at school had asked her to draw a picture of her family, she'd always drawn a mommy and a daddy and herself in the middle.

"You don't actually see us as a couple, do you?" he said.

She shook her head because he so obviously wanted her to. "Look," she said, "I guess I just panicked and thought when I felt so sick that I couldn't do this alone. Maybe I would have been stronger before...but now... I have no money. No allies. No family really...other than Daddy, who's been indicted."

"And you're so used to money, you don't know how to get by without it."

"My life hasn't been what you think. I don't believe I have any friends left in Louisiana. Everybody here blames me for what they think Daddy did."

"*Because of what he did!* And what you helped him do in all probability. Whose fault is that?"

"Right. You think I schemed to steal millions of dollars from Houses for Hurricane Victims and his bank? And that I deliberately set out to destroy your good name?"

"Well, your father damn sure did, that's for sure."

"I think my father's innocent."

"Then where's the money he managed? Why can't we find any records to prove he ever invested a single dollar? Maybe you don't know how the charity world operates, so I'll fill you in on a little secret. At the first hint of scandal, all future funding dries up. So now poor families, who were counting on me to build them homes, won't get them. Because of my close association to the charity, funding for my architectural projects is drying up as well. It would be financial suicide for me to associate myself with you right now. And now you want me to marry you?"

"The government has been investigating him for the past six weeks, and so far they've found nothing to link me to any of it. Doesn't that tell you anything about me? I never volunteered for that organization. I never worked at Daddy's bank or the shipyard either."

"Maybe you're good at covering your tracks."

"Or maybe I'm innocent. I was an editor and a writer."

"I wasn't born yesterday. You got that job because of your father's connections."

"Maybe."

"Maybe you're a taker like your father. Maybe you came to me yesterday hoping I'd help you financially."

"Is everything really just money to you?"

He leaned toward her. "How dare *you* ask *me* that?"

"Then what about our child? I want our baby to have his or her father's name…and his love, if that's possible. Your love. That's very important to me. Do you want to play a role in his or her life, or not?"

He was silent.

"Because if you don't, one of my oldest and dearest friends lives in London. Her name's Carol Lawton, and when she heard about my problems, she offered me a job in a publishing firm over there. It would mean leaving Louisiana…"

"No!"

"You wouldn't have to stay married to me for very long to give him his name. You could even tell people why you had to marry me."

"No. I couldn't do that." He hesitated, his gaze sweeping her. "So, what kind of theoretical marriage do you imagine we could possibly have? Hell, the only plus we have going for us is that we're great together in bed."

"No sex," she asserted in a low, breathy rush.

"What? You expect me to tie myself to you without even that as a fringe benefit?" He stared through her. "What about you? After the way you kissed me yesterday, are you sure that's what you want?"

"Who are you kidding? You ran off to the swamp yesterday because you couldn't take the heat from that kiss. Our marriage should be about the baby—not us. I, for one—definitely—don't think we should complicate our confusing situation with more sex."

"Definitely?" The edges of his tense mouth relaxed. "You sound so…er…determined."

She wished. Who was she kidding? Jake had such a devastating effect on her, she wondered if she'd be able to resist him if he chose to exploit that weakness some night when she was feeling particularly lonely and unloved.

"So, we're talking about a marriage of convenience. Doubtless, you'll demand a sizable settlement when we split up?" he said.

"No settlement."

"Right. A Butler who isn't after my money. What a refreshing development."

"I'll sign a prenup if you want me to. If you help me find a job somewhere…or help me get started in London, that would be wonderful. We…we wouldn't even have to live together while we're married either. I just want the baby to feel his father wanted him."

"So, no sex and no settlement, huh?"

"I told you, this isn't about sex or money. It's about what's best for the baby. I grew up with all the money in the world, but…"

"But with a real bastard for a father, who never gave a damn about you. Poor little rich girl."

"Please…don't run him down." She stopped, feeling bleak at the dark feelings his words too easily stirred within her. Her childhood with her father may have been loveless, but that didn't mean she could bear other people sitting in judgment of him. Especially not now when he was under house arrest and she herself was uncertain as to his guilt of innocence.

Turning away so he wouldn't read the longing that

welled up inside her, she watched a happy young couple leave the medical building. They were laughing and holding hands. When they reached their battered, compact car, the man pulled the woman into his arms and kissed her fervently. Maybe they, too, had learned they were going to have a baby—only they were both thrilled.

Color me green, she thought.

Watching them, too, Jake stiffened. "Sorry…for what I just said about your dad," he said in a gentler tone.

"It's okay," she whispered. "Our marriage would hardly be a fairy tale with the promise of happily-ever-after like we both dreamed we might know with someone we would have freely chosen some day. And believe me, my father won't be happy about any of this when he finds out."

"If you're determined to get married, we live together," Jake growled.

"Why—when you didn't even want to spend the night with me last night?"

"Who the hell knows? Maybe because I don't trust you as far as I can throw you. As long as you're my wife, I'll keep you close so I can keep an eye on you. Besides, who'll look after you if I'm not around?"

Against her better judgment, at this softer sentiment her heart warmed to him a little.

"My house is big," he said. "You can use the bedroom downstairs that you slept in last night. I'll live on the second floor just like always. But while we're married, you're to have nothing to do with your father."

"But Jake…."

"That's nonnegotiable. I don't trust him or you—and I especially don't trust the two of you together."

"But, he's been arrested. He's alone and in trouble.

I know how that feels. I can't just turn my back on him."

"No involvement. So long as you're my wife, you're not to associate with him. Not even a phone call. You're to stay away from his trial, too. Do you understand me?"

She turned and stared mutely out the window at the cars speeding by beyond the parking lot. What if her father was innocent and she deserted him?

"Do you want to marry me or not?" Jake demanded, hard finality in his voice.

Uncertain, she froze. Finally she nodded. "But only for the baby's sake."

He frowned. "Then you'll agree to stay away from him while we're married?"

"Yes," she whispered in a tone that was so faint it was nearly inaudible.

"There can be no other men in your life while we're married."

"What?" she murmured, feeling crushed that he thought her so low. But then, all he knew was that she'd made love to him the first night she'd met him. How could he possibly realize how special he'd been, how profoundly connected she'd felt to him?

"Since our marriage will upset a lot of people, including my clients and employees, I want it to appear respectable. I don't want to give the press or your numerous enemies anything extra to chew on. So you'll have to agree not to be seen out with other men."

"Of course," she said quietly even as anger began to bubble inside her. "What about you, Mr. High And Mighty? Will the same rule apply to you?"

"I will abide by the same rule—for the same reason."

"Not out of any loyalty to me. But then, why should you feel the slightest loyalty? You don't want to marry me any more than I want to marry you."

"Maybe we're finally beginning to understand each other. Will you be faithful?"

"I said yes already!" she snapped. "Did you really spend the night alone last night?"

He smiled. "So you care a little, too?"

She shook her head much too vigorously, because his quick white smile, the beautiful smile that had seduced her, broadened, causing her blood to heat.

"Were you really alone?" she persisted, furious at him for being so attractive to her just because of a smile and at herself for being so susceptible to his virile brand of sexiness.

"I was. So, when you're my wife, a wife who, for the record, refuses to sleep with me, will you expect me to answer questions like that if I choose not to come home some night?"

"Look…I shouldn't have asked about last night. Forget I did it! I don't care what you do…."

"Okay." Grinning, he held up his hands in a gesture of mock innocence. "But just in case you do care…a tiny bit…I spent the night alone like I said. I was in a houseboat in the swamp behind Belle Rose that I told you about. The only time I left it was when I built a fire on a muddy bank and cooked out."

"What did you cook?"

"A squirrel. There's not much to a squirrel. So it was a long, hungry night spent *alone*."

She frowned. "You killed a little squirrel?"

"I threw my knife. He died in a flash."

"I can't believe you'd be so cruel!"

"What? Do you think I like killing animals? I like to

eat. Do you think you're morally superior because your meat comes in plastic-covered packages in the grocery store?"

Unable to refute his logic but not liking the thought of him eating a helpless, little squirrel any better than she originally had, she began to twirl a strand of her hair and fume as she stared into the distance.

"Look, I had to get away," he said. "Firing everybody... you showing up saying you might be pregnant...was too much for one day. I didn't want to be with you...or any other woman. I know it sounds unusual, going off alone into the wilderness on the spur of the moment, but it's something I do fairly frequently when I need to chill. I'll probably do it again during our marriage—if we're married any time. Happy now?"

"I wish."

"Okay. Back to the plan. We marry. At some point after our child is born, we go our separate ways. No settlement. Just custody arrangements."

"Fine," she agreed, feeling dismal at that prospect.

"That's all you really want?"

"I don't want any of this!"

"You wanted me *that* night," he reminded her.

The memory of it, plus the knowledge that she still wanted him, was not her favorite fun fact.

"You knew how desperate I felt that night...because my father had just told me he was caught in a credit crunch and was on the verge of losing everything, including the bank, if the merger between his shipyard and Claiborne Energy didn't work out."

He nodded.

Knowing that she'd had a date with Logan that night to his grandfather's eightieth birthday, her father had ordered her to do everything in her power to charm

Logan and lull his suspicions that anything might be amiss with the Butler empire. But Logan had been interested only in Cici.

"I felt shy that night at Belle Rose when Logan abandoned me to dance with Cici. I didn't know anyone. Then you started smiling at me from across the room. I smiled back and you came up to me and were so nice, I began to enjoy myself and open up. When you said you were involved with my father in that charity, I told you how worried I was about him. I had no idea you were planning to gang up with Hayes Daniels and accuse him of all those crimes or that maybe the only reason you took an interest in me was to get more information out of me."

"I wasn't planning anything. I had no idea your father was guilty of anything that night. Cici simply wanted to spend time with Logan, and she asked me to take care of you. Hayes didn't clue me in about Mitchell until the next morning. But after the credit problems you'd hinted your father was having, I thought you must have known everything your father was doing and that you were involved. So I was furious at you for deceiving me…and seducing me. I thought maybe you did all that in an effort to buy my silence where your father was concerned. I called you because I wanted to give you a chance to defend yourself. When you wouldn't take my calls, I took that to mean you were guilty."

She hadn't answered the phone because she'd thought him the most treacherous human being alive for seducing her to gain information about her father.

"I was very lonely that night, too," he said. "Being with my family always makes me feel like I don't know my place in the world. Then Logan abandoned you. And you were very, very beautiful."

She blushed, feeling shyly pleased.

"You weren't what I was expecting," he said. "I thought you'd be more like your father but you were nothing like him. You swept me off my feet, as you probably know."

Had he felt the same incredible rush of thrilling excitement in her presence she'd found in his? She wanted to believe that so much.

"Later I wondered if you'd been setting me up," Jake said, killing the softness she'd been feeling toward him. "What about this pregnancy? Did you get pregnant on purpose? Maybe to buy me off?"

"You have to know I didn't. I would never deliberately bring a baby into a mess like this! You seemed so nice that night, and idiot that I was, I trusted you enough to confide in you…and sleep with you."

He stared into her eyes for a long time.

"Okay," he muttered as he finally put the SUV into gear and pulled out into traffic. "Okay."

"The morning after we slept together my father called me and told me about the missing money from the Houses for Hurricane Victims. He said you took it, and that you set him up."

"Well, I didn't. So do you always believe everything your father says?"

"I try to see his side of things…because he's my father and the only parent I have left."

"Look," he growled, "I was nice to you that night because… Hell, I already told you why…." He swore under his breath. "If I'm already damned in your eyes, why should I bother to defend myself?"

After that final question, the thick silence that fell between them grew increasingly strained.

Her mind drifted, and she remembered all too well

how Jake had coaxed her to confide in him their first night together. He'd pretended to listen to her fears concerning her father and to understand; pretended to care about her, and, she, as always, too eager and made happy by any kindness, however small, had ended up in his bed.

But not before she'd told him too much. Pretending sympathy and passion after her confidences, Jake had soothingly kissed her mouth, her face, her throat, her breasts, until he'd made her feel safe and breathless with desire for him.

"It's going to be all right," he'd whispered in a kindly tone. "Dark moments are part of life. They teach us lessons we need to learn."

Soon she'd been clinging, longing for more than his compassion. Forgetting her father and his troubles, she'd begged Jake to make love to her and he'd complied, showering her with all the warmth and passion she'd craved.

Then the next morning Jake had gone out. Later her father had called her and cruelly informed her that the merger was in trouble—and that Jake Claiborne, along with Hayes Daniels, Logan's CEO, had joined forces and reported him to the feds.

Her father and his bank and shipyard had gone down in flames, and Jake was at least partially responsible. Every time she'd thought of how she'd bared her soul and given her body to a man who'd spent the night with her, maybe to milk her for information about her father she'd felt freshly used and humiliated. She'd told herself she shouldn't ever see Jake again or even take his calls.

Not so easy when he'd continued to call her and all her friends had cut her dead.

Most of the time she'd ignored his calls, but once

when he'd phoned her after some particularly vicious stories about her had filled the Internet and newspapers, she'd actually wanted to hear his voice so much she'd answered. They'd soon quarreled, but she'd had the feeling he'd been concerned about her. Then she'd seen him at Logan's wedding. Not that they'd spoken.

She forced her mind back to the present and their new reality. Jake was driving so fast, she was clutching the armrest while houses and strip malls flew by in a blur. When they reached his sprawling home, half a dozen reporters' vans were still lined up in front of his house.

Van doors popped open and reporters rushed toward his SUV as he swerved into his drive. Ignoring them, Jake drove the large vehicle slowly toward a gate that opened electronically and then shut behind them, locking out the invasive horde.

In his garage Jake cut the engine and turned slowly to face her. "Okay, you told me what you want and what you think about me, didn't you?"

"I guess," she replied.

"So, here's what I want out of this disastrous affair. First, we involve as few people as possible in our little scheme. I don't want my grandfather hurt. I'm not on the easiest terms with Logan or his new wife, Cici, so the less they know about this, the better. My grandfather's lonely. I don't want him forming an unsuitable attachment to a woman I don't plan to keep in my life any longer than necessary."

"But he was so friendly to me at his party. Do you really want me to be rude to him?"

"Be polite but cool. In case you didn't realize it, you're natural at that role."

"Thanks...for nothing," she whispered.

"Not for nothing, sweetheart. I agreed to marry you, didn't I? For me—that's a big step."

"For me, too," she said.

His weary expression told her he didn't believe her. "You...proposed."

"Not because I wanted to," she flared.

"So—I guess the next step is to plan our wedding. Are you up to that or do you want me to get Vanessa to handle it?"

As a child her mother had let her decorate for all her parties. Excitedly they'd cut out cardboard stars and glued glitter on them. They'd hung posters and sent out invitations. Once her mother had rented ponies and Alicia and all her friends had ridden in the back yard. But after her mother's death, the celebration of Alicia's birthdays, when remembered, and of the important milestones in her life had always been planned by her father's employees.

No way was she going to let her wedding, such as it was, be planned by Jake's office staff.

"I'll plan it," she whispered, hurt beyond words that he'd suggested such a thing even though she knew her feelings were utterly illogical.

Pregnancy. Hormones. A marriage of convenience to Jake. She was definitely in for a roller-coaster ride.

Six

How ironic that St. Anthony's Garden, the spot his bride had chosen for their wedding, had once been the most popular dueling ground in New Orleans. Too bad the twenty-first century was more civilized. If Jake could have called his bride's father out and shot him, he would have.

Tonight peace reigned. Birds chirped high in the oak trees. A great sculpture of the Sacred Heart reigned in the shady nook that smelled so sweetly of olives. Beyond the garden, tourists chattered as they posed in Pirate's Alley snapping pictures. In the distance street musicians played jazz.

Jake wanted to hate Alicia for complicating his life but reason told him he was equally to blame. He didn't want to marry her, but with every word that the priest uttered binding him to Alicia Butler, his desire for her grew until it felt like a crushing weight. Indeed, ever since he'd agreed to the marriage, thoughts of a naked and eagerly writhing Alicia in his bed had consumed him. All night long he'd lain awake in his bed and thought of her lying in hers downstairs, and he'd wondered if she was thinking of him.

Why did she have to stand so close to him in the dense, humid air so that with every breath he inhaled her perfume?

They say a little piece of paper doesn't matter; that it changes nothing.

They don't know crap. He felt trapped—doomed. At the same time his body raged to have her again. And again. He burned as if he had a fever. His feelings for this woman were illogical and out of proportion to any he'd ever felt for another.

Get a grip.

To distract himself Jake stared up at the triple spires of St. Louis Cathedral towering above their small wedding party hunched together beneath the hurricane-damaged trees. The only guests were his secretary and her bored-looking son, whose dark head was bent over some electronic device.

Thankfully, no member of his own family or Alicia's was present to witness this farce.

It didn't console him that Alicia seemed equally miserable. Her slim fingers that gripped his arm for support shook. Her carriage was rigid; her lovely face ashen.

His heart caught. Why should he sympathize? With a little imagination, surely she could have dreamed up a better solution than a sexless marriage that was already driving him crazy.

A man forced into a shotgun marriage should get

something for his trouble, Jake thought gloomily. Why had he stupidly agreed not to sleep with her?

He'd been sober, that was why. He never thought straight sober.

Too bad he wasn't sober now. Thanks to the shots of whiskey he'd drunk to give him the courage to show up, he felt dangerously near some breaking point.

The late-evening sunlight sifting through the oaks caressed her high, classic brow and made her creamy skin glow. Every time their glances met, her large, dark eyes shot sparks. Why did she keep licking her plump, sensual mouth? Didn't she know that the sight of her tongue had him remembering all the erotic places her moist lips and tongue had touched him with deft little strokes?

His gaze drifted over her straight chiseled nose, her delicate chin and her long graceful neck. Her white lace sheath was skintight, showing off her flawless figure even as the purity of its color made her look virginal. How could a pregnant woman whose breasts were swollen look so untouched and sexy?

Hell.

"Jake, will you have this woman to be your wedded wife, to love her, comfort her, honor and keep her, forsaking all others, so long as you both shall live?" Father Alex asked.

Alicia's hot, dark eyes flashed when they met Jake's again, causing his blood to quicken.

"I will," he whispered hoarsely through clenched teeth.

No matter how he fought to blank out her soft response as she pledged herself to him forever, when her husky voice said, "I will," something shifted inside him and the dark need to claim her obsessed him all over again.

Suddenly he couldn't wait to slip his ring on her finger. He didn't want other men looking at her or touching her without knowing who she belonged to.

She was his wife. His. Period.

As the priest continued to drone, Jake's blood buzzed with fierce passion. Damn it, he wanted to at least kiss her. Wasn't that part of this hellish ceremony?

After an interminable amount of sanctimonious verbiage, the priest finally pronounced them man and wife. "You may kiss your bride," he said.

In a flutter, Alicia tried to turn away, but Jake grabbed her slim wrist and spun her into his hard arms. Cutting off her startled cry of protest, he claimed her mouth with his.

Her hands came up to push against his wide chest, but at the first touch of his lips, she sighed and then whispered his name.

"Jake, oh, Jake…" Her dark eyes were aflame with needs as deep and dark as his own. Rising onto her tiptoes, her arms circling his neck, she clung, leaning into his body.

She was soft and warm. Waves of hot pleasure washed through him. Her lips parted, inviting more.

Maybe everything about their marriage was wrong, but this felt right. Too right.

She was shaking, and so was he as his tongue swept inside her warm, honeyed mouth.

His kiss was needlessly aggressive, possessive and primitive. Once he'd started kissing her, some force outside him took over, and he couldn't stop himself.

He'd married her, hadn't he? She was his. If his pulse

had been racing before the kiss, her satiny mouth and honeyed taste made it accelerate to rocket speed.

Ever since he'd kissed her that afternoon she'd shown up on his doorstep, he'd thought about doing it again, thought about it too damn much. The night he'd spent in the swamp to get his head straight had changed nothing.

His arms crushed her body to his. He wanted her to moan, to press her slim body and heavy breasts closer, and to go limp and beg. The longer he kissed her, the more he wanted from her.

"Jake, we're in public," she whispered shyly. Her slender hands fells away from his neck and wedged themselves between their bodies. Pushing against him, she stared up at him with eyes filled with a mixture of longing and embarrassment.

Slowly her puny efforts penetrated his lust-charged brain, and he realized he was way out of line.

What the hell was he doing? Cursing his damnable weakness for her, he let her go and pivoted free.

Blushing, Alicia fell back a few feet. Turning her back to him, she wiped her mouth and smoothed her hair with hands that trembled.

When Vanessa's sharp, questioning gaze sought his, he felt like an idiot, so he scowled back at her, willing to keep her damn mouth shut and mind her own business for once. She did, but her expression softened as she regarded first him and then his wife.

Then he realized Vanessa wasn't the only member of their little party who was gazing at them with rapt fascination. Her son had stopped playing with his electronic device, and Father Alex had dropped his Bible and looked agitated as he stooped to pick it up.

Feeling a growing pressure to say something or do

something, he turned on Alicia. "Well, now that we've gotten the ceremony out of the way, Vanessa can drive you home. I'm going back to my office."

Alicia's cheeks flamed with wounded pride. "But it's Saturday."

"So?"

"But…I mean…when will you be home?"

He didn't want her to know how profoundly she affected him. He didn't want any of them to know.

"This is hardly a real marriage," he said beneath his breath. "So don't wait up. Watch a movie. Read a book. Pet the beast. Frankly, I don't care what you do."

She turned so white, he was afraid she'd faint. He was reaching for her when Vanessa rushed to her side.

More than anything he wanted to take Alicia in his arms again. He wanted to drive her home and spend the night with her, but his feelings were too raw and charged.

His bride's stricken expression made him feel like a heel. He'd hurt her, and he felt bad about that, too.

How the hell had she turned the tables on him? Her father had stolen money from his charity and from thousands of other innocent people. She was probably in on the entire scam.

But was she?

Damn it. Fool that he was, he very much wanted to believe she was innocent.

"Some honeymoon, huh?" Vanessa smiled as she stood on Jake's front porch. "I'd come in and stay for a while if I didn't have Rick in the car."

"I'll be fine."

"Look, I don't know what's going on with my boss, and I don't really know you, other than what I've read, but if you feel like talking to somebody, remember my home phone is number two on your speed dial. I'll be home with the kids all evening." Vanessa smiled at her.

"Thanks." Just knowing that someone was out there was reassuring. "And thanks for coming today," Alicia said. "I…I always dreamed of a different kind of wedding."

"Don't we all? I had a great wedding and a lousy marriage. Maybe you'll have the reverse. It could happen. Jake's a good man, better than most—but he is a man. Sure, he has his limitations. Trust me, he already had a lot on his plate before you showed up on his doorstep."

"I know. And he thinks it's all my fault."

"I'm beginning to doubt that. You hang in there… and he'll see you for who you really are. Be patient…. Oh, who am I to talk? I'm really the last thing from a romantic."

Vanessa reached for her and pulled her into her arms. After hugging her, she whispered, "Good luck. You deserve it. For what it's worth, you were a very beautiful bride. I think you knocked Jake off his feet. He'll be back, probably sooner than you expect."

"You'd better be calling to tell me you didn't go through with it!" Mitchell roared.

Alicia sagged against a wall as she gripped the telephone. A small voice did ask why he couldn't once take her side. Vanessa, who didn't even know her, was at least trying not judge her.

"But Daddy…."

In spite of the fact that Jake had forbidden her to call her father, she had. While Jake had been at work, she'd left her father a message yesterday informing him of her intention to marry Jake today. Besides, what was the harm? She hadn't told him where or when, so it wasn't as if she'd invited him and he might show up and upset Jake or anything.

As was his custom, Mitchell hadn't even bothered to return her call in a timely fashion.

"So you married him?"

"I called because I didn't want you learn about it by reading it in the newspapers or on the Web."

"As if it matters how I learn it! Where is he now? Is he listening? Gloating?"

"No. He left…right after the marriage ceremony. I don't know where he is or if he's ever coming home. It's not like he wanted to marry me."

"What? Then why the hell… Never mind! It's your funeral. You were a fool to marry him, so you deserve whatever misery he dishes out—which will be plenty, I assure you. You made your bed—now lie in it!" With that her father, who wasn't known for his patience or gentleness, hung up on her, leaving her alone in Jake's big house to enjoy what was left of her wedding day.

As if she could enjoy anything now, trapped in this house, knowing she'd married a man who didn't care for her, knowing that by doing so, she'd turned her father completely against her. She should have realized how totally empty and bereft she'd feel once she truly alienated him.

Laying down her cordless phone, she went in search of Gus. Naturally, he wouldn't come or even mew when she called. When she couldn't find him anywhere on the first floor, she climbed the stairs and found him reclining in the hall outside Jake's locked, bedroom door, thumping his tail while waiting for the master of the house to come home.

"You little traitor. You're worthless sometimes, you know that?"

Gus's eyes remained shut. He looked much too serene as his head remained on his crossed paws even as his tail began to twitch faster.

When she leaned down and picked him up, he meowed loudly and swished his tail to show that he was very much annoyed.

"Traitor! You're my cat, you know, not his," she said, kissing the tip of his ear.

The ear whipped against his skull as she headed down the stairs with him. His yellow eyes stared into hers with a feral look that said he didn't know any such thing. He was his own cat, thank you very much, and, of course, he refused to purr and began to strain to get away.

When she reached the bottom floor, he twisted sharply. A claw from a back paw caught in her forearm as he jumped to the floor. Then he leaped back up the stairs, no doubt to resume his stubborn vigil outside Jake's door.

"He doesn't want you any more than he wants me, you know," she yelled. "Maybe less!" Then she stalked to the hall bathroom, and washed off the beads of blood and toweled her arm dry.

What had she done? Why had she ever thought marrying Jake even for a short time would be a solution to anything? She'd completely alienated her father now, and that loss filled her with a mixture of guilt and regret. Maybe he hadn't been the most attentive of fathers but he'd always been there, at least in the background. Until now.

He was probably going to prison and she'd married the man who was responsible. Tears flooded her eyes but she brushed them aside, refusing to surrender to emotional turmoil or self-doubt. She'd done what she had to do for her baby.

Marching into the kitchen, she poured herself a glass of ice water and then gobbled three dill pickles and a slice of cheese. Then she hurried to her bedroom where she undressed and got ready for a long evening of watching television and reading the books and magazines on her nightstand. All of Jake's magazines had to do with outdoor adventures, especially in Alaska, which sounded like a freezing hell with way too many mosquitoes, not to mention bears. Funny, but hadn't he told her that first night that he sometimes went there to be all alone when he was feeling most stressed?

Later, as she climbed into the big bed all by herself and pulled the sheets up to her neck, loneliness washed over her. She wanted Jake, which was stupid and illogical, considering their circumstances. He had kissed her, yes. Passionately. And then he'd hated them both for it.

Why should she think she could matter to Jake, her father's enemy, who'd been forced to marry her, when she hadn't ever mattered to anyone else before? Not even her own father.

Except Mother.

Don't think about any of that. Or even the present. You will get through this. Concentrate on the future.

Thinking of her own baby, her spirits gradually brightened. She wanted her child fiercely and she was willing to fight for the best possible life for her baby—and that included giving her baby a father. Like her mother, she would create a beautiful nursery. Like her mother, she would spend as much time as possible with her child. And maybe…maybe in time what her father had done or hadn't done would become clear. And Jake's attitude toward her and their child would change.

For no reason at all she remembered how he'd held her hand and listened so intently that first night she'd confided in him. Then he'd taken her in his arms the day she'd shown up on his doorstep and told him she was pregnant. Today he'd kissed her passionately. Maybe it wasn't so foolish to believe he had it in him to make a wonderful father and even a good husband.

She had to hold on to that possibility…and fight for it.

Seven

Alicia woke the next morning feeling stronger—until she caught the thick scent of boudin sausage, frying eggs and steaming chicory-flavored coffee wafting out of the air-conditioning vent.

Obviously Jake had come home. Smiling because she was glad he was home, she sat up. At that slight movement her stomach became hollow and her mouth was suddenly too dry for her to swallow. Throwing her sheets aside, she rushed for the bathroom, intending to splash cold water on her face.

In her haste, she slammed into a low table. The china teacup and saucer she'd forgotten to return to the kitchen last night shattered on the oak floor. With a little cry, she kept running.

After bathing her face, the nausea gradually passed.

Last night to cheer herself up she'd watched a couple of comedies on television, which had eased her depression and caused her to laugh until she'd nearly cried. She'd fallen asleep feeling more hopeful about the future.

At the sound of the bedroom door opening and closing and heavy, male footsteps approaching, she turned slowly.

"Jake?"

"Who else? Are you all right?" he rumbled in his deep, insistent voice.

"Just a touch of morning sickness, but I'm fine. Or at least I will be…soon," she whispered. "Give me a minute. I don't want you to see me like this."

"Are you naked again?" He sounded hopeful.

"You would think of that."

"I'm a man. You're a beautiful woman, who's now my wife. A woman I have a sexual history with. Of course I imagine you naked. All the time."

"Beautiful? I haven't brushed my hair and I've got mascara smudged under my eyes." She groaned.

"I was just trying to make you forget how rotten you feel."

"Just go away."

Then he was there beside her with the disloyal Gus Dear close at his heels. The feline devil had the gall to purr as his black tail curled around Jake's legs and then hers.

"Please leave me—both of you," she begged even as Jake's hand against her back and Gus's silky tail raised goose bumps. "I'll be okay. Really! Go eat your sausage…and give Gus some tuna or something. Oh, God, tuna!" At the thought of tuna, she fought to swallow.

"So it was the smell of our breakfast that made you feel sick."

"Partly, but I just wake up that way a lot of mornings."

"I'm sorry. I shouldn't have left you alone last night."

Jake turned on the faucet, wet a rag and then shut it off. His arms circled her waist gently and he bathed her warm face and lips with a cool rag while Gus's intent yellow eyes watched them both.

"How did you even know I felt queasy?"

"I heard a sound and wanted to make sure you were all right."

"Probably the cup I broke when I ran in here. I'm sorry—"

"Forget it. I'll sweep it up in a minute."

"You must have been very late last night," she said, finally looking up at him. Where was her pride? Why had she admitted she'd even noticed the hour?

His icy blue eyes were shadowed, with exhaustion she thought, and his dark face looked ravaged.

"Yes, I was late. Your light was out. I didn't think you heard me come in."

She wasn't about to admit that she hadn't, even though after her comedies she'd lain alone in the dark for hours listening to every sound the mansion had made. How had she missed his return?

"I didn't want to bother you," he said.

Not for the first time she wondered why he had insisted that they live together if her mere presence was such a torture to him he couldn't stand to be in the same house with her.

"I didn't get much sleep because your cat insisted on sleeping with me."

"You should have locked him out then."

"I did, but he yowled and scratched at my door until

I let him back in. Then he lay on top of me purring for the rest of the night."

"I tried to coax him downstairs to sleep with me earlier but I'm afraid he insisted on lying in wait for you outside your door."

"Stubborn creatures, cats," Jake said.

"Disloyal!" she snapped.

"They know what they want, and they never give up."

Jake's hard glance sought her face and then raked her body, causing confused emotions to course through her. Then he smiled. "I have a feeling he's going to make a real nuisance of himself while we're married. Funny thing—I sort of enjoyed his company last night. I didn't feel like sleeping alone."

If Gus was winning him so easily maybe there was a chance for her....

A chance for what, you fool? This isn't a real marriage. Jake's lost lots of money and his reputation is in shreds. He blames you. Daddy's been indicted because of him. You can't forget any of that—ever!

And yet people dealt with crises and moved on, didn't they?

"I'm all right now, so you can go," she whispered, struggling to stand.

"Are you sure?" he asked.

The warmth of his hands lingered so caressingly on her arms that she was almost seduced into allowing herself the pleasure of his touch. Then she remembered how he'd cut her at their wedding and left her alone all last night. Shakily, she drew herself up taller and pushed his hands away.

"I know you don't like me," she said.

"Is this your perverse way of seeking a compliment?"

"No! Of course not!"

"I think it is, so I'll have to dream one up." He scratched his dark head.

If she didn't know better, she would have thought his quick smile endearingly tender.

"You make it sound like that's very difficult to do."

His hand touched the back of her waist gently and then brushed her fingertips. "Not so difficult as you might think. It's impossible to hate you, *cher*...knowing that you are carrying my child," he murmured.

He squeezed her hand. "You were very beautiful yesterday. Okay. Enough compliments." Then he threw his dark head back and laughed. "Be a good girl. It's early. Quit looking for trouble. Take a shower and comb your hair. You'll feel better, and maybe you won't be so set on bringing out the worst in me—which is fairly easy for you to do—as I'm sure you know."

Thirty minutes later a freshly showered Alicia walked into the kitchen and was surprised to find her husband sprawled at the table in crisp, pressed jeans and a white shirt, looking much too relaxed and handsome with his cup of coffee as he read the paper.

He'd eaten, washed his dishes and cooking utensils and put them away. So why was her husband, who preferred to avoid her, still hanging out in his tidy kitchen? Surely he wasn't eagerly waiting for his temporary bride to appear.

Sunshine streamed through the windows, filling the mostly white room with golden light. He looked so content with his dark head bent over his paper, for a second she could almost forget how angrily he'd loomed beside her at their wedding yesterday before vanishing on their wedding night. She could almost imagine herself a happy bride.

Then their reality slammed her anew. He was her sworn enemy. Kindness from him was not to be counted on or treasured. It was to be distrusted. Thus, when he looked up at her with an amiable smile on his dark face, she frowned.

"What?" He sat up straighter and finger-combed his dark hair. "Am I guilty of some awful new crime or do I just have a crumb on my lip? Or nose?"

As he brushed his mouth and nose with his napkin, she laughed in spite of herself.

"No."

"You want me gone so you can have the kitchen to yourself? Well, I won't be bullied out of my own house."

"I assumed you'd be at the office, avoiding me again...like last night," she said.

"Right," he said, "we're the weirdo newlyweds who did some very interesting variations on sex—positions that are probably still illegal in some states—on this very table, but now we are supposed to have an aversion to sex."

Maybe because he was so preoccupied with sex or the lack of it, she remembered lying naked on the kitchen table in this very room, crying out his name in the heat of her passion. She'd loved him that night, incoherently. With his every touch, with every flick of his tongue, he'd awakened a fire inside her she hadn't known existed, and the embers of that fire still hadn't gone out.

As he stared at the table, she began to sizzle.

Sensing an advantage when she blushed, he moved his hand back and forth across the smooth finish of the tabletop in the way he might stroke a woman. "You know you could change your mind about that. I won't object."

"But you don't even like me."

"I'm a man." He ran his hand along the tabletop again, caressing it. "I can compartmentalize. Let's just say my body likes yours, and it wonders…upon occasion… rather frequently—hell, all the time—how yours feels about mine. If you want the truth, I don't think I slept a wink last night. I kept thinking of you in your bed and me upstairs sleeping with a cat."

She moved to set a kettle boiling on the stove. "You make us sound like we're no better than animals."

"You're in my house, cute as hell…available. I wouldn't be normal if you didn't tempt me."

"Even though you hate my father?"

"*He* isn't here. With any luck he'll be sent to a place where he can't hurt any more people."

Fortunately, the tea kettle whistled. With hands that shook she pulled an egg out of the fridge and placed it in the middle of a pot. As she poured boiling water over it, the egg cracked. She set the pot on the stove top anyway. She was almost glad he'd reminded her of her father's plight and the satisfaction he took in it. The knowledge helped her build up her defenses.

"I'm just being honest," he said. "There's a bit of the wild in us all. Why else do we have to spend years and years civilizing our young? Why else did we behave like we did *that* night? On this very table?"

"Stop…."

"You brought out the beast. I think you liked it, too. In fact, I know you did."

She wet her lips with her tongue and was too aware of his avid eyes glued to her moist lips. For six weeks she'd been a virtual prisoner in her apartment, hated by all. Loneliness and the desire for companionship had built into an almost palpable need. If he stuck around in the same room where she'd been so crazy to have him, saying he wanted her, she wasn't sure how well she'd control her attraction for him.

"Can we please please change the subject?" she pleaded.

Newspapers rustled as he set his paper aside. "You mean…from sex?" he murmured thickly.

Afraid he'd see her flushed cheeks again and understand just how much he affected her, she kept her back to him. "Yes."

"Okay," he muttered. "Sure. Hey, here's some good news for you that has nothing to do with sex. Nowhere in this newspaper did I see any mention of our marriage. Looks like we're still flying under the radar. When people find out, I'll be bombarded at the office. No telling who else will fire me."

"I'm sorry for ruining your life. If you've finished your own breakfast, you don't have to stay here just to entertain me, you know," she whispered.

"I wanted to discuss a few more things—other than sex."

The word sent more tingles through her. "Grrrr."

He laughed. "I think you're running as hot as I am. Maybe hotter."

"What things did you want to discuss?" she said through gritted teeth, too hatefully aware of her heart racing.

"For starters, tomorrow I want to make some financial arrangements for you. Open a new account you can sign on, so you won't feel so dependent on me."

"Why would you do that when I imagine you want

revenge for all those crimes you believe my father and
I committed against you?"

"I didn't dream up what you or your father did, so
I'm under no illusions about your character. Or his.
Especially his. But like you pointed out, you have no
money or allies. You're my wife and you're carrying
my baby. You need to buy things for yourself and our
baby."

"I couldn't possibly accept—"

"Anything from me—the enemy." His lips had
tightened. "I'm afraid you'll have to. What choice do
either of us have? Much as I might want to treat you
like a pauper, it would make me look bad. Much as you
want to treat me as the enemy, you have no one else who
cares as much as I do.

"Our baby needs a nursery. Supplies. A baby bed.
God only knows what else. Am I right?"

She sighed. "I do want to create a charming nursery.
I guess since I always had money, I never thought much
about it. My job as an editor didn't pay much, but it
didn't matter. I loved writing and editing, and I could
rely on the trust fund money. So, now that the money's
all gone, I've got to get used to a new way of living. And
thinking. I'll need to think about a career."

"True. But not now. Until the baby's born, I'm going
to take care of you. And the baby. That's final."

"Do your people always do what you say, when you
say?"

"You're my wife. My broke, pregnant wife. You're
my responsibility. You don't have a choice. Why is that
so difficult for you to grasp?"

"Maybe because ours is the last thing from a real
marriage."

"Right. So, let's be sure and make ourselves just as

miserable as we can at every possible opportunity. Is that your goal?"

No, this morning she just wanted to stay out of his arms…and his bed. His talking about sex had stirred her up.

Jake grabbed his paper and stood up.

Good. She wanted him gone, needed him gone. The sooner, the better. His kindness and concern for her this morning mixed with his sexiness unnerved her. She, who always read too much into kindnesses and into making love, didn't want to soften toward him.

It wouldn't be just sex for her as it would be for him. She would weave all sorts of interlocking emotions around an act that meant next to nothing to him, and each time she went to bed with him, her feelings for him would deepen. Pretty soon she'd be thinking they had a real relationship. He would be thinking she was easy and very replaceable the minute their baby was born. She would be thinking he would become a real husband and father.

Theirs was a marriage of convenience. She was living with him for the baby's sake, so he might grow attached to it even before it was born.

For her own emotional safety, she had to keep her distance.

But could she?

Eight

By eight o'clock Monday morning, everybody who was anybody in New Orleans knew Jake Claiborne had married Alicia Butler. Their enemies, and they had legions, viewed their match with immense suspicion, just as Jake had known they would. Like vultures circling, the boldest and meanest were the first to pounce and tear off their pound of flesh.

No sooner was Jake in his building and striding down the hall toward Vanessa's office with his briefcase, than he heard his phones buzzing. Vanessa would answer one, quickly and efficiently, put the caller on hold and catch the next.

Then Jake walked into her office. Swiveling in her chair, Vanessa frowned and cupped the phone, waving him over with a swift motion.

"It's Coulter, the city manager. Line two. Third time he's called. Says it's urgent. I've got Davis on one."

Blake Davis was a heavy donor for Houses for Hurricane Victims.

"He sounds really annoyed," she said. "He isn't the only one. The phones have been ringing off the wall." She handed him a list of names and phone numbers.

Jake had expected trouble, and he was prepared to deal with it. Under no circumstances would he have even considered abandoning Alicia and their newborn baby. In time, the trouble would blow over.

"I'll take them in my office."

Without preamble Coulter told Jake he'd learned about his marriage to Miss Butler from concerned taxpayers, so he was afraid he was going to have to hire a new architect to finish the concert hall near the French Quarter.

"Sorry, Claiborne, I know she's not her father, but with her last name and his close association to you through Houses for Hurricane Victims, there'd be too much political fallout if we didn't terminate our relationship with you. We can't have any taint of scandal on this public project, especially after Katrina."

Jake picked up line one next.

"I was very disappointed by the news of your marriage to Mitchell Butler's daughter," Blake Davis said. "*Very disappointed*. Until this, I told myself you weren't involved in all that money disappearing. Needless to say, your marrying Butler's daughter would give even a naïve fool second thoughts. I'd look like an idiot if I didn't bail, damn it."

Before Jake could defend Alicia, Raymond Lewis, his top designer, barged into his office and slammed a legal document on his desk.

Jake waved the phone at Lewis, indicating he was busy. Ignoring Lewis, he spoke into the mouthpiece.

"I'm not involved with the money disappearing. Neither is my wife. She has nothing to do with any of her father's illegal activities."

"Save it for the jury. George is going to call you a little later and withdraw his support as well. Without us, HFHV is history."

"You know who you're punishing—the people who've been waiting for houses for two years."

"That should keep you up nights—not me!"

Jake sighed. He'd known when he'd married Alicia there would be fallout. What he hadn't realized was how determined he would feel about protecting Alicia.

No sooner had Davis hung up than Lewis leaned threateningly over his desk.

"What?" Jake set the receiver down. "What's wrong?"

"Your wife for starters. My letter of resignation is on your desk."

Jake glanced down, speed-reading the document. He tore it in two. "This is ridiculous."

"Not to me. When you fired all my top designers the other day, I still believed you were a man of integrity who was being unfairly judged by the media," Lewis said. "When I heard you secretly married, I wised up about you fast."

"Sorry you feel that way. I believe my wife is innocent."

"Who do you think you're kidding? Mitchell must have bought and paid for you. You're dirty, and he's threatened to spill what he knows unless you promise to take care of his little girl while he's in the slammer."

"You're very wrong. I wouldn't give that bastard the time of day."

Lewis didn't stay to argue the point. Turning on his

heel, he stalked out, banging as many doors as he could, thereby causing such a ruckus, people stopped what they were doing and stepped out of their offices to watch.

Vanessa rushed into Jake's office. "Your face is a dangerous shade of red. I'd tell you to sit down, but you're already sitting. What exactly happened in here?"

"Lewis called me a crook and quit. Unfortunately, it's becoming a familiar refrain. Not that I didn't expect something like this when word got out."

"Sorry the honeymoon had to end so fast."

What honeymoon? Jake thought bleakly.

"What do you say we get back to work—unless you're going to call me a crook and quit on me, too."

"I can't afford high-minded principles. I've got three growing sons to support. You should see my grocery bills." She smiled encouragingly.

"Glad somebody believes in my character."

She laughed. "Cheer up. When you've sunk this low, there's nowhere to go but up. Your wife's a beautiful woman. Seems kind of sweet, too. You could have done worse."

"You think so?"

She nodded.

Odd the way Vanessa's faith in Alicia eased his tension. Vanessa had excellent instincts.

"And she's a breeder. You don't always know that when you tie the knot. Your kid will be better off if the two of you figure out how to be happy together. I hope you give her a chance."

"You are not my therapist! Out!"

"That's my cue." She saluted him and made a brisk exit.

You could have done worse. And she's a breeder.

Jake leaned back in his chair and massaged his brow.

He'd been married to Alicia what, two nights? Not that he felt married exactly. No—he felt frustrated and lonely.

He never felt lonely. He liked being alone. Hell, besides having had no sex, they'd hardly spent any time together. Why was this bothering him so much when he hadn't even wanted to marry her?

Yesterday after breakfast, even though she'd locked herself in her bedroom, he hadn't wanted to leave her. To give her the run of the house, he'd stayed outside doing odd maintenance jobs like throwing out a plastic storage box full of mildewed life preservers. And all that time, he'd been wondering if she was as aware of him as he was of her.

So much for the first day of his marriage to his very sexy wife. This morning, he'd hoped that when he left for work he'd quit thinking about her. He'd been glad that, unlike her, he had somewhere to go where maybe he could get his mind off her. But even here he hadn't been able to stop thinking about her.

He'd known their marriage would cause more problems, at least in the short term. Not that it was fun to deal with the onslaught of attacks from all directions. Still, they were going to have a baby. Every time he remembered how pale and haunted Alicia had looked when she'd turned up on his doorstep with her news, he felt more determined than ever to stand by her.

When the phone rang again, he cringed. Fortunately it was only his twin brother.

"You're a lucky man," Logan said.

"Good to know somebody thinks so."

"Alicia didn't know a damn thing her father was up to."

"What makes you so sure?"

"Mitchell lied to and manipulated everybody. I know how he was with her because she and I went out…for a while. But then, you already know that," Logan trailed off awkwardly.

"Right."

Jake didn't like Logan reminding him he'd been there first with Alicia any better than he'd ever liked Logan telling him what to do or think.

"Every time I took her anywhere, people envied me," Logan said.

Jake frowned. "Well, she's married to me now."

"True. And how did that happen so fast? Last time we talked, you said she didn't want to date anybody. Then my CEO and you went to the feds and Butler really crashed in flames."

If he'd felt closer to Logan, maybe he would have told him about the pregnancy and explained the sense of responsibility he felt toward Alicia. But for a lot of years Jake had kept Logan in the dark about his life. So, for now, Jake wanted to keep it that way.

"Look, I'm sorry I didn't invite you to the wedding. If it makes you feel any better, we didn't invite anyone. Well…except for my secretary, who brought her son…but only because we needed a witnesses. Frankly, Alicia and I wanted to keep our marriage quiet as long as possible. Not easy when satellite trucks and photographers are camped on our doorstep."

"Well, the papers and Internet are full of it this morning."

"They're all damning me as a crook the equal of Butler—so you see why I wanted to keep things quiet."

"It'll blow over. Alicia's a wonderful woman."

Jake appreciated his brother's vote of confidence—not that he voiced this.

"No matter what it costs you, she'll be worth it."

Vanessa had said almost the same thing. Difficult as his relationship with Logan had been in the past, Jake respected his opinion.

"Treat her right—you hear? Someday you might have a family together."

A family. At the thought of the child that she was already secretly carrying, he felt his neck grow hot.

"Like you know everything because you're ten minutes older," Jake said.

"Being first is everything." Logan laughed.

Jake was silent.

"Well, Cici will be calling Alicia to invite you all out here to Belle Rose for dinner, so we can at least celebrate this with Grand-père, who's thrilled, by the way. The two of you could spend the weekend."

Jake's skin heated at the thought of sharing a double bed in an upstairs guest room with Alicia all night and trying to keep his hands off her.

"That's not necessary."

"Sure it is. We're family. It's about time we started acting like one."

Family. Heavy word coming from Logan, Jake thought before he said goodbye.

He began to think about his wife, wondering what Alicia could possibly be doing at home all by herself. He wanted to call her and see how she felt. He hoped she wasn't feeling nauseated.

Don't think about her. You did what she asked. You married her, didn't you? That's all you owe her.

Why didn't he feel like it was? Why did he feel… sorry for her…concerned even?

Hell. He felt a whole lot more than that. When her father had been indicted, her whole world had been destroyed. She'd lost her job and her friends in Louisiana. Maybe he was having problems himself right now, but his battles were nothing compared to hers.

Concerned about her father, she'd seemed so genuine and sweet the first night they'd met. She hadn't acted as if she had anything to hide.

If only he could stop remembering their lovemaking in such excruciating detail. She'd been so slick and warm and tight when he'd been inside her.

He wanted her again—badly.

Alicia arose from the computer, sure that if she didn't stop reading Basil Bienville's revolting blog about her marriage and her father along with the scathing comments posted by his readers, her morning sickness would return.

Those of us who've followed the scandals involving Butler Bank and Houses for Hurricane Victims shouldn't really be so amazed to learn that Alicia Butler has been living openly with Jake Claiborne. Or surprised that now we know why. According to a source close to the bride, Claiborne married the daughter of the man he turned over to the feds and publicly claims to hate Saturday evening in St. Anthony's Garden.

Why so hush-hush? Who's really responsible for the funds missing from Houses for Hurricane Victims? Does this marriage confirm what we already suspected—that Claiborne is as big a thief as Butler?

"Damn sure confirms it for me," wrote an angry reader.

If Jake hadn't married her, nobody would want to nail him to the cross.

Feeling isolated, she began to pace, wondering if there was anything lonelier than being in a house alone that wasn't one's own, especially when you were upset and needed to talk to someone—anyone. In one's own house, there were always a million little tasks to perform to distract oneself.

Not so in Jake's house—unless she read his outdoor adventure magazines or decided to answer his phone, which had rung nonstop ever since he'd left for the office. For a while she'd been too nauseated to move, so answering it had been out of the question. But her nausea seemed to be in the past now.

If in the six weeks before her marriage she'd felt as if she were dead to everybody she'd ever known, now she truly felt buried alive.

If only Carol, the one friend who'd stood by her, didn't live in London…. Damn the time difference.

Feeling the need to talk to a real friend, she sat down and dialed Carol.

Carol's voice mail picked up.

"Carol here. Sorry we're not home…."

Alicia listened to her friend's message until it ended with a beep. She almost felt like calling her back so she could hear her voice again. Instead, she left a message and then called Kimberly, who formerly had been her best friend at work. They'd gone out together to movies and concerts and for the occasional drink or dinner.

"It's me, Alicia," she said when Kim answered.

There was a telling pause. "I…I read in the paper that you got married this past weekend," Kim finally said.

"You can't believe everything you read, you know."

"I know. Still… Well, I hope you'll be very happy."

"Thanks." Alicia paused. "So, how have you been?"

"Busy. Deadlines. A couple of writers are late with their stuff. We're juggling. You know how it is."

"I've missed you so much. Missed work, too. I really need to talk to someone."

"I have missed you…. Look, Alicia, I'd love to talk. Really I would, but Sam's waving at me to get off the phone now, so I…I really do have to go."

"But, Kim, please—"

"Bye for now, Alicia. Sorry. I'll call you when I have a minute. Really I will."

Then Kim was gone. Just like Alicia's entire life was gone.

She closed her eyes and let the silence of the empty house fill her for a long moment. Deliberately trying to blank her mind, she kept them shut for ten minutes. When at last she opened them, she felt as if something inside her had shifted.

Just because things looked bad now, they didn't have to stay that way. She was pregnant. Her baby meant she had a future. Maybe a future she couldn't imagine yet, but a future. She shouldn't dwell on the past—she should make plans for the months and years ahead. Not easy when she was under siege in this house with nothing to do and her heart feeling like a heavy lump in her chest. But she could do it.

Where to start? What did people who stayed home do all day?

They had lives. They went out with their friends. They shopped. They went to their gyms. They could do these things because they still had friends and their bank accounts weren't frozen. They planned parties, fundraisers. They weren't their federally-indicted father's number one scapegoat.

Alicia walked over to a kitchen window. Lifting the drape, she stared out at the overgrown yard and beds. As a child she'd gardened with her mother. Her job and her apartment hadn't made gardening a feasible hobby. Maybe there was something outside she could do. She couldn't face days and days inside the house watching television.

Scarcely knowing what she did, she ran to her room to change. Then she let herself out the back door, banging the screen door behind her.

Curious, Gus slipped out behind her. She went into the garage and dug through drawers and shelves until she found a large straw hat, a pair of old gardening gloves that were too large and some gardening tools. Then she began to attack the beds, weeding, pruning, turning the rich, loamy soil.

Most of the yard was shaded by magnolia and oak trees. It felt good to be outdoors. Since she couldn't hear the phone, she didn't stress about the hate calls.

Once or twice she took a break and drank a tall glass of water sitting on the rocker on the veranda. The rocker made her think of the baby and how nice it might be to bring her or him out here for a feeding.

When it was time for lunch, she made herself a sandwich. After a short break, she tackled a second bed.

At least she was no longer cooped up inside. Her shoulders and lower back began to ache so much, she almost looked forward to going inside and reading an Alaska adventure story, even one that focused on bears and mosquitoes.

She was smiling at that thought when something large crashed behind her. Whirling, she stared at the hedge that lined the fence separating the front yard from the back.

"Hell," fumed a hoarse voice.

Mumbled curses were followed by more branches thrashing about and then by heavy, stumbling footsteps.

Muddy spade in hand, she stood up just as a wild-eyed, grizzled man leapt out of the azalea bushes at her.

"Well! Looky here! Caught you!" he said.

"You're not supposed to be back here, so you'd better go!"

"Or you'll what—*Mrs. Claiborne?* Scream? For your new husband? Well, he's not here, as you probably know. You won't answer your phone. You won't come to your door. How else could I talk to you?"

She didn't know whether he was dangerous or not, but her pulse was pounding in her throat as she began backing swiftly toward her kitchen door.

"Who are you?" she asked, determined to keep him talking.

"Just one of your father's investors who lost everything. Now I can't support my wife or daughter. Or put my grandchildren through college. Not that you care…"

"But I do."

"He probably spent it on you! I hoped you'd get yours when they kicked you out on the street. But you've landed on your feet, haven't you, living in this mansion with your brand-new husband! You think you're so smart you don't have to pay for what you did!"

"What do you want?"

"My money! That's what I want! Why shouldn't you pay me back what your father took?"

"Because I have no money of my own."

"Liar. Look at this house."

"Rented."

Just as he lunged toward her, the automatic gate to the driveway began to slide open. A second later Jake's big black SUV rushed down the driveway and slammed to a standstill. Jake jumped out.

It was too early for him to be home, but Alicia had never been happier to see him.

"Hey!" he yelled, shouting her name as he rushed toward her.

"Who the hell are you?" Jake demanded, stepping between Alicia and the stranger. "What the hell do you think you're doing here? Get lost. Now."

The older man stared at Jake, whose lean body looked massive and powerful even in his tailored suit. Then the man nodded slowly, as if something of Jake's meaning had penetrated.

"I'll go," he said wearily. "I'm finished here. She and her father have finished me and my whole family. You'd better be careful boy, before she finishes you, too. Or maybe you're as bad as she is."

Alicia stood behind Jake as he relocked the gate after the man had exited. Reporters eager for his story swarmed the stranger, their mikes held high.

"It's early for you to be home," Alicia said shakily to Jake.

He turned. "When I couldn't reach you by phone during lunch either on your cell or the house line, I got nervous. So I decided to drive home and check on you myself. I'm certainly glad I did."

"Me, too," she agreed weakly.

"That guy had clearly lost it."

"With good reason," she said. "He's lost all his life savings."

"Still, there's no telling what he might have done."

"I think he just wanted to vent."

"People are very angry about this. I'm going to hire you a driver, someone who'll double as your bodyguard."

"No…" She didn't want to be any more of a burden than she already was.

"So you can go out some. So you won't be totally alone here all the time."

"No!"

"I'm afraid I'm going to insist. It's for the baby's safety. Not just yours."

"Oh." His words stung a little. He didn't care about her. Still, the good part was he cared about the baby.

"So, you've been digging in the flowerbeds, I see."

"How can you tell?" she asked.

Leaning toward her, he wiped a speck of dirt off her nose and then another off her chin. Then his mouth quirked into a lopsided smile that made him too handsome to believe. "Trust me. It didn't take Sherlock Holmes."

"I was very scared before you came," she said, her voice breaking in heartfelt gratitude.

"And I felt crazier and crazier at the office when you didn't answer." He caught himself. Clearly he felt awkward about revealing his concern. "Well, speaking of the office, I'd better get back to work."

"Yes. Sorry to be such a bother. I'll try to be better behaved."

He smiled. "Then promise me you won't go into the

backyard alone until I find someone to see after you. And why don't you get a new cell phone number so I can reach you."

Feeling pleased that he was so protective, and a little shy, she nodded.

When he left, she stood at a front window and watched him drive away. Long after he'd disappeared she continued to stare at the lengthy shadows beneath the trees across the street.

When she finally turned back to face the empty house, she didn't feel quite as lonely as she had before. Her heart felt lighter, her mood brighter. She actually looked forward to making plans for the future and shopping for the baby with a driver.

Jake had come home because of her.

He'd protected her and the baby.

For no reason at all she kept remembering the way he'd smiled so tenderly when he'd wiped the dirt off her nose.

He didn't really care. Not about her.

Still…it felt nice to pretend that he might.

Nine

The more Alicia tried to ignore Jake, the more fascinated by him she grew.

She knew that there were no photographs or personal memorabilia in his house. It was as if he wanted no link to his past. Why? Had he had a difficult past too?

She knew the exact hour he left for work. Seven-thirty. On the dot.

She knew the exact hour he came home. Six-thirty.

She knew that he had trouble sleeping, that he often paced at night, pausing at her door. The knob would turn and she would sit up, listening in the dark, charged with the hope and fear that he might open it.

She knew what he ate for dinner—fast food because she found the wadded wrappers and boxes in the trash. Pizza mostly. Way too much pizza.

It's none of your business that he never eats vegetables.

A real wife would at least cook healthier choices for him. But it was dangerous to even think she might ever be that woman.

Too often Alicia thought about Jake rescuing her from that man in the garden. It seemed uncanny that he'd known just when to come home. It was as if he were tuned into her in a psychic way.

When she relived that scene, she wished she'd kissed him.

Stupid. A kiss wouldn't change anything. She was the woman he'd married reluctantly and kept hidden away from his business associates, friends and family; the woman he chose never to be seen with in public.

After two whole weeks of living such separate lives, Alicia felt like she was going mad. She longed to eat with him, to talk to him—to know him better, to know why he looked so increasingly tense.

"He sounds nicer than I pictured him," Carol said during one of their morning chats as Alicia prepared a beef stew for her dinner. "And his photographs on the Web are absolutely hunky."

Tell me about it.

"Coming home like that…at just the right moment when that man was in your backyard, it's no wonder…"

"No wonder what?"

"No wonder that you're having these fantasies and starting to like him."

Grrrrr. "I am not having fantasies or starting to like him," she grumbled, hating that she was so easy to read even over an overseas phone call.

"If you say so, love."

For some reason Alicia didn't snap back with a sassy retort.

Carol had started calling her a couple of times a week after she'd heard Alicia's message when Alicia had phoned her when she'd been so depressed.

"You should never have stayed in Louisiana," Carol said. "You should have come to London and taken that job I found you."

"I know. Part of me agrees. But I felt I had to give him a chance...for the baby's sake... Being here, at least, means the baby is part of his life."

"Well, that was very generous of you, under the circumstances."

"I know what it feels like to be without a parent. Really without any parents. What if I died, and the baby ended up with strangers?"

"Still, I can't help thinking you would have been better off to have gotten clean away from that whole mess, started over here in the U.K., you know what I mean. Nobody's ever heard of Dear Old Daddy being accused of anything over here."

"Sounds lovely. Jake thinks Daddy's a criminal, and since he sees me solely as Daddy's daughter, well...he probably thinks I'm guilty, too."

"Are you sure about that?"

"Well, he's said it often enough."

He hadn't said it lately. But that was only because they barely spoke.

"Well, after you have the baby and the baby's old enough, I'll whisk you and the baby over here and take care of you. I have so many friends, many of them men, and they'll all adore you. You'll forget Jake in no time. You'll meet a handsome Brit, fall madly in love and live happily ever after."

Carol's supportive attitude warmed her. But the

thought of leaving Jake and then their child growing up far from its father did not.

That evening when Jake came home early, she was still out in the backyard digging. Victor, her bodyguard/ chauffeur, had helped her buy a crib for the nursery, more azaleas and a birdcage to house an injured mourning dove she'd rescued on the back veranda as well as several bird feeders. Victor had set up the birdcage, the crib and the feeders, but she hadn't yet finished preparing the soil to plant the azaleas. She hadn't come inside and eaten the beef stew she'd cooked. She was tired but eager to finish what she'd started.

Suddenly Jake was just there, towering behind her as he watched her attack his flowerbed like a dog burying a treasured bone. Since she didn't know he was there, she slung a shovel load of dirt onto his expensive Italian loafer.

"Hey," he said, chuckling as he shook his foot. "Aren't you getting a little carried away? If you don't stop that we'll have to shower together."

She whirled. His eyes were shadowed despite his amusement. He looked exhausted, both physically and mentally.

But when their glances touched, he smiled, that quick, sexy flash of straight white teeth that always made her stomach feel hollow…but in that good way. She felt a zing.

Before she thought, she smiled right back at him. The thought of showering with him held way too much appeal.

He knelt and cupped her elbow lightly. "I'll bet that'll wait until tomorrow. You don't want to overtire yourself."

Her breath caught. "What are you doing home this early?"

"I brought some work home."

"Oh." She turned back to the flowerbed and continued to dig, but not quite so vigorously as before. She was too aware of the electric heat of his touch, of his nearness, of the desire to be held closely in his arms.

"You know, I think there are fewer trucks outside. Maybe the media's interest in us is lessening just a bit."

"Hope so."

He let her go and stood up. "I met Victor out front. Told him he could go home for the day, that I'd see about you this afternoon."

She was too conscious of his long shadow falling across her. She wished he'd kneel again and touch her. Just her elbow would be enough.

Instead he took a step backward. He'd been being polite, that was all.

"Well, I guess I'll go inside and get to work," he said after watching her for a while longer.

No doubt he'd quickly vanish upstairs and lock her out of his office. Gus would probably follow him as he usually did, and she would be as lonely as she was every night. Only lonelier because she'd feel left out after Jake had been so nice.

That cat of hers was incorrigible. He would never stay in her room once Jake came home. If she tried to force him, he would go to the door and yowl and paw until she let him out. If she ever felt lonely enough to crack her door to see what was going on in the rest of the house, she would sometimes hear violent blasts of sound from Jake's television set upstairs and imagine her cat napping serenely at Jake's feet while macho actors gunned each other down.

If she went into the kitchen to find a snack, she would discover Jake's fast-food wrappers in the garbage and guilt about his bad diet would gnaw even as she reminded herself what he wanted was no wife at all.

When the screen door banged behind him, she raced after him, slowing her pace when she neared the kitchen because she did not want him to think her in a mad hurry to catch up to him, although she was.

"Smells good," he said, sounding almost wistful when she walked into the kitchen.

"Beef stew. Nothing fancy."

"Reminds me that I was so tired and ready to get home I forgot to stop and get anything to eat tonight. Pizza every night gets old."

Was that a hint? "Would you like some stew? There's enough for two."

"I think I would…if you don't mind. Why don't you wash up while I set the table?"

Did that mean he was calling a truce?

"Okay. I'll just be a second," she whispered in a voice that was much too breathy and eager.

He grinned broadly. "I think it may take you longer than that."

"Do I look that horrible?"

"Loaded question, *cher.* But no, you don't look horrible. You look cute that way."

What way? She ran to her bedroom, only to let out a little shriek and stomp her feet when she saw her filthy reflection in the mirror. Did she only imagine his chuckle? Flecks of black dirt spotted her face, shirt and shorts and greased her arms.

She kicked off her muddy shoes and shed her grimy

clothes. Showering quickly, she tied her hair in a red ribbon and put on a pair of red capris and a white shirt. Then she slipped on gold bangles and a pair of gold sandals. The last thing she did was dab her wrists with perfume.

When she returned to the kitchen the flash of heat in Jake's blue eyes and his crooked grin told her that she looked presentable.

He'd poured himself a glass of wine and her a glass of sparkling water garnished with a slice of lime. He'd put on music and had set the table for two in the dining room. A contented Gus lay in the middle of the kitchen, his tail lazily thumping the tile as he waited for the stew to come out of the oven. She knew that behind her back, Jake fed Gus table scraps. The scene felt too domestic and comfortable and was much too close to her dream of a fantasy marriage with a man she loved.

"So, how was your day?" he asked, his interested gaze sweeping her and making her feel hot and strange.

"Same as always," she replied, her tone clipped as she sipped her icy water and fought to shore up her defenses.

"The yard's looking good."

"At least it's given me something to do. And I feel happy outside. And your day?"

"Still putting out fires that have to do with my association with your father and now my marriage to you," he said coolly. "Today was particularly bad. The entire Houses for Hurricane Victims board dropped by and demanded my resignation. After that meeting, I decided to come home."

"I'm sorry."

"It was a cause close to my heart…so, bad subject. What do you say we change it?"

"What would you prefer to talk about?"

"You," he said.

"We already did that. The first night we met when I stupidly confided my entire life story to you…before I knew who you really were and what you were about to do to my father. Remember?"

Fire flashed in his eyes and she regretted goading him.

"All right, then. You choose what we talk about," he said.

"You."

"Boring subject."

"Maybe to you."

"All right. What do you want to know?"

"Why were you estranged from your family for nine years?"

He flinched involuntarily, and just for an instant she thought she saw pain shadow his eyes. Then his features hardened into that neutral mask that was all too familiar. It was his habit to shut people out, to keep them at a distance.

"My brother took the woman I'd loved all my life away from me, so I left," he said, so bitterly she felt as if a fist had grabbed her heart and squeezed hard.

Ask a tough question, you get a tough answer.

"You mean Cici?" she whispered.

"Do we have to talk about this?" He yanked at the knot of his silk tie as if his collar had suddenly tightened to the point it was choking him. Then he unbuttoned the top two buttons of his shirt.

At the strip of dark hair now visible at the base of his throat, she sucked in her breath.

"Was it Cici?" she said.

"Yes," he said. *"Cici.* He took her and discarded her

to save me, he said. He broke her heart and married a wealthy, suitable girl."

Savagely he slung his tie across a kitchen chair. "I found that hard to forgive."

Because his heart, the heart he guarded so closely, had been shattered.

"What happened to Logan's first wife?"

"She died."

"And you… Are you still in love with Cici?" She hated the way her husky voice was suddenly quivering.

"No. But that doesn't mean I trust my brother."

Maybe he wasn't being entirely honest about no longer loving Cici. Alicia knew she shouldn't care. Then why did she feel as if that awful fist around her heart had tightened?

"But you came back," she whispered, her tone barely audible.

"This is my home. When Katrina struck, and so many people needed houses and help of the most basic kind, I had the right skills to make a difference. I felt compelled to return. Though I wasn't ready to connect with a family I believed to be ruthlessly materialistic and cruel. Do you understand why I had at least some sympathy for your problems with your father that night? But then, Hayes Daniels hadn't filled me in on the whole story yet."

Jake's eyes were blazing suddenly.

"I'll get the stew," she said quietly, not wanting to push him—or herself—any closer to such dangerous subjects. Not that she could forget that he'd made a play for her that first night only after Cici had gone after Logan.

"Why don't we eat out on the back veranda? I need some fresh air," he said.

"Okay," she agreed.

In silence he moved the place settings to the table outside while she got their dinner ready to serve. He did not look at her or speak to her again as they spooned food onto their plates and carried them along with their drinks outside.

Despite the humidity it was a lovely evening with voluminous, pink thunderheads looming in the west. Oblivious to the distant storms, birds sang in the trees as they settled down for the night. She could hear a child playing with a barking dog in a nearby yard. But most of all she was conscious of Jake sitting across the table from her. He looked tall and dark, smoldering even, as the delicious scent of his aftershave wafted toward her disturbingly.

For a while he ate in brooding silence, his spoon clinking against his bowl. And all the while as she started at every clink, she felt like she was holding her breath.

One question thrummed in her primitive, female brain—was he still in love with Cici? He'd said he wasn't. Why couldn't she just take him at his word?

"So, where did you go?" Alicia finally said, persisting despite the agony in her heart.

He looked up, his gaze so intense she had to inhale a steadying breath.

"What?"

"When you left Louisiana all those years ago. Where did you go? What did you do?"

"You don't give up easily, do you?"

"I was an editor. It goes with the territory."

Much to her surprise he unleashed a wary grin. "Like you said, you told me everything *that* first night…."

"Except the embarrassing location of my heart-shaped birthmark."

When his grin grew wicked and his gaze drifted to her left breast and lingered, heat suffused her throat and spread upward to her cheeks. She could have kicked herself for that slip.

"I found that out for myself, didn't I? A most delightful discovery, by the way. But I'm sure I told you that when I made love to you."

His last sentence seemed to hang in the air. The quick, volcanic burst of fire that washed through her had nothing to do with the summer evening and everything to do with the memory of his sensual mouth nibbling her breasts and sucking her nipples, of his large male body pressing close.

Wishing with all her heart that she could erase the vision of his virile mating, she sat up taller. "You were about to tell me where you went," she reminded him.

"Where all young American men with something to prove have always gone traditionally. Out West. To Utah, Arizona, Colorado, New Mexico…California. And then to Alaska. I traveled with a friend…Paul…for a while." His voice darkened. "We hiked, kayaked, camped out, rock climbed, did manual labor to pay our way."

"Where's Paul now?"

"He died. Because of a damn fool idea of mine to go rock climbing. He fell."

He paused, and she was stunned at the sudden pain that welled up in his eyes, which were now dark blue pools.

"I'm so sorry," she said.

"It was a long time ago. I'm over it." His expression was blank and cold.

Was he? Was he over Cici as well? Guilt and love

could have very long tails. "Still, it's too bad that he…" Her voice was soft, gentle, consoling.

"His death taught me life is too short to waste. So I got a grip on my anger and pulled myself together. I went back to school. I found that I liked building things. I think I became an architect because I envisioned myself building houses that would be homes for happy couples. Not that I know anything about being part of a happy family. When I graduated I went to work, and I got lucky. Or maybe luck comes to the driven. All I know is that as long as I was working, I was fairly happy for a while, at least professionally. Then one day my luck ran out."

"When was that?"

"The day I nominated your father to the board of Houses for Hurricane Victims. The only reason he was unanimously elected was because of my recommendation."

The sudden harshness in his voice and eyes brought her up short. Maybe because she hadn't seen the blow coming, she felt more vulnerable than usual. It hurt more. It was as if he'd reached across the table and struck her.

"He'll always be between us, won't he? You'll always hate me for what you think he did." Maybe Cici would be between them, too, for that matter. But she didn't dare throw Cici at him. What if he told her flat out he loved Cici?

"He did it. That's not even in question," Jake said.

She shut her eyes, hating herself for doubting her father. "So, you'll never in a thousand years be able to forgive me for being the daughter of the man you believe cost you so much."

With a sharp intake of breath, he clenched his hands.

"Am I right?" she demanded.

He glanced angrily away from her toward the yard.

"You won't," she said. "I accept that. Look, I…I think I made a mistake to eat with you," she said. "I don't know why I ever thought you and I could have a civil conversation…even for one meal. I'll eat later. By myself." She stood up to go.

He rushed to his feet, too. "The hell you will."

His eyes were so fierce her chest tightened, and suddenly she could barely breathe.

How could this happen? One minute they'd been eating dinner, talking. Then their conversation had veered into forbidden territory. Now suddenly she felt herself caught in a swirling conflagration of conflicting, hot-blooded emotions.

"I don't understand what you want with me," she whispered. "You've ignored me ever since we married and now…"

"I made it clear from the first I want you in my bed."

"And I told you why that's not possible. Good night, Jake."

"Like hell," he muttered.

She intended to whip past him and head inside to safety, but he was faster. He caught up to her in a single stride. Clamping his strong hand around her upper arm, he yanked her against his hard body.

When she was too stunned to fight him, he swung her even tighter against his body and then walked her backward until they stood, his body flattening her breasts and pressing her spine against the wall of his house.

The mask was gone. His blue eyes blazed. "For days I've wanted to touch you and hold you. God, you feel good."

Oh, so did he. She felt like she was melting into him, every cell in her body dissolving and flowing into his.

"I don't want to want you, but I do. More and more. Every day," he said.

"You do?"

"Then I think about what your father did and feel torn."

She felt torn about her father, too. Growing up, she'd always known he was ruthlessly ambitious. In business it was so easy for those in power to ride roughshod over the little people. Of late, it was increasingly difficult for her to believe that her father was innocent, and yet she felt deeply conflicted about that. She wanted to stand by him.

"You're driving me crazy," Jake said. "There's you and the baby on one side, and him and what happened, what's still happening, on the other. I feel like I'm living in hell."

"Me, too."

"Time to end it," he whispered. His hand cupped her chin. For a long moment, his eyes searched hers as if asking her for something. Then his lips took hers in a searing kiss.

"Don't," she pleaded, tearing her mouth free.

"We're getting a divorce eventually, remember? I won't complicate this horrible mess further."

"Shut up," he said, his voice hoarse. Then his mouth came down on hers again, claiming her in a raw act of possession while his hands and body crushed her closer.

After he explored the sweet wetness of her mouth

thoroughly, warmth from his lips and tongue slowly stole through her body, making her ache for more. After feeling so alone all day, indeed for weeks, it felt thrillingly wonderful to be held and kissed with such wild abandon by a man so determined to control his emotions.

Deep down she had wanted this, too. Wanted him. Obsessed about this. Most of all she wanted to be wanted this much. When she felt his aroused manhood pushing against her thighs, his intense physical need was a healing balm to the deep psychological wound that her father's indifference had inflicted. At least Jake wasn't indifferent. She wanted to be loved so much. To be wanted...even just for this.

When the thrusts of Jake's tongue took on a sexual rhythm, instead of protesting, her hands circled his neck. Her body tingling all the ways to her toes, she clung to him and sighed. She was on the verge of surrendering everything to him when she heard the sound of glass shattering at the front of the house. People in the front yard began to shout and curse.

Panting hard, furious, he jerked free of her. "Damn it, what's going on now?"

"Sounds like another brick through your window."

His eyes were wild as he gently smoothed her hair. "Don't you move a single inch, sweetheart. I'm coming right back to finish what we've started."

Then he was gone.

Like a sick, love-struck fool she remained paralyzed for long minutes, her blood humming. But when he didn't come back, and her pulse slowed, her power to reason gradually returned.

Knowing all that stood between them, she could not

let her passions rule her. She would not surrender so easily.

Very deliberately she walked into the house and down the hall to her bedroom.

Ten

When Jake strode back inside the front door, he was still on fire for Alicia. She wasn't where he'd left her and she searched the house.

Breathing hard, he returned to the nursery and stood in the doorway for a long moment. Every night lately, after the constant attacks at work, he'd come here and had found comfort in this room with the soft yellow quilts and valences with blue bunnies on them. He would imagine her holding their baby, playing with it, reading to it. Imagine himself joining in, imagine them down on their knees, playing with their baby together.

He would put his arm around her and her dark eyes would shine with shared tenderness. Their baby would not want its parents to hate each other or live apart from each other. Surely she would see that.

Was he a fool to imagine such scenes? Strangely, he had begun to look forward to coming home at night just to see what else she'd done in here. He'd begun to wish she wanted to spend time with him, to wish he'd treated her differently right from the first. He hated how he'd prejudged her, blaming her for every crime her father had committed. He'd begun to wonder if he'd been wrong.

In two short weeks she'd made it a real nursery. His child had become more real to him and infinitely precious.

Even though adjusting to having her as his wife was still difficult for him and very costly professionally, he knew he'd get through this. Every evening he looked forward to leaving the office and opening this door. It was like stepping into an entirely new world, one that was full of possibility…and hope.

Was it ridiculous to dream of such a future with her when there was so much bad blood between them?

Quietly he left the nursery. Her bedroom door was closed, but the sliver brightness that lit its bottom made him suspect she was probably inside hiding from him.

Well, after the stunt he'd pulled, he damn sure had it coming. Fisting his hand, he raised it to her door. Instead of knocking, he froze as he often did in the dead of the night. The last thing he wanted to do was to scare her again.

"Alicia?" he whispered.

Something rustled on the other side of the door. Then, to his amazement, the door opened, if just a crack. Had she been waiting for him all the time?

He couldn't see that much of her, but with her big brown eyes glimmering up at him in confusion while her dark hair fell in tangles about her throat, she was too sexy for words. It didn't hurt that her red lips were still moist and swollen from being so thoroughly kissed.

If ever a woman looked like she needed more kissing, it was Alicia.

The permanent knot in his throat tightened and his blood began to burn again. His groin ached.

How could he live in the same house with her another night if he didn't sleep with her? He clenched his hands and struggled to control his harsh breathing.

"I regret the caveman tactics," he heard himself mutter hoarsely.

"I understand," she said. Her soft voice cut his heart like sharp glass. "You're forgiven."

She didn't sound like she was over their encounter any more than he was, but he didn't call her on it.

"That's very generous of you," he said.

"So, what was all the excitement out front about?"

At least she hadn't shut her door in his face.

"The usual. Another angry investor got drunk and threw a rock through our window."

"Same window?"

"Afraid so. Luckily a couple of the reporters made themselves useful and tackled him. I told the self-righteous vandal to go home and sleep it off. Then they all wanted to interview me."

"This is all my fault."

"Don't…. He's gone for now. I'm on my way out to the garage to get a board and some nails to cover the window."

"I'll help you with that if you want," she said, almost eagerly. He felt an answering excitement because her offer pleased him far too much.

He nodded.

"I'll just get my shoes," she said.

He liked hearing her soft-soled footsteps trailing behind him all the way out to the garage. Despite the

reporters taking pictures and the hecklers yelling at
them from the front yard, he enjoyed her carrying the
nails for him and holding the board steady while he
nailed it.

"I'll call someone tomorrow to repair it," he said
when he was through hammering and they were safely
back inside the house.

"No, let me. I'm home all day. It's the least I can do."

She was so sweet and so eager to please. Surely that
was a good sign. "Okay. Thank you."

She turned to go. He ached to seize her and kiss her
again. But even though his heart pounded violently, he
didn't.

As her slim, solitary figure moved gracefully down
the hall, he stood transfixed watching the gentle sway
of her hips. Dear God… The memory of their recent
kiss had him so hot with desire to hold her and kiss her
again that he couldn't resist calling after her.

"Alicia—" He caught himself then, afraid she'd see
or hear something that would make her know how acute
his need was.

She pivoted sharply. Light from the chandelier in
the dining room slanted across her long neck. Her gaze
was sharp, almost piercing. Why did she have to be so
damned beautiful?

Too beautiful to hate.

With a start he began to dwell on the reality that
he didn't dislike her and that maybe he never had. Not
even from the first. His wanting her wasn't just lust
anymore—if it ever had been. Then what was it?

What was going on here? What was happening to
him?

He had thought he loved Cici, but what he felt now
for Alicia was even more powerful.

He hadn't fought for Cici. Even though Alicia was Butler's daughter, he knew that if any man threatened her, he'd give his life to protect her.

He would never have chosen Alicia as his wife, but now that she was, he couldn't imagine anyone else ever taking her place any more than he could imagine ever wanting to let her go. Why had he ever thought he could easily divorce her?

Maybe he would just have to accept that there were some things between a man and woman that couldn't be explained. He didn't know why or when she'd come to matter to him so much. But matter she did—and more every day.

The terms of his marriage which included never touching her again and divorcing her as soon as possible now seemed hellish and impossible.

"Alicia…" His voice broke.

"Yes, Jake," she said in that soft honeyed tone that could turn him to mush.

"I was thinking…that maybe…I mean if you want to…" He sounded worse than a horny teenager awkwardly asking a girl he had a crush on out for the first time. "I mean maybe I could take you out to dinner… tomorrow night."

Her eyes shone for a moment. "That's not necessary, Jake. I've cost you as much as you've cost me."

"I know it's not necessary. That's not the point. I want things to be different between us. Better. I mean, hell, we're going to have a baby together. Maybe we should try to at least be cordial to each other. Friends?"

He could never be friends with her.

"All right then," she agreed. "Dinner."

"I'll look forward to it."

He held his breath, willing her to walk into his arms.

Instead, she shyly lowered her eyes, turned on her slender heel and vanished, leaving him staring after her. Marriage, he thought bitterly as he stood in the gloom, had become his own peculiar brand of hell.

"Goodbye, Jake," Alicia said as she followed him him as he went out the back door.

Walking with him to his car every morning when he left for his office had become a pleasant routine this past month.

He turned around and waited for her. His red tie slanted across his broad chest at a cockeyed angle. If she had been his real wife, she would have reached up and straightened it. Maybe she would have kissed him on his tanned cheek and then whispered in his ear not to forget that today was her birthday.

He would ask her what she wanted and she would either tell him or tease him, saying she wanted him to surprise her.

Instead she said, "Your tie is crooked." After a quick glance at her, he said a gruff "thanks" and straightened it.

"Is it all right now?" he asked with a smile.

A wealth of emotions hung in the air as their eyes touched briefly.

She was standing on the exact spot on the veranda where he'd seized her and kissed her a month ago.

She sighed. "Perfect."

Although they were on much friendlier terms, she hadn't told him today was her special day. If he didn't know, how could he disappoint her?

Not that she hadn't wanted to tell him. She'd held back mainly because her father had always forgotten or ignored her birthdays, and she didn't want to risk Jake being indifferent, too.

"Who has the time for birthdays?" her father had said on more than one occasion when she'd dared complain.

Yes, a whole month had passed since Jake had kissed her against her will right here and then had apologized by taking her out to eat the next evening to an elegant meal at her favorite French restaurant in the Quarter. That night he'd gone overboard being nice and polite to her, repeating that he'd desired a less hostile relationship with the future mother of his child.

"But could you ever really forgive me?" she'd asked as the candle on their table had lit the right side of his face and eyes with golden light.

"Could you forgive me for blowing the whistle on your father? For conspiring with my brother's CEO, Hayes Daniels, to set him up for prison?" he'd countered.

Neither had said they could. Even so, ever since he'd been exceptionally deferential toward her. She now looked forward to being with him and dreaded her evenings alone when he was away on one of his frequent business trips to Orlando.

In a state of wistful longing, she stood on the veranda until the gates closed and his SUV disappeared from view. When the phone began to ring, she ran back inside the kitchen and then stopped short when she saw the familiar name blazing on the caller ID.

She picked it up anyway. "Hello, Daddy."

"Happy birthday, pumpkin," he said, stunning her into silence.

"You remembered," she finally whispered, pleased in spite of herself. Maybe he was adjusting to her marriage after all.

"I'd invite you to lunch or something…take you shopping…but…but you understand why that's not possible."

Since he didn't mention he was under house arrest, neither did she. "I know. And that's okay. I mean…it's not okay…but—"

He interrupted her. "I know what you mean. I'd like to see you. I've missed you. We could still have lunch, if you brought a pizza or hamburgers over here…or carry-out from any restaurant you'd like."

"I…I'm afraid I can't come," she said. Her promise to Jake stood between them.

"Oh." His voice sounded dead and lost. "Is it because of him?"

"Yes," she admitted. "He doesn't think I should see you. I'm sorry."

"It's okay."

But it wasn't. He sounded so down. And who could blame him?

"Are you all right?" she asked.

"No. It's your birthday…and God knows I've missed enough of your birthdays in my time. Your mother always made such a fuss—over both of us. I missed the fuss as much as you did. I thought this year I might make it up to you."

"I'll be there within the hour," she promised. He sounded so bleak. But as she held the phone so tightly her fingers ached she wondered how she'd ever pull a stunt like this off without Jake finding out.

"Do you need anything?" she asked.

"Razors. Toothpaste. Sugarless gum."

He sounded so diminished. How could she possibly say no?

* * *

"I feel like a spy," Alicia said as she slipped across her father's threshold and he quickly shut the door behind her.

She pulled her scarves and sunglasses off and shook out her hair. When she handed her father a sack containing the items he'd requested, his hard gaze swept her. A guard slipped forward to inspect what she'd brought. Nodding, the guard backed away.

"Marriage doesn't suit you. You look exhausted."

In the past he'd rarely commented on her appearance if it didn't involve the public; he'd always been too self-involved.

She could have said he looked tired, too, because he did, worrisomely so. The strong and powerful-looking father she'd admired and feared was gone. The man before her had dark rings around his eyes and was so shrunken in stature she was now several inches taller than he was. His hair was snow-white.

"Daddy, do we have to quarrel? Today?"

"I suppose not...since it's your birthday," he said.

She didn't have much time to be with him. She'd told Victor she wanted to shop for the nursery in the French Quarter. Then she'd lost him and had taken a cab to her father's mansion across town. She doubted her sunglasses and scarves had concealed her identity from the single reporter camped outside her father's home.

She felt guilty about giving Victor the slip and deceiving Jake, and she needed to get back to the French Quarter to find Victor within the hour. Otherwise he wouldn't grow alarmed and alert Jake. If Jake found out she'd gone off on her own, he'd probably fire Victor.

"How could you betray me by marrying Claiborne?" her father asked.

"You never give up," she said.

"Does he?"

"Look, I didn't exactly want to marry him, okay?" She stopped herself. The last thing she wanted was to discuss Jake or her pregnancy.

"Well, at least you haven't totally lost your senses. Why did you do it then? How'd he make you? What does he have on you?"

"Let's not talk about Jake or why I married him. It's not a good subject for us."

"To say the least."

After a brief pause she changed tacks. "I brought pizza. Pepperoni. Your favorite." It was Jake's favorite, too, but, of course, she couldn't say that.

He gave the pizza box a long look and then shrugged before leading her into the dining room away from the guard, who remained in the living room. She set the table and her father ate in gloomy silence while she sipped tea.

His tomblike house was a whole lot quieter and lonelier than it used to be. He'd always been a man of action who worked all day and went out all night. When he'd been home, phones had rung constantly. How did he stand the silence and inactivity?

"You're not eating?" he asked after a while.

"I'll eat later." She didn't tell him that pizza upset her stomach if she ate it this early in the day. If she told him she sometimes suffered from nausea in the mornings, he'd put two and two together.

"I have a present for you," her father said after his cup of coffee.

"There's no need…really…."

Glancing toward the living room where the guard was on his cell phone, he got up and pulled a black ebony box that she recognized as her mother's out of a drawer and handed it to her.

Upon opening the lacquered box, she gasped. With shaking fingers she lifted the sparkling diamond pin in the shape of a starfish from the bed of black velvet. Smiling at him, she caressed each point of the star with a fingertip, just to make sure they were all there.

"Your mother wore it every day," he said, his deep voice rough behind her.

"I know."

"It was her mother's and maybe her mother's before her I think."

Sudden tears pricked Alicia's lashes but she wiped them away. She remembered too well how the pin used to flash on her dear mother's collar. Alicia had always loved this piece of jewelry. She remembered sneaking into her mother's room sometimes when she'd played dressup and opening the lacquered box just to gaze at it and count the points of the star.

"No, it's too valuable," she said, replacing the pin in the box and handing it to him. "Besides, the authorities said they own everything now."

"Forget them." He glanced toward the guard, who was still on his phone. "They'd take everything if we let them. This'll be our little secret. Like I said, this was your grandmother's before it was your mother's. I know how much you loved your mother. I loved her, too. Pumpkin, one reason I wasn't around much after she was gone was because you reminded me too much of her."

"Oh?" Was that really true? she wondered.

"Also, I told myself that I was making all that money for you."

"Daddy, I can't take it."

"She would have wanted you to have it. Besides, it's your birthday. If I end up in prison, it may be the last present I can ever give you on your birthday."

"Don't say that."

"Well, like I said, I've missed too many of your birthdays. I didn't want to ignore this one…because it could be my last chance…"

"Daddy, that's really so sweet, but if I took it, it might get you into more trouble."

"Okay. I understand." Closing the box, he replaced it in the drawer.

He looked so disappointed she got up and put her arms around him. "But Daddy, thank you so much for thinking of me!"

He stiffened and refused to look at her, since she wasn't doing what he wanted.

Touching his cheek, she said, "Maybe you won't go to prison. Maybe you'll be exonerated."

"Dream on," he said wearily. "A lot of liars like your husband, who will stop at nothing, are conspiring to frame me."

Hesitantly she said, "Jake told me about the money missing from Houses for Hurricane Victims. He said you were in charge of investing those funds. If you didn't take that money, then surely you must have an idea of who did."

"He would say that, of course! And you're always so gullible, you believed him." Letting her go, he stared at her as if she had become someone he didn't really know. "He's getting to you, isn't he? Turning you against me?"

"Did you take that money, Daddy? From the charity? From the bank?"

He turned away. "Who do you think you are—to

accuse me? You're married to the real crook. When he's through with you, he'll toss you out like so much garbage."

"You didn't answer my question."

"Because I never thought I'd live to see the day when a daughter of mine would ask me such a thing. *You know me.*"

"Do I?"

Her father grew morose and silent. After sitting with him for ten more minutes and trying in vain to make small talk, she finally gave up and told him she had to go. He nodded indifferently.

The guard checked her purse and shopping bags again at the door, but then at the last minute her father said something, so she went back to give him a goodbye hug. Throwing up his hands to ward off her embrace, he sent her purse and bags flying, spilling their contents under his couch and easy chair.

"Sorry," he muttered as he knelt to retrieve her things.

"I'll do it," she whispered.

"No! Stay where you are," he thundered as he pulled a lipstick out from under a chair. "You caused enough trouble—by marrying Jake Claiborne."

When her father stood up, he was panting hard. He slammed the purse and bags into her hands.

"Goodbye," she whispered.

Turning away, he slumped back in his chair. She took a taxi back to the Quarter, where she found Victor. Later when she was safely back home, she went to her desk, intending to file the receipts for the things she'd bought for the nursery. But when she opened her shopping bags to look for the receipts, she found the lacquered box her father had tried to give her. When she lifted the lid, dazzling sparks of light glinted from her mother's lovely pin.

"Oh, no!"

She sagged against her chair, her heart pounding. Why did her father have to be so hardheaded? Why couldn't he just once take no for an answer? He was under house arrest. Didn't he realize how serious that was? Even if this pin had belonged to her mother, he should abide by the terms of his arrest.

She loved the pin, and he knew it. He'd thought she should have it for her birthday, so he'd found a way to slip it into a bag after the guard had checked them. If she took the pin back, she would get him into even worse trouble. A second trip would risk involving Jake again.

Torn, she closed the box and stared at it for what seemed an eternity. After a long while she got up, carried it to her bedroom and slid it under her mattress. Later she would figure out what to do about the pin.

Right now she wanted to concentrate on happier things...like Jake and her baby. Gathering her shopping bags, she hurried to the nursery and began putting away the things she'd bought for the baby.

Eleven

Alicia was straightening up the nursery when the phone rang.

Had the authorities missed her mother's pin so soon?

Or was it Jake calling to ask about her day? How could she talk to him without mentioning her visit to her father and the pin, which were so heavy on her mind? She would—she had to.

Then, hoping the caller actually was her husband, she ran out into the hall to catch the phone.

"Alicia?" The lilting, feminine voice was vaguely familiar, yet she couldn't place it.

"Yes."

"It's Cici! Logan's wife. I don't know if you remember me. We met at Pierre's birthday party."

As if she could ever forget her dancing so wildly with

Logan, who'd been her date, or anything else about *that* night.

"I remember," she said.

Even though he said he was over her, Alicia felt too unsure of their relationship to feel totally secure around a woman he'd once been involved with. She wished she could stop remembering how erotically Cici had danced with Logan.

"Logan and I want to invite you and Jake to dinner. Here at Belle Rose with Pierre."

"Oh? How nice."

Sounding sincerely friendly, Cici rushed on, giving her possible dates, saying they had some happy news too, suggesting a Friday or a Saturday so they could stay over and avoid a late night drive back to New Orleans.

"I'll talk to Jake and get back to you later today."

"That would be lovely. We can't wait to see you both and congratulate you. We're very happy you're family."

"Thank you."

She asked after Pierre. After a brief conversation, they hung up.

Alicia felt more uncertain than ever as she held the phone. The pin hidden under her mattress worried her, as did Cici's warmth and eagerness to entertain them and celebrate their marriage. What if seeing Logan and Cici together made Jake focus on his past love?

Still she should call Jake and tell him about the invitation. No. She would go to his office. Better to see his face when she told him Cici had called.

Jake was thumbing through an annual report on a project in Orlando while deep in conversation with his head man on that venture when Vanessa suddenly burst into his office. Expecting bad news, he stared up at her.

"Sorry to be a bother, but your wife is here, sir." Her voice was tight and low. "She's been here awhile and I have to tell you—she's upsetting the natives. The sooner you see her, the better."

Jake didn't say a word; he was too surprised. Quickly he terminated his call and rushed out to Vanessa's office.

"I hope you're not too busy," Alicia began as she stood up, glancing uncertainly at Vanessa before she looked at him. "Some of your employees weren't happy to see me in the elevator."

"I'm sorry if my people were rude. It's as much my fault as yours that tensions have been running so high around here of late. As far as I'm concerned, this is a pleasant surprise." Frowning at his secretary, who was watching them with excessive interest, he took his wife's arm and led her into his office. "We'd like coffee, if that's not too much to ask, Vanessa."

She hesitated and then smiled at his bride. "Right away, sir."

"Decaf for me, please," Alicia said.

Alicia's dark hair was drawn back from her fine-boned face and held by a pair of fat, gold clips. She wore a dark, tailored suit that made her look elegant but much too thin. Pregnant women were supposed to put on weight, not lose it. Was she all right?

Had she dressed up for him? He wondered because Victor had called him from the Quarter. When Victor had said he'd lost her for a while, he'd described her clothes. She hadn't been wearing a dark suit when she'd gone shopping earlier.

He wouldn't have thought much about her disappearance except he knew that her father had had a mysterious visitor today. A veiled lady. Basil Bienville, the infamous blogger had started the rumor that the woman was Alicia. He'd speculated she'd visited him because today was her birthday.

Vanessa brought in a coffee tray, set it down without asking Alicia if she took cream or sugar and left them.

"Why are you here?" he asked Alicia when they were alone.

Was she here to tell him where she'd gone when she'd disappeared? Wondering if Basil was right, he braced himself for her confession.

"I came because…" She flushed as she poured herself a cup of decaf coffee and watched him with an intensity that made him even more uneasy. She looked guilty of something. Then she said, "Cici called."

"Cici?"

Alicia licked her lips and waited. When he said nothing more, she began in a rush, "She and Logan want us to come to Belle Rose for dinner. She said we should come on a Friday or a Saturday so we could stay the night."

"Do you want to go?"

"They're your family. It's your decision."

"They'd expect us to share a bedroom…and a bed… like a normal, married couple. Is that something you really want to do?"

Her face reddened. "Oh. I didn't think."

She looked away as an answering tide of heat swept him. The dinner invitation was beginning to appeal to him. Yet…

"We plan to separate after the child is born. I think it's unwise to make this more difficult on ourselves or to involve other people, especially my family. We've discussed this before," he said.

"I'll call her and decline."

Damn. "No, leave Cici to me."

Some emotion flashed in her eyes. Then she blushed. "Of course. I understand. You would use any excuse to talk to her, wouldn't you?"

"What's that supposed to mean?"

"Nothing."

When she whitened and turned quickly away, he wondered why she was so upset. Did it bother her that he'd once been in love with Cici? Why be jealous of a relationship that had been dead for years?

"You do still see it that way, that we have to live by the rules we set, don't you?" he said smoothly, hoping she'd indicate she didn't.

"Yes. It's all perfectly logical." Her voice was too soft and her spine too straight, and she was wringing her hands in her lap.

"As if anything in our situation is logical." She was his enemy's daughter, but he wanted her more with every passing day. Wanted her enough to take her home to visit his family—just so he'd have an excuse to share her bed. "Are you sure nothing's wrong?" he asked.

"I'm fine."

"Separate bedrooms was your idea, remember?"

She whirled on him. "I said I'm fine!"

"Then why do you sound upset as hell?"

"I don't know. I don't know anything anymore. It's like my life has spun out of control. My dad getting into trouble. You. The pregnancy. Our marriage. I don't have anything to hold on to."

"Why did Cici's call upset you so much?"

"Who said it did?"

"It did. I can tell."

"I don't know. You've been so nice lately, it's impossible to hate you. And if I can't even hold on to that, what does that leave me?"

"A chance to start over maybe. Look, I heard a rumor that today's your birthday. Is that true?"

She lowered her head shyly and he knew it was.

"Why didn't you tell me?" he whispered.

"We barely know each other. This wasn't supposed to happen."

"What?" he demanded.

She stood up. "I'd better go home so you can work in peace."

He sprang to his feet. "Hey there—you can't just start something and then run. Alicia, I want to know what's going on. Are you jealous of Cici?"

"No!"

She was hell-bent for his door now, so he stopped her the only way he knew how—by clamping a strong hand over her arm and swinging her around into his arms.

"It's you I want. Not her." He tilted her chin, then lowered his gaze to her lips that were so provocatively close to his. He was starving for another kiss. Starving. "Do you ever think about that night? I do. I want to do all the things we did that night again."

When she gazed at his mouth, he said, "I think it's way past time we changed the dynamics of our marriage. Don't normal people in normal relationships just let things progress to the next level sometimes? Like we did *that* night?"

"That's how we got in this mess."

"It's what brought us together. We took risks that night because we wanted each other."

"Everybody who works for you hates me. You don't want me near your family."

"Look, you're my wife, a wife I very much want to get along with better. I'd like us to agree that our being together because of the baby was our start, but maybe that doesn't have to always be the only reason we're together. I know I said we should keep my family out of this if our marriage was going to be temporary. What if I want to change the rules?"

"How? Why?"

"I think it's stupid to plan for failure. Our baby will need us together more after he or she is born. Why don't we give our marriage a chance? What if I call Cici and suggest that since today's your birthday, we'll drive out for dinner Saturday night and have birthday cake with candles and presents, the works…with the whole family? I'll tell her how proud I am of you, that I want to show you off to my family. Then—what if tonight I take you out for dinner, just the two of us, and celebrate your birthday?"

She shook her head. "I—I can't believe you mean this. Not when I'm who I am and you're who you are."

"I don't want to fight. I think it's way past time we started considering new options—other than fighting—don't you?"

He moved to take her into his arms, but before he could touch her, a light knock on the door stopped him cold.

Vanessa swept inside with a stack of documents in her arms. "Oh, I'm so sorry," she exclaimed. "Am I interrupting something?"

Alicia blushed. "No, I was just going."

And just like that, the moment was lost. Jake clenched his hands, then forced himself to unclench them.

"Don't go," he whispered to his wife, who froze.

"Sorry," Vanessa said softly as she set the documents on his desk.

"Me, too," he muttered.

When Vanessa tiptocd outside, Jake turned back to his wife. "I'd very much like a fresh start."

"I would, too. If only such a thing were possible."

"I believe we have to make our own opportunities," he said, his hungry gaze on her beautiful lips again.

Leaning into her, he put his hands on her shoulders and drew her closer. A pulse was beating madly in her throat.

"Happy birthday," he murmured, caressing her arms in an effort to ease her tension.

Her eyes lit up.

Seizing his chance, he kissed her. She expelled a delicious sigh and clasped him tighter.

The kiss went on and on. Finally her dark eyes opened slowly and rose to his. He ran a light fingertip down her cheek. "Nice," he whispered.

Long after she'd said goodbye and left him, her taste and scent lingered.

The hours dragged. He couldn't wait to get home.

Twelve

The SUV was speeding along the Interstate lined on both sides by moss-covered live oaks and cypress trees and the occasional chemical plant. Not that Alicia was paying much attention to the semitropical abundance of greenery. She was too conscious of her husband behind the wheel. Ever since her birthday, he'd made it plain how much he wanted her.

She wanted him, too, but reckless sex was what had caused their problems. If they were going to parent a child, their relationship needed to be based on something deeper than mere animal attraction. He needed to like her and respect her. They needed to trust each other. That said, she'd taken great pains with her hair and makeup and white linen dress.

"Why do you keep fidgeting with the strap of your purse?" he asked.

"I'm not fidgeting." She pushed the straw purse onto

the floorboard, so she wouldn't be tempted to keep tracing the rough edges of the stitched leather strap.

"We don't have to go to Belle Rose, you know. My family always makes me feel…"

"What? How do they make you feel?"

"Let's just say I'd rather spend the weekend alone with you. I'll turn around. We'll call Cici on my cell."

"No. They've probably already cooked dinner for us."

"So, they can eat it themselves and have more leftovers to enjoy."

"You know that people always go to more trouble for guests. They spend hours doing all sorts of things they'd never do otherwise."

"Things they need to do."

"I don't want to be rude to your family just because I feel nervous about going there pretending I'm your wife."

"You *are* my wife. I told you I'd like to try to make this work."

Heat washed over her. When she made no comment, he didn't push as he often did, and for that she should have been grateful. But when he didn't speak to her until he pulled into the oak alley that led up to the pillared mansion where he'd grown up, she grew more nervous.

The deep shade and banks of flowers made the house look like something out of a dream. Could they make a go of it? Would she ever feel she belonged here?

"I'd forgotten how beautiful your boyhood home is."

His knuckles were white; his face was tense. "I never forgot, no matter how long I stayed away. And believe me, I tried. Time and again I told myself I'd never come back here. There was too much emotion to deal with."

"So, here we are," she said lightly.

He parked as far as possible from the house, maybe so his family wouldn't hear the car and come out to greet them. Was he trying to put off seeing them for as long as possible?

Sunlight sifted through the trees and leaves crackled underneath her feet as they walked through the humid heat up to the house, pulling their overnight bags behind them.

"It's not quite so hot here as it is in the city," she said, trying to lighten the mood with conversation again.

He nodded but didn't elaborate.

Like a child eager for Christmas morning, Noonoon must have been watching for Jake. No sooner had he planted one long foot on the bottom stair that led up to the veranda than she opened the door in a rush and hurled herself into Jake's arms.

"Mister Jake, you don't get home near often enough." Her dark eyes shone with pleasure.

After a moment, he said, "Have you met my wife, Alicia?"

"We met before," Noonoon said, smiling as she released Jake so he could include Alicia in a three-way hug.

When his family heard the commotion, they spilled out onto the veranda too. Hayes Daniels, Logan's CEO and best friend, who was tall and dark, was with them. Alicia wasn't too thrilled to see him, because he'd been a key player in bringing her father down. She avoided his stony gaze. Obviously he didn't approve of her. Logan kept his distance—maybe because they'd dated in the past.

Cici had a red scarf in her curls, gold earrings dangling from her ears and gold bangles on her arms. She wore a soft white dress. The skirt swirled around her slim ankles every time she moved, and she moved a lot. She looked beautiful and wild and too thrilled to see Jake. Or was she simply so exuberant because she was newly married herself?

Hard to tell for Alicia, since the green monster held her in thrall.

Everybody talked and laughed at once—nervously, Alicia thought. Was that because they were all trying too hard?

More hugs were exchanged, and it seemed to Alicia that Jake embraced Cici much longer than he held anyone else. When Jake released Cici, did Alicia imagine that Logan and Jake barely shook hands? Jake was definitely ill at ease around his family, especially his brother.

Logan took their bags and carried them upstairs. Even though Alicia had always longed for a close, loving family, her spirits sank every time Cici smiled at Jake.

Then Pierre, who was eighty, hobbled up to Alicia on a cane and told her how glad he was to see her again. He alone seemed relaxed and unaware of any familial undercurrents.

Taking her hand in his cool, shaky grip, he led her inside and invited her to sit beside him so that he could get a good look at her. Jake joined them. Logan returned and put his arm around Cici and held her possessively on the other side of the room. Cici, her eyes alight, tossed her blond curls back and kissed her husband on the cheek. She did seem to be deeply in love with Logan.

Although Jake's family asked her questions about her life as a new bride, Alicia felt so shy and tongue-tied that Jake did most of the talking. He told them how she'd improved his backyard. He spoke of their evenings out at some of the better New Orleans restaurants, making it sound as if they were truly and happily married.

Acting the part, she smiled while he talked. Maybe he really did want to make their marriage work. Gradually she relaxed. With all her heart she longed to be the happy, carefree couple he described even as she wondered if it would ever be possible.

"When are you going to go on a honeymoon?" Hayes Daniels asked suspiciously as Noonoon served the first course.

"What do you think, darling?" Jake brushed Alicia's fingertips with his lips. "After things settle down? Maybe in eight or nine months?"

Dazzled by his expectant gaze and unexpected touch, she couldn't think straight. The baby might be old enough to leave for a long weekend by then she thought—if they were still together. *If* was the key word.

"Who knows?" she whispered.

"You two seem so good together," Logan said. "And to think I never saw it coming."

Guilt made Alicia's pulse quicken.

"It took us by surprise, too," Jake said.

"Funny how things work out," Hayes added as he turned to Jake. "You and Mitchell Butler's daughter together. You were so angry that morning we went to the feds."

"Yes I was."

"Well, it's good having you back in Louisiana, Jake," Logan said. "Now that you're settled, do you think you'll stay awhile? There's still a lot to rebuild."

"A year ago I would have said no unequivocally," Jake said.

"And now?"

"Would it matter? You've always been busy with Claiborne Energy. You never needed me."

"You're wrong. That was just your perception of the way things were," Logan said. "The truth is Grand-père and I regretted our part in the estrangement. We're glad you're back in Louisiana, and all of us want you to stay. On a side note, we've decided we need a bigger building for our headquarters downtown and we want you to design it."

"That's wonderful," Alicia said, smiling until she looked at Jake and saw that he wasn't.

"I'd prefer not to discuss the past or business tonight," he said.

Logan nodded. "So I'll call you Monday."

"Fine."

Cici smiled at Alicia. "We think you're a wonderful addition to the family. Logan, can I please please tell her our news?"

When he nodded, she beamed. "I'm pregnant! That's why I'm wearing this full skirt. We felt the baby move this morning."

Wistfully Alicia placed her hand on her abdomen. She hadn't yet experienced that.

"Congratulations," Jake said even as his gaze followed her hand.

He made a toast. "To the future. To more babies in the family."

Alicia blushed when all eyes focused on her. No sooner was dinner over than Noonoon brought in a white birthday cake with candles. Then everybody, including Noonoon, sang "Happy Birthday" to Alicia.

Their radiantly smiling faces blurred as emotion overwhelmed her.

"Thank you," she whispered. "I've never had such a wonderful birthday celebration."

"Wait, we have a birthday present for you, too." Cici handed Alicia a small white box wrapped with gold ribbon.

The tiny card on the gift read, "With love to our new sister, Alicia." "The earrings inside belonged to Logan's and Jake's great-grandmother."

After Alicia tore the paper off, she held her breath when she saw the exquisite diamond earrings inside the box.

"Françoise, our grandmother, didn't want to be accused of pride or vanity, so she painted them black. That was about one hundred years ago."

Alicia smiled.

"The earrings were Pierre's idea, but Jake was in on it, too," Logan said.

"But they should go to Cici," Alicia said.

"I have her ring," Cici said.

"Even so, I...I can't accept them."

"Why not?" Jake asked.

"Because this isn't...real! Because..."

"What isn't real?" Logan looked confused. "I can assure you, the stones are genuine. We had the last of the black paint removed by a professional, but they're real."

"That's not what I meant!"

Jake was frowning at her as he took her hand and pressed her fingertips.

"Look, this was very kind of all of you. But I—I need a minute. To freshen up. Where's our guest room?"

"Down the hall," Cici said. "Then you go upstairs. First door on the right. Are you sure you're feeling well? Do you want me to take you up to it?"

"No! If you'll just excuse me, I'll find it on my own. I'll be fine in a minute."

Folding her napkin into a perfect square and placing it on the table to the left of her plate very precisely, Alicia stood. As soon as she'd escaped the brilliantly lit dining room and their concerned faces, she took in a deep breath and tried to calm down.

She was beginning to want it all—love, a real marriage, a future. Jake had said he wanted to try to make their relationship work, and now his family was being so accepting. And yet her father and all the crimes he was accused of stood between them. Part of her wanted to do as Jake said he wanted and go with the flow, but another part was afraid to trust in her wildest hopes.

Walking down the hall and up the stairs, she opened the door of their guest room and sat down on the bed. She shut her eyes and was fighting to control her conflicting emotions when the door opened and closed, and she heard heavy footsteps striding toward her.

"What's wrong now?" Jake said from behind her.

She whirled. "I can't lie anymore—at least not to your family. I certainly can't take family heirlooms."

"You're the mother of my child. That's real. I want you to have the earrings."

"No. It will be easier if we break up if I never wear them and treasure them as a gift from you and your family. Don't you see, it will be one less thing to lose?"

He was silent for a long moment. "All right. I can understand that. I'll talk to my family. But while we're on the subject of lying, I have a question." His gaze had hardened. "Did you go visit your father on your birthday?"

Swallowing a quick breath, she shut her eyes briefly and then looked away from him. "Yes."

He hissed in air.

"I'm sorry."

"One of the terms of our marriage was that you would stay away from him."

"I couldn't."

"Damn it, you agreed."

"I know. But he called me. Usually he ignores my birthday. It meant a lot to me that he called—and wanted to see me."

"So why didn't he ignore it this year? What did he really want? He wanted something. I'd bet money on it."

She cringed when she remembered the pin hidden under her mattress. She wanted to tell him about that, but she couldn't—not without hurting her father. Not without making a mess of everything.

"What we feel for each other is too fragile to withstand all the pressures from the outside world," she said. "I'm Mitchell Butler's daughter. You couldn't possibly ever really care…" She hated the passion that had crept into her soft voice, exposing her vulnerability as well as her most heartfelt longings.

"I care," he whispered, his low tone heavier and huskier suddenly. "You don't really want me to go, do you?"

She took a quiet pleasure in him asking her that, even though she knew she should tell him to go.

"I don't intend to leave," he whispered.

He leaned down. When he stroked the length of her spine, his warm, caressing hands caused an involuntary shiver. "We've both fought this too long."

"J-Jake, you have to go." Not that she tried to twist

away. His touch was too pleasant, too consoling. Too sexually arousing. In seconds he had her on fire.

"What I have to do is kiss you," he said.

"We have to go back down!"

She felt his hand stroke up the length of her spine again. Then he turned her around. When his gaze locked with hers, his hand moved to her neckline. Slowly he began to unbutton her white linen dress.

Staring into his eyes again, she couldn't resist the hot, naked desire she saw there.

"Here. Now," he whispered.

Thirteen

His mouth was on her breast. "Delicious birthmark," he murmured.

To his surprise she arched her back to draw him nearer. Not only was she not putting up a struggle, but her pulse was beating faster and faster.

Her hands came up and cupped his rough chin. Slowly her soft fingertips guided his mouth down to hers. He knew longing when he saw it. Her eyes burned with need. Her fingertips shook.

"You're as ravenous as I am," he whispered.

"No…"

"Wanna bet?"

He could feel the tension in her even as her warm lips that quivered under his made him want more. He ran his hands through her soft hair soothingly. He knew he should probably let her go, but he wanted her too much.

He'd been on his own so damn long…and so had

she. In a way they were alike, fearing attachment for different reasons. She'd sought love and had never found it, while he'd hated being manipulated by those who'd loved him and had a habit of running if anybody got close.

Her hands and lips fell away. "I don't want to play sexual games," she said, but her voice was a velvet purr that lured him.

"I'm not playing games." His lips slid down her throat to the other nipple that he'd neglected before. He began to suck it in a leisurely way until it was wet and flushed and hard and she lay trembling beneath him.

"You don't want me for anything but sex," she whispered.

"Lucky you," he teased.

"This isn't a game. If we don't go back down soon… what will your family think?"

"That we're newlyweds. That I can't keep my hands off you, which is all too true."

He wanted to touch her, to kiss her, to feel her silken flesh beneath his, to feel the muscles of her legs contract around his waist when he first entered her. He wanted to make her writhe and explode with passion at the exact same moment he did. He wanted to crush her close, to possess her completely again and again, for the next forty years.

That last thought stunned him. It wasn't that he no longer cared if her last name was Butler or that her father had robbed him and ruined his hard-won reputation. Still, for her, he would throw everything away and start over. He wanted to make this work even though he knew it wouldn't be easy.

He kissed Alicia on the mouth again, taking his time, nibbling her lips until her hands began to roam his body and she began to kiss him back. Her lips parted to accept his tongue. As always she tasted like honey. His mouth didn't leave hers until she was making little moans of ecstasy and begging him for much more than chaste kisses.

"I want you inside me," she whispered, hunger making her voice rasp and her eyelids droop lazily.

When he slid his body over hers and probed her sleek, wet entrance with the tip of his erection, she cried out. He fused his mouth to hers and drove into her. Their tongues mated. Their bodies grew hotter and hotter. With each thrust, her fingers dug into his shoulder and her legs tightened around his waist. Her excitement fed his, pushing him even nearer the edge. When it came, their crisis was mutual and spontaneous, shuddering through them both like a hot wave of pleasure.

With a voice muffled by passion, she said those three little words that shouldn't matter but did. Too profoundly.

"I love you."

He didn't want to hear them, so he tried to blot them out. But she repeated them.

"I love you, Jake. I think I've loved you from the first. I want your child more than I've ever wanted anything. And I want you…like this…close to me…always…again and again. Inside me. I don't want a divorce. I want to be your real wife, and that scares me."

He froze, wishing she'd stop.

Love. Marriage. A lifetime together. Children. Grandchildren.

"Alicia…" He put a fingertip to her lips.

"Okay…okay… I'll stop." But her shining eyes continued to caress him with unguarded emotion for another long moment.

"Sorry I said all that mushy stuff," she whispered as she curled herself into his body.

"Don't worry about it," he said, tracing his thumb around the curve of her earlobe.

She squirmed, and soon he felt hooked by her soft arms and legs that wrapped themselves warmly around his. Slowly the need to answer her in words dissolved as he slipped into a black, welcoming unconsciousness.

When he woke up hours later, she was still there, was breathtakingly lovely as ever in his arms as she slept.

He wanted her again, but if he kissed her, he would awaken her. And she might start asking all those troubling questions he wasn't ready to answer.

He was the one who'd pushed for more, and now that she was trying to take their relationship to the next level, he wasn't sure how to deal with it. Suddenly his marriage to Alicia felt like way more than he'd bargained for.

"What are you doing?" Alicia was standing just inside the bedroom door of Jake's New Orleans home.

Ridiculous question. It was plain as day that he was unpacking his suitcase from their overnight trip and repacking a backpack.

If only she could be as cool and suave as he was. If she were a clever bride maybe she'd be able to ignore his coldness and reserve—hold her tongue and bide her time.

Why did she wear her heart on her sleeve and feel compelled to throw herself at people when she craved their love? Last night he'd made wild, impassioned love to her, and she'd been so profoundly touched she'd told him how she felt.

The first hint that something was wrong had been when she'd awakened at Belle Rose and reached for him and found she was alone in their bed. She'd dressed and run downstairs, only to discover him finishing breakfast with Cici and Logan. As soon as she'd entered the dining room, he'd announced they would leave as soon as she ate breakfast.

"I asked what you are doing," Alicia repeated from his New Orleans doorway as he grabbed a tackle box.

Without so much as a glance her way, he slung a pair of jeans and a frayed plaid shirt into his backpack. "I would think it's pretty obvious. I'm packing."

Gus lay in the middle of his bed, watching them both as he thumped his tail and purred. Alicia resented his simple happiness.

"Why? Are you moving out?"

"No." He didn't look up. "I'll be gone a week at most."

"Going where for a week? I don't understand."

"I need solitude. Why did you go see your father when he called? Because you're made that way. Because you had to. I need to get away."

"Can't we just talk about last night?"

"We can talk when I get back. Maybe then I'll have something to say."

"You're making me crazy."

"I'm sorry. That's not my intention."

"What about your work?"

"Things are slow."

He didn't have to explain that. She knew he and his staff believed she or her father were to blame for most of his firm's business problems. "Okay," she said. "Go. Just tell me where you're going."

"To my cabin in Alaska probably." His voice was harsh and loud.

Alaska? As far as possible, in other words.

She hated herself, because if she'd thought it would do any good she would have gotten on her knees and begged him to stay. She wanted to know what he was thinking and feeling. If she'd thought it would do any good, she would have yelled at him until he told her.

For her, the sex last night had been more than wonderful. She'd felt as if her soul had been welded to his, as if it still was—but he was shutting her out, going to Alaska of all places.

"Okay," she said. "Alaska. I'll let you concentrate on your packing."

As she walked slowly out of his room and then downstairs, her heart constricted.

Alaska. She couldn't believe this. Not after last night.

Sucking in a breath, she decided to brew herself a cup of tea. Fifteen minutes later Alicia was sitting quietly in her rocker on the back porch, sipping from her mug, when she heard him in the kitchen.

He'd married her only because of the baby. He'd wanted sex, but obviously he hadn't wanted her saying she loved him. Well, she had a right to her feelings and a right to express them. And she wasn't going to take any of it back. She would just have to deal with this, and so would he.

Not that it was fun. No—she was utterly miserable at the thought of him leaving.

She heard the screen door open. Then his footsteps sounded as he approached her. She notched her chin up and met his gaze.

"I don't want to quarrel," he said. "I'm going—so I can figure myself out. Vanessa will call later to check on you."

"I'll be okay."

A muscle pulled in his jaw as he nodded. "Good."

Her stomach tightened. Her mouth felt too dry to speak, but someone she managed to whisper, "Goodbye."

"Goodbye." Slinging his backpack over his shoulder, he walked across the backyard to the garage.

When the garage door went up and his SUV backed out, she stood and walked to the edge of the porch with her hand on her heart.

He stopped, rolled his window down and waved to her.

She took a deep breath and waved back. Then she held up her hand a blew him a kiss.

He nodded mutely. Then his tinted window went up.

When the gate closed behind him and she finally went back inside, the stillness within the house seemed deafening.

Fourteen

Alicia couldn't bear Jake's big, quiet house after he'd left, so she called Carol.

"Why don't you come to London?" Carol said as soon as Alicia had told her everything.

Why couldn't she go somewhere? Who said she was stuck here just because he'd left?

"You're right. I could take a little trip of my own."

Suddenly there was a loud knock at her front door.

"Somebody's outside," Alicia said.

"Maybe it's him—come to his senses."

"He has a key. No, it's either Vanesa or our land-lady."

Curious, Alicia told Carol she'd call her back after she saw who it was, then she hung up.

When she crept to the front of the house and lifted the shade, Vanessa waved at her.

Disappointment swamped Alicia as she cracked the

door. "Okay, you did your job," she said. "I'm fine, so you can go home to your sons."

"They're not there right now. So—are you going to invite me in to your pity party or not?"

"Am I that obvious?"

"Who wouldn't be in your shoes? You're a beautiful bride, and your big dope of a husband runs off to Alaska."

Alicia didn't know what to say, so she stood aside and let Vanessa sweep boldly across her threshold.

"I know Jake asked you to check on me, but it's not necessary. I'm fine."

"I tried to call, but your line was busy. I thought if you were free, maybe we could go out to dinner."

"Like I said, it's not necessary."

"If I'm going to remain Jake's secretary, allow me to disagree. Besides, I'd get brownie points from Jake if you'd say yes."

"He doesn't really care about me."

"Then why did he run all the way to Alaska?"

"He runs as far as he can—and this is proof he cares?"

"I'd put money on it. What did you do to scare the socks off him?"

"Scare him?"

"Don't look so wide-eyed and innocent. I know scared when I see scared. If I didn't know better, I'd say he's in love. He just doesn't know it yet."

Was that true? The image of Jake's large body on top of hers flashed in her mind. He'd felt so wonderful. So right. Everything had been perfect until she'd told him she loved him. Not that she could tell his nosy secretary about their great sex.

"Look…er…" Alicia began.

"Okay, I get it. What if I promise to quit prying into my boss's love life, not to mention yours? Will you say yes to dinner then?"

Vanessa probably knew Jake better than anybody else. If she thought he was scared, maybe Alicia could learn more about what scared him if she spent time with this woman. Besides, she was friendly and seemed like fun.

"It's not like I have anything better to do," Alicia said.

"What do you say we exact revenge on your honey and go somewhere really, really expensive? I mean somewhere I could never afford on what he pays me?"

Alicia laughed. "I'll get dressed." A wild idea had begun to germinate in the back of her mind.

"Do you know where exactly he is in Alaska?" Alicia asked.

"Who do you think made arrangements for his favorite bush pilot to drop him and a week's worth of supplies up at his cabin south of Denali National Park? He goes there every year around this time in the summer. He says the place clears his mind."

"What does he do there?"

"It's wild country. He hunts and fishes. Not my thing, but he always returns tanned and happier. Some summers I can actually stand him for a whole month. The year he broke a bone in his knee when he fell running from a grizzly he was happy for three months. You know what I heard him say? 'I had fun. I nearly died.' *Men!*"

"What if I wanted to join him for a...er...a belated honeymoon? Could you make the same arrangements for me?"

The idea that had begun to germinate as Alicia was

getting dressed blossomed. Suddenly she knew exactly where she wanted to spend the next week and what she wanted to do.

"His cabin doesn't have electricity or running water. You have to carry water from the river to bathe. And like I said, it's grizzly bear country."

"I really want to understand him, I need to make this trip."

"You know what they say—if you love him let him go. If he doesn't come back, hunt him down and kill him."

"Next time. I'd prefer to surprise him."

"You're one gutsy girl."

"So will you help me?" Alicia asked.

"Can I finish my margarita first? When we're done here, we'll go back to the office, where I have all the phone numbers. Oh…and before we leave, don't let me forget to snap a picture of you and the delectable Javier."

"Who's Javier?"

"Honey, he's the yummy bartender who's been giving me the eye all night."

"Jake said you don't like men."

"Wrong. I've got three children, haven't I?"

Jake was looking forward to a meal of mild-flavored grayling as he laid his heavy stringer of fish on the rocky ground and stared at the cloud-shrouded peaks of the wild range extending east and west as far as he could see. He'd build a fire, sit out in the open and enjoy the view. He was tired after having spent fourteen hours hip-deep in icy rapids fishing.

Sucking in a long breath, he wished Alicia was standing here beside him. He wanted to share with her the extraordinary sensation of freedom and release this big land gave him. Then he frowned as he realized he was thinking of her again.

What was wrong with him? He'd come here to get some distance from his feelings for her, to enjoy the land that had always been such a comfort. So, why couldn't he shake her hold even here? He liked being on his own.

Usually there was nothing like a couple of days in the wild to change his view of the world and make him realize that what had been bothering him back home wasn't really much of a problem.

Twice already he'd let his thoughts of her distract him to the point of endangering himself. He'd gotten too close to a blond grizzly with black legs and a moose intent on gobbling river vegetation right where he wanted to fish. Even though he'd had a gun, he'd let the moose and grizzly have his fishing hole.

Suddenly he heard the thin drone of a single-engine plane flying low, which was odd because few people came up here. His heart leapt. Hill wasn't due back to pick him up for four days, but if he was here dropping another hunter, and if he could wave him down, there was no reason he couldn't return early to his bride.

Scanning the sky, he tried to locate the plane. But no matter how hard he squinted and strained, he never saw the plane. The noise grew fainter and Jake cursed in frustration. When all was silent again, he dropped to his knees. The wilderness felt alien and lonely. He'd had enough of it, and he knew it was because he needed Alicia too much.

She'd said she loved him. His feelings for her were so powerful he was afraid to analyze them. So, he wouldn't.

He'd just live with them and try to get used to them before he put a name on them.

Slowly he picked up his stringer and resumed trudging the last three miles to his cabin that stood on top of the ridge. He was a mile out when he saw wisps of dark smoke curling into the air. Somebody was at his cabin. That somebody had built a fire.

Hugging herself, Alicia stood on the porch of Jake's one-room log cabin. She'd been so sure coming here was the right thing to do.

So sure—until she'd gotten here and Hill had flown away and left her with only the whispery stillness of the trees for company. Without Jake she felt too alone.

Was it only an hour ago that she'd fibbed bravely to Hill that Jake was expecting her, and, no, Hill didn't have to wait and make sure she was all right, that he could take off?

"He didn't say nothin' about you coming," Hill had insisted, repeating that he'd be glad to wait. "He always comes by hisself."

Her heart had quickened but she'd said, "Our plans were tentative, like I told you."

He'd cocked a bushy eyebrow and had eyed her suspiciously. "I'll even stay the night if you like. I can sleep in my plane. You wouldn't even know I was here. Unless there was trouble."

"He'll be here."

"All right, then. If you're sure… Tell you what—I'll do a flyby tomorrow just to make sure you're all right." He'd instructed her as to what hand signals to use to wave him down or send him on his way. "Don't want to land unnecessarily," he'd said gruffly. "Waste of fuel."

Without further ado he'd taken off for Fairbanks.

She'd toted the single bag Hill had allowed her to fly with to the cabin and had busied herself gathering wood and building a fire, all the while keeping an eye out for any kind of bear. Not just a grizzly.

"There's no such thing as a good bear in Alaska," Hill had warned her. "They're all wild and unpredictable, especially this time of year. And don't leave any food out."

She felt sick to her stomach with worry. What if Jake was furious? What if he hated her for following him?

So what? He was her husband. She had to know what he felt. That's why she'd come here. She had to know if they had a chance. Every day she was investing more of herself into this marriage.

Suddenly she glimpsed movement against the horizon—a tiny figure was heading purposefully for the cabin. Maybe a lone moose or caribou, she told herself, trying not to get her hopes up that it was Jake, even as she hoped that it was.

Finally she made out a tall man with long legs and a familiar gait. *Jake.* He had something heavy slung over a broad shoulder that caused him to lean to one side as he strode toward her.

"Jake? Jake!" She tore down the steps and ran toward him. *"Jake!"*

He must have heard her. After a pause, he started running, too. She was breathless when they both stopped a few yards from each other.

Without taking his eyes off her, he knelt and carefully laid his fat stringer of heavy fish on the ground.

"Nice fish," she whispered, feeling uncertain suddenly.

He stood again and contemplated the fish and then the scuffed toes of his boots for a long moment.

"I got lucky. Real lucky." His gaze climbed her slowly, lingering on her mouth, and she didn't think he was talking about his catch.

She hissed in a breath. Was he really as glad to see her as she was to see him? His handsome face was flushed. His chocolate-brown hair fell across his brow. She swallowed, waited.

A sheepish grin crept across his features as he reached for her. The fierce emotion that tore through him, causing him to shudder as he pulled her to him, shredded her, too.

Giving a little cry, she smothered her lips in his thick hair, which smelled of wood smoke and damp forest.

"So what are you doing way up here?" he whispered huskily in an odd voice he'd never used before. When she didn't answer at first, his grip around her body tightened.

She was thrilled that he kept holding her, but still afraid that once he got over the shock that she was here, he might be angry.

"Are you all right?" he demanded. "Is the baby all right?"

"Yes! I had to come. I had to know what you felt. I couldn't go on loving you, wondering if you hate me, or if I'm too clingy and not what you want. I know I shouldn't have chased you, and I'll stay out of your way while I'm here."

"Shut up." His voice was suddenly so harsh and cold, she was terrified that as soon as he was sure the baby was okay, he was going to send her away. She felt his arms knot with tension. For a long moment he said nothing else.

"What am I going to do about you?" His arms

tightened around her shoulders and he pulled her closer.

"I know I probably shouldn't have come," she whispered. "I should have never have suggested marriage...and made you feel so trapped that you had to run all the way up here."

"What?" Suddenly he burst out laughing.

"Don't laugh at me," she begged. "Whatever you do, don't laugh."

"I'm not laughing at you. I'm glad you're here, you little fool. I missed you hellishly. I admire your honesty. I was an ass. It took a lot of guts on your part to come here. But I'm glad you did."

"You are?"

"*Very* glad. I kept saying I wanted to take our relationship to the next level. I guess I got my wish. And for the record, I'm not talking just about sex."

As Alicia clung to him, her eyes filled with tears of joy.

"Don't cry," he whispered.

"It's just that I'm so happy."

Leaning down, he cupped her chin. Gently he brushed her trembling lips with his own, and a wild piercing joy such as she had never known filled her. When he deepened the kiss, Alicia's knees went limp.

A long time later he said, "Let's go inside. Unless you want me looking over your shoulder for a grizzly the whole time we're making love."

She laughed and he let go of the long dark strands of her hair that had become tangled in his fist at her nape.

"I was wishing that I'd brought you with me," he said. "I wanted to share all this with you so much."

I love you, she thought, but this time she knew better than to say it aloud.

He didn't say it either, and he probably wasn't close to thinking it, but the light in his eyes every time he looked at her coupled with the thrilled grin that dazzled her was enough.

At least for now.

Fifteen

Jake brought the fish inside and set them in his ice cooler.

"I'll clean them later." He turned to her. "You can't leave anything edible outside here—including your delectable self."

"Hill told me that."

"That old rascal…flying you here and leaving you all alone…. What if I'd been camping out?"

"He didn't want to. And he promised to fly over and check on me tomorrow."

"Well, you're not giving the orders from now on. You're not to go outside—not without me—ever. Especially not at night, even though it only gets dark for an hour…and not completely dark even then."

"Bears?"

"This is wild country."

Alicia's confidence soared. He was obviously glad

she was here and he was being so protective. Maybe he didn't love her, but he definitely felt something.

"Come here," he whispered.

She hesitated but only for a moment. "Aren't you starving? You've been fishing all day. And you walked…"

"We'll eat later. After…"

"After what?" she teased.

"I'm hungrier for you than for anything else. The past two days felt like the longest in my life. You're becoming a habit."

"Is that all I am?"

"Withdrawal was hell." His laugh was husky and tinged with desire. "Worst of all, I think you're beginning to know your power over me."

"Is it so hard to trust me?" Would her father always be between them?

Jake didn't answer.

When he took her in his arms, she closed her eyes at the surge of joy that filled her. With calloused fingers rasping across her silken skin he slowly removed her clothes. First he unbuttoned her blouse and then reached inside her waistband and unsnapped her jeans and pulled both jeans and satin panties down. Last he unhooked her lacy black bra so that her breasts swung free. Then it was her turn to strip him. She couldn't tear off his clothes fast enough, tossing them in heap on top of hers.

She swept her hand over his flat stomach and pectoral muscles. Sinking to her knees she began to use her mouth.

He sucked in a savage breath when the tip of her tongue stroked the length of his erection. "Not yet," he whispered raggedly, dragging her down onto a low cot draped with his sleeping bag.

"Still scared of losing control?" she teased.

"Who me? No, I just want to take my time…and make you happy, too."

"I am happy."

"Happier then."

But in the end, he couldn't wait any more than she could. When he plunged inside her, she wrapped her legs around him and held on tight. As he began to move in that rhythmical dance as ancient as time, she grew hotter and wetter until finally she couldn't bear it and they exploded together, waves of passion crashing over them.

The second time he let her please him with her mouth. The third time he took her hard and fast again. After the fourth, they were so tired they slept curled against each others' bodies. When they woke up, it was still light.

"I'm starving," he said. "Time to clean the fish and build a fire. Time to feed you."

"I brought a jar of peanut butter and jelly and two loaves of bread," she whispered. "Just in case…"

"Cheater."

"Appetizers," she amended.

He laughed. "Smart girl. Let's make sandwiches. Who wants to clean fish when I can lie in bed holding you?"

He wasn't professing love, but he wasn't indifferent. That was something, wasn't it?

"Alicia! Wake up! You've got to see this!"

At first she was so groggy, she was afraid something was wrong, but when he crashed back into the cabin without bothering to shut the door, her worry dissolved.

Wrapping her in a blanket, he led her by the hand

across the rough planks of the floor to the porch. Once there, he put his arm around her and hugged her close.

"It's the northern lights," he said. "You almost never see them in the summer. The sky isn't dark enough for long enough."

Undulating ribbons of light shimmered against the horizon. Streaks of green, orange, yellow and dark red danced like flame.

Together, in silence, they enjoyed the miraculous display that seemed like it had been designed for them alone.

"I feel like we're the last man and woman on earth," she finally said.

"Adam and Eve in the Garden of Paradise?"

"Sort of. But since they were naked, I always imagined their paradise as being tropical."

"We got naked."

"In a cabin."

When the display ended, he took her back to bed and made love to her again.

Then it was over and he held her close, caressing her hair and silken skin.

"I wish we never had to go home," she said.

"Me, too. But we do, of course," he murmured.

"Like Adam and Eve thrown out of paradise?"

"So I did make you happy."

"Very happy. So happy."

And yet some part of her still felt unsure when she thought about their future.

It was midnight. Except for a sliver of brilliant silver light fringing the horizon, low, dark clouds wrapped Fairbanks International Airport. Since their jet to the lower forty-eight was late, Alicia had had time to charge her cell phone, its battery having run down up at the cabin. No service.

When she checked it after charging it and saw that her father had called repeatedly, leaving several increasingly urgent messages begging her to call him, alarm made her heart pound.

"Jake, I'll just be a minute," she said, pointing toward the ladies' room.

He nodded absently and went back to his newspaper.

When her father didn't answer any of the numbers he'd left and his home phone indicated that his home number had been disconnected, she tried to ignore the sinking feeling in the pit of her stomach. Had the stress gotten to him? Had he had a heart attack or something? Even though it was the middle of the night in Louisiana, wouldn't he have answered his phone if he was okay?

Reluctantly she slipped her phone into a pocket of her purse and returned to Jake.

"What's wrong?" He looked up from his paper and studied her much too closely.

Twisting a strand of her hair, she glanced away uneasily. For the first time in days, she thought about the pin her father had slipped into her shopping bag and that she'd hidden. She hadn't tried to return it because she hadn't wanted to get him into more trouble. Or complicate her situation with Jake. Now she wished she'd marched back to her father's house, sans scarves, and had handed it over to the guard the same day she'd discovered it.

If her father was okay, she'd do that as soon as they got back to New Orleans. From now on she wanted to be honest with Jake about everything. He was her future.

"What's this little worry line between your brows?" Jake asked, gently touching it. "Why won't you look at me?"

When she pulled back, his hand fell to his newspaper.

She bit her lips. "It's about my father. He tried to call me—repeatedly. I just tried to call him back, but he doesn't answer. I know it's the middle of the night in Louisiana, but he should be home. I'm afraid something's happened to him."

Jake's gaze was hard and piercing as he pulled his own cell phone out of his pocket and snapped it open. "I'll call Logan. Maybe he knows something."

"Okay," she whispered tightly.

Their time in Alaska had been the next best thing to a honeymoon. They'd spent days hiking and fishing and exploring. He'd shown her all his favorite fishing holes and vistas. At night they'd cooked outside and then had made love in the cabin before a glowing fire until all hours. She'd given herself to him completely, hoping that he'd break down and do the same. He'd come close a time or two, but somehow he'd always held some part of himself in check.

Even so, she hadn't wanted their special time to end, but now it had—with a bang.

As she watched him punch in Logan's number, her throat felt dry. Suddenly there was a bad taste in her mouth.

Shortly into his call to her brother, he shot her a dark look that told her the news wasn't good. Jake's face grew increasingly tense as he listened. His own replies were so cryptic and terse, she couldn't tell what was going on. Something was definitely up. Then he said goodbye and shoved his phone into his breast pocket.

She inhaled a long breath. "What's going on?"

"Your father has violated the terms of his parole and fled to Brazil. Apparently he'd distributed lots of valuables to people he was close to."

"Valuables?" she repeated in a croaky voice. Her first guilty thought concerned her mother's pin.

"Jewelry. Diamonds. Cash. He went to certain people before he left and asked that his property be returned. When they complied, he left the country. For good. Of course, the feds consider the money and diamonds theirs."

"Oh, no! Not before his trial! This makes him look... so guilty."

"Yes. It does. You've got to face the fact that he ran because he's guilty. He intends to sell the diamonds and live in Brazil. The last thing he's ever wanted is justice! Or you!"

She shut her eyes, but she could not shut out the horrible truth. If her father wasn't guilty, who else could have done what he'd been accused of? Why had he run?

"Did he give you money? Or diamonds? Did he? Because if he did, you'd better call the feds and tell them right now."

Watching him, she chewed her lips, feeling torn and uncertain about Logan's news. Slowly the last illusion about her father that she'd clung to dissolved. He had to be guilty.

"Jake, I just need to sit here quietly and digest this."

"Fine. You do that."

He turned his back and pretended to read his paper. She knew he was pretending, because he never turned a page. He just sat there, statue still, his spine rigid, fighting to ignore her.

She'd been fooling herself. They'd never had a chance. There was too much between them. She was Mitchell Butler's daughter, and therefore doomed forever to be his enemy.

As soon as they got home, she would call that awful agent who'd evicted her from her apartment and tell him she had her mother's pin.

Jake would never believe that she hadn't taken it on purpose.

He would never forgive her.

She would face that when they were home in New Orleans.

Sixteen

Alicia was anxiously unpacking in her downstairs bedroom when the doorbell chimed. She rushed out into the hall, but Jake was already stomping down the stairs ahead of her, taking them two and three at a time, with Gus trotting behind him.

"I'll get it," she said.

"No, I will," he replied, not looking at her.

"But it's for me," she whispered.

They'd barely spoken on the long flight home or on the shorter taxi ride to the house. She was dead with exhaustion, sick with worry about her father and her relationship with Jake. On top of all that, she dreaded this interview that she'd set up with the federal agent from Seattle when they'd landed to change planes.

Gus's silken tail curved around her legs as she stood in the hall and waited as Jake opened the door.

"FBI," said a familiar voice. "Is Mrs. Claiborne home?"

"What do you want with her?"

"I'm here to question her about her father, Mitchell Butler."

"She's been in Alaska on a honeymoon with me, so she's not involved with his flight to Brazil."

"She did call us and set this appointment up herself."

"What?"

"From Seattle," she whispered, walking slowly to Jake's side. "As soon as I heard the facts about my father, I knew there was something I had to tell this man. And you."

Jake stood where he was, statue still, his face blank and cold.

Her heart sank. He would never believe that she hadn't taken the pin deliberately because she'd intended to help her father escape.

"I'd prefer that she have an attorney present," Jake said, surprising her.

The self-righteous FBI agent who'd evicted her lifted his bulbous nose and stared at her so accusingly through his wire-rimmed glasses, she began to feel a little faint.

She must have whitened, because Jake slid a protective arm around her. Then he suggested everybody sit down in the living room. Flat-eared, Gus hunched down on all fours and watched the agent with wary yellow eyes.

The agent leaned toward her. "Why don't we get to the point? Why exactly did you call us?"

She felt Jake tense beside her.

"On the morning of my birthday my father called me and said he wanted to wish me a happy birthday.

He invited me over, so I went. While I was there, he tried to give me a birthday gift, a pin I've always loved that belonged to my mother. I refused to take it, but somehow, I don't know how, he managed to hide it in one of my shopping bags. I didn't discover it until I got home."

Jake's hand on her shoulders fell away. She was aware of him stiffening rigidly beside her.

"As you may remember," the agent said, his eyes on both of them, "when your father agreed to the terms of his house arrest, he signed papers saying he would give no assets of any kind away. Not to you. Not to anybody."

"I really think she needs an attorney present," Jake said.

"Our sources think he gave you diamonds," the agent persisted.

"He gave me an heirloom pin that had belonged to my mother. I've been trying to figure out how to return it to him without making things worse for him."

Jake sucked in a breath and stood up. Then he strode to a far corner of the room, where he stared coldly out the window.

"Your father was in no position to give you anything—as I've explained to you repeatedly, in some detail. Isn't that right?" the agent demanded.

"Yes," she whispered.

"So you knew you should have called us immediately," he said. "Didn't you?"

"Yes."

"May I see it—the gift?"

Slowly she got up and went to her room. Within minutes she returned with the lacquered box. The agent took it and opened it. He removed the pin and then tossed it to her impatiently as he continued to manhandle the box.

Turning it over, he shook it.

"There's nothing in it," she said just as he opened a secret drawer and removed a small envelope.

"Nothing, you say?" He began unfolding the tissue paper. As he pulled back the last bit of paper, hundreds of diamonds caught the light and shot sparks.

"Nothing?" The agent whistled. "Investment grade, if I'm not mistaken," he said, lifting his hard gaze to hers.

Slowly he rewrapped the tissue around the diamonds and returned them to the envelope. He replaced the envelope in the box. Last of all, he took her mother's pin from her and put it in the top drawer.

She turned to Jake, but his back was to her as he stood frozen at the window.

"I knew I shouldn't have kept the pin, Jake, and like I said, I didn't intend to keep it. But I didn't know those diamonds were there. I didn't!"

"I'm sure your father would say the same thing." The agent snapped the lid of the box shut.

"Don't say another word to this man, Alicia. Not without my attorney present," Jake said.

"Good day, Mrs. Claiborne. We'll be contacting you very soon." He nodded in Jake's direction. "Mr. Claiborne, I will give you the benefit of the doubt and assume you knew nothing about this."

Jake's icy gaze swept over her.

"Of course, he didn't," Alicia said. "He wanted me to have nothing to do with him."

"You should have listened to your husband."

* * *

Her heart full of pain, Alicia stared into those cold blue eyes she no longer recognized.

"Jake, I swear I didn't know the diamonds were there," she said.

"Save your breath," he said in a low, hard tone.

"All my life I wanted my father to love me. I wanted to believe maybe he'd softened...that maybe the birthday gift really meant something. Just like I thought Alaska meant something."

"You're unbelievable! You know what? You almost had me believing that Alaska meant something, too. Now I don't know. Funny, when people lie to you, it's hard to know where the lies end and the truth begins. All I know is that I want out of this marriage."

"My father knew how much I loved my mother and how much I would treasure that pin," she said brokenly. "I really was planning to take it back."

"Your father wanted to use you to hide portable wealth, and you went along with him. You let him use you."

"You're right. I did. I should have returned that pin that day." Her stomach knotted in pain. She bit her lips. "Maybe...deep down...I knew his having hidden that pin showed how dishonest he was, but he was my father. I've spent my whole life trying to believe in him."

"I'll do what I can, hire you the best lawyers to help you get out of this mess he's caused. But I'm moving out."

"When?"

"Now." Without looking at her again he turned and headed for the stairs.

A rising tide of pain enveloped her. He was leaving

her. Forever. She didn't want Jake to go, but how could she stop him?

When he came back down the stairs, he was carrying a suitcase.

"Until our marriage ends officially, we live apart," he said. "I should have listened to you. You were right about us not having a real marriage."

He turned his back on her then and headed toward the kitchen. Silently she watched his broad shoulders disappear down the hall. Their marriage was over, and it was her fault.

A door opened and closed. Then she was alone.

For a moment as she thought of a lifetime without him, her throat was so tight she felt like she might strangle.

"I can't think about that now," she thought, hugging herself. "I have to think about our baby. I have to be strong for our baby."

Suddenly there was tiny movement like the wings of a butterfly in her abdomen.

The baby. She'd felt their baby.

When their precious child kicked her again, she smiled.

"You don't look too good, boss man," Vanessa said as she dumped a stack of file folders onto his desk.

"What's this?" he growled as he picked up a folder.

"Maybe you should call your wife. She doesn't look so hot either."

Jake had given Vanessa a bonus to check on Alicia every day and report back to him. Because of this she seemed to think he'd given her a license to interfere. "You said she was fine."

"She misses you."

"And you know this how?"

"I know. She's heartbroken, and I'm tired of going over there and seeing her pale face and shadowed eyes. The girl looks haggard, and she resents me...for not being you."

"She crossed a line. She'd not the woman I'd begun to think she was."

"Okay, so what if her father hid a few diamonds in a gift he snuck into her shopping bag. So she didn't tell you, since, big surprise, you've been such a jerk on the subject of her father. I wouldn't have told you either."

"If she's telling the truth, she should have called the feds about that pin as soon as she discovered it. Lots of people probably think I knew she had the diamonds all along. I have no reputation now."

"What about her? She didn't know what that slimeball was up to either, because she's not a criminal. Then after the bastard betrayed her, you walked out on her, too."

"Damn it! That's not how it was! And I'm paying for her legal defense! Why can't you ever, just once, be on my side?"

"I am on your side. That's why I'm telling you to work things out."

"I've got a better idea. Get your nose out of my personal life, so we can get back to work."

She shrugged.

It irritated the hell out of him that Vanessa had been giving him a hard time the past four days. He'd had four miserable nights on Bos's houseboat because he couldn't trust himself to stay in the same city with Alicia and not call her. Alicia had betrayed him. Besides that, she'd reduced him to a needy, clingy, besotted idiot.

Some part of him didn't care if she'd lied to him and

betrayed him. The nights on the houseboat had been even worse than being in Alaska on his own.

The woman had gotten under his skin. She'd hooked him, and no matter how hard he tried to wriggle free, the hook just kept sinking deeper. He'd said he was leaving her. What a joke. He couldn't get through an hour without pining for her.

This was what he'd always feared—that love would take him over again and destroy him as it had before. Only this felt a thousand times worse. He'd fought to become strong and self-reliant. She was a liar and a cheat. Why couldn't he stop wanting her?

Well, he'd said he was finished, hadn't he? He wouldn't go back to her. He wouldn't.

One minute Jake was alone in a jungle of dwarf palmettos and water tupelo as the bull alligators roared and the next he saw a willowy figure paddling a kayak gracefully through the dark waters toward the houseboat.

"Alicia?"

"No, it's just me," Cici said, tossing her blond curls. "Who's the only person crazy enough to follow you into the swamp?"

"Does Logan know where you are?"

"I like to keep him guessing. What are wives for?"

"As long as you don't get me shot."

"He's your brother."

"Right. Family loyalties run deep in the South, and all that rot."

"Deeper than we sometimes realize. You came back, didn't you? And so did I."

She threw him the bowline and he pulled her

kayak snug against the houseboat. Then he helped her disembark. "Want a drink?"

She shook her head. "I just want to talk." She paused. "You've been doing a lot of hiding out…ever since you got married," she said.

"I'd rather not talk about her."

"I'm sure." She hesitated. "Vanessa called me, so I went to see Alicia."

"Vanessa is a real rabble-rouser."

"Alicia's every bit as unhappy as you are."

"The hell I'm unhappy!"

"Right. Just look at you. When was the last time your jaw saw a razor? The only way to end your mutual misery is for you to go back to her."

"She lied."

"You lied, too…about how you feel. Did you ever make her feel like you wanted to marry her? Didn't she have to practically beg you? She had a rotten childhood. Maybe she's tired of begging people to love her."

"That's her problem."

"Then why do you look so awful?"

"Thanks. You look great, by the way."

"Alicia loves you and you love her. You're hurting her terribly because you're so determined to be strong and hard and never care about anybody because you don't want them close enough to hurt you…the way I hurt you. I'm sorry, by the way…."

He didn't say anything.

"But you and me—we're ancient history. What about Alicia, not to mention the baby?" Cici said. "Don't you care that you're hurting them? She told me it moved."

And he hadn't been there.

"What if you're throwing away your one chance at true happiness? Jake, I know what you went through in the past. Believe it or not, I got hurt, too. I ran away and stayed away because I couldn't deal with it. But at some point I learned that maybe there comes a time when you've got to stop running or you'll always have an empty, meaningless life. Sometimes you've got to face who you are and what you need. You're going to be a father. It's obvious to everyone who knows you that you need her. Why don't you forget your pride and put aside your fear of being hurt again? For once in your life—just go for it!"

Seventeen

"Alicia!"

Jake's footsteps rang on the hard floors as he strode through the downstairs shouting her name. His house had never sounded so scarily empty. Usually Gus came trotting up to him when he came home. Not this time.

Where was his wife? And her damned nuisance of a cat? What if she'd already gone to London and taken Gus with her?

Jake tore out the back door and then stopped, expelling a long sigh of relief when he saw a tall, slim woman in a red shirt and jeans tucking a tiny plant into the soft earth as gently as a mother would put a baby to sleep. Alicia's dark, tousled hair fell about her shoulders like a silken veil. She was so damned beautiful. Beside her sat a black-and-white cat, his tail twitching in a lively manner as he eyed a yellow butterfly.

Jake let the screen slam behind him so she'd look

up. She turned as he walked toward her slowly, her eyes widening when she saw him. Their glances touched, held. Neither seemed able to look away.

Finally he stopped at the edge of the lush grass. She stood, warm heat suffusing her cheeks, coloring them prettily. Her eyes were so brilliant and her smile so sweet, he felt a thrilling rush of emotion.

Did she still love him? If so, he would welcome her love and cherish her because he needed her, craved her. She made him feel alive, happy—happy in a way he'd never been happy before.

Clasping her hands together, she waited as he walked across the thick lawn toward her. In the next moment he enfolded her in a crushing embrace.

"Alicia, I've missed you so much!"

She sighed. "I was hoping against hope you'd come back," she whispered breathlessly.

"I'm sorry I walked out on you."

"Your behavior was perfectly understandable under the circumstances."

"That's garbage, and you know it. Forgive me?"

"The minute I saw you standing there." She hesitated. "I love you."

"I can't live without you," he said. "I love you more than anything in the world."

"I think I've been waiting my whole life to feel like this."

He clasped her tightly, burying his face against the smooth skin of her warm, silky throat, inhaling her sweet scent.

She took his hand and placed it on her tummy so that he could feel their baby kick.

"Wow," he whispered.

She was his wife, his love, his everything. He couldn't wait to take her to bed.

He handed her a black velvet box. "I have something for you."

She opened it and expelled an amazed breath. "My mother's pin! How did you get this?" With reverent fingers she caressed each point of the sparkling star just as she used to when she'd been a little girl.

"Let's just say that it cost me a fortune to buy it before the feds' auction, but you're worth it. The feds are going to let you off the hook, too. It took a few legal maneuvers, but we cut a deal."

"Oh, Jake," she whispered clutching the diamond pin to her heart.

He handed her a second velvet jewelry box.

"What's this?"

"My grandmother's earrings. You wouldn't take them when my family gave them to you for your birthday."

She laughed. "I couldn't accept them when I thought our marriage wasn't real."

Holding the box, she hurled herself into his arms and held on tight.

He folded her against his chest, crushing her against him. "I want to design you a house with lots of bedrooms…so we'll have room for more children."

Unable to speak, she stared up at him, her eyes shining with such excitement that he knew she had to feel the same way he did.

* * * * *

His kiss was consuming and she wanted to be consumed.

And with that want, she realized what a dangerous path she trod right now—how very much was at stake. Every single reason why she had never let herself dwell on the memory of her time with Benedict flashed through her mind—his touch, his taste, their mutual pleasure.

And then reality had hit—hard.

Mia stepped away from him. Her heart fluttered in her chest like a bird trapped in a net. All in all, that was exactly how she felt. Trapped.

Dear Reader,

When I knew I was setting this story in Queenstown, one of the most picturesque and fun-filled tourist centres of New Zealand, I also knew I just needed to spend a little extra time there. After all, a hastily snatched lunch with friends about twenty years ago wasn't going to be enough, was it?

I'll never forget the descent into Queenstown, how we literally flew down a valley between two mountains and how awesome and amazing that view was. Queenstown itself is every bit as gorgeous as the promotional pictures suggest and if you're ever lucky enough to go there I'd encourage you to allow several days to enjoy the environs—seriously. You may even need weeks to do everything properly. My most exciting moment, though, was on the last day there, when I saw the location I'd been looking for, for Parker's Retreat, during a cruise on the lake. What better for my story than a property accessed only by air or boat? How exclusive and private could that be?

In this story, not only does Mia Parker come face to face with the worst judgement call of her life, but Benedict del Castillo finds his answer to the family curse. An answer he thought would be lost to him forever. Balancing Ben's determination with Mia's protective instincts was, at times, quite a challenge for this author, and I hope you will enjoy *For the Sake of the Secret Child* and Ben and Mia's hard-fought journey to their own happy ever after.

Happy reading and very best wishes,

Yvonne Lindsay

3 Months Free

when you subscribe for 12 Months

SAVE OVER £31

SEE OVERLEAF
FOR DETAILS

www.millsandboon.co.uk/subscriptions

SAVE OVER £31

Subscribe to Desire today to get 4 stories
a month delivered to your door for 12 months
saving a fantastic £31.80.

Alternatively, subscribe for 6 months and save
£12.72, that's still an impressive 20% off!

FULL PRICE	YOUR PRICE	SAVINGS	MONTHS
£127.20	£95.40	25%	12
£63.60	£50.88	20%	6

As a welcome gift we will also
send you a FREE L'Occitane
gift set worth £10

**PLUS, by becoming a member you
will also receive these additional benefits:**

🌹 FREE P&P Your books delivered to your
   door every month at no extra charge

🌹 Be the first to receive new titles two
   months ahead of the shops

🌹 Exclusive monthly newsletter

🌹 Excellent Special offers

🌹 Membership to our Special Rewards programme

No Obligation- You can cancel your subscription at any time by writing
to us at Mills & Boon Book Club, PO Box 676, Richmond. TW9 1WU.

To subscribe, visit
www.millsandboon.co.uk/subscriptions

MILLS
BOON

FOR THE SAKE OF
THE SECRET CHILD

BY
YVONNE LINDSAY

All the characters in this book have no existence outside the imagination of
the author, and have no relation whatsoever to anyone bearing the same name
or names. They are not even distantly inspired by any individual known or
unknown to the author, and all the incidents are pure invention.

Published in Great Britain 2011
by Mills & Boon, an imprint of Harlequin (UK) Limited,
Eton House, 18-24 Paradise Road, Richmond, Surrey TW9 1SR

© Dolce Vita Trust 2010

ISBN: 978 0 263 88319 0

51-1011

Harlequin (UK) policy is to use papers that are natural, renewable and
recyclable products and made from wood grown in sustainable forests. The
logging and manufacturing processes conform to the legal environmental
regulations of the country of origin.

Printed and bound in Spain
by Blackprint CPI, Barcelona

New Zealand-born to Dutch immigrant parents, **Yvonne Lindsay** became an avid romance reader at the age of thirteen. Now married to her "blind date" and with two surprisingly amenable teenagers, she remains a firm believer in the power of romance. Yvonne feels privileged to be able to bring to her readers the stories of her heart. In her spare time, when not writing, she can be found with her nose firmly in a book, reliving the power of love in all walks of life. She can be contacted via her website, www.yvonnelindsay.com.

This book is dedicated to Kate Gordon with grateful thanks for all her patience and help regarding so many questions relating to Queenstown.

One

Waiting on her private dock at the edge of Lake Wakatipu, Mia Parker smoothed her uniform for the umpteenth time. She was as curious to meet the new guest for Parker's Retreat as she was nervous. The prickle of unease that had started around 3:00 a.m. this morning was now a deep-seated knot of tension situated between her shoulder blades.

"What do you think he'll be like?" her mother asked from her side.

"I don't know, but he's paying us well enough not to wonder too much," Mia answered with a tight smile.

She told herself, not for the first time, that her sudden anxiety was completely unfounded. From what her friend, Rina Woodville, had explained to her, Mia knew that Benedict del Castillo came from a wealthy family and was looking for a quiet and private respite while he recovered from a car accident. Despite that, she couldn't help wondering what type of man had the kind of money to book out her entire boutique hotel and health spa for a whole month *and* pay her a considerable bonus at the same time.

With that much wealth, why come all the way to her private oasis in one of New Zealand's busiest tourist spots? The fabulous spas and resorts of Europe would have been much closer to his Mediterranean island home. And they were more accustomed to providing the type of luxurious anonymity Mr. del Castillo seemed to require. What had happened to make the man want to travel so far?

"With any luck he'll be tall, dark and handsome and in the market for a wife," her mother persisted.

"Mom, I didn't know you were in the market for a new husband," Mia teased, knowing full well her mother was still grieving over Reuben Parker's death three years ago.

To her surprise her mother blushed, but then quickly resumed her not-so-subtle assault. "You know full well I'm talking about you, young lady. Don't think you can change the subject. It's about time you got back with the real world and stopped hiding yourself away here."

"I'm not hiding, I'm building a business. And this guy, well, he's our ticket to some much-needed financial security. That's more important to me right now than romance."

Mia closed her eyes for a moment, reliving the rush of relief and excitement that had swamped her when his first half payment had been confirmed in her bank account. Knowing she'd be able to cover her staff's wages for the duration of his stay and for a good month beyond that had brought a peace of mind she hadn't known in a very long time. The sensation was addictive, making it easy for her to justify not investigating the background of her guest further—telling herself she was merely respecting his request for privacy.

A sound on the water caught her attention, making her

open her eyes. The boat was coming and, with it, the man who would be the sole focus of the retreat's staff for the next thirty days. She could see the sleek lines of the luxury thirty-eight footer as it cut through the slight chop on the surface of the lake. She was glad she'd ignored the bank manager's advice to sell the boat after her father's death and the true state of their family's affairs had been revealed.

At times like this, the boat was a vital, and impressive, link to the outside world. A statement that, despite Reuben Parker's choice to take his own life rather than face his debtors, the Parkers would survive.

The vessel was closer now and she could see three figures standing on the flying bridge—one she easily identified as Don, her boat captain and all-round handyman at Parker's Retreat. The others must be her guest and his personal trainer, because she could already see Don's seventy-one-year-old father—and self-proclaimed boat boy—standing on the main deck, ready to cast the mooring lines.

Again that knot in between her shoulder blades tightened. Everything about her reclusive guest's visit was integral to the survival of her business. Everything.

"Everything's perfect, isn't it?" She turned and asked her mother, suddenly stricken with an irrational fear that she'd forgotten something.

"Mia, relax. You know we've done everything. Mr. del Castillo is in the Summit Suite, his trainer's accommodation is sorted, the kitchen has Mr. del Castillo's food and beverage preferences, the car and driver in Queenstown are on constant standby and you yourself have his spa visit schedule organized like a military exercise. Stop worrying so much. Besides, in the unlikely event we've overlooked anything, we can fix it without it causing any problems, I'm sure."

"Right. We'll be fine," Mia said, more for her own peace of mind than in agreement with her mother's calming words.

She stepped forward and grabbed the bow line being thrown from the boat and tied it off on the dock as Don's father nimbly sprang to do the same to secure the rear.

As soon as the boat was secured and the gangway bridged the short distance between the vessel and the dock, she painted on a smile. First to disembark was a whipcord-lean blond man, dressed casually in jeans and a lightweight ski jacket to ward off the chill winter air. The personal trainer, she guessed. She'd assumed that the trainer might be a woman, when told that her guest would be arriving with one other person, and had suspected the moniker to be one of convenience only. But the suppressed energy in the blond man's gait said otherwise. Mr. del Castillo must be taking his recuperation seriously if this was the man he'd hired for the task.

"Hi," he said, taking her hand and pumping it enthusiastically. "I'm Andre Silvain, pleased to meet you."

French, she noted, judging by his accent. "Welcome to Parker's Retreat, Mr. Silvain. I think you'll find we have all the equipment you said you would need for the duration of your stay. This is my mother, Elsa Parker. She acts as chatelaine here."

"Call me Andre." He smiled back charmingly and looked around. "This place is amazing. I'm sure Ben and I will accomplish great things together here."

His enthusiasm was almost overwhelming and Mia felt her cheeks start to ache as she turned to watch the tall, dark-haired man now limping down the gangway. Dressed all in black and clearly suffering from the contrast in temperature between his native Isla Sagrado and a southern New Zealand winter, he guided himself slowly, one hand resting on the hand rail.

Though she couldn't yet see his face, there was something familiar about him, she thought as she watched the wind tug at the silk paisley scarf he wore looped around his collar and lower jaw. The finely woven fabric slid down, exposing a shadow of a beard and a pallor to his skin at odds with the Mediterranean summer weather she knew he'd come from. The wind tousled his slightly overlong black hair, lifting it from the smooth wide plane of his forehead. The sense of familiarity increased as he lifted his head and dark chocolate-brown eyes caught with hers.

The knot in her spine intensified and sent a spear of shock straight to her heart as her worst judgment call, ever, walked back into her life.

Benedict del Castillo shivered under the heavy black wool of his knee-length coat, his hand tightening on the gangway rail as he made eye contact with the young woman standing on the dock. Instant recognition and something unexpected—something hot and feral—fired through his veins.

Just over three and a half years ago, at the weekend-long, high-society party where they'd met, he'd only known her as "M." But despite that virtual anonymity, his body knew hers with a depth of intimacy he'd shared with very few. What were the odds, he wondered, that she would be here?

Ben's eyes raked her from head to toe and he noted her not quite form-fitting uniform with distaste. The jacket and trousers were designed to conceal, rather than reveal and—if his memory served him correctly—her attributes were well worth revealing.

"Welcome to Parker's Retreat, Mr. del Castillo. I'm Mia Parker. I hope you will be comfortable here."

"So formal, M?"

He saw the fear that clouded her eyes straight away. The reaction intrigued him. Obviously, she hadn't planned to acknowledge the fact that the last time they'd been together they'd done just about every single physical thing a couple could do in the pursuit of mutual sexual satisfaction. He could understand the coolness, he supposed; given the circumstances. They had a business arrangement in place for the next month—it was not surprising that she would wish to be professional. But fear? What on earth did she have to be afraid of?

He took her hand and lifted it to his lips, pressing them to her cold knuckles. He sensed the tremor that rocked through her at his touch and he allowed his mouth to curl into a smile as he released her hand. To his amusement, she snatched it away, rubbing her knuckles against those god-awful trousers and stiffening her posture.

"I believe you'll find everything here to your satisfaction. My staff has worked hard to ensure that all your specific requirements are met."

"And you, *querida?* Do you plan to meet my—" he paused for effect, unable to resist baiting her "—specific requirements also?"

A bright flush of color stained her cheeks and her voice shook a little when she replied.

"Obviously, I'll be working closely with your trainer to ensure your recovery is as swift as it can possibly be."

His recovery. Self-disgust gouged through him, cooling his amusement as effectively as the glacier that had long ago formed the lake behind him. The memory of the car crash infuriated him, especially since it came with the knowledge that it was his stupidity and reckless taunt at fate that had come back and bitten him painfully hard. That was still a bitter pill to swallow. He tamped down the feelings that had riddled him since his accident and shifted his focus to M's obvious discomfort. A man had to find his amusements where he could and right now Mia Parker was looking very good indeed.

"Obviously," he finally responded. "And who is this charming lady here with you?"

"Oh, I am sorry." Mia flushed with embarrassment. "This is my mother, Elsa Parker. Together, we run Parker's Retreat."

"Pleased to meet you, Mr. del Castillo, although you'll have to forgive my daughter for underselling herself. She's responsible for just about everything around here."

"Is that so?" Ben replied, taking Elsa's hand and offering her the same "olde worlde" courtesy he'd just shown her daughter.

To her credit, the older woman carried herself with a great deal more aplomb than Mia but then again, she had no idea of just how well he knew her daughter.

Mia gestured to one of two golf carts parked by the dock.

"If you'd like to take a seat, Don will take you and Andre up to the main guest house. Mother and I will follow with your luggage."

She wasn't about to be rid of him that easily.

"Actually, it's only a short distance, isn't it? After all that flying, I think I'd rather walk. You go on up, Andre," he said to his trainer. "Ms. Parker can accompany me to the hotel building."

"What about your crutches, Ben? I think you left them on the boat," Andre said, his meaning clear.

"They can stay there. The sooner I learn to live without them the better, as far as I'm concerned."

"Your call, *mon ami*. I believe you would be more comfortable with them for now, but given that it's only been a couple of weeks since you came out of hospital I insist you at least use a walking stick. I have a collapsible cane here near the top of my case for exactly this purpose."

Ben grimaced as Andre handed him the cane. He'd had enough of taking it easy, and enough of being poked, prodded and mollycoddled. Coming here was his chance to build himself back up to peak strength in privacy and without prying eyes or media conjecture as to any long-term damage to his body. His family was too wealthy, too famous for him to hide his recovery from the public eye if he had stayed in the Mediterranean, but here on the other side of the world, he could finally have the seclusion he needed. The seclusion his contract with Parker's Retreat had guaranteed.

It was past time his recalcitrant body returned to the level of fitness he was used to, so he could return to his usual activities—*all* of his usual activities. He cast a sideways glance at his reluctant escort and felt a ribbon of anticipation thread through him. And he knew just where he was going to start.

He'd changed, Mia thought as she adjusted her pace to walk slowly toward the main hotel building. Gone was the affable and self-assured man who'd swept her off her feet and into his bed the summer before her world turned upside down. Oh, he was still most definitely self-assured, but there was an edge to him now. Something else lay beneath the surface of his charm that hadn't been there before and she remembered "before" in all its Technicolor glory.

Her hand still tingled where he'd kissed her. Why couldn't he have simply settled for a handshake like everyone else? But then he wouldn't be Benedict del Castillo, her alter ego replied silently. He wouldn't be the man whom she'd met at a New Year's Eve gathering at one of the Gibbston Valley vineyards. The man who'd instantly caught her attention and then held it for every split second of the hours they'd spent together during one whole glorious day and two even more glorious nights, until his departure back overseas.

A man who, even now, sent her blood thrumming through her veins. She couldn't afford to let him affect her this way. He was a guest at the retreat and she had to see him in that light and that light only.

Oh Lord. A thought suddenly occurred to her. How on earth would she cope when it came time for his sessions at the spa? She'd given her other massage therapists a vacation for the duration of the del Castillo party's stay, intending to handle the sessions herself. She was a certified massage therapist, and had thought that personally undertaking Mr. del Castillo's treatment would show her commitment to maintaining his privacy and comfort. But now she couldn't help but wonder what she'd gotten herself into.

Touching him, stroking him. Letting her hands reacquaint themselves with his body. And what a body. Even now she had no difficulty recalling the smooth tanned texture of his chest, the way his dark brown nipples would tighten beneath her tongue. The taste of him.

She clamped down on her wayward thoughts. This was most definitely not the way for her to be thinking.

She wasn't the same girl she'd been when she'd shared his bed. She had a new life now, and new responsibilities. In the past three years, she'd lost her wealth, lost her father... and gained a son. Jasper, she had to think of Jasper. To remind herself why she was working so hard to make the retreat a success. Why it was so important to her to provide some form of security for her son and her mother, as well as for herself.

But even as she did so, the memories of that long-ago tryst

still kept on filtering through her mind. She'd only had to see him to feel that sense of excitement and anticipation again.

Don't even go there, she argued with herself. What they had shared was in the past. Very firmly in the past. She wasn't that woman anymore. She was a mother, a daughter, an employer—not the wild party girl who'd always had more money to throw around than sense to realize how lucky she'd been.

Mia started to silently recite a number in her head. The exact amount of money she owed the bank. It would be years before she could honestly say she was easily holding her head above water but for as long as she could paddle and break even, she would. Benedict del Castillo's financial arrangement for the privacy he so craved, paying full occupancy rates for the hotel for a month, plus a thirty percent premium provided his needs were met, would go a long way toward her immediate security. She couldn't afford to do anything that would breach that arrangement.

But what if he wanted to resume where they'd left off? The thought came and blindsided her. She simply could not afford to upset or reject him in any way, and she could hardly be surprised if he craved a repeat of the passion and intensity they'd shared during their last encounter. Even she had to admit she found the idea arousing. It had been so long since she'd let herself indulge in an affair.

No, she shook her head slightly, ridding herself of the notion before it could bloom and take hold in her mind. As tempting as it might be, it was certainly not a part of the professional persona she now maintained.

And there was far more at stake than her professional persona now.

Jasper.

Just thinking about her little boy, nearly three months shy of his third birthday, made her know that the choices and the sacrifices she'd made were for a darn good purpose. Taking care of him—and protecting his future by focusing on growing and stabilizing her business—had to take priority. He was something she'd done all on her own and something she'd done right, for the first time in her life. She'd do anything to protect him. Anything.

She fixed her eyes firmly on the building ahead, trying to ignore the man who walked slowly beside her. The man who could undoubtedly make or break her future security.

The man who had no idea that he was the father of her child.

Two

"The spa bath is right through there and, if you prefer a shower, you'll find it has multiple adjustable jets and a bench built into the stall."

A bench.

Benedict closed his eyes briefly and bit back the sharp retort that had become his standard response when faced with the assumption he was infirm. That he'd need to sit down in the shower.

She was merely extolling the features of her facility, he reminded himself. She wasn't one of the long parade of ex-girlfriends who'd turned up at his house wanting to "care" for him straight out of hospital—and sell their stories to the highest tabloid bidder.

He'd eventually sought sanctuary in the castillo where his family had lived for three hundred years. He'd been warmly welcomed by his grandfather and oldest brother—and gently cared for by his brother's wife—but even there the concern of his family and their retainers had become suffocating.

He was a survivor, dammit. For all those hours he'd been trapped in the wreckage of his car, he'd fought against the inky blackness of unconsciousness with that thought. No matter how much pain he'd been in, he knew he'd survive—he had to. No deals with the devil for him. Instead, the experience had given him a new perspective on things. A knowledge that life was indeed precious and not to be taken for granted—that time was not something to be wasted, because no one knew when that time could be cut short. In the deep dark of that night he'd also grasped the importance of family, and that promises to family were, above all other things, to be honored. His life, as he'd known it, had ended there and then—exposed for the shallow and somewhat hedonistic behavior it had been. He would no longer take his carefree and privileged lifestyle for granted.

He opened his eyes and looked out the massive picture window that framed the retreat's gardens, showing the path that led to the shore of the lake. A long, low, gray cloud snaked a line between the mountains that ringed Wakatipu. A blemish on an otherwise perfect scene. A perfect example of his life.

Blemished. Flawed.

Resentment—his constant friend since doctors had delivered the news that, despite the best microsurgery available, his injuries had left him infertile—tasted bitter on his tongue.

He turned from the vista, from the reminder that despite all outward appearances, he was no longer like other men. That he could never provide a child for his family and, with it, the assurance that the ancient governess's curse could be broken once and for all.

The old myth had haunted his family for years, but neither Ben nor his brothers had taken it seriously—until their grandfather grew ill. If *Abuelo* believed that some old curse required the three brothers to marry and have children, then that was precisely what they would do. Or rather, that was what the *others* had done.

His eldest brother, Alex, was happily married and would no doubt be announcing an impending heir sometime soon. Even Reynard, his second eldest brother, was engaged and surprisingly besotted with his fiancée. Their grandfather, the whole reason they'd embarked on the pact that had seen both his brothers race into relationships to placate the old man's fears, was beginning to relax.

However, he hadn't relaxed sufficiently. The words *Abuelo* had spoken to Ben before he'd left Isla Sagrado still rang in his ears.

"It's up to you now, Benedict. You're the last one. Without you, the curse will not be broken and the del Castillo family will be wiped from existence."

No pressure there. Thanks, *Abuelo*, Ben thought cynically as he let Mia's voice wash over him as she showed him how to operate the entertainment center, discreetly hidden behind painted silk screens that slid aside at the touch of a button. It wasn't as if he even believed in the blasted curse anyway. What relevance did a jumble of words thrown out by his ancestor's scorned lover have in today's world?

But no matter what his feelings on the subject were, he had made a pact with his brothers to do whatever it took to make *Abuelo*'s last years as happy as they could be. And it was his inability to live up to his part of the pact that now weighed heavy on his heart. The old man had stepped in when their parents had died in a skiing accident and had raised them through their turbulent teens to adulthood. They owed him. Big time. And no matter what Ben thought, *Abuelo* believed in the curse with every cell in his body.

And Ben's promise, made only four months ago, was now something upon which he could never deliver.

An all too familiar lash of anger flicked through his veins. Anger tempered with a fair serving of frustration at his own stupidity in having brought himself to this situation in the first place. He'd known as he drove his car along the coast road that he was taking a risk but, as with everything in his life, he'd wanted to push it to the absolute limits. Unfortunately for him, and the tangled pile of metal that was all that was left of a couple of hundred thousand dollars worth of car, he'd well exceeded them.

He looked at Mia, still without really listening to a word she said. The afternoon sun slanted in through the massive window and bathed her in its light, glancing off the spun gold of her hair neatly tied back from her heart-shaped face. His fingers itched to loosen her hair from its bonds—to run his fingers through it and discover whether it still felt as silky soft, to bury his face in it and find out if it still smelled the same. Then, to lose himself and his failings in the exquisite beauty of her welcoming body.

"So, if that's everything, I'll leave you to settle in. Please don't hesitate to contact reception if there's anything at all that you need."

Mia stood by the door to his suite. Clearly she was finished explaining everything, and he'd missed most of it. He fixed his gaze upon her again. Remembering anew the passion they'd shared. The passion he now craved again.

"Anything?" he answered, raising a brow.

He couldn't help it. He loved to see that cool professional facade she presented suddenly flush with heat. Heat and knowing. Remembering. If she thought that hiding her body in those shapeless rags—not to mention concealing the vibrant personality he remembered, behind a businesslike mask—would keep him from seeing her as a woman, she was vastly mistaken. It just made it more enticing to tease out a reaction in the face of her reluctance.

"We work hard to cater to our clients' specific needs, Mr. del Castillo—"

"Call me Ben," he interrupted. "After all, we're hardly on a formal footing, are we?"

He crossed the short distance between them and raised his hand to her face, one knuckle softly stroking the elegant line of her jaw. She jerked her head away, breaking the contact, but not before he felt the sizzle of electricity tingle up his arm. Oh yes—Mia Parker was exactly what he needed to aid in his recovery.

"That wouldn't be appropriate, Mr. del Castillo. Should you require company, however, I'm sure you will be able to accommodate your needs in town."

Her tone was glacial and to add insult to injury, she took a step back from him. He was not the kind of man who pushed himself on any woman—had never needed to. But they hadn't parted on bad terms. Was it so far out of the realms of possibility to want to revisit what they had shared—especially when he'd had so much taken from him already?

"*Querida,* I do not recall you ever worrying whether your behavior could be considered *appropriate* before," he drawled.

He heard the sharp intake of her breath. Saw the battle for composure flit across her features. Noted the flare of green fire in her eyes before she responded.

"That was then. I've changed."

"People don't change that much, Mia. Not if they're honest with themselves." He let his words linger on the air between them before continuing. "What we had was special—unique. Can you honestly tell me you have no wish to revisit that bond again?"

"No, I do not."

Her voice was emphatic, but he didn't miss the telltale flick of the pulse at her neck, or the sudden dilation of her pupils.

"Now, if you'll excuse me, I have work to do."

She spun away from him and let herself out of his suite, closing the door behind her with a careful "click" that spoke volumes as to the control she exhibited. As appealing as the new Mia was, with her buttoned down exterior, he wished he could see a glimpse of the old Mia who'd so absorbed him. She couldn't be too far beneath the surface, he was sure of it. Finding her—now, there was the challenge.

With every nerve in her body on full stinging alert, Mia forced herself to walk, not run, from Benedict's rooms. She'd hoped against hope that he'd be gentleman enough not to bring up their previous liaison—she should have known that such a wish was impossible. She couldn't deny that he'd spoken the truth. What they'd shared *had* been unique. But no matter how spectacular it had been, she wasn't about to throw everything she'd worked so hard for down the drain purely for the chance to rediscover the heights of pleasure she'd found in his arms. The old Mia would have jumped at the chance to renew their fling—but she wasn't that girl anymore. Couldn't be. Never would be again.

Mud had a habit of sticking, especially the kind of mud associated with her old behaviors, not to mention her father's financial misdemeanors. It had only been in the past eighteen months or so that she'd felt as if she could raise her head in a professional sphere and be recognized for her achievements here at Parker's Retreat, rather than her exploits in the latest women's magazines. She wasn't going to risk that hard-won respect for anything or any man—no matter how tempting he was.

By the time she reached the sanctuary of her office, at the end of the accommodation wing, she almost had the trembling under control. She shut the door behind her and leaned back against the paneled wooden surface.

Not for anything would she jeopardize the life she'd fought so hard to rebuild for her family. What her father had done had been the biggest abuse of trust and love he could ever have committed. It had taken all of her energy to pull her mother back from the brink of abject despair. Mia wouldn't let Elsa—or Jasper—down now. Not after all she'd accomplished.

When disaster first struck, keeping their family home had been paramount. She'd succeeded in making that happen, albeit in an entirely different manner from what they had enjoyed before. They now lived in what had once been their guest house. Guests now enjoyed the trappings Mia and Elsa had taken for granted would always be theirs, but at least she and her mother—and Jasper—still had a roof over their heads and she sure as heck planned to ensure it stayed that way.

She raised a now steady hand to her jaw. Retraced the line of skin he'd touched so very gently. It was tempting, so very tempting, to give in to the past. To take some relief from the constant daily pressures of balancing the tasks of running the hotel and spa and being a good mother and daughter.

She'd taken so much for granted during her first twenty-three years. Had lived with a silver spoon in her mouth with never a care or a thought as to what was around the next corner of her adult life. She hadn't even taken seriously the training she'd undergone as a massage therapist—at least, not until it looked as though it was the only way she was going to be able to make any money. Even then she'd had to spend vital funds on retraining before she could pick up the reins again.

Well, she'd certainly learned to grow up in a hurry. First, with the news that she was pregnant with the child of a man she hadn't—to her eternal shame—even known the name of and then second, with her father's admission of gross financial failure, followed shortly by him taking his own life.

Those had been dark days—seemingly endless with sorrow, accusations and confusion. Days when her lifestyle choices became fair game for the media—when people pointed the finger at her and apportioned their own blame on her for her father's downfall. But she'd pulled them through it. She—Mia Parker, party girl—had done what it took to hold on to what she could. And she would keep hold of what was hers.

Benedict del Castillo was only here a short time. He need never know that their blazing passion had resulted in a child. Jasper was *her* son. She wasn't about to lose another member of her family.

Besides, who knew what kind of man Benedict really was? He'd been as flip and casual as she had that summer. Had been just as happy to play along with the ridiculous game of anonymity she'd suggested. Was he capable of handling the responsibility of fatherhood? Sure, he seemed more intense now, his mood darker, but he hadn't hesitated to suggest they take up where they left off. A leopard didn't change its spots—he said as much himself. Did she really want a man like that in Jasper's life?

There had been a brief time when she'd contemplated trying to track him down. To tell him he had a fiscal responsibility to his unborn child, if not an emotional one. But the reality that such a request could backfire on her—could even have seen her declared an unfit parent and lose Jasper, given her less-than-circumspect behavior in the past and her difficulty in supporting him—had been overwhelming. She'd already lost so very much. She couldn't stand to lose her son as well. So she'd made do with less herself. Had poured her energy into supporting her mother and fighting to keep their home—a home where they could feel safe and, finally, proud of what they'd achieved together.

Her son had stability here—the love of his grandmother, his friends at day care, and all the care and love and guidance he would ever need from his mother. Ensuring Jasper didn't run across his father wouldn't be so difficult. Elsa took care of him while he wasn't at day care and during the business hours that occupied Mia's attention. She could easily keep him away from Ben. And she'd keep her distance from Benedict, as well.

Mia was not about to do a single thing that would cast a ripple on the smooth waters of their new life. Not a single thing. The terms of her arrangement with Benedict were simple. Exclusivity, privacy and therapy—for all of which she was being paid extremely well. He'd get what he paid for, and that was it.

A knock on the door behind her made her start, setting her heart to race in her chest. She took a deep breath and turned around, her hand on the doorknob before she could change her mind and pretend she wasn't in her office. She'd trained herself to face her fears, and if her current fear, Ben del Castillo, stood on the other side of that door, she'd face him, too.

"I hope I'm not disturbing you," Andre Silvain said through a charming smile. "It seems the gym is locked and I was wondering if you could show me through the facilities."

"Of course," she answered, willing her heartbeat back to some semblance of normality. "Usually we provide our guests with their own swipe key to access the pool and gym. Why don't we go to reception? I'll get that sorted out for you right now."

In a matter of minutes, Mia had organized a key for both Andre and Benedict and was leading Andre through the glass corridor that connected the accommodation wing of the hotel and the purpose-built gym she'd added to the already existing indoor swimming pool. The pool had been another of her father's extravagances—an extravagance she'd been grateful he'd indulged in as she'd never have been able to afford to have a pool installed with her current financial position.

Andre made several noises of appreciation as she showed him the facilities together with her treatment rooms.

"Since it will only be yourself and Mr. del Castillo here for the month, my usual gym and spa staff have been given a leave of absence. I will be attending to Mr. del Castillo's treatments myself."

It was a decision that had seemed like a good idea at the time, and the staff involved had accepted the offer of a month's leave, at what was usually their busiest time, with alacrity. However, now she'd learned exactly who her guest was, Mia was ruing her decision to provide the therapy herself.

"That's fine. As his trainer, I won't need anyone else in the gym. I've worked up a mixed bag of programs for him, starting tomorrow with swimming in the morning and then a gentle hike later in the afternoon, if he's up to it," Andre said. "After the hike he'll probably need some work on those muscles of his. I understand he was pretty fit before his accident, and despite his injuries I don't think it'll take too long before he's almost back to normal again."

Mia's stomach pitched on the thought of the type of injuries Benedict had sustained.

"Were they severe?" she couldn't help asking.

"Yes—mostly internal and tissue damage. His knee was also dislocated."

"Dislocated? That's unusual in a car accident, isn't it?"

"From what I've learned, it's a minor miracle he didn't break any bones. The driver's side of his car bore the full impact of the accident. It was only due to the safety features of the car that he survived at all. That and the fact that emergency services got to him in time. If they hadn't found him when they did, he could have lost his leg. A dislocation like that can do untold damage to nerves and cause blood supply to the foot to be interrupted. And that's not taking into account the internal bleeding from his injuries."

A chill ran through Mia's body. Ben could have died. She'd never really stopped to consider that before. While she'd never expected to see Jasper's father again, she had also never considered how she'd feel if she knew he didn't walk the face of the earth anymore, either. It didn't bear thinking about, she told herself sternly.

"He seems to have made a remarkable recovery. It's been, what, six or seven weeks since the accident?"

"Probably closer to five, and yes, he's one stubborn piece of work. We started his recovery program shortly before he was released from hospital. Of course, he was still getting over abdominal surgery at that stage and his knee was still splinted. He's a proud man, though, which makes it hard work. He doesn't like anyone to see him struggle or witness his pain."

Mia nodded. That made perfect sense. Even when she'd first met him, Ben had carried himself with an air of pride and entitlement that had been instantly appealing to her. After all, she'd borne herself in much the same way.

She knew what a struggle it was emotionally to come to terms with a massive change in circumstances, and felt a begrudging respect for how far Ben had come with his physical recovery from the accident. Perhaps his victory over death had given him that dark edge she now sensed hung around him like an invisible cloak.

"Well, this all looks really good," Andre continued. "I didn't expect your facilities to be as comprehensive as this but I'm impressed."

"We aim to please," Mia said, smiling. "And I like to believe that most of the time, we succeed. A lot of our business is now by referral or from returning clientele. Mr. del Castillo's booking certainly threw a bit of a spanner in the works but fortunately we were able to accommodate everything and everyone. I have to say I was surprised he was prepared to come all this way, though. Surely he could have completed his recovery at home, or at least nearer to home."

"The media wouldn't leave him alone long enough, and like I said before, he's a proud man. He didn't want pictures of himself plastered through the European papers looking anything less than his old self. Plus, he's made it quite clear to me that when he returns to Sagradan society he wants to do so in peak fitness."

Just privately, she didn't blame Ben one bit for seeking anonymity. In the aftermath of her father's death, his shame had been broadcast the length and breadth of the country. Her mother had retreated from the public eye, refusing to work on the charities that had once been a part of her life and slowly but surely severing all ties with her old friends. It had been up to Mia to hold her head high and to meet the public gaze upon their lives. She hadn't liked it one bit, but one of them at least had had to hold it all together.

She wondered whether Ben had a special someone

waiting in the wings for him when he went back home.
Someone who'd appreciate that peak fitness. Someone he
was perhaps too proud to allow to see him less than perfect.
Somehow the thought of another woman waiting for him
rankled her on a level she really didn't want to acknowledge,
because doing so would mean she had feelings for him,
wouldn't it? And she couldn't afford that. Not under any
circumstances.

Three

Mia moved around her treatment room, dimming the lights and ensuring the room temperature was comfortable. Once she was satisfied, she lit a candle in the oil diffuser she used to permeate the air with relaxing scents. Whether that relaxation was more for her benefit or for Ben's she couldn't honestly answer. The prospect of having his prone form beneath her hands while she gave him a massage was something she'd been working to keep from her mind all day.

She'd seen the two men return from their hike about an hour ago. Ben was limping more than he had when she'd caught a glimpse of him earlier today. When she'd mentioned it to Andre, he'd merely rolled his eyes and said that his client had been unimpressed with the gentle workout Andre'd mapped out for him and had insisted they take a more arduous trek. Nothing he'd been able to say had swayed Benedict's insistence and rather than leave him to go off and potentially hurt himself again, Andre had gone along with him in an attempt to at least temper the hike with enough rest stops and stretches to ensure he didn't undo any of the work they'd achieved to date.

Clearly Ben was driven to get well again as fast as he could. She carefully blended the cold-pressed carrier oil she preferred to use for massage with a few drops of pure essential oil that would aid his muscle recovery. As she did so, she wondered what drove him so hard. Was it just typical male stubbornness, or was it the prospect of returning home and getting back to his old life, and whoever was a part of that life?

Either way, it was none of her business. All she was here for today was to ensure that his workouts didn't leave him with painfully tight muscles that would keep him from his program for the next few days. Although she doubted that anything would sway him from his task. She'd seen the determination in his eyes as he'd gone through to the pool this morning and then later as he and Andre had set out for their hike. But despite the fact it wasn't her business, she couldn't deny that this new, more serious Benedict del Castillo was infinitely more appealing than the fun-loving guy she'd met the first time around.

If he'd been any other kind of man she would have thought he was pushing himself too hard. Risking further damage to an already traumatized body. But she had a feeling he knew his boundaries and that he was merely determined to extend those boundaries as far as possible.

"Where do you want me?"

Mia whirled around at Ben's voice, startled he'd managed to sneak up behind her and surprise her like that. She composed her features into what she hoped was a serene expression. He looked tired, she thought as she made eye contact with him for the first time since yesterday, and there were fine lines of strain about his eyes and mouth.

By all appearances, he was not in the mood to make small talk.

"Please, remove your clothes and then lie facedown on the table with the covers up to your waist. You can leave your briefs on. I'll leave you to get comfortable and I'll be back in a few minutes."

Without giving him a chance to respond she slipped out of her treatment room and closed the door behind her. The instant there was a solid barrier between them, Mia put a hand to her throat and took a deep breath. She could do this. She absolutely could do this—and without allowing it to affect her equilibrium. She'd remain professional at all times.

After waiting what she felt should be long enough for him to disrobe and position himself on the table, she knocked gently on the treatment room door and let herself back in. Her gaze flicked over the exposed expanse of skin of his shoulders and back and down to the tapered narrow width of his waist. He'd yanked the covers up unevenly so she took a moment to straighten them before facing the moment of truth where she would have to touch him.

"Have you had an aromatherapy massage before?" she asked, keeping her voice low as she cupped her left hand firmly over the base of his skull, while pressing her right hand flat against his upper back. She repeated the movement and pressure in segments down his back to his lumbar region. His skin was smooth and hot to touch. Achingly familiar, yet foreign at the same time.

"Not the kind you're thinking of," Ben said, his voice muffled in the purpose-built cavity for his face.

Mia fought a smile. She got that kind of comment a lot from guests using the spa. Some serious, some definitely not so.

"Then just let yourself relax. I think you'll find you'll enjoy it."

"You're touching me, aren't you? Of course I'll enjoy it."

There was a note to his voice, something unspoken, and just like that her mind filled with images of them enjoying one another. Mia shook her head slightly, and willed the images away. It was just mind over matter.

She released the gentle pressure she'd applied to his neck and used her fingertips to press individual points leading up to his skull. Beneath her touch she felt the tension in the corded muscles of his neck slowly release. Silently nodding to herself, she slid her fingers along his skull up to the tip of his head, her fingers dragging through the dark silk of his hair, before withdrawing her touch completely.

"Is that it?" he groused from on the table.

"That's just the beginning. Relax, Mr. del Castillo. Try and focus on your breathing and let your mind go."

"Ben. I told you to call me Ben."

"Fine," she breathed out a soft sigh of capitulation. "Ben, it is."

She turned from the table briefly to pour a measure of the blended massage oil into her palm, and then warmed it in her hands before applying her hands to his back. Immediately, she began the movements that now came to her as instinctively as breathing. Bit by bit, as she worked first in long sliding strokes, she could feel him respond to the soothing touch.

His muscle tissue became more malleable, his breathing deepened—and her fingers felt as if a warm buzz was building up beneath them. A warm buzz that tingled and crackled up her arms and charged her entire body. It had been so long since she'd touched him, and yet the sensations it evoked came pouring back from deep within her.

She shook her head slightly, determined to rid herself of her pitiful lack of personal control, but she couldn't deny the heated heaviness that now built inside her, or the glowing ember of need that smoldered at her core.

Mia worked her hands up from his lower back and to his shoulders, remembering the first time she'd felt his strength beneath her hands. Despite the injuries he'd sustained in the car wreck he still had pretty good muscle definition, she noted in the dim lighting of the room. His shoulders were still broad and strong—the muscles leading from his neck to the tops of his shoulders defined yet not overpowering. She let her hand slide down one arm, her fingers stimulating pressure points inside his elbow and wrist as she worked before mirroring her actions on his other side.

In fact, she was surprised not to have seen any scar tissue on his body. So far, she'd only seen the starburst tattoo he bore on the back of his right shoulder—the same tattoo she'd traced intimately with the tip of her tongue the last time he'd lain prone before her.

Her inner muscles clenched tight and an almost all-consuming flood of heat washed over her body. She always kept her treatment rooms warm but the temperature that radiated off her now had nothing to do with central heating. A demanding tremor of need shot through her, making her hands tremble ever so slightly in their ministrations.

Focus on the work, she all but shouted in her mind. The work and not the man, and most definitely not the past.

But her focus became blurred as she completed her work on his upper body and she shifted the covers to expose his legs. She worked for longer than usual on his feet and calves, avoiding the moment when she'd run her hands up along the backs of his thighs and higher, almost to his buttocks. Somehow she managed to hold it together—to regulate her breathing and to keep herself from combusting internally.

She was temporarily distracted by his knee, and took special care around the site of the damage—some residual swelling and bruising reminding her of the severity of the injury. To think he may have lost his lower leg completely if his circulation had been cut off completely to his foot. She couldn't imagine how devastating that would have been for him. A constant physical reminder of the crash.

Despite what Andre had told her of his injuries, Ben did seem to have gotten off very lightly, she thought— until she bade him to roll over while she held the covers a circumspect distance from his body. As she settled the covers in a fold down below his waist she fought to hold back a gasp at the livid lines of scarring that bisected his abdomen and crept, in lightning bolts of knotted tissue, to his hip on one side and lower, beneath the blanket, on the other.

"What happened to you?" she asked, before she could stop the words ejecting from her mouth.

Ben opened his eyes and their darkness glittered in the soft lighting of the room. His hands grasped the edge of the covers and eased them over his scars, hiding them from view.

"It's in the past. I do not wish to discuss it," he said, the words clipped and leaving her in no doubt he meant every one of them.

"I'm sorry, I didn't mean to pry. Are you comfortable with me continuing the massage or are you still abdominally tender?"

"Stay above the blanket. I'll let you know if I want you to stop."

He closed his eyes again and she studied him for a moment before adding another measure of oil to her hands and positioning herself at the head of the table. She took a deep steadying breath and began anew, trying not to think about the damage that had been wrought on his body. While some of his scars were clearly surgical, others looked as if he'd been torn into by a wild beast.

She fought back a shudder as she imagined what it must have been like to be trapped in a jumble of metal—in pain and alone, wondering when, or even if, rescue would come. The mental toughness required to survive such a thing was monumental.

As would be the mental toughness she'd need to get through the next month. Already, touching him was proving to be a torture all of its own. The long, slow strokes reminded her of another time—a time when all their attention had been solely for one another. When those strokes had led to other kinds of intimacies that had brought each of them immeasurable pleasure. Again she felt that tautening deep in her belly, that undeniable pull that ached with emptiness—ached for him. And not just for the intimate memories they had shared, but for what she wanted *now*. The very thought saw Mia nearly halt in her movements but she forced herself to continue, and forced her mind away from the treacherous thoughts that could lead only to more trouble than she could deal with right now.

By the time she neared the end of his massage, she was a mass of knotted nerves herself. Normally a full body massage left her wrung out, both physically and mentally. But for some reason, touching Benedict today, working out the knots under his skin, had energized her. Instead of her usual reviving cup of herbal tea, she wanted to do nothing more than swim off all this vitality now coursing through her veins.

Mia concentrated on the circular movements of her

fingers around his ankles and then up across the tops of his legs, finally bringing the session to an end by placing her hands flat on the soles of Ben's feet.

"We're all done for today," she said softly. "If you'd like a few minutes to gather your thoughts before heading back to your suite, feel free to take your time. I'll go and get you a glass of water to have before you go. Keep drinking plenty of water through the rest of today—it'll help you flush away the toxins that were released by the massage. Now, is there anything else you'd like from me?"

Ben pushed himself upright and swung his legs over the side of the table, the covers sliding down past his waist and revealing the hollow lines of definition that started at the top of each side of his hips. Mia rapidly averted her gaze.

"Before you go, there is just one more thing," he said.

Before she could ask what that was, Ben caught one of her hands in his and tugged her toward him, nestling her between his legs. His free hand caught the back of her neck, his fingers curling gently into the knot of hair at her nape and pulling free the clip that secured it.

He moved so swiftly she barely had a moment to realize what was happening, until he leaned forward, his mouth slanting across her lips, capturing her gasp of shock.

Ben couldn't say what had driven him to kiss her, but he knew the second his lips touched hers that he'd done the right thing. Lying prone on the table while she'd massaged his aching body, draining away what had felt like a lifetime's worth of tension, had been the kind of pleasure-pain he'd never thought he'd actively welcome into his life.

But under her long delicate fingers he'd felt the stirrings of desire—desire that demanded to be acknowledged and acted upon. Since discovering his infertility—and adding that on to the knowledge that due to his recklessness, he was directly responsible for that state—he'd wondered if he'd ever even want to make love again. Goodness only knew the pain of rehabilitation had driven all thoughts of sex from his mind.

Here, now, though, it was all different. While he might never father the son or daughter he'd always dreamed of having, he could at the very least reclaim his manhood, and with who better than the woman who'd remained on the periphery of his memory for more than three years? A woman who'd made all others since pale in comparison.

Beneath his touch he felt her resistance, the rigidity with which she held her body, her reluctance to part her lips. He teased the seam of her mouth with the tip of his tongue then gently caught her lower lip between his teeth and, ever so softly, tugged. Her capitulation was audible in the moan that rippled from her throat—tangible in the way her body relaxed into his. Ben felt a celebration of triumph as her mouth opened for him, gaining him access to her special sweet flavor and the passion she'd been hiding from him since his arrival.

Beneath his fingers her pulse bumped in a rapid beat at her wrist. He recognized its rhythm—it matched his own. Ben deepened their kiss, savoring her taste, the texture of her tongue as it danced with his.

Yes, this was what he'd needed. The unabashed, passionate response of a woman who was as attuned to his needs as he was to hers. He slid both his hands to her waist, pulling her more firmly against him, before easing his hands under the fitted T-shirt she wore, up across the satin smoothness of her belly, over her ribcage and finally over the cotton-covered mounds of her breasts.

Her nipples pebbled against the fabric of her bra and she

shuddered as he cupped her in his palms. But he wanted no barriers between them now. He wanted to feel her—all of her. He slipped one hand to her back and released the catch. The material of her T-shirt was too snug, so he eased it up over her body, pushing her bra up along with it and exposing her full rose-tipped breasts. He cupped them briefly before tearing his lips from hers and placing them around one puckered nub and laving it with his tongue, drawing it deeper into his mouth.

Mia pressed her lower body deeper into the cradle of his hips, her hands gripping his shoulders, her head dropping back and arching her breasts toward him in supplication, wordlessly begging for more. He did not plan to disappoint her. His body continued to quicken, to respond to her unabashed desire. His hands dropped to the waistband of her trousers, sliding the button from its keeper before easing the zipper open—and then everything changed.

She stiffened in his arms—one hand fluttering down from where her nails had only seconds ago been digging into his skin to halt him and to push his hand from her.

"N-no," she breathed.

He kissed her again, sweeping his tongue across her lip. "Yes."

"We can't," she said, pulling away from him. "*I* can't."

He let his hands drop from her, watching as she struggled to do up her bra and pull her T-shirt back down. In the dim lighting of the room her eyes were shadowed, but he could see the moisture that gathered at their corners and threatened to spill over.

"Mia—" He reached for her again.

"No! Don't touch me. Please, just go." Her voice broke on the last word.

"I didn't force you, Mia. There's no need to act like

an outraged virgin when we both know nothing could be further from the truth."

Frustration clawed at his insides. Frustration tempered with unaccustomed shame at the harshness of his words. He hadn't meant to lash out like that. He certainly hadn't wanted to make her cry.

One solitary tear spilled over the rim of her lower eyelid and tracked a line of silver down her cheek. She dashed it away with a shaking hand.

"I should never have let it go that far. I apologize. It was most unprofessional of me." She turned and grabbed a robe from behind the door and thrust it at him. "Please, use this. I'll see to it that your clothing is laundered and returned to your room by the morning."

He accepted the robe and wrapped it around his body. He wasn't about to let her pretend that nothing had happened. Not when that all-too-brief embrace had made him feel more alive than anything else had since his accident.

"This isn't over between us," he growled as he pulled open the door and stepped out into the foyer of the spa.

"Over? It never began. I'm not the person you think I am."

"I know this much," he said, "you ache for me just about as much as I do for you right now and we *will* see this to its natural conclusion."

He yanked the belt into a knot at his waist and stalked off, his body vibrating with a tension which warred with the cold hard truth that the nascent desire which had begun to blossom within him, was now dormant again.

He fought back the irritation he felt and instead brought forth a new resolve. He would break down the barriers of Mia's resistance, piece by piece. And he would delight in every minute of it.

Four

Mia collapsed against the table the instant he walked out the door. So much for being strong and in control. If he hadn't listened to her, hadn't stopped when she'd asked, she had no doubt he'd be making love to her right now.

God, she was so *weak!* He'd been here one day. One! And still, just a touch, a kiss from him, was all it had taken to turn her into a scrambled mess of seething need. He had her on every level and she was apparently helpless against his sensual onslaught.

Even now, after he was gone, her entire body continued to hum with desire for his touch, her nipples still contracted and abrading the soft cotton of her bra. The taste of him still on her tongue. She clenched her hands in the covers on the massage table and dragged in a deep, steadying breath.

She had to harden up. Rebuild that control she'd forged in the past three years. Remember what was most important.

Slipping into automatic mode, Mia stripped the table and remade it to be ready for the next day. Ready for Ben. She quelled the shiver of apprehension that rippled down her spine. Each day she would have to go through this again. Well, she'd just have to pull on her big-girl panties and get on with it, she told herself sternly. And find something particularly nasty to think about while she did it so that there was no fear he'd ambush her again like he had today.

She reached for the jumble of clothes Ben had left on the chair in the corner of the room and gathered them up. The crisp, citrusy scent of his aftershave wafted up to her in a wave that hit her with the subtlety of a sledgehammer. Somehow she didn't quite think that big-girl panties were going to cut it this time. Something in cast iron, perhaps, she thought with a cynical laugh out loud.

Mia bagged his clothes and set them aside to be attended to by the laundry staff overnight and finished tidying the room. It was getting late and if she didn't hurry, she'd miss Jasper's bath time and story before bed. It was precious time they spent together—just mother and son. Right now she couldn't wait to wrap her arms around his sturdy little body and ground herself again.

Later that night, after Jasper had gone to bed and Mia's mother, Elsa, had returned to her own private apartment at the back of what had been the guest house, Mia fired up her personal computer and did an Internet search on Benedict del Castillo. Many of the results that popped up in a list on her screen were in Spanish—a language she'd always loved to hear but didn't understand a single word of.

She quickly scanned through them, searching for anything with an English translation, and fortunately, there were plenty of them. Mostly tabloid links to pictures of Ben with an ever-changing bevy of beautiful women hanging off his arm at one celebrity-studded function after another. Then she found what she'd been looking for. The details of his accident.

It made for chilling reading. Apparently, he'd been speeding on the coast road toward his home when for some reason his car had gone into a skid. There was conjecture that he'd swerved to miss something on the road and that when his rear tires had hit some loose gravel, he hadn't been able to regain control. Either way, it had been early the next morning when one of his vineyard workers had noticed the marks on the bitumen and investigated the trail of rubber to the edge.

Rescue workers called his survival nothing short of a miracle. A stand of trees clinging to the steep hillside had prevented his car from tumbling to the rocks and sea below. However, those trees had exacted their own damage when a branch had penetrated the vehicle and quite literally pinned him in the wreckage.

Mia leaned back in her chair. No wonder the scarring to his lower abdomen had been so ragged. And no wonder, if he'd survived all of that, that his demeanor should be so different to that of the laugh-a-minute sex god who'd swept her off her feet when they'd first met. An experience like that changed a person—irrevocably. She knew that herself. While the damage to her life hadn't been physical, the emotional toll had been huge. The fight to survive both monumental and ongoing.

She could understand the complexities that made up Benedict del Castillo a little better now, she thought. But as she shut down her computer and got ready for bed she forced herself to acknowledge that understanding him would not make it any easier to resist him. She could only hope against hope that she would remain strong.

She slept surprisingly deeply and dreamlessly and was

woken only by a sharp cry from Jasper's bedroom. She flung off her sheets and ran to his room.

The nightlight in the corner cast a warm glow over his bed. She felt a pang of regret that her baby boy was growing up so fast. He'd transferred from his crib and into a "big boy's bed" about six months ago after she'd lost patience with the number of times he'd climbed from the crib and she'd found him pattering around the apartment. Since he'd been in the bed, however, he'd been an angel. Never once rising through the night unless he needed the potty or had a bad dream.

Checking her tearful son now, though, gave her cause for concern. His forehead was hot and his voice croaky as he tried to talk. She scooped him into her arms and took him through to the bathroom. After soaking a face cloth with cool water and squeezing out the excess, she wiped his little red face. Once he'd settled somewhat, she gave him a drink of water but swallowing just had him crying all over again. She scoured her medicine cabinet for the infant pain reliever she knew should be there somewhere and used a tiny dropper to encourage him to take the liquid.

At times like this she felt so incredibly alone. What would it be like, she wondered, to be able to share these kinds of concerns with a broad pair of shoulders at her side? Mia tried to settle Jasper back in his bed but he was having none of it.

"Mommy's bed," he cried and the big fat tears rolling from his dark brown eyes, eyes so like his father's, were her total undoing.

"Just for tonight, then," she whispered. "But don't tell Grandma, okay?"

Her mother was a stickler for children sleeping in their own beds but sometimes rules were meant to be stretched.

"Okay," Jasper croaked with a conspiratorial wee smile.

Mia was relieved to see he was feeling better with the pain reliever but she had no doubts that once it wore off he'd be miserable again. She put the bottle and dropper next to her side of the bed. At least this way, if he woke again within the prescribed time, she could administer more without disturbing either of them unduly.

The morning brought her a very unhappy little boy and a weariness in herself that had come from calming him several times over the past few hours. It was at times like this that Mia sorely missed the convenience of living in town, as she had when she'd been footloose and fancy-free. In Queenstown, she could have taken Jasper to an emergency doctor during the night and he could already have been receiving medical care. Now, she'd have to rely on her mother to take Jasper, who was becoming clingier by the minute, to their family doctor.

In an ideal world she'd be able to take him herself, but she had a staff meeting this morning and a telephone conference scheduled with her bank manager just before midday. She was no different from any other working mother, she reminded herself. Women the world over faced tough decisions about their children's care every day. But the reminder was no consolation when her mother came to share breakfast with them and the time approached when Mia would have to turn her sick baby over to someone else's care.

Elsa readily agreed to take Jasper to the doctor that morning, and made the necessary calls to the surgery and let Don know what time they'd need the boat, while Mia dressed for work.

"There, it's all sorted. It's probably just a bit of a cold coming on. You know, in my day we didn't race off to the doctor at the hint of a snuffle like you young mothers do today," Elsa said, but her smile belied the censure in her words.

"I know, Mom, but he had a fever through the night. I'd just like him checked over," Mia responded firmly.

"Of course you would. And you're going to be right as rain in no time, aren't you, Jasper?" Elsa ruffled her grandson's hair with a loving hand and pulled him into her lap for a cuddle. "How's it going with the new guest? Did he settle in all right?"

"Seems to have. I haven't had a great deal to do with him so far."

Mia felt her cheeks burn at the lie she told her mother. Under no extreme of imagination could their kiss ever be described as "not a great deal."

"What's he like?" her mother pressed. "I got the impression you two had met before."

"Just once, years ago. Besides, you saw what he's like. Tall, dark, handsome."

"Single?"

"Mom!"

"Well, it doesn't hurt to ask. I take it you're not interested in him, then?" Elsa arched one perfectly plucked brow in her daughter's direction. "It's about time you started dating again. You've worn your hair shirt for quite long enough."

The hair-shirt comment stung. Mia had done her best to atone for what she'd realized were her shortcomings. If she'd been a better daughter she might have seen her father's business concerns before they'd overwhelmed him. She could most certainly have cut back on her own extravagant lifestyle if she'd had any idea of the toll it was taking on their financial position.

Since Reuben Parker's death, she'd done everything in her power to restore some semblance of normality into their lives. Now that she was almost there, she didn't want to do a single thing that would rock the fragile balance of this particular boat.

"If and when I feel ready to date again, I will," she replied stiffly.

"No need to get all huffy on me, Mia." Elsa put one hand on Mia's across the table. "I know how hard you've worked and I appreciate it. None of it was your fault, you know."

"Mom—"

"No, you need to listen to me. You've been an absolute rock since your father died and it's past time I stepped up and helped out a bit more. You've had far more responsibility on your shoulders than you deserved. I know you call me your chatelaine, but I'm not so stupid or selfish that I haven't noticed that I haven't been much help to you. Honey, I'm ready now. You gave me my time to grieve and I appreciate that, even when I know it must have been so hard for you on your own. Now I want to do my bit."

Tears pricked at Mia's eyes at her mother's words. She knew firsthand how devastated and betrayed Elsa had been when all the bad stuff had hit the proverbial fan. It had been a hard lesson for them all. Her mother still rocked Jasper absently in her arms, the little boy already starting to doze again, his cheeks still flushed with a trace of fever. Having her grandson to focus upon had been an anchor for Elsa, one that had helped both mother and daughter immeasurably.

"Mom, you already help me more than you know by being here for Jasper."

"Yes, but he isn't going to need me forever. Before you know it, he'll be five and in new entrants at school. I need to get back in the saddle, so to speak. It's time I reengaged my mind on matters other than what we've lost."

Mia squeezed her mother's hand. This was the strongest she'd seen, or heard, Elsa be in years. Before everything had fallen apart, Elsa Parker had been a force to be reckoned with, leading the charitable organizations where she volunteered with her organizational skills and efficiency. It had been a double blow for Mia that after her father's death, she'd also lost sight of the strong, confident, capable woman her mother had always been. It would be an enormous relief to have her back. To be able to begin to share some of the responsibility for the hotel and spa would be monumental, even if she knew that realistically it would take some time for her mother to get up to speed with how things were run.

"Thanks, Mom. Let's take it in small steps first—see if you even like what we do here."

Elsa laughed. "Like it or not, it's our livelihood. I'll learn to love it—just you wait and see."

Mia's cell phone chirped in her trouser pocket. "That's my reminder. I'd better get into the office."

She bent and kissed Jasper, who promptly woke and broke into tears. He insisted on a very long cuddle before he'd go to his grandmother again. It was with a worried frown that Mia left the house and headed for the hotel. She hoped he'd settle and be good for her mother, and she hoped like mad that all would be okay at the doctor. With Benedict del Castillo here at the hotel she couldn't afford for her concentration to be off, not by as much as a single thought.

From his window, Ben looked out straight across the lake. The water was an inky gray, a reflection of the dark clouds gathering in the skies above and completely at odds with his memory of it during the New Zealand summer he was here. A movement on the path caught his attention and he quickly identified Mia as she walked across from her accommodation to the hotel. He hoped her night had been as fractured as his had. Far from relaxing him, her massage had left him restless and with his blood pounding through his veins.

Massage, hell, it had been much more than that. She'd aroused his body from a slumber from which he'd wondered if it would ever awake. He was keen to see if she could do it again, except this time there'd be no going back. He smiled. It was good to actually *feel* alive again—to have a new purpose. He turned from the window and headed out of his suite, determined to intercept her before she could hide in her office or elsewhere on the property.

The single-story sprawl of the hotel suited his purposes beautifully. Mia was just about at the main entrance when he caught up with her. There were dark shadows under her eyes, and the sharp icy wind had brought spots of rosy color to her cheeks.

"Mr. del Castillo," she said as soon as she saw him in her path. "Good morning."

She didn't betray her nerves with as much as a flicker of an eyelid. He had to hand it to her. She could be one cool customer. But he knew he had the power to change that, and it was a power he relished.

"We agreed you would call me Ben," he reminded her with a slow smile.

To his delight, the color in her cheeks heightened and her slender hands, hands that had stroked all over his body yesterday, tightened into small fists.

"What can I do for you, Ben?" she asked, planting her feet a small distance apart as if she was bracing herself for a blow.

"Dinner, tonight."

"I don't usually dine with our guests," she hedged.

"Don't tell me you're going to relegate Andre and me to solitary splendor in the hotel dining room every night of our stay."

"You did request exclusivity," she reminded him coolly. "I can arrange for you to dine in a smaller room if you'd prefer."

"That won't be necessary if you join us every now and then to break the monotony."

Her eyes brightened with a hint of humor. "Are you tired of Andre's company already? I'm sure he'd be crushed to hear that."

Ben allowed himself a small smile. "Not exactly, but we'd both appreciate your company at dinner tonight. Say, eight o'clock?"

He could see the idea turning around in the back of her mind.

"I'm sorry, tonight's really not a good night for me." She paused and looked at her watch. "You'll need to excuse me, I'm on my way to a meeting."

She went to pass him but he shot out a hand and caught her arm. The instant he touched her, she went rigid. She stared at his hand then cast him a look that spoke volumes. He didn't let go.

"You can tell me you've changed your mind when I come for my massage today," he said, locking his gaze with hers.

He released her, his fingers uncurling slowly, and took a step away.

"About the massage..." she started.

"Daily, as per our agreement, remember?"

She shot him a look, a flash of fear suddenly visible in her eyes. "Yes, I remember. I'll see you at four, then."

"So you will," he replied and watched her walk away.

Her reluctance to rekindle their earlier affair challenged him. He'd seen no evidence of any ring on her finger to say she was otherwise spoken for, so in his opinion that left the field well and truly open. Any man fool enough to let her out of his sight for longer than a day deserved to lose her to a worthier man, and that included him. He should have prolonged his last stay here in New Zealand until he and Mia could have worked one another out of their systems. If he had, maybe he wouldn't be so hungry for her today. Ah, but then he wouldn't have the delight of looking forward to cracking that shell of resistance she wore like some flimsy armor now.

Ben turned back to his room to gear up for the day's activities. After a supervised gym workout today, he and Andre were heading into Queenstown to go tandem paragliding—his trainer having vehemently vetoed the idea of bungee jumping at Skipper's Canyon, citing Ben's barely healed knee. Between the paragliding and his appointment with Mia this afternoon, he wasn't sure which he looked forward to more.

Five

Mia applied long, steady strokes along Benedict's back and forced her mind to divorce itself from the man and think only about him as a prone form in need of massage therapy. It worked. Up to a point. Unfortunately, while she could separate her *mind* from the action, her *body* seemed to have a mind of its own.

She tried to simply relax into the movements and let her thoughts wander to other things. Things like the staff meeting this morning where some of the staff had expressed a certain amount of boredom in their day-to-day activity now that the hotel only catered to two guests. Mia shook her head. You'd have thought they'd have been glad for the respite. Things would certainly hot up again when Benedict and his trainer were gone.

Twenty-seven more days. It seemed like a lifetime.

In an attempt to ease some of the staff's frustration, she'd worked with them to alter their rosters, giving them more time off and shorter shifts at Parker's Retreat. Of course, all of that only reminded Mia that, even though she'd have a skeleton staff here at all times, there would be less buffers between herself and Ben for the rest of the time he was here.

She sighed inwardly, concentrating her energy on working out a bunch of knots Ben had in his upper back and shoulders and tried to ignore the nagging pains that built up in her own.

Managing the hotel, as small and select as it was, was a great deal more difficult than she'd ever anticipated. Some days just topped the "too hard" list and today was very definitely shaping up to be one of those. Even the discussion with her bank manager hadn't been promising. He'd wanted to warn her that the fixed-term loan she'd originally negotiated was coming up for renewal. She had the choice of fixing it again or allowing the interest rates to float with the market. It was at times like this that Mia most missed having a partner to share the major decisions with. So much rode on her every choice.

And then, over everything, were her responsibilities to Jasper. How on earth could she be a good mother when nearly her every waking thought was consumed by work? Today she'd been torn in two leaving him with her mother. He'd been tearful and feverish and even her mother's call, once they'd returned from the doctor, to say it was a mild throat infection, hadn't allowed her to settle.

It should have been her that took Jasper to the doctor. She owed it to her little boy. She'd popped home after her discussion with the bank manager and checked on him, but he'd been asleep, her mother catching up on tidying Mia's apartment and putting away washing that had accumulated on the sofa.

She'd stood in Jasper's bedroom doorway and watched

as her son slept off his illness, his multicolored stuffed tuatara clutched in his small hands, the traces of tears dried on his cheeks. Her own tears had been easy to hide but the pain in her chest had stayed with her all afternoon.

She shifted her attention to Benedict's legs before asking him to roll over onto his back.

"Is everything okay?" he asked.

She started a little. "Of course it is. Why do you ask?"

"You keep sighing all the time," he answered.

"I'm fine. Just a lot on my mind."

"Want to share some of it? I hear it helps."

Mia shook her head. There was no way she was spilling the beans about her problems to Ben. She didn't trust him not to use the knowledge against her somehow, although even as she had the thought she wondered just where it had come from. He'd never struck her as manipulative before so why should she feel that way about him now?

Perhaps it was his dogged determination to get her to agree to his request to join him for dinner tonight.

She forced herself to smile. "No, I'll be fine. Now, let's get back to work here, hmmm?"

To her relief Ben closed his eyes again and she felt his body relax into the table as she recommenced his massage. She was on the verge of finishing up when the sound of a child's miserable wail penetrated the walls of the treatment room.

Instantly she stiffened. Oh, no. Please no. Don't let it be Jasper at the spa, she thought frantically. She couldn't deal with that on top of everything else. She should have told her mother to keep Jasper well away from the hotel, but she hadn't thought that necessary. In his usual day-to-day care, when he was well and happy, the problem never arose. But with him sick? He was hardly ever ill, so it was no surprise that he'd become difficult and clingy.

"I want my mommy!"

The distressed cry shot straight to her heart and splintered it in two. She flattened her hands on the soles of Ben's feet, as she had yesterday, to signal the end of the session.

"I'll go and get your water," she said, "and I'll be back in a minute."

She slipped from the room before he could answer. Before he could ask about the commotion outside in the spa foyer.

"I'm so sorry, Mia," Elsa said, looking far more flustered than her usual aplomb would allow, "but he was just so upset. Nothing would calm him until I said I'd bring him to you."

Elsa had tears in her eyes and Mia could see by the lines of strain on her face that Jasper had no doubt been a demanding handful. She held her arms out to her little boy and enveloped him in her hold.

"It's okay, Mom," she whispered over the top of Jasper's dark head. "I know you wouldn't have come here unless absolutely necessary."

Jasper's hand crept up her neck and started to play with the ponytail she'd pulled her hair into today. Whenever he was fractious it seemed to soothe him to play with her hair. Before long, his hiccoughing sobs had settled into regular breathing, but the instant she tried to give him back to his grandmother, he wailed again.

Mia shot a nervous look to the door to her treatment room. "Mom, I have Mr. del Castillo in there. I've finished his massage, but I still need to give him a glass of water and we really need to get Jasper away from here."

"Surely the man would understand. You are a mother, after all," Elsa countered. "Here, I'll get the water for him."

"It's not that," Mia started, suddenly wishing she'd shared the truth of Jasper's parentage with her mother earlier. "Please, Mom, take him. I know he'll be upset, but I'll try to make it up to him later. I'll be home again in about twenty minutes. Just give me some time to see Ben off and then tidy up."

"Ben, is it?" Her mother arched a brow at Mia and reached again for Jasper, who shook his head and burrowed more deeply against Mia's shoulder.

"It's not like that—he insisted on the informality. Now, please, take Jasper."

But Jasper wasn't in the mood to cooperate and set up an almighty howl as Elsa tried to pluck him from Mia's arms. Mia was almost in tears herself when a sound from behind her sent a chill of dread down her spine.

"Is everything all right?" Ben asked.

Oh no, it was her worst nightmare come true. She wheeled around, holding Jasper close to her, her hand on the back of his head and keeping it turned away from his father's curious gaze. Ben stood framed in the doorway. He'd dressed during the time she'd been out of the room and she felt at a complete disadvantage as he fixed her with a dark-eyed look.

"I'm sorry. My son, he isn't well."

"And he wants his mother. Understandable."

At the sound of Ben's voice, Jasper lifted his head and fought free of his mother's gentle hold. And in that moment all of Mia's worst fears over the past two days coalesced into a solid lump of lead in the middle of her chest. She tried to reposition the little boy, but he was determined to see who the newcomer was.

"Who's dat?" Jasper asked, letting go of Mia's hair to point at Ben.

"It's rude to point, Jasper," Mia said, grabbing his little hand and pulling it back down against his side.

Ben took a step toward them and smiled at Jasper. "I'm Ben," he said gently.

Jasper's curiosity morphed into instant shyness when the object of his attention answered him and he turned his head back into Mia's shoulder. Mia fought back her surprise at the tone in Ben's voice, but all his gentleness was apparently only for the wee person in her arms, because the look Ben gave her in the next minute was anything but.

Sensing something was very definitely amiss, Elsa stepped forward.

"Mr. del Castillo, I hope you're enjoying your stay at Parker's Retreat. I'm so sorry we had to disturb you today."

"It is nothing," he said smoothly, but Mia noted he didn't shift his gaze from Jasper for a moment.

Every nerve in Mia's body stretched until they were so taut she thought she'd snap in two. Her tension must have transferred to Jasper, because he started to wriggle in her arms, reaching for Elsa.

"Want Grandma now," he demanded.

With a sigh of relief Mia handed him over to her mother.

"It was nice to see you again, Mr. del Castillo," Elsa said. "Perhaps you can share a meal or two with us while you're here. I'm sure you don't want to be on your own all the time."

Mia groaned inwardly and cursed herself anew for not apprising her mother of the situation between her and Ben earlier.

"I'd like that, but please, call me Ben."

"Only if you'll call me Elsa," her mother replied coquettishly.

Oh, my God, was her mother flirting with him? Mia couldn't believe her eyes, and all the while her stomach was churning. She hadn't missed the sharp perusal Ben had given Jasper, nor the very pointed question in the look he'd given her earlier. She'd never been a good liar, but somehow she was going to have to put on a performance worthy of Meryl Streep to field what was most definitely coming her way.

"Mom, I think Jasper needs to head back home now."

"Oh, of course." Elsa smiled. "We'll see you later on, then. Say bye to Mommy."

"Bye, Mommy."

Jasper leaned away from his grandmother long enough to plant a wet kiss smack on Mia's cheek and she gave him a kiss and smile in return.

"See you at bath time, munchkin."

After Elsa and Jasper had gone, Mia bustled over to a cabinet set against the wall and extracted a glass before filling it from the water cooler she had in the corner by the reception desk.

"Here, you'll need this."

Ben's fingers grazed hers as she handed him the glass.

"Actually, I think I might need something stronger."

"I wouldn't, if I were you. You need to concentrate on flushing toxins from your body right now," she said, deliberately misconstruing his meaning.

Ben followed her back into the treatment room, where she fluttered about—stripping the table and remaking it, tipping out the balance of the oil and washing the container. His mind whirled with the details of what he'd just witnessed and there was a deep ache in his chest he couldn't quite define.

A son. Mia Parker had a son. One who was probably somewhere near three years old, if he could hazard a guess, given the child's size and vocabulary—not that he was any expert on children. But if he was right, and he firmly believed he was, it would make young Jasper's date of conception around the time he and Mia had enjoyed their all-too-brief affair.

Shock that she could have had his child and not made any attempt to find him, or even tell him the truth when he arrived here at Parker's Retreat, hit him with the subtlety of a wrecking ball, along with the big question—why would she deliberately try to *hide* his son from him? But then a new realization slowly dawned that, despite his injuries, he might actually be able to meet the terms of the agreement he and his brothers had come to.

But first he had to know for sure if Jasper was his. He could almost have been persuaded on appearances alone. Jasper was nothing like his mother in build or coloring.

The boy's body was sturdy, his hair dark, his eyes a rich deep brown—just like Ben's own. He fought the urge to grab Mia by the arms and shake the truth from her, to force her to state the words that would both turn his world upside down and at the same time make everything right. But appearances aside, he knew on a gut level that went far, far deeper than a simple need to be Jasper's father that the boy was of his making.

He would get to the truth, one way or another.

He drained the last of the water from his glass and set it down on the bench top with a loud "crack" of sound. Mia flinched, very clearly on edge.

"You never mentioned you had a son," he said evenly.

"It has no bearing on my ability to do my job or on your booking here. Why should I have mentioned it?"

"Oh, I don't know." He stepped to one side, blocking her attempt to walk out of the room. "Maybe because I could be his father?"

"That's ridiculous."

She tried to walk around him, but it took little effort to shift his weight and prevent her from getting past.

"Ridiculous? I would have thought it far more ridiculous to try and hide the truth."

Despite his desire to remain fully in control, he couldn't help the edge of anger that permeated his words.

"He's my son. I carried him, I bore him and I'm raising him to the best of my ability. That's the truth."

"The truth? Then who is Jasper's father, if not me?"

Ben caught her chin between his strong fingers and forced her to meet his gaze.

"Mia, tell me Jasper is my son."

She jerked herself free.

"I will tell you no such thing. Now, please let me pass. I have work to complete and a sick child to attend to. Since you're so worried about his welfare, perhaps you'd do well to remember it's you who is holding me up from being with him right now."

"We have not finished discussing this," he warned.

"I beg to differ. We have totally exhausted the subject."

She pushed past him and went to stand at the door to the entrance of the spa, holding it open for him—her foot none too subtly tapping on the floor.

"I understand you need to be with Jasper tonight, but we will talk about this further tomorrow."

"There is nothing to talk about. I told you that already."

"So you say. However, your eyes betray you, Mia."

"There is nothing to betray," she insisted, but behind her words he heard a note of anxiety.

And it was that very note that gave him purpose.

"Then meet me for dinner tonight as I suggested this

morning. Tell me about Jasper's father. Prove to me that I'm not him."

"I don't need to have dinner with you to prove you have no claim on my son."

Every muscle in her body was rigid and her face had paled, making her eyes shine with the brilliance of unflawed emeralds against her white cheeks.

"Then you have nothing to fear, do you?"

"Mr. del Castillo, my son is ill and needs his mother. Tell me, why on earth would I choose to spend time with you rather than comforting him?"

"You will call me Ben, and I am certain Jasper will fall asleep at some stage this evening. When he does, you can come to my rooms. I will wait for you. It is no matter to me—I'm used to dining late anyway."

"And if he doesn't settle and I don't come?"

"Well, then, I will have to come to you instead."

"I'll see what I can do," she eventually replied through lips thinned with anger.

He watched her as she locked the door of the spa behind them and stalked off toward the doors leading outside. He took a moment to indulge in the sheer masculine pleasure of watching the sway of her hips and the sharply straight set of her shoulders.

She would not dodge his need to know precisely who Jasper's father was and, if she tried to prevent him, she'd learn exactly what it was like to nay-say a del Castillo.

Six

Ben waited until nine-thirty before calling reception and asking to speak with Mia. Irritation at her delaying tactics danced along his spine as he paced the confines of his sitting room, the cordless phone glued to his ear, and stared out the window at the black velvet blanket of night beyond.

"I'm sorry, sir, but Ms. Parker is off duty until tomorrow morning. Could someone else help you?"

Not unless someone else could tell him every single thing that Mia had done since he'd left Queenstown after the New Year's celebrations that had surpassed all New Year's celebrations in his memory.

"Ms. Parker is expecting my call. Please put me through to her quarters."

He sensed the night receptionist's hesitation before she continued.

"Let me check with Ms. Parker first."

Her staff's loyalty and attention to observing privacy was commendable. However, he could barely stop himself from grinding his teeth in frustration.

"I'm putting you through," the receptionist breezed a moment later.

"Muchas gracias," Ben replied, forcing himself to continue to inject civility into his voice.

There was a short delay on the line before he heard a woman's voice on the other end.

"Mr. del Castillo?"

"Elsa, how are you this evening? I thought we'd agreed you'd call me Ben." He injected as much warmth as he could into his voice. If he was to get to Mia, he wasn't averse to using whatever powers he had to work through the people she had around her. "Would it be possible to speak with Mia?"

"I'm sorry but Mia is sleeping. She had a very troubled night with Jasper last night and she fell asleep shortly after his bath time this evening. I'm staying here tonight to help out in case he has another bad one. Perhaps I can take a message for you."

Ben considered Elsa's words. Was Mia truly asleep, or had she coached her mother to screen her calls?

"No, no message. I will speak with her tomorrow. I hope you all rest well and that Jasper is much improved by morning."

The words stuck on his tongue as it suddenly struck him that if he was truly Jasper's father it should be him helping Mia through the night with their son—*would* have been him, if she had done him the courtesy of informing him of her pregnancy at the time. The thought cut him to his core. He'd never stopped to consider what it meant to be a father before. Certainly hadn't given it a thought when he and Reynard had agreed to Alex's harebrained scheme to marry and start families to prove their grandfather's fears about the curse as unfounded.

In fact, truth be told, he had no idea how he would have reacted had Mia tracked him down and told him about her pregnancy from the start. Fatherhood was something he'd always assumed would happen when he was older, ready to settle down by choice rather than by some ancient dictate. But now he knew, deep in his soul, that he wanted this responsibility in his life more than anything he'd ever wanted before.

He ended the call and let the phone drop from his hands onto the sofa beside him. More than anything he wanted to know the truth about Jasper. But how was he to go about it when Mia kept stonewalling him every step of the way?

Maybe he was going at this all wrong, he thought. There was more than one way to reel in a fish, but to hook them you needed the right bait. And the question was, what was Mia's bait?

The next afternoon, when Ben turned up for his massage, he was surprised to find a different woman waiting for him at the spa.

"You must be Mr. del Castillo," the brunette said as she stepped forward to welcome him. "I'm Cassie Edwards. Mia asked me to stand in for her today as she's not well."

"Not well?"

His distrust of her statement must have been obvious, because she hastened to add, "Apparently she's come down with the same illness as her son."

Has she, now? Ben thought to himself. It was something that would be quite simple to check out and he resolved to do that the moment his session with Cassie was over.

Cassie was good, he acknowledged later, once the massage was over, but she wasn't Mia. He missed the gentle strength of her fingers as they glided over his body, even missed the way she worked out the knots in his shoulders and lower, down his back. But most of all, he missed her touch. Knowing it was her and her alone who soothed his tortured muscles.

After he was finished, he went to his suite to shower and change and decided to pay Mia and Jasper a visit. A quick call to room service soon saw a basket delivered to his door laden with fresh bread, chicken soup in a generous thermos and a selection of fresh fruit.

It was only a short walk to the building where he knew Mia stayed. He deduced the building, built around the turn of the last century, had probably been the original station house when the property was a working farm station. Literature in the hotel had told him that about three years ago most of the grazing acreage of the station had been sold and the property converted into the boutique hotel and spa it was now.

Reading between the lines, Benedict began to wonder what exactly had prompted the sudden and massive change in such a short period of time. He made a mental note to do a little more investigating. Tomorrow would be soon enough, as he planned to spend some time in Queenstown catching up with the friends he'd stayed with during his last visit to the area. A few careful questions here and there should give him the information he needed.

For now, though, his most immediate concern was finding out whether or not Mia was indeed unwell, or simply avoiding him.

When he reached the building he followed the first path that led him to a paneled green door. He rapped his knuckles against the surface and waited. After a few minutes he heard the sound of footsteps inside and eventually the door swung open.

Mia stood in front of him, her blond hair loose rather than in the ponytail or twist she usually wore. The rings under her eyes were even more prominent than the day before and her eyes shone, as if she had a mild fever.

Suddenly feeling ridiculous for his suspicions, Ben lifted the basket he'd brought.

"I heard you weren't feeling well and I thought you might like this. Can I come in?"

"Aren't you worried you'll catch whatever we have?" she rasped.

"I think if I were to get it, I would have already caught whatever it is from you," Ben answered, giving her a pointed look.

The slight flush on her cheeks deepened as he alluded to the kiss they'd shared two days ago.

"Your choice," she said, ducking her head and standing to one side to let him through. "Frankly, I'm too tired to argue with you."

"That makes a pleasant change," he quipped, brushing past her and stepping into a large open-plan sitting-cum-dining area.

Toys were scattered across the floor and the couch had been made up into a bed.

"I'm sorry for the mess. Just didn't have the energy to pick up after Jas today."

"Understandable, if you're not well. Here, sit down, before you fall down."

He took her by the elbow, guided her onto the couch and lifted her feet up before pulling the blanket over her. The fact that she didn't so much as raise a single objection spoke volumes as to how unwell she was.

"Is Elsa not here today?"

Mia shook her head. "She's staying in town for an early

appointment with her cardiologist tomorrow. He only visits Queenstown every so often so I wouldn't let her cancel."

"How has Jasper been today?"

She gave a weak smile. "Oh, he's been much better today. The antibiotics are working a treat and he's full of beans. Too many beans, actually. He's asleep now." She gestured to the chaos of the sitting room. "I probably should have tried to keep him up to closer to his usual bedtime, because now he's going to be up far too late tonight, but when he just dropped, I had to tuck him into bed."

"Have you eaten anything today?"

She shook her head. "Not much. Hurts to eat."

"I brought soup. I think you should try some. Your chef assures me it's his grandmother's secret recipe and bound to have you feeling better in no time."

"Why?"

"Why what?"

"Why are you doing this for me?"

Ben hesitated. To be honest, he didn't really know. Sure, at first he'd just wanted to prove to himself that she wasn't just avoiding him—and more to the point, avoiding his questions about Jasper. But since he'd seen her at the door he'd been filled with a disquieting need to make sure she was okay. He reached in his mind for something to say, settling on the first thing that came.

"Oh, it's nothing philanthropic, I can assure you. It's all about me. I want my usual massage therapist back as soon as possible. Cassie's good, but she's not as good as you."

She made a strangled sound, halfway between a laugh and a groan of pain.

He flung her a glance. "Is that so hard to believe?"

"No, no it's not, not when you put it like that," she said with a weak smile before struggling to get off the couch again.

"Where do you think you're going?"

"To the kitchen to get some bowls for the soup."

"Tell me where to find everything. You can stay right where you are."

Ben readjusted the blanket across her jean-clad legs, noting with approval that her jeans were a far better fit than the uniform she usually wore day-to-day around the hotel. Her spa attire was a little more revealing but nowhere near as good as his memory. And that memory became more and more distinct with every day he spent time with her again.

Under her directions, he went into her compact kitchen and found the necessary utensils and a tray. He retrieved the basket from the sitting room and set the tray for one. A fact she protested about when he brought the bowl of soup and a slice of buttered bread through to her.

"Aren't you eating, too?"

"No, I brought this for you. My mother didn't have much to do in our kitchens when we were growing up but I always remember her bringing me her chicken soup when I was sick."

Mia eyed him over the tray he'd propped onto her lap. This Benedict del Castillo was a different man from the one who'd all but threatened her over Jasper yesterday afternoon. What had brought about the change? Surely it wasn't just because she was unwell. Deep down she knew he must have an ulterior motive of some description but she felt so utterly rotten she couldn't fight through the fugue of her mind to pin it down.

She scooped her spoon into the soup and brought it to her lips. The subtle flavors of chicken, celery and some other vegetable that she couldn't quite place immediately, slid over her tongue and down her raw throat like a balm.

"This is really good—you should have some," she said, her voice not quite as raspy as before.

"Maybe. See how much you feel like, first."

Under his watchful gaze she dipped a corner of the bread into the soup and brought it to her mouth. She felt a drop of soup linger on the edge of her lip and she swept it with her tongue, her gaze flitting to Ben's when he roughly cleared his throat and looked away. A hot flush raced through her that had nothing whatsoever to do with the fever she'd been running most of the day.

Crazy. Her reactions to him were totally off the scale of reasonable behavior. Here she was, sick, and still she wanted him. Mia focused on her soup and trying to get it all down her sore throat.

No wonder Jasper had been so fractious yesterday if this was how he'd felt. She'd weighed up going to the doctor herself today but decided against it. Bed rest and plenty of fluids were all she needed, she was sure of it. If she didn't show an improvement in the next day or two she'd go to the doctor, but for now she was sure she could beat this on her own. Besides, being unwell had given her an excuse to call in Cassie, one of the therapists she usually had working at the spa during full capacity of the hotel, to take on her responsibilities with Ben.

So much for her attempts to avoid him, though, she thought as she stole another glance at him. He'd risen from his chair and was now picking up Jasper's scatter of toys and putting them in the big toy barrel she kept in the room. Usually she made Jasper tidy after himself, but today everything was just too much.

Actually, now she thought about it, even keeping her eyes open defied every ounce of willpower she had. Her head dropped back against the pillow behind her and her eyelids slid shut. She'd close them for only a minute, that was all, and then she'd be all right again.

She could tell it was much later when she next opened her eyes. The gray light of the winter afternoon had darkened to night and the tray that had still been on her lap when she'd drifted off was now gone. She felt a little better for the food and rest, though her mouth felt fuzzy and her eyes burned as if they had a week's worth of household dust behind her lids. Still weak, she pushed the blanket off and forced herself to her feet. She had to check on Jasper, and take a much-needed bathroom break, she realized.

The room spun a little and she took a moment to check her bearings. The sitting room was a heck of a lot tidier than it had been when she'd fallen asleep. Not only had her tray been cleared away, but the coffee table tidied, and from the overhead light still on in the kitchen she could see that someone had cleared up in there also.

Had Ben done all of that? The almost overwhelming sense of relief at having someone who could share the load with her was short-lived as a flush of shame and embarrassment swept through her. No doubt that would give him even more ammunition to use against her when he questioned her parenting skills. And she had no doubt that he'd use every weapon available to him when it came time to fight. It struck her that she now accepted that the fight for Jasper was only a matter of time away. The realization struck dread into her heart.

She took a look at the wall clock above the kitchen bench. It was past midnight. Good grief. She really had to check on Jasper. He'd been due another dose of the liquid antibiotic his doctor had prescribed at around seven. But first, the bathroom.

After she'd taken care of her needs and washed her

hands and face, she moved as quickly and carefully as she could across the hall to Jasper's room. She gently pushed open his door and froze in the doorway. There on Jasper's "big boy's bed," curled up with their son in his arms, lay Benedict del Castillo. Her heart lurched as she saw the two dark heads so close together.

They each had the same bone structure. A strong, broad forehead with heavy dark brows sweeping in a slight arch over their thick, dark lash-tipped eyes. Eyes that were closed in slumber, but that she knew to be the same rich, dark hue. Ben's long, straight nose was different from Jasper's, the little boy's still holding some of the lack of definition of infanthood. But their lips showed every sign of bearing the same haughty line even if Ben's were outlined with the shadow of a day's growth of beard. They even had the same indentation in their chins.

Stupid tears burned at the back of her eyes and she backed out of the room. Somehow, she must have made a noise though, because Ben's eyes flicked open. He pursed his lips in a silent "shhh" and carefully moved, tucking Jasper under his covers and joining her at the bedroom door.

He took her by the hand, his long, warm fingers clasping hers as if the action was totally normal and everyday between them. Once they were back in the sitting room he put his free hand against her forehead.

"You feel cooler than before."

"What were you doing?" she asked. "Have you been here all this time?"

"You needed the rest and I didn't see the point in disturbing you. Jasper woke shortly after you dozed off. We made it a game to see how quiet he could be. He's a very good boy for his age."

"But your dinner, his dinner—"

"I scrambled Jasper some eggs and made toast with some of the bread I brought over earlier. He wolfed it down and then reminded me he was supposed to take his medicine."

Mia was overwhelmed. This international jet-setting playboy had settled into her son's evening routine and taken care of him and she'd been totally oblivious. Her legs became too unsteady to hold her up any longer and she sat down heavily on a chair, her eyes still locked on Ben.

"I don't know how to thank you. Really, I don't. You should have woken me so you could get back to the hotel."

"It's not like I had anything more pressing to do," he said as he sat down opposite her. "Besides, you looked like you were spiking quite a fever there for a while. It was easier to let you sleep it off and take care of Jasper for you."

"What time did he go back to bed?"

"He fell asleep about nine, after insisting on several stories."

She smiled. "He's like that."

"I told him about my home country and what it was like growing up there in my family's castillo. He was fascinated. I promised him I'd take him there one day."

Mia's spine snapped straight and an icy fist closed around her heart.

"You what? You had no right to do that," she cried.

"I have every right. He *is* my son, after all, isn't he?"

Mia struggled to deny his words. So far she had managed not to lie outright to Ben—it shouldn't be all that difficult to do, should it? But right now the words of denial froze on her lips as Ben sat back in his chair and stretched out his legs.

"He told me when his birthday is—showed me on the

calendar on his bedroom wall. He was conceived when we were together, wasn't he, Mia?"

She swallowed against the sudden painful dryness of her throat and tried to draw a breath into lungs that were suddenly too constricted to fill.

"I'm not proud of my behavior back then but, honestly, any man I slept with that summer could be his father," she finally managed in a strained voice.

Ben's eyes narrowed and she saw the flare of anger reflected in their depths making them look black rather than brown. Instantly she wished her words back. It was true she wasn't proud of her behavior from that period in her life, but when it came to physical intimacy, she had little to be ashamed of. Benedict del Castillo had been the *only* man she'd shared her body with that summer.

"Why won't you just tell me the truth?" he asked, his voice as cold and steady as a surgeon's blade.

"Because I owe you nothing. Even if you were Jasper's father, why on earth would I tell you? You're hardly the kind of man I'd want in his life. Sure, I used to behave fast and loose, but all that changed when I had Jas. You, however, well—the Internet is full of your exploits and your conquests all over Europe. You change your women as frequently as you change your suits.

"You go from adventure to adventure—whether it's street racing in Monaco, rock climbing in Switzerland or anything else that catches your fancy for a moment, and then is quickly discarded again. None of that makes you father material in my book, and as far as I'm concerned you're certainly not the kind of man Jasper deserves in his life. Right now, to you, he's merely something to possess. You know nothing about him and yet because of a vague physical resemblance you expect me to give you rights you probably don't even really want."

"You know nothing about what I really want, but you will find out. Trust me on this."

"Trust you?" She forced a broken laugh. "I wouldn't trust you as far as I could kick you, and right now that wouldn't be any distance at all. Look, I appreciate what you did for me tonight but, please, leave now. You will not hear what you want to from me. Not now. Not ever."

"You're making a bad mistake, Mia."

"Oh, believe me, I'm not. If I wasn't bound to you by that stupid contract you'd be leaving here right now."

"You're bound to me by more than a contract, Mia, and don't you forget it."

As Mia watched him leave the room and let himself out she sagged back in her seat and wondered just what she was letting herself in for. It was clear he wasn't going to give up on this quest of his and, in the end, where would that leave her and her son?

Seven

Ben looked back at Queenstown as the boat motored away from the public dock of the bustling town center. A wonderfully relaxing day in the Gibbston Valley with his friends, Jim and Cathy Samson, had taken the edge off of his fury over Mia's stubbornness last night, but it had done nothing to soften his determination. Although he had no conclusive proof, he knew to the depths of his soul that Jasper was his son. Even now he felt a bond with the little boy he'd never have imagined possible.

Her words had spun in his head all night. So she didn't think he was father material, did she? At first the words had incensed him…but as he'd tossed and turned during the sleepless night, he'd been forced to admit to himself that he could understand some of her fears. Nothing from their brief, anonymous interlude would have given her the impression that he had any immediate intention of becoming a husband, much less a father. It hadn't been on his radar then at all.

But on the other side of the coin, he knew that motherhood hadn't been in her plans, either. And yet she had risen to the challenge, capably loving and caring for their child in the years since. Did she think he was unable to achieve the same growth and maturity? Was that why she'd been so determined to keep him at a distance ever since his arrival in New Zealand? Did she truly believe he was incapable of treating anyone—woman or child—as more than a temporary diversion? The thought stung, and made him all the more unwavering in his resolve to stay the course on this challenge. He *would* gain rights to his son, even if it meant fighting it all out in court.

He hunched into his wool coat and pushed his hands deeper into his pockets. It didn't have to be like this. All she'd had to do was acknowledge him as Jasper's father and they'd have been able to find a common ground on which to base their parenthood. But no. She had to fight him. Deny him his rights.

In the distance now, he could see the driver and car that had been assigned to him for today pull away from the no-stopping area on the dock. It seemed that Mia had managed to follow all his stipulations on his contract to the letter so far. For some reason, that rankled rather than satisfied him. Now he understood how important the financial side of their agreement was for her, it would have been interesting to play her a little and see just how far she was prepared to go to protect her livelihood. But he'd been unable to fault anything so far.

This morning when he'd arrived in Queenstown, he'd been whisked away from the dock in leather-seated, climate-controlled comfort, and headed out to the Gibbston Highway where his friends' vineyard and winery were situated. The scenery en route to the Gibbston Valley was at a complete contrast to his last visit but he'd found the cool white and gray beauty of the landscape equally as striking as the summer heat and colors.

His lips curled in a bitter smile. The difference in climate between this visit and last was a perfect mirror for his reception from Mia. The first time, full of heat and intensity, the second, the complete antithesis.

Except for when he'd kissed her. That had been incendiary. Yet that memory, too, was tainted by the realization that even as she'd responded to his kiss, she'd been hiding the truth from him about their son.

Well, incendiary or not, she'd soon learn that he didn't back down from what was important in his life, and his son was the most important thing to him right now. Today he'd begun to gather information about Mia with the intention of proving he was the better option to be Jasper's parent. While his objective had been clear in his own mind, he hadn't anticipated discovering how far off the mark he'd been about her. The information he'd gleaned from the conversation with his friends during the day had been eye-opening and had shown a side of Mia he hadn't expected. A side that demonstrated her grit and determination. He supposed he had to allow for some admiration of how hard she'd worked to keep her family home in the face of her father's financial failures and the fallout after his death. It couldn't have been easy for her.

Jim and Cathy had been full of praise for her—how strong she'd been for her mother, how she'd adapted to their straitened circumstances, how she'd built the hotel/spa business out of nothing, even how she'd slid into mother-hood as if it was as natural to her as breathing.

A kernel of guilt unfurled deep inside. She'd gone through hell and was holding on to her life by the tips of her fingers. It wasn't his intention to rip it all away from her. But she, in turn, had to understand that there was more at stake than merely her balking at admitting his paternity of Jasper. His entire family was counting on him now. Even if he couldn't fulfill both terms of his agreement with his brothers—to marry and start a family—at least he could produce a son to prove to his grandfather that the del Castillos would continue for at least another generation, despite *Abuelo*'s fears to the contrary.

For centuries the prosperity of the people of Isla Sagrado had been tied into the success of the del Castillo family. They had all seen some difficult times and had fought against adversity to be where they were today. While he may not officially carry the name, Jasper was a del Castillo. He deserved the chance to know his father's family, see his father's home. And Ben deserved the chance to know Jasper, too.

Ben had spent only a few hours with the boy the night before, but that brief time had been infinitely precious. To see his son smile, to hear him laugh, to have the opportunity to care for him and get to know him—it was a gift Ben had never thought he'd be able to have after he'd learned the results of the car crash. Mia had no right to take that away from him. Especially not if she was motivated by some misguided belief that he was not able to love and care for his son.

She would learn, though, that when the chips were down, the del Castillos didn't give up. Ben was not about to give up on his son. Not under any circumstances.

While Mia waited in the spa for Benedict to arrive for his massage, she filled her time with a mini inventory of supplies. Anything to take her mind off their impending time together. She'd been tempted to take another sick day.

She still felt wrung out and her throat was still a little sore but she'd realized this morning that hiding from him wasn't going to solve anything. He'd struck her as the kind of man who approached things head-on. At least if she spent whatever time necessary with him, he was less likely to be able to ambush her.

Jasper was almost a hundred percent well again today, although she'd carefully instructed Elsa on when his antibiotics were due through the day. With any luck he'd be fit for day care again soon. As far as she was concerned, right now, the less time Jasper spent in Ben's vicinity, the better.

A sound at the doorway made her stop what she was doing. She forced herself to calmly turn around and place the clipboard and pen she'd been using onto the reception desk in front of her.

"I didn't expect to see you here today," Ben said.

"I was feeling a bit better so thought I'd let Cassie off the hook." She stepped out from behind the reception desk and crossed the short distance to the door to her treatment room and gestured to Ben to go inside. "You know the drill. I'll be in when you're ready."

For a moment he hesitated, as if he was about to say something, but then he simply went into the room and closed the door behind him. Mia pressed a hand to her throat. She could feel her pulse racing beneath her fingertips. Maybe doing this when she wasn't quite up to speed hadn't been such a great idea after all. Just seeing him was enough to upset the rhythm of her breathing, let alone her heart rate.

He'd turned up today in designer jeans and a long-sleeved black polo shirt and the effect was mouthwatering. The fabric clung to the lines of his sculpted body, a body she knew all too well. A body that even in her semi-well state sent all her receptors pinging on full alert. She closed her eyes and drew in a steadying breath. She'd done this before and she could do it again. He was a mass of muscle and tissue and skin and bone. Her job was to massage, relax and provide muscular relief.

Opening her eyes, Mia knocked gently on the door before letting herself in. As usual, the calming scent she had burning in the oil burner hit her immediately, relaxing her and settling her mind into work mode. As she had done the last two times, she straightened the covers over Ben's legs and buttocks before starting her routine.

"How was your day?" she asked conversationally as she pressed her hands against his warm, smooth skin.

"Do you really want to know, or are you merely being polite?" Ben answered from beneath her.

"I'm being polite," she said carefully, determined to keep control of both her temper and her nerves.

He snorted a derisive laugh. "Well, at least you're honest. I suppose if I were to be as honest I'd tell you that I found out some interesting things about you today."

Mia stilled her movements. "You were asking about me? Who? Where?"

He mentioned the Samsons, where they'd met at the New Year's Eve party three and a half years ago.

"Oh," she said quietly, suddenly wishing she'd never embarked upon this conversation in the first place. "I haven't seen them since."

"They said that, too. Seems you haven't made any effort to stay in touch with your old crowd. Why is that, Mia?"

"Like I've said to you before, people change. *I* changed, to be more precise. I couldn't operate on their level anymore and I didn't want to feel as if I had to. Besides, I didn't really know them all that well."

She remembered all too vividly the well-meaning phone

calls, the gently probing questions about how she was managing. Sure, a handful of her old friends had been genuine in their concern but some had simply been digging for gossip, as if the horrible newspaper headlines hadn't been revealing enough. Mia had had enough to focus on with her mother's fragile state and her own pregnancy to have to worry about what her friends and acquaintances thought and who she could trust anymore.

The media had been vicious about her father's financial ruin. Nothing had been sacred. She well remembered the photos plastered in the papers every time she set foot in Queenstown or even further afield—their captions speculating on how much of her daddy's money Mia would be spending on that occasion. Each shot, each conjecture, had been yet another nail in her father's coffin and eventually he hadn't been able to continue any longer.

And then they'd really grown nasty, insinuating how maintaining the lifestyle expected of his women had driven Reuben Parker to take a rope to one of the trees at the back of the property and take his life. It hadn't taken long before Mia had found herself second-guessing every word of condolence, every gesture of comfort, from the people she'd counted among her friends. Eventually it was simply easier to refuse all invitations, issue none herself and retreat into the world her father had left for them. A world she had painstakingly rebuilt piece by piece.

Her bank manager had asked her why she didn't just sell up entirely, settle the outstanding debts and strike out somewhere anew. But Parker's Retreat had been in her father's family for generations. His forebears had hacked out an existence in hostile land to build a dream for generations. She wasn't prepared to let that all go, especially not when she harbored a precious new generation within her own body. And especially not when she felt as if much of it had been her fault.

"You know Jim and Cathy aren't like that. They don't judge people by everyone else's standards."

Mia made a non-committal noise and moved into the next stage of the massage, hoping he'd drop the subject. She should have known better.

"So just how much in debt are you, Mia? Converting this property into a hotel and spa can't have been cheap. Not on top of the other debts I understand you took responsibility for."

"That's between me and my bank manager," she said carefully, hoping her flare of anger didn't color her words. How dare he ask such a personal question?

"I'm guessing with the current economic climate you haven't exactly been running at full capacity, have you?"

"We're doing okay," she insisted.

In all honesty, though, they were barely making ends meet. Yes, they'd done well building up a client base and securing bookings, but she knew that she'd been ambitious with her plans for the hotel and spa. Not wanting to take it in increments by building first the hotel and then the treatment side of the business over time, she'd done it all at once. She'd gone into business in the same manner she'd gone into everything in her life—boots and all. It was all paying off this time—but slowly.

"The contract we signed must have been a godsend, hmmm?"

"I won't deny it was welcome, until I found out exactly who it was with."

He chuckled and beneath her hands she felt his shoulder muscles tense.

"You think you struck a deal with the Devil?"

"You could say that," she said carefully. After all, it was his phrasing, not hers.

"Then you'd do well not to tax my generosity."

Oh boy. Here it came. His demands. She had to concede he definitely had a way about him. Circle slowly, show concern—care, even, if last night was any indicator—and then go straight for the jugular.

"Are you dissatisfied with your stay here?" she asked.

"Not yet, but it's early days."

She focused her energy on a particularly taut section of muscle at the top of his hip and was rewarded by his grunt of discomfort as she did so.

"I shall consider myself warned then," she answered through tight lips and made a silent resolve to ensure her staff was one hundred percent up to speed with the conditions of his occupancy.

There would be no mistakes. None.

The next day, Mia took the morning off. Jasper's doctor had a brief Saturday morning surgery at the clinic, and Mia wanted to take Jasper back into Queenstown to be rechecked. She herself was pleased with his progress, though. Right now he behaved as if he'd never been sick, whereas she was still struggling to recover. It didn't help that her nights were now fractured with dreams of Benedict del Castillo. Dreams which delved into the one day and two nights they'd shared, leaving her aching and irritable when she woke.

Jasper always loved the trips into town and especially loved to watch the gondolas climb the side of the mountain leading up to the Skyline complex. For his third birthday, coming up in just over two and a half months, she planned to take him for a ride to the top and a special birthday meal in the restaurant. She wasn't sure if she was brave enough to take him on the luge ride just yet and hoped he'd be satisfied with watching this year. Right now, though, her little boy was happy to be sitting on Don's lap, pretending to skipper the boat as they drew closer to the public dock.

"Don't worry about waiting for us," she said to Don, "we'll probably head out to the Remarkables Shopping Centre for a bit and after that we'll just get a water taxi home."

"If you're sure," Don said. "I don't mind waiting, you know that."

"Yes, but I think it's more important you be available for Mr. del Castillo should he want the boat for any reason today. Let's not do anything that might ruffle his feathers, hmmm?"

"Anything you say. You're the boss."

Don gave her his trademark smile and ruffled Jasper's hair with one of his work-roughened hands. "So, skipper. Are we ready to dock?"

Jasper nodded enthusiastically and hopped off the older man's lap and made his way to another seat so he wasn't in the way. Mia watched him with pride. So young and yet already so responsible. She'd done a good job so far with him, she told herself. And nothing and no one was going to jeopardize that, no matter how big their threats or how much money they had to wield at their disposal.

The visit to the doctor went smoothly and to Mia's relief, Jas was given the all clear to go back to day care on Monday. As lovely as it had been to have him home, he was rather wearing for her mother on a full-day basis. Something that would only become more obvious as his need for stimulation became more demanding.

Well, she consoled herself, for as long as she kept Parker's Retreat running smoothly, there would be no problem with affording his day care's fees or the fees for the next level of pre-school provided by the facility. Her heart crunched a little on the knowledge that her son was fast growing up. Every day with him was a gift she readily accepted with open arms.

Jasper was excited on the bus ride to the shopping center and jiggled up and down on his seat asking umpteen questions as they passed along the main bus route. The trip to Frankton didn't take long and Mia held his hand firmly as they alighted from the bus. She'd promised him a special treat from the large multipurpose store there, followed by lunch at the café right by the bus stop.

It was as they were moving up and down the toy aisles in the store that Mia suddenly had the sensation she was being watched. She turned her head, catching a glimpse of a young woman staring at her intently before rapidly averting her head and showing a sudden interest in a stand of action figures. Maybe she was just being paranoid, but Mia moved Jasper on to another aisle, distracting him with a junior construction set he'd seen on television and had been nagging at her to get for days now.

The pack was a great deal more expensive than the "treat" she'd planned for him, but the other woman's perusal had left her feeling edgy. For some strange reason it reminded her too much of the way she'd been hounded when her father's scandal had hit the news. Right now she was keen to follow her instincts and get back on the next bus to Queenstown.

At the checkout, she quickly made her purchase and hurried Jasper back to the bus stop.

"I want lunch, Mommy. You said lunch," Jasper complained, and started pulling at her with one hand as he pointed with the other to the café doors.

"I know, honey, but I remembered I have to get back

home. I promise I'll get you something in Queenstown before we get the water taxi back. Okay?"

"No." Jasper's lower lip began to wobble ominously. "I want lunch now."

Juggling her bag and the bulky construction kit, Mia bent to pick Jasper up, but he wasn't having any of it. Simultaneously, she sensed someone beside her. The woman from the store—except now she had someone with her. A man with a camera, its shutter working flat out as he took several photos of her and one very unhappy little boy.

"Ms. Parker, is it true that Benedict del Castillo is staying at your hotel?" the woman asked, her tone smug and more than a little pushy.

"What? I'm sorry, I don't know what you're talking about."

"Come on now, Mia. Benedict del Castillo was seen in Queenstown yesterday and he's news wherever he goes, particularly since his accident. A source tells us you two were lovers some time ago. Is his visit now a reunion?"

Bile rose in Mia's throat and she pulled Jasper up into her arms and turned his head into her shoulder.

"As I said," she answered as calmly as she could, "I have no idea what you're talking about. Now please, you're distressing my son. Stop taking those photos. You're invading my privacy."

She glared at the photographer, who completely ignored her.

"We're in a public area, Mia," the reporter reminded her with a smile that was anything but friendly. "Tell me, how does one of Europe's most sought-after bachelors feel about being a father?"

Eight

Mia clutched Jasper to her so tight he wriggled in protest. She felt a sting of remorse, but right now, having the photographer's camera thrust right in her face hard on the heels of the reporter's last question, she was determined to protect her son's privacy by preventing them from capturing another image of his face. She could only hope against hope that they hadn't already done so.

To her relief, a taxi pulled into the shopping-center car park, disgorging a very obvious pair of foreign tourists. She shot across the roadway and climbed in the open door, pushing Jasper down on the seat beside her.

"I'm sorry, miss," the driver said. "But my current fare is paying me to stay and wait for them."

"Please, I need to get away from those people. I'll pay you double the fare to take me back to the wharf in town. Triple! Just please get us away from here."

"Just a minute, then," he said, and alighted from the car.

Mia watched from behind locked doors as he jogged over to the tourist couple and with a series of gestures indicated he would be back in half an hour. When they nodded Mia groaned with relief.

Beside her, Jasper lay facedown on the car seat, sobbing his little heart out. Mia shrugged out of her coat and covered him with it, her hand stroking his narrow wee shoulders through the material. The driver returned to the cab and got behind the wheel. All the way back to the town center she looked out the back of the cab, noting the red hatchback that followed them every kilometer of the way. For the second time in her life she rued living in what was a relatively small town. There really was no escape. Nothing to even stop them hiring another water taxi and following her out to Parker's Retreat if they really wanted to.

Jasper had finally quieted, she noted with relief, but though the tears had stopped, he still seemed upset and confused. Her heart throbbed for him. He didn't deserve this. Not a bar of it. He was an innocent. A cold chill settled deep inside her. She knew what the media were like. Relentless when they thought they were onto a good story. The prospect of them dragging her innocent child into their gutter press filled her with equal parts of fear and anger.

Of even greater concern was how on earth they'd even found out about Ben's relationship to Jasper, let alone the short-lived affair she and Ben had indulged in. Even her own mother hadn't been privy to the truth.

Just out of Frankton, Mia noticed the red car slow down and pull over to the side of the road. She could see the female reporter with her cell phone to her ear, her free hand gesticulating wildly as she spoke. In the passenger seat the photographer trained his camera on Mia's face and she quickly turned her head away, relieved to see they'd given up the chase for now.

Within fifteen minutes, the cab pulled up at the Queenstown wharf. Her whole body trembling, Mia reached into her purse and pulled out all the money she had in there. She knew it was far more than the fare—even more than triple the fare—but she was so grateful to finally be away from the reporter she didn't even care.

She scooped Jasper from his seat and grabbed the shopping bag with his treat inside—and as she did so, she heard the cab driver's mobile phone chime. He picked it up and answered, his gaze suddenly fixing on hers as she began to get out of the car. Another chill ran down her spine as she watched him end the call and press a few buttons on his phone—which he then aimed directly at her and Jasper. Before she could block his view of them both she heard the telltale click of her picture being taken. Even her knight in shining armor had his price, it seemed.

The reporter must have called the cab company and somehow been patched through to the driver, she surmised as she hustled away toward the water-taxi jetty. She wondered just how much money he'd agreed to, to give her privacy away.

"Come on, Jas, let's get to the boat and get home, hmmm?" she said, trying to keep her voice as upbeat as possible.

"Lunch?" he asked, his voice once again a tear-soaked whimper.

"I'm so sorry, baby. We have to get home."

The construction set bumped against her leg as she half walked, half ran to the jetty. She only hoped that she'd be able to persuade the skipper of the vessel to break his schedule to take her out to Parker's Retreat right now rather than wait for other concession passengers on his regular service.

Thankfully, the skipper was amenable, agreeing to bill the trip—with a premium—to the Parker's Retreat account. As they headed out past the Queenstown Gardens and into the lake Mia finally allowed herself to relax. The rush of adrenaline that had propelled her from the shopping center to here had run its course and right now she felt completely deflated.

Deflated and worried sick about what she was going to do next. She knew she shouldn't be surprised that Ben had been spotted in Queenstown—he'd told her himself that he'd gone out to see friends—but how on earth had they made the connection between him and her? Who amongst her old friends had spilled the beans about their previous affair? Few people had known about it at the time. Jim and Cathy Samson—the couple Ben had seen yesterday—and one of her old girlfriends were the only three that sprang to mind.

She knew for a fact that the Samsons were as fierce about their privacy as anyone could be. But her old girlfriend? Much as it pained her to admit it, Sue had always had a bit of an ax to grind as far as Mia had been concerned. In the shallow social pond in which they'd swum, Mia had always shrugged it off as a touch of misplaced envy, but she'd never believed Sue could be malicious.

She knew Sue worked in the CBD of Queenstown in a building overlooking the wharf. Had she caught a glimpse of Ben when he'd gone into town yesterday? Maybe she'd gone so far as to call the local paper and tell them what little she'd known.

Yes, she was definitely the most likely culprit, though the idea that someone she'd known so well could turn into an enemy so easily really hurt. No matter what the circumstances were, Mia knew she could never do something like that. But the knowledge was cold comfort in the face of what she now had ahead of her.

* * *

Mia saw Ben standing on the dock at Parker's Retreat when the water taxi pulled up behind the Parker's launch. The cream wool Aran-knit sweater that he wore emphasized the width of his shoulders and his stone-washed jeans hugged his hips and thighs in all the right places. He looked strong and confident and put together—all the things that she wasn't, at the moment.

As traumatic as her day had become, she couldn't help but feel a sense of relief that he was here waiting for them. She was going to have to tell him what had happened and she'd rather deal with it sooner than later. First, though, she had some serious making up to do with her little boy.

A little boy who seemed all too happy to be lifted into Benedict's arms rather than be held by his mother a moment longer. Mia didn't blame him for wanting to have nothing to do with her right now. He'd been frightened, had promises broken, and now, without a doubt, he was terribly hungry, as well.

"There have been helicopters overhead all morning," Ben said to her after the water taxi had motored away from the dock.

Mia nodded and swallowed against the lump in her throat.

"Can we talk about it after I've fed Jasper? I promised him lunch back in town, but something happened and we had to leave before he could get anything."

Ben shot her a piercing look. "Something happened?"

"I will tell you the minute he's been fed, I promise."

"Well, then," he said, lifting Jasper high and settling the squealing boy on his shoulders, "we'd better get you some lunch, young man."

Mia was painfully aware of Ben's gaze upon her the whole time she prepared a bowl with nacho chips, tomato ketchup and melted grated cheese for Jasper. Once she'd settled him on the couch with his fuzzy blanket, the bowl of nachos and his favorite DVD on the television, she knew it was time to face the music.

"Tell me, then, why has the place been buzzing with helicopters all morning?" Ben demanded the minute they were more or less alone in the kitchen.

Mia cast a glance at her son, reassuring herself he was happily occupied before answering.

"I think you were spotted during your outing yesterday and that the rumor mill has been well and truly put into action."

"Rumor mill?"

"Jas and I were bailed up outside a shopping center just outside Queenstown late this morning."

She shuddered at the memory—at the sheer and utter helplessness she'd felt with nowhere to turn and no way out.

"And?" Ben prompted.

Mia suddenly wished she'd had more time to think about exactly what she had to say to Ben. More precisely, exactly *how* she was going to say what she had to. One thing she was absolutely positive about. She would not tell him about the questions about Jasper being Benedict's son. It would give him too much power over her—would force her to admit his paternity and with it, his rights to Jas. She wasn't in any way ready to do that.

"Someone has told them about our affair during your last visit," she said bluntly. "They asked me if your being here was a reunion."

"To which you replied?"

"I told them I had no idea what they were talking about, of course. Then I got in a taxi and came back home."

Ben gave her another probing stare. "I have a feeling you're leaving something out."

Mia shook her head. "I've told you what happened. It was horrible the way they harassed us. Jas was so upset."

"They? How many were there?"

"A reporter and a photographer."

"So I imagine we can expect to see some photos of the two of you in the near future."

Mia bristled with anger. "Is that it? Is that all you can say?"

"What else is there to say, Mia? Unless, of course, something else happened that you're holding back from me?"

She tamped down on her fury and dragged in a deep breath. "There's nothing else to say. We had a bad experience that left us both upset. Obviously the helicopters were here taking aerial shots of the retreat and hoping for a glimpse of you. No doubt, no matter what I said, they'll just make up their own stories to suit themselves."

"Exactly," said Ben. "I'll talk to Andre and we'll concentrate on a program that'll keep me away from the public eye. And I'll put any sightseeing trips we'd planned on hold for now. Don't worry, if I know the paparazzi—and I've had some experience with them—they'll disappear as soon as they realize that there's no story here."

Mia nodded, but deep inside she was still very afraid. She, too, had had up close and personal experience with the paparazzi and she knew full well that for as long as they thought they had a lead on something, they'd be more tenacious than a starving dog with a bone. But without giving Ben the full truth about what had happened today, she had no way of telling him how wrong his perception was.

* * *

The following Monday Elsa took Jasper to day care but was quite flustered when she returned back on the boat with Don and, unfortunately, a very teary grandson.

"What happened?" Mia asked her the minute she heard they were both back home.

"It was awful, Mia. A wretched woman came up to me at the wharf and started to follow us, asking all sorts of questions about you and Mr. del Castillo. I didn't even give her the time of day and eventually she disappeared but when we reached day care there were a whole swag of them there. Reporters, photographers. Poor Jasper was terrified and I have to say that the other parents and the staff weren't happy at all."

Mia's heart sunk to the soles of her shoes. Were they not even able to go about their everyday lives now? As much as the money from Benedict's stay was a lifesaver, right now she wished she'd never taken his booking. Her entire world had been turned upside down.

"We'll just have to keep Jasper home until it dies down."

"Dies down? What exactly is 'it,' Mia? Why this sudden interest in our lives again?" her mother pressed.

Mia looked into her worried eyes and realized it was past time for her to tell her mother the truth about Ben and Jasper. To her credit, her mother took the news pretty well.

"So what now? Does he expect to share custody?" Elsa asked.

"I don't know, Mom. To be honest, I haven't even admitted to him that he is Jasper's dad. I'm terrified of what he'll do if he knows for certain."

"He has rights, you know. You can't hide the truth from him forever."

"I know," Mia acknowledged with a weary sigh. "But I'm afraid of just how far he'll try to take those rights. I can't fight someone like him in court. He's from a wealthy family so money is no object if he decided to go for full custody of Jas. You know what will happen. He has enough money for his lawyers to track down every single person I knew before I fell pregnant. If they're put on a stand in the family court, they won't exactly paint a picture of the perfect mother, will they? And then there's our financial position. We're only just making ends meet, here. I can't spare the funds for a protracted legal battle—not after all we've done to hold on to our home."

Her mother put one hand on Mia's shoulder. "Sweetheart, think about what's important here. There's no way to keep the truth a secret forever. If this is going to turn into a battle, you have to face it head-on. You can't hide with your head in the sand. That's exactly what your father did, and look where that left him—where it left us. This," she gestured to the buildings and the land beyond, "it's all just *things*. If you want to keep your son, you're going to have to be prepared to fight for him."

"But Mom, even if we sold another parcel of land, or even the entire complex, we'd have so little to work with. By the time we paid off the business loan…" Her voice trailed off as the helplessness of her situation struck her anew.

"Well, whatever we decide, we'll do it together."

Mia gave her mother a weak smile but deep down there was a deep-seated fear that absolutely nothing she could do at this stage could make things all right again. Even if she could send Ben packing back to Isla Sagrado, she'd have to refund him the money he'd already paid and if that happened, her next mortgage repayment simply wouldn't happen. It would be impossible then to keep the wolves from the door. She felt totally hemmed in. A captive in her own home.

"Would you care to explain the meaning of these?"

Mia looked up from her desk as Benedict came stalking into her office. Her heart gave an all-too-familiar lurch at the sight of him, but that rapidly changed when he slapped not one, but three various issues of New Zealand's weekly women's magazines in front of her. Her hand shook as she reached for the top one.

There, in all their reluctant glory, were Jasper and she at the bus stop at the shopping center. To the right screamed a headline that made her blood turn cold. *Mediterranean Millionaire's Love Child Exposed!*

She dropped the magazine as if it had burned her fingers, and in doing so, saw the cover of the next one with the picture that had obviously been taken by the cab driver. A similar caption burst from the paper. She didn't need to see the next one to know what their feature article was.

"Didn't you say they'd lose interest soon enough?" Mia said in a voice that was not quite steady.

Ben made a raw sound of disgust. "What I can't understand is why you'd admit Jasper is my son to some tabloid gossipmonger but continue to refuse to afford me the same truth."

"I never said anything to them about you or Jasper. In fact, I very clearly told them I had nothing to say and to leave me alone."

"Then where did they get their information?"

Mia shivered. She'd never heard Benedict's voice so cold and controlled. Her emotional defenses rose like a solid wall—the only wall she'd been able to erect during that awful time after her father's death. It had seen her through then and it would hopefully see her through this, too. She gathered her strength to her like some kind of barrier and, imitating his tone, threw out the first words that came to mind.

"For all I know, *you* could have been the one to tip off the media."

She knew the words were a mistake the instant they left her lips.

"If you'll recall, one of the major stipulations in our contract was that you would ensure my privacy. That privacy is well and truly violated now, wouldn't you say? I think we can safely say I had nothing to do with this invasion and I would like to point out that as you have not met this particular term of our agreement, you are in breach. Unless you would like me to rescind our contract, and the second half payment and bonus that would still have been due to you, I suggest you pay attention. I repeat—where did they get their information?"

Mia knew when she was beaten. "I believe one of my old friends may have spilled the beans about our little fling. She was a guest at the party where we met, too—and I had a feeling at the time that she knew who you were, even though she never told me your name. She was…less than pleased that you chose to spend the weekend with me rather than her.

"She moves in the same circles as Jim and Cathy. They could have mentioned to her that you're here, or she may have seen you herself, last Friday, and tipped off the media. She's the type of person who wouldn't hesitate to capitalize on anything that could even remotely show me in a bad light."

"Some friend. I hope she's been paid extremely well, because I intend to see to it that she doesn't make another cent from her knowledge."

"How on earth are you going to do that?" Mia asked, bewildered.

What her friend—her ex-friend, she corrected herself— had done was nasty but it was only hearsay. Which was exactly what these magazines fed on, unfortunately.

"There will be injunctions on everyone involved with this debacle—" He broke off as his cell phone chimed from his pocket.

With a muttered curse he dragged it out and answered.

"Hola."

Mia watched as his face lightened, his expression becoming warm and friendly before rapidly returning to become the hard mask of anger he'd worn a moment ago.

"Sí. It is true. I will speak to you as soon as I have confirmation or if there are any further developments."

Ben reverted to rapid Spanish for several minutes, then ended the call and returned his phone to his pocket. She didn't like the look he pinned her with. Somehow she knew she wasn't going to be able to evade him, or the truth, for very much longer.

"It seems the news has reached my home. That was my brother, Alex, demanding to know why I had not yet informed him he was an uncle and that my grandfather is now a great-grandfather."

"Oh, no."

Suddenly it was as if the walls were closing in on her. Her breath caught, trapped in her chest, and her heart began to accelerate. The news had gone global? How on earth could that have happened so very fast? Bile rose in her throat and she reached for the glass of water she constantly kept full on her desk, desperate to ease the sick, burning sensation that spread through her like wildfire.

"Oh, yes." Ben sat down in the visitor's chair opposite

her desk and leaned forward, his elbows resting on the wooden barrier between them. "Now, I want you to tell me everything that happened the other day from the moment you stepped off at the pier until the second I saw you come back."

"It's too late, though, isn't it? There's nothing you can do to undo this."

Mia gestured to the magazines, realizing as she did so that the third one had also printed an old photo of her father's next to that of her and Jasper. Her gut twisted painfully. So they were not even going to leave her father to rest in peace? Hadn't they already done enough when they pilloried him for his financial collapse and drove him to his death?

"I cannot turn back the clock, Mia. Would that I could! But I can make sure that not another scurrilous word is printed about my family. My grandfather is not in the best of health. The last thing he needs right now is something else to add to his troubles." He leaned back in his chair and fixed her with another one of those hard-edged looks he was so painfully good at. "Tell me, and this time, leave nothing out."

By the time Mia had recounted what had happened, Ben was pacing the small confines of her office.

"You mean even the cab driver took a photo of you and Jasper?" His voice boiled with barely restrained fury. "He will regret that action most dearly."

Mia rose from her desk and put a hand on Ben's arm. Beneath her fingers she could feel the heat of his skin through the fine silk of his shirt. She tried to ignore the tingling sensation it aroused in her. There were far more important things to consider here.

"Ben, please, as you said, you can't turn back the clock.

Can we not just focus on making sure they go no further?" she implored him.

"He should pay for what he did to you. What he did to Jasper."

"I know, but don't you see? If you take action against him, even if you take action against Sue, they're only going to make things worse. People like that always do. I don't think I can go through that again. It was bad enough with Dad—it went on for months and months." She prodded her forefinger against the magazine that had included her father's photo on the cover. "It will destroy Mom to have to relive all that. She's only just started grasping her life with both hands again. I can't let her go through that for a second time, too, not to mention how it'll make life impossible for Jasper. I can't do it, Ben. I just can't."

Her voice broke on her final words and to her horror her eyes flooded with tears. And that was when Ben did the last thing she'd imagined he would. He took her in his arms. The solid strength of his body, the firm way he held her, was seductively comforting. His silent support encouraged her to give in, to surrender control. It would be so easy, she thought, and then all thought was suspended as, with the tip of his index finger under her chin, he lifted her face to his and kissed her.

Nine

The taste of him invaded her senses and her body responded like she was starved for physical attention. She kissed him back with all the frustration and tamped down desire she'd suffered from since the moment they'd last touched. Her hands slid over his shoulders, allowing her body to mold against his, to feel the hard core of his strength bolstering her. A sturdy anchor in a sea of fear and concern.

She worked her fingers into his hair, holding him to her, relishing the feel of the silky dark strands threaded through her fingers.

His kiss was consuming and she wanted to be consumed. She wanted everything she'd been too afraid to want for such a very long time. And with that want, she realized what a dangerous path she trod right now—how very much was at stake. Every single reason why she had never let herself dwell on the memory of her time with Benedict flashed through her mind—his touch, his taste, their mutual pleasure. It had been indescribably beautiful and yet over after only thirty-six hours. And then reality had hit—hard.

Mia tore her lips from his and lowered her hands to his shoulders to give him a firm push away from her—though the breaking of contact was almost a physical hurt.

"No, this isn't right," she cried, panting. "It just complicates things."

"*Sí*, it is more than right. We need to do this, Mia. We cannot fight what exists between us. Let me show you how special we can be. Let me be there for you, protect you, make love to you."

Mia gathered all her strength and stepped away from him. Her heart fluttered in her chest like a bird trapped in a net. All in all, that was exactly how she felt. Trapped. When had life become so complicated? She hadn't allowed herself to yearn for the past, for the time when life was more carefree and fun. It was a waste of time in her new world.

She shook her head slowly. "No, Ben. Even if I wanted to, I am not that kind of woman anymore. I have responsibilities to my son and my mother. I have to be there for them one hundred percent. I can't falter."

Ben reached out to take both her hands in his and pressed them flat against his chest.

"Mia, let me share your burden."

If he had read her mind he couldn't have said any words that spoke more directly to her heart.

"I'm afraid."

"Afraid of me?"

Twin lines of concern pulled his brows into a frown.

"Of you? Not exactly. More of what you're capable of doing to me."

"If you let me into your life, I would never hurt you."

"Not physically, no. But you have so much power over me. I'm afraid if I relinquish what control I have left over my life I'll lose everything I've worked so hard for. I don't think you understand how much it means to me."

"I understand. I know what it is like to have the expectations of so many others like a weight on your shoulders. But I also know that no one can do everything on their own."

He bent forward and pressed a kiss to her forehead. The simplicity and sheer undemanding gentleness of the action became her undoing.

"Help me, then. Please?"

He nodded. "First, I think we need to make sure Jasper and Elsa aren't dragged into this any more than they have been already."

Over the next couple of hours they made plans. For Mia it was scarily easy to not only share her responsibilities but to relinquish their control to Ben. After discussions with Don, who suggested Elsa and Jas stay at his daughter's farm just out of Glenorchy, it was merely a matter of waiting for the cover of darkness to let them slip away. Elsa had originally protested, saying she needed to be there for Mia, but Ben had been firm. So too, surprisingly, had Don. When he'd heard what had happened he'd shown an unexpected determination about protecting both Elsa and Jas from any further media intrusion. Eventually Elsa had capitulated. Jas was beside himself at the prospect of being able to go pony riding on the farm and Mia had to fight back tears that he was so happy to leave her.

She rationalized her misery with the relief that Jas would be out of reach to the media until Ben could get the injunctions in place.

Later she watched the boat draw away from the dock

and head down the lake until she saw its navigation lights no longer. The tears that had been all too near the surface all day couldn't be held back a moment longer.

Ben put a comforting arm around her shoulders and guided her back into the hotel.

"I need to go to my apartment," she protested.

"You shouldn't be alone," he said, his voice low and reassuring. "Stay with me tonight."

"Stay with you?"

"I will not force you to do anything you do not want, Mia. I promise you."

She let him take her by her hand. In minutes they were in his suite. His presence was surprisingly soothing and, by increments, Mia felt the tension in her body begin to ease.

"They'll be all right there, won't they?" she asked.

"Don assures me that he will call and let us know when they've arrived and settled in. His daughter's place is quite remote and I'm certain no one followed them. Trust me, Mia. I will do everything in my power to keep Jasper safe, and your mother, too."

"I know," she whispered.

It felt so foreign to have someone else to lean upon, someone to share her worries and concerns. Foreign, and yet distinctly appealing at the same time. The emptiness inside her, opened even wider by Jasper and Elsa's departure, began to fill with something else. Something she was almost too afraid to acknowledge.

Ben still held her hand. His fingers were warm and strong and entangled in her own, securing a link between them that she couldn't ignore any longer. She looked up at him, to the face that had haunted her dreams for the past three and a half years, and knew that she had to be honest with him.

"Jasper is your son," she said, her voice soft and barely audible.

An almost feral glow of possession shone in Ben's eyes before he closed them briefly and tilted his head slightly back. His lips firmed in a straight line and his jaw clenched tight. When he opened his eyes again and looked in hers, she saw a shimmer in their dark brown depths that evidenced the deep and raw emotion there.

The play of emotion on his face was heartrending. Shock, perhaps, that she'd finally stopped stonewalling him, warred with pleasure and then an intensity that she recognized on a gut level. It was the exact same intensity she felt when she looked at Jas—pride, parental ownership and a sense of wonder that this child was her very own. Except now she shared him, with Ben.

"Thank you," he said, and lowered his face to hers, his lips possessing her own in a kiss that was on a different scale to anything they had shared before.

His mouth was almost unbearably gentle as it took hers, supping from her as if she was the sweetest nectar. His hands cupped her face, holding her tenderly and making her feel as though she was the most precious thing in the world to him. Her lonely heart cracked open, as she took everything he offered her. Her arms roped around his waist, her hands splaying across his strongly muscled back as if she was afraid to let go and be cast adrift. To be totally alone again.

Ben carefully drew back from her and rested his forehead against hers.

"What are we going to do now?" Mia asked, almost afraid of the answer he'd give her. "What do you want to do about Jasper?"

"It's been quite a day and we both have had a lot to take in. We can discuss everything later. Besides, right now, I'm sure you need your rest. You take the master suite. I'll go and sleep in the spare room."

Mia shook her head. "No, I can't chase you from your bed. Won't you at least share it with me?"

"Mia, I am only a man. A man who is fiercely attracted to you. I cannot, in all honesty, say I can sleep with you and not want to make love with you."

She placed a finger on his lips and looked him solemnly in the eye.

"Then make love to me, Ben. Please?"

He didn't answer, merely took her by the hand and led her into his bedroom and closed the doors firmly behind them. Tiny shudders rocked Mia's body—part fear, part anticipation. There was no going back now.

He couldn't believe she'd finally opened herself up to him. Even as she stood in front of him now he half expected her to bolt like a frightened doe.

He reached for her jacket, and slowly slid it from her shoulders. Beneath his hands he could feel the tremors that ran through her. Nerves, or desire, he wondered. Perhaps a mix of both. He fought with his own desire to rush this. To push their clothing aside and take her with the passion that had built in him each day he'd been here—the same level of passion that had lain semi-dormant since he'd rolled from their sheets and caught his flight back home to Isla Sagrado all those years ago. She was like a drug in his system. Once taken, forever desired.

But he'd waited this long for their reunion. He could tame his urge to hasten, and shower her with the gentleness and care she seemed to need so badly. It would be no hardship to take his time. Some things were best savored.

He smiled at Mia as he let her jacket fall to the thickly carpeted floor. Her blouse soon followed suit, although her gasp as his knuckles brushed the soft swell of her breast while he undid the buttons almost destroyed the vestiges of control he so stringently held.

Ben closed his eyes a moment, and took a breath, before opening them and feasting his eyes on her translucent skin, bound in delicate white lace.

"You are exquisite," he murmured, trailing his fingertips over one faint blue vein to where it disappeared into the scalloped edge of her bra cup.

He bent his head and traced the line with the tip of his tongue. The scent of her skin invaded his nostrils, urging him to breathe her more deeply. His hands went to the snap at her waist, undoing it and then reaching for her zipper. The rasp as it slid open was a sigh on the air. Her pants fell to her feet and he supported her as she stepped free and kicked off the low-heeled pumps she wore beneath them.

He took a moment to drink in the sight of her, her curves lushly feminine, her secrets innocently hidden behind the white lace of her lingerie. Blood heated in his groin, sending an age-old message to his brain.

His. She was all his.

He reached for the clips that bound her hair in a twist and smiled again as the honey-blond strands fell to caress her neck and shoulders. She'd been stunningly beautiful the first time he'd met her, but there was a luminescence about her now that spoke volumes about the woman she'd become.

She took a tentative step forward, so close now that he could feel her warmth through the thin barrier of his shirt. Then her hands were at his clothes, except they shook so much she could barely undo each button on his shirt. He closed his hands over hers and pulled, sending buttons flying as they popped from the silk fabric. It took only a matter of seconds to toe out of his loafers, undo his belt buckle and drop his trousers.

For the briefest moment his reluctance to let her see his scars, to touch them, froze him, but then she dropped one hand to his boxer briefs and hooked the other around his neck to pull his face to hers and the last vestige of hesitancy fled.

She took his lips in a kiss that almost saw him lose it right there. In fact, when she lightly trailed her fingernails over the hard ridge in his briefs, he couldn't stop himself from groaning into her mouth and thrusting his hands into her hair, holding her to him. Giving her full access to his mouth, his face, his throat. He backed her up against the bed, felt her knees buckle and her body drop onto the wide mattress before following her. Her skin against his was a sensation he'd totally underestimated. Every nerve in his body leaped to full life, doubly sensitized to her every touch.

Ben reached between them and stroked her through her panties. She flexed her hips upward, increasing the pressure of his fingers against her. She was already damp with desire and the knowledge made him feel stronger than he'd ever felt in his lifetime.

"I have dreamed of being with you again, *querida*. Over and over and over again until I began to fear I was a madman, obsessed with you," he said, his voice shaking.

"I have dreamed of you, too. Too many times to count. But this—touching you, feeling you with me—is so much better than a dream and so much better than I remembered."

Ben's fingers slid inside the elastic of her panties and grazed against the nest of curls that protected her inner softness.

"Oh yes," he said, "better, definitely very much better."

He slid one finger along the wet crease of her core—back and forth, back and forth, until she squirmed.

"More, Ben, please more."

He smiled and laid a trail of hot wet kisses down her belly.

"You want more?" he asked.

She nodded, her eyes glittering green pools in her exquisite face. As he watched her, he eased his finger inside her heat, instantly feeling her muscles clamp tight around him.

"Like this?" he asked again.

"More. I want you, Ben. All of you."

"Not yet," he said softly.

He eased another finger inside her, stroking her long and deep. Mia dropped her head back on the bed and closed her eyes, finally giving herself over to the sensations he aroused in her. Knowing her every focus was now on what he was doing to her he pressed his mouth against her mound, tasting her through the fine fabric of her panties and hearing her moan with uninhibited pleasure.

He blew a warm breath through the material then pressed another, firmer kiss against her. She pressed back against him, forcing his fingers deeper inside her, increasing the pressure of his mouth against her. He eased aside the damp fabric and fixed his mouth to the part of her he knew would send her skyward. His tongue flicked the hooded nub nestled in her blond curls and beneath him he felt her shudder, her internal muscles closing on his fingers, holding them tight, tighter. Alternately his tongue swirled then flicked, first slow, then with increasing tempo and he felt her body grow taut as her orgasm built and built but still remained out of reach as he refused to give her what she almost incoherently begged for.

He drew her out for as long as he could bear, relishing

the sounds she made, knowing he had the power to drive her to this edge of sweet madness. It was time to take her over that edge. Ben closed his lips around her rigid bud, suckling it until, with a sharp cry, she tumbled—her body clenching and releasing as the waves crashed over her. He shifted on the bed, quickly yanking off his briefs before more gently easing Mia's down her glorious long legs and then reaching behind her to unclasp her bra. When he took her he wanted there to be nothing between them. Nothing at all.

Her breasts spilled free of the restraining fabric and he could see the faint tracery of silver lines that were her badge of motherhood. If anything the markings only served to make him want her even more. Ben was even more amazed at what she'd achieved on her own.

He eased himself between her legs and positioned himself at her entrance.

"Look at me, Mia," he demanded.

She opened her eyes and he saw the haze of satiation that blurred her vision. Slowly he edged inside her, the thick head of his penis probing bluntly past her inner lips. Her eyes sharpened, awareness flooding back into them. Awareness...and anticipation.

He sank into her welcoming heat, almost coming straight away. Mia wound her legs behind his, holding him close to her. His arms shook as he fought back his climax, as he tried to control the overwhelming urge to lose himself in her, but she began to move beneath him, a smile softly curving her mouth.

Her smile was his undoing. He had been determined to take it slow. To woo her body back to full consciousness before driving her into blissful oblivion again. But he was not strong enough to hold back another second. His hips pistoned against her, and she met his every thrust, until every cell in his body drew tight then released in a rhythmic flood of ecstasy.

She cried out again, and through his pleasure he felt her join him on the wave. Eventually he lowered himself onto her, then rolled slightly to one side and tucked her firmly against his body. He'd been right. Being with Mia again had broken through the barriers that had rendered him useless after the crash. She'd brought him through the darkness and made him feel almost whole again.

Benedict nuzzled against the side of her neck and Mia relished the contact. Her body still fired with aftershocks of pleasure. What they had was amazing—like nothing she'd ever shared with anyone else. Their connection in bed was off the scale and she couldn't help but feel a twinge of sorrow that out of the grip of passion, all they seemed to be able to do was fight.

"You realize this changes things now, don't you?" he said.

"Changes things? Why should it?"

"Now that I know that Jasper is my son, I want to be a part of his life. I'm his father. He has other family who deserve to know him also—*Abuelo,* my brothers. He has a whole other world waiting for him in Isla Sagrado."

A shiver of fear ran across Mia's skin. She snatched up the sheet that had tangled near their feet and wrapped it around her, desperate for some type of shield. She fought her way off the bed and struggled to her feet, clutching the bed linen in a tight fist.

"You're going to take him from me?"

"That would not be the ideal solution."

But it is an option, hung in the air between them.

"Then what is?"

Ben got off the bed and casually walked across the floor to where he'd dropped his pants. He shoved his feet inside the legs and pulled them up. Again Mia's gaze was drawn to the scar tissue that ran in rivers across his lower abdomen. He'd nearly died. Again the realization struck her like a physical blow, and with it the solid truth that her feelings for him had shifted, had somehow irrevocably changed. That now he was far more important to her than she'd ever believed possible. She tried to push the thoughts from her mind, from her heart, but failed miserably.

All the breath sucked out of her body and she lowered herself back down to the edge of the bed. How much worse could this get?

Ben came and sat beside her, the warmth of his body penetrating the cold shell of disbelief that surrounded her. Deep inside she wanted to welcome that warmth—to share the burden of parenthood, to share the burden of rebuilding her family name and building a new business. But she'd done it on her own for so long the prospect of relinquishing control was as terrifying as it was appealing.

"I can make all your troubles go away, Mia. The press, your financial pressures. Everything. But I want you to agree to some things first."

The very idea of allowing him to take charge of the rapidly degenerating situation that was her life was almost as seductive as the sensation of his breath against her neck. But, she reminded herself, a man like Benedict would have a proviso riding on something as far-reaching as "making her troubles go away," and she had a fair idea of what that proviso might be.

She took a second to take stock. In exchange for him solving her problems with the media, etc., he'd have uncontested access to Jasper. A few days ago, she would have refused him outright, but everything had changed since then. Now she realized that she had misjudged Ben before. He *was* capable of being a good father, a man that Jasper could depend on. A man that *she* could depend on, if she would simply allow herself to do so. It sounded like a win-win situation no matter which angle she looked at it. And frankly, she knew when she was beaten. She didn't know if she could fight back one more time.

"Anything. I'll agree to anything."

"First, I want Jasper to undergo a paternity test. It's noninvasive and the results are available promptly."

Mia nodded, "I have no problem with that."

"My second condition hinges on the first. Once we have medical and legal proof that Jasper is my son, we will marry and return to Isla Sagrado. It is my home and it should be Jasper's home, too."

"No!"

The single syllable ripped from her mouth before she could stop it.

Ben narrowed his eyes. "It is not such an impossible thing to ask, is it? You agreed to my conditions just a moment ago, and I'm prepared to be generous with you—to give you my protection, my name and my home. I'm giving you a chance to get away from all the scandal and the unhappy reminders you have here. A chance to watch your son grow to adulthood in a secure and loving environment."

Mia didn't trust herself to speak. Her chin wobbled as she fought back the words she wanted to say—that she was taking everything back; that she'd rather face the media without his help rather than give up her home. Ben could obviously see the battle behind her eyes because he appeared to choose his next words very carefully.

"I would not like to be forced to assert my parental rights

to Jasper by legal means, Mia. If such a thing happened I would seek full custody and I would bring the might of the greatest legal minds in family law, both here and in Isla Sagrado, to fight for what is my right as Jasper's father. And I will win. You can be certain of that."

Ten

"Why? Why would you do that to him? Why would you be so cruel as to tear him from the only home he has ever known—the only family he's ever had?"

Ben huffed out a breath and pushed himself up off the bed before crossing the room to stand before the window. His shoulders were set in a straight line, his spine equally rigid.

"He has another family, *my* family. We are the last of a dying line, which makes him all the more precious. He's a sign of hope for the future."

"That's a heck of a lot of pressure to put on one little boy, Ben. You told me you have brothers—that hardly seems like a dying line. Aren't you being unrealistic about Jasper's importance?" she asked, stricken by the heavy portent of his words.

"Not according to the curse."

"Curse?"

Ben sighed. "Let me explain it to you fully. Three hundred years ago one of my ancestors took a lover—the governess whom he'd hired to teach his daughters. Over time, she bore him three sons—sons he needed to carry on the family name especially as his wife had borne him three more daughters. He raised the boys as if they were his own legitimate issue. When his wife died, his lover expected him to marry her. After all, he'd already gifted her with *La Verdad del Corazon*—the Heart's Truth—a ruby necklace traditionally given as a betrothal gift to a del Castillo bride-to-be.

"But he chose to marry another and on the wedding day his lover broke into the celebrations and made an accusation before everyone assembled there that he had stolen her sons from her. My ancestor declared her mad and ordered her to be taken away. The stories say that she implored her sons to be true to their real mother, but they stood by their father and told her their real mother was dead. Before the guards could remove her from the banquet hall, the governess flung a curse upon the del Castillo family and swore that if in nine generations we could not learn to live our lives by our family motto of honor, truth and love, every branch of the family would die out.

"The guards took her into custody then, but she broke free and jumped off the cliffs onto the rocks below. Before she fell, she tore the necklace from her neck and threw it into the ocean screaming that only when the curse was broken would it be returned to the family again. Her body was recovered, but the necklace never was."

Mia sat in stunned silence. Surely he didn't believe all that. It was preposterous. A legend of what, three hundred years, having a bearing on her son? She cleared her throat carefully before speaking.

"And you and your brothers, you believe in this curse?"

Ben's shoulders sagged momentarily. "No, we did not. But our grandfather most certainly does and it is for him that we have all agreed to marry and start families so that his final years can be happy ones, surrounded by the great-grandchildren who can prove to him that we are not cursed."

"And here you are, with a ready-made family." Mia could not keep the bitterness from infiltrating her words.

"Mia, this is not something of my own choosing. Each of my brothers and I made a pact, a vow of honor to one another that we are sworn to uphold. It may sound archaic to you, but both Alex and Reynard have taken the first steps to make this right for our grandfather. Now it is up to me."

"But why does it have to be Jasper? Why can't you marry someone else and start a family with them?"

The second the words exited her body she was struck with a fierce shaft of jealousy such as she'd never experienced before. The mere thought of Benedict having children with another woman was poison to her mind.

He turned from the window and faced her before answering with words that suddenly robbed her of breath.

"Because I can no longer father a child."

She didn't even question the veracity of his statement; she could see it in his eyes. He told the truth and it was killing him inside.

"The accident? Your injuries? Is that why?"

He gave her a curt nod.

Suddenly it all made awful sense—why he'd been so adamant that Jasper was his son, why he'd wanted her to admit it and, now, why he'd insisted that she agree to paternity testing so he had irrevocable proof that he had a child of his own.

But she still couldn't help feeling that Jas was being used as a tool in all this. Sure, she could understand that after being injured so severely Ben would feel justified in considering the discovery of his son as a gift. But the whole curse thing and the pact between the brothers? It just didn't sit right with her. He'd said nothing of love, for Jasper even if not for her. How could she agree to her little boy going to a world he didn't know, to have his life mapped out by a man who didn't even love him?

But what else could she do? He literally had her over a financial barrel.

"Do we have to live on Isla Sagrado?" she eventually asked, her voice strained.

"It is my home and the home of my family. My business is there, as is everything else I hold dear."

His words struck at her like pebbles thrown against glass. He couldn't have made it clearer that she and her son were not a part of what he held dear. Not in any way, shape or form. Jasper was a means to fulfill a promise he'd made to his brothers. A promise that was designed to make the final years of an old man happy. And she was merely a step to acquiring that goal—a step that he could and would dispense with, if she persisted in refusing him.

Her father had many failings but one thing Mia never doubted was his love for her and her mother. That very emotion was part of the reason why she was so riddled with guilt for her contribution to what had become more than he could control or eventually bear. How could she agree to let Jasper go with a man who made no mention of offering unconditional love?

"And what of my home, my family, my business? This is where Jasper was born. Parker's Retreat is part of his heritage, too," she argued.

"We can install a manager to run Parker's Retreat for

you and via the Internet and phone I'm sure you can keep a hand in the running of the place. If you wish to continue with your massage therapy I have no doubt that Alex would find your skills a welcome addition to our family's resort facilities on the island.

"As to your remaining family, Elsa is more than welcome to relocate with us. In fact, I'd prefer it because I know it would only cause you concern if you were each on opposite sides of the world."

"How generous of you," Mia responded scornfully.

"It is generous of me, Mia, and you would do well to remember that. You will not suffer for this, I promise you. And on those occasions when we return to New Zealand, you will have the anonymity and privacy that my money can provide for you." His voice hardened. "Bear in mind, I am giving you every incentive to do this the right way but if you don't, I will invoke the clause of our current contract that provides for me to be fully refunded if you have not satisfied the terms as laid out."

He gestured beyond the darkened gardens to where the media's boats would undoubtedly return at daybreak.

"I believe what has been happening here is irrefutable evidence that you are in forfeit, Mia."

Mia swallowed against the solid lump of emotion in her throat. She would not cry. She would not give in to the overwhelming sense of failure that assailed her. Had he no idea how much this place meant to her? It was her life, her identity. It was tangible proof that she could make a success of *something*—be someone her son could not only love, but also admire and aspire to. If she walked away now it was admitting she had bombed in the worst way possible. She not only failed herself, but she'd failed her father's memory as well.

But there was no other option. Through circumstances

over which she'd had no control, she was now forced to adhere to his demands. Mia wound the sheet more tightly around her and stood to face him, her chin up, her eyes clear of the tears she would shed in private.

"Fine, I'll do what you say. But only because you give me no other choice."

Mia was alternately surprised and horrified at the speed with which the paternity testing was completed and the results delivered back to them at Parker's Retreat. The results only bore out what she knew already but Benedict became fired by a new energy when he received the news.

As soon as proof had been delivered, Ben must have taken action against the press because the media had slowly disappeared from the lake near the property. Even a trip to Queenstown didn't bring them back out of the woodwork. Whatever power and money Ben had thrown at the situation, it must have been impressive because Jas and Elsa had been able to return from Glenorchy and Jasper had been able to resume going to his day care. Even Mia was now able to go about her occasional business in town with no more than a random finger pointed from behind a café menu.

And then there was the wedding. Elsa's initial reaction of excitement at the news was tempered with concern, especially when the hollow emptiness in Mia's eyes had made her ask her daughter if she was certain she was doing the right thing.

"I'm doing the only thing, Mom," Mia said as she stared at her reflection in the full-length mirror in her mother's bedroom. "Jasper deserves to know his father, and Ben insisted that it happen on these terms."

The woman staring back was a virtual stranger in the

vintage 1920s wedding gown that had been in her mother's family for generations. It was not quite as impactful as a three-hundred-year-old curse, Mia thought cynically, but it still carried with it the weight of all the dreams and hopes of many brides-to-be—all of whom, if family history was correct—had married for love.

"Well, if you're certain, but it seems to me you are both rushing into this marriage," her mother answered through a mouthful of pins as she marked where the side seams needed to be altered. "I've always been a strong advocate of a couple sharing their child-rearing responsibilities, but usually they've had time to know one another first. You and Ben, well, you can hardly say you know one another all that well, can you?"

Know him? She certainly knew him in the biblical sense, if nothing else. Her inner muscles clenched on the sudden sharp pull of desire that drew through her at the thought of their lovemaking.

"I'm certain, Mom. It's for the best."

"For everyone else, sure, but is it the best thing for you?"

Mia forced a smile. "Why wouldn't it be? He's handsome, he's rich and most importantly, he's Jasper's father."

"But does he love you?"

"He doesn't hate me, so that's a start, right?"

She tried to inject a little humor into the conversation but her mother simply gave her a quelling look. It shouldn't have been so easily done when on her knees and with a mouth looking like she'd consumed a porcupine but she managed. Suddenly Mia realized how far her mother had come from the broken widow of three years ago. It gave her a start to see glimpses of her mother's old strength coming back.

"I just think that this marriage is a little hasty. Couldn't you just take some more time?" Elsa asked.

"Mom, he's due back on Isla Sagrado at the end of the month. It made sense for us to go ahead with the wedding now rather than later. At least we're having it here at home."

"Well, that's another thing. Isn't it strange that he isn't having any of his family here for the wedding? I thought you said they're all very close?"

"We'll have another ceremony there. Did I tell you they have their own chapel in their own castle?" Mia tried to change the subject but not terribly successfully.

Elsa gave her another one of *those* looks before putting her pins away and standing up to cup Mia's face in her hands.

"I love you, darling. I just want you to be happy. You've sacrificed so much at your own emotional expense for too long now. I just wish I didn't feel as if that's what you're still doing in marrying Ben." She pressed a kiss on Mia's forehead then let her go. "Right, then. You'd better get that dress off so I can make those alterations and you'll be all ready for Friday night."

Friday night. It would come soon enough. Mia had been amazed at how quickly the legal side of arranging a marriage here in New Zealand could be taken care of. Despite the rush, Elsa had insisted on everything being done properly and that meant that Mia would be wearing what had originally been Elsa's grandmother's wedding gown.

She and Ben had agreed that they wanted only her mother and Andre as witnesses for the evening ceremony. If anything, as far as Mia was concerned, it would help keep this all from feeling too real.

Mia tried to quell the squadron of butterflies that had taken flight in her stomach as she waited outside the old ballroom, which was now the main dining room of the hotel. Inside, waiting by the deep bay window overlooking the gardens and the lake, was the man she'd lost her heart to. Her heart and her whole life.

She gripped the simple bouquet of dusky pink rosebuds and gypsophila and nodded to the staff member waiting for her signal to open the double doors into the ballroom. While not massive by any standard, the ballroom suddenly appeared to be longer than she remembered. The aisle that had been created between the dining tables was now strewn with flower petals and lined with creamy-colored candles on tall pedestals.

It was a fairytale setting for the kind of wedding she'd always wanted and yet it felt all wrong. Her father should have been walking at her side, and the room should have been filled with friends and colleagues. It should have been a joyful celebration of a mutual love that would endure forever.

Mia closed her eyes briefly on the dreams she'd once had. When she opened them again her gaze found Ben at the end of the aisle. Waiting for her. Somber and dark in a tuxedo, he stood tall and proud—every part of his Spanish-Franco lineage visible in his bearing.

Mia hesitated on the threshold. She loved him enough that a large part of her truly *wanted* to marry him—to go to his side and take vows to become his wife. But by taking that step, she'd be giving up everything else. Her home. Her past. The life she had built for herself. All in exchange for a man who had shown no signs of returning her love. Each particle of her body froze as all her instincts urged her to flee. But where could she go? There were no other choices open to her now. She forced one ballet-slippered foot in front of the other, stepping carefully in time to the music played on the sound system. Elsa stood to the left of the makeshift altar, Jasper's hand held firmly in hers as he stood on a chair and watched the proceedings with eager interest. Mia felt a flicker of surprise to see Don standing close by her mother's other side, looking austerely handsome in a sharply pressed dark suit.

While she knew her mother's eyes were on her, she couldn't look at her. Couldn't stand to see the concern she knew would be mirrored in Elsa's gaze. Instead, Mia kept moving forward, keeping her eyes very firmly on the man she was about to pledge herself to.

As she drew closer to Benedict she grew more and more aware of the flare of satisfaction in his eyes. Her body thrummed to life in answer to the glow. At least that was one side of their marriage she knew would be fulfilling even if their emotional compatibility was unbalanced. But in her heart of hearts she wondered if that would ever be enough. She wanted it all. Could she settle for anything less?

Mia was only a few steps away from the altar when Ben came toward her and took her by the hand, leading her the final distance to where the celebrant waited to conduct the short ceremony that would tie her to Benedict del Castillo forever.

An unexpected thrill shot through her. One of anticipation and laced with threads of hope. She already loved him. Surely it was not impossible to believe that he would come to love her also? A tremulous smile spread across her lips as she looked across to her mother and sent her a silent message that everything would be okay. She knew Elsa understood when her mother gave her a small nod and an answering smile.

The service was simple and without the flowering expectations of a marriage based on mutual love. Still, when Ben promised to honor and keep her all the days of his life a solid feeling of permanence seeped through her, buoying her spirits a little higher. When the celebrant declared them husband and wife, Ben stepped forward to kiss her and as she lost herself in his caress, Mia allowed herself to be imbued by a deep sense of rightness in their being bonded together.

By the time she and Ben stepped forward to sign the marriage certificate and complete the legal undertakings of their marriage Mia had almost convinced herself she felt happy, genuinely happy, for the first time in a very long while.

Her staff had prepared a simple three-course meal for them to share in the restaurant after the service and by the time the last plate had been cleared away, Mia was longing for some alone time with her husband. He'd been attentive throughout their meal, but also gave Jasper the attention he demanded. When Elsa suggested it was time for Jas to be taken to bed and for the newlyweds to be left alone, Mia felt her heart skip a beat.

Ben had barely touched her since they'd made love nearly two weeks ago. Thinking back on it now, it was probably one of the reasons why Elsa was so concerned about whether or not Mia was doing the right thing—their lack of visible connection as a couple. Thankfully, one thing Elsa hadn't had to worry about was the rapport between Jasper and Ben. Already, Mia could see the very positive aspects of Jasper having a father figure in his life.

Their little boy had adapted to Ben's presence already and clamored for Ben's company all the time. Ben treated Jasper with remarkable patience and warmth, stepping into the role of father as if he'd been there all along. Mia was pleased and relieved to see their growing connection, but it only made her more sharply aware of the distance that still remained between her and Ben. But she couldn't afford to think about that now.

Right now there was another aspect of their marriage she was about to focus on. Their wedding night. Tension coiled tight in her gut. She'd thought about this long and hard in the past few days. Been forced to examine her own growing feelings for the man she had agreed to marry. If they were to be married, to provide a strong example to their son, there had to be some communication between them. This marriage had to work. Against all the odds, she wanted to be able to believe that one day her husband could fall in love with her too. Because if he didn't, what on earth was she doing giving up everything she'd worked so hard for?

Eleven

After they'd bid everyone a good-night, they walked arm in arm to Ben's suite. Once inside, Mia suddenly felt awkward. What if he didn't want their marriage to be a normal one? They hadn't exactly discussed what would happen after the ceremony. She swallowed against the sudden dryness in her throat and searched for something to say.

"That went rather well, don't you think?" she eventually managed.

"Of course," Ben replied, shrugging out of his jacket and undoing the gold cufflinks at his wrists. "Did you expect anything less?"

"No, not really. I have good staff. Once they heard we were marrying I didn't have to lift another finger. Between them and my mom they handled it perfectly."

Ben wrenched his tie loose and cast it on an easy chair beside him.

"Actually, I thought you were the perfect one tonight," he said, his voice deep and laced with a very strong note of pride. "You are truly beautiful."

Mia felt a flush of warmth spread through her at his words, all the way to her cheeks, which suddenly felt uncomfortably warm in the face of his praise. She ducked her head slightly, only to feel the heat of his fingertips at her chin as he raised her head to meet his gaze. His very heated and possessive gaze.

Her stomach knotted on a hard pull of desire. One look, one touch, was all it took and she became a melting puddle of need. Her breasts, unfettered by a bra due to the design of her gown, swelled against the chiffon, her nipples drawing into tight, aching beads.

He bent his head to kiss her and Mia met him halfway, a sound of satisfaction sounding deep in her throat as their lips meshed and his arms curved around her, pulling her hard against him, settling her hips to the clear evidence that his desire for her was as palpable as hers for him. He tore his lips from hers, his breathing ragged, his eyes burning with a heat she knew was reflected in her own.

"I would hate to damage that rather delicate gown you're wearing. Let me help you out of it before I lose all control."

His words thrilled her and imbued her with a sense of power. By his own admission, being with her put him at the verge of his control. Knowing the kind of man he was, that was an incredible power, indeed. Surely he had to have some feelings for her? Feelings that went beyond the physical.

She slowly turned around, and pointed over her shoulder to the long trail of pearl beads that tapered down her spine. A smile pulled at her lips when she heard his groan of dismay.

"I suppose it is too much to hope that those are merely for aesthetic appeal and that they hide a zipper instead?"

Mia laughed, a light bubble of joy on the air. "Yes, it is too much to hope for. I don't think zippers even became popular in women's clothing until a good ten years after this was originally made."

"*Dios,* and no one thought to modernize the thing in all this time?" he grumbled teasingly as his fingers began to deftly slide the beads free, exposing her back inch by inch.

Mia laughed again, then gasped as his fingers stroked her uncovered skin, his touch sending tiny fire-bursts through her body.

"Ah, now I understand the principle," Ben murmured and she could hear the smile on his face. "It's to torment you, not me."

Her breath caught again as she felt his lips where his fingers had lingered only seconds before.

"I think I can slip out of it now," she choked, suddenly desperate to disrobe herself of the gown.

"What? And spoil the fun? I don't think so."

It felt as if he moved even slower than before, prolonging the wait for the moment when he could hold apart the gaping edges of the back of her dress and free her from the layers of gossamer-fine silk chiffon and hand embroidery. When his hands finally touched her shoulders and gently pushed the dress off her body, she nearly wept with relief. She stepped free of the dress, eased off her ballet slippers, and stood before him in only a pair of shell pink satin tap pants and a pair of hold up stockings edged in the same shade of shell pink lace.

"*Te desero,*" Ben groaned as he reached for her, palming her naked breasts and lowering his head to place a kiss at the sensitive spot where her shoulder and her neck merged together.

"I want you, too," she whispered, tilting her head to allow him clearer access and relishing the increasing spears of pleasure that rocketed through her as she felt his tongue burn a path along her skin.

This time, it was she who took him by the hand and led him to the bedroom. She who swiftly divested him of his clothing and then stood back in a moment of silent awe as she took in the sight of him—roped muscle and power, smooth skin and silky fine hair, his arousal heavy and engorged—proudly jutting from the dark nest of hair at the apex of his thighs.

She trailed her fingers over his shoulders, down his arms and back up again, before tracing the strength of his chest, the delineation of his ribs and lower toward the scars that evidenced the damage he'd suffered. Ben grabbed her hands and pulled them back up to his chest and kissed her, slowly half walking, half dancing her to the bed.

Ben reached down and pushed his hands inside the waistband of her tap pants and began to ease them off her hips, his fingers brushing over her buttocks and down the back of her thighs. Then he bent to his good knee and slowly rolled down her stockings, pressing soft kisses against the sensitive skin of her inner thighs as he did so.

Mia's legs were trembling and her entire body ached for him. Ben stood up, rubbing his body against her. His erection bumped against her lower belly as he wrapped her in his arms and tumbled with her onto the covers, supporting her weight with his body as they sank into the mattress. Their legs instinctively entwined, their hands skimmed over one another's bodies as their lips fused in a hot wet kiss that she wished would never end.

She loved the feel of him, loved that he was now hers to

take and to touch. She placed her knees on either side of his hips and raised her torso from his so she could better enjoy him with her hands. This was different to when she massaged him. This was personal—both exhilarating and wonderful all at the same time.

Between her legs she could feel the hardness of his arousal, of his desire and need for her. He surged up against her and she fought the urge to give in to his silent demand. First, she wanted to explore him a little more—reacquaint herself with the little things that drove him wild.

She placed her lips very gently around one of his nipples, her tongue spiraling round the flat brown disk from its outer edge to its hardened tip. Her own nipples mirrored his response, in fact it was as if every cell and nerve ending in her body had tautened and honed itself to what thrilled Ben and Ben alone.

Her fingers traced a similar line on his other nipple before she coasted her hand down over his ribs. Beneath her she felt him tense as her fingers neared his scars.

"What is it?" she whispered. "Does that hurt? I thought you were okay with me touching you there."

"Just don't, okay? I don't need the reminder. Not now."

"Ben, your scars are a part of you and they certainly don't scare me or turn me off. Do you want to talk about it? The accident?"

"What, you want to counsel me now? I think I liked it better when we were making love," Ben said and tried to distract her by flipping her over onto her back and pinning her hands at her sides.

His body hovered over hers, his heat all but enveloping her and when he bent to tease her nipples with his tongue, the same way she'd teased him, she nearly lost all sense of reason. But there'd been an edge to Ben's voice that struck at her heart. She pushed back against the fog of desire that threatened to cloud her mind.

"Ben? Why won't you talk about it? Please, I only want to know you better, to understand you. We're married now. As husband and wife we need to be able to talk to one another about anything."

He shoved himself away from her and got up off the bed.

"I thought this was our wedding night, not a therapy session. Now, we can either resume where we left off, or we can sleep apart tonight. It's up to you."

Mia could only stare at him in shock. Why did he refuse to open up to her? In the face of her silence he gave his head a brief shake and turned and stalked out of the bedroom.

"Ben!" she called, suddenly gaining her voice back and getting up to run after him, but as she reached the door to the main bedroom she heard the telltale snick of the lock being turned on the second bedroom, the one that was to be Jasper's, on the other side of the suite.

Stunned, she stared at the door. Barely daring to believe that her husband had walked out on her on their wedding night and over something so trivial. Was this how it was to be between them? Her wanting to give Ben everything she had and Ben holding everything back?

Ben threw himself onto the narrow bed and stared up at the luminous star-studded ceiling, his body taut with unrelieved tension. Why did she have to try and force the issue? They'd been married less than a few hours and already she wanted to delve inside his head. Even *he* didn't want to go there. Didn't want to face the mortality that had so terrified him while he'd been locked in the metal cage that had almost become his coffin. Didn't want to face the failure he'd become. Didn't want his wife to see that side of him.

Ben knew that Mia needed him to be strong, to be able to take care of her and Jasper. Without his strength—without his power and wealth and authority to shield her from the press, to protect her family and reputation—she'd never have succumbed to his need to make her and Jasper *his*. She had resisted him for far too long, but he had her now—her and Jasper. They were the family he'd despaired of ever being able to create, and he wasn't going to do anything to risk losing them. If his wife needed him to be strong, he'd be strong. And he would allow no sign of weakness. Not even at her request.

Instead, he would focus on what he had, rather than what he'd lost. He had a wife and a son and that was all that mattered. That and ensuring Jasper and Mia had all the best of everything that life had to offer—including his unwavering protection to keep them both safe all his days.

He had fulfilled his obligations to the rest of his family, as well. The curse, such as it was, had to be broken now. *Abuelo* could rest easy. Hell, they could all rest easy.

But as he pulled the covers over his naked body he had to force himself to shut out the sense that somewhere he had still failed. As a man. As a husband. And as a father.

After a fitful night spent tossing and turning alone in her bed, Mia woke to hear rain driving against the windows. She lay in the bed and tried again to make sense of what had happened last night. Ben had shut down completely— emotionally and physically—when she'd pressed him to talk about his accident. That it had been harrowing she had no doubt, but to refuse to talk about it altogether? It just wasn't healthy. Why didn't he trust her to help him?

A sound at the bedroom door made her stiffen in the sheets. She turned to watch the door swing slowly open. Ben stood framed in the doorway, a towel wrapped around his waist.

"Did I wake you?" he asked.

"No, I was already awake."

In the gloom of early morning it was hard to make out his expression. Ben lifted a hand to rub at his eyes, the action showing her an unexpected vulnerability. He took a step into the room, hesitated, then took another until he was beside the bed.

"I'm sorry about last night. I spoke too harshly."

Mia merely watched him, her eyes searching his face to see if he really meant the words or if he was merely paying lip service. Even in the semi-dark of the room she could see anguish behind Ben's eyes. The honest emotion struck her to her core and without realizing what she was doing she reached for him, tugging him down onto the bed beside her.

Ben's arms enfolded her body and as her sheet slid away she felt the heat of his skin sear hers. Their coming together was not as intense as their first coupling had been, nor was it as loaded with heat and anticipation as last night's abortive lovemaking. Instead, it was as if there was a flow of give and take. A mingling of minds and bodies.

When her climax wrung her body, the sensation was so bittersweet that Mia felt tears spring to her eyes. As Ben reached his own pinnacle she couldn't help feeling that even though, in this moment, they were as together as a couple could be, there still lay an unbreachable gulf between them.

They drifted off to sleep in the aftermath, their bodies touching, Ben's fingers entwined in her own, and yet somehow she still felt unspeakably alone.

When she woke again, the sun was full in the sky and the rain had stopped. Outside the window, she could see the freshness of the rain-washed gardens—their brilliant greens a symbol of all that was fresh and new. She hoped that it was equally symbolic of the beginning of her marriage to Benedict del Castillo but she couldn't quite nudge away the sense that the path ahead of them would not be smooth.

Ben had already woken and she could hear him in the bathroom. If they'd been any other normal married couple, she would be in there with him by now, perhaps even sharing the shower stall, lathering up one another's bodies before indulging again in sating one another's appetites. But they weren't a normal couple, and they wouldn't be a normal family either, she realized. Not as long as there was this imbalance between them. Benedict would always have the financial upper hand. He'd always have Jasper to use as leverage over her. And once they moved to Isla Sagrado—a place she'd never even seen—the advantage would be even stronger on his side. As much as she loved her son's father, she wished their reunion could have been so very much different.

The bathroom door opened and Ben came through, dressed in his usual workout gear. Before the wedding, they'd agreed to continue with their daily routines as normal, suggesting they'd enjoy a honeymoon together once they were on Isla Sagrado. Everyone had accepted their choice without much demur but right now it just made Mia feel even more as if she was simply the means to an end in Ben's world.

"What time is Elsa bringing Jasper today?" Ben asked, confirming her belief.

"After lunch."

"I'll get him earlier, after my session today. I really want us to spend as much time together as possible before we head home."

But this is our home. Mia bit back the words that begged to be spoken and took a deep breath.

"Sure," she said.

She slid from the bed, crossed to the sliding doors of the closet and grabbed a robe. The empty hanger jangled on the rod. She sensed Ben's gaze on her body as if it was a physical caress and she wrapped the robe around her—her choice of armor flimsy, but effective.

"You cannot blame me for being eager to spend time with my son."

"No, you're right, I can't." And she was pleased that he seemed so committed to spending time with Jasper. She just wished he showed more interest in spending time with *her*—outside of bed, that is. "Would you like me to pull him from day care next week also? After all, we'll be leaving at the end of the week anyway."

Ben shook his head. "No, let's keep him in his routine for now. But I'll adjust my schedule with Andre so I can take him to day care and collect him myself."

Mia nodded her understanding.

"I'll still see you alone for my massage this afternoon, *sí?*" he asked as he bent to tie the laces on his trainers. "Your mother will still take care of Jasper in the afternoon as usual?"

She shot him a look of surprise. "Of course she will, but do you still want to go through with those?"

"They are a part of my rehabilitation and our original contract, are they not?"

Ben moved swiftly to close the distance between them. His hands slipped inside her robe to cup her breasts. The instant he touched her, her nipples beaded into tight buds against the palms of his hands and a flame of desire licked through her, warming her nether regions with a heat that shamed her. She still wanted him with every breath, with every thought, with every touch. She was hopelessly trapped in a snare of her own making.

"Yes, they are indeed," she said through suddenly dry lips.

"Then I look forward to it, and you, later."

He bent and kissed each aching tip before fastening his lips on hers in a kiss that left her in some doubt as to whether his massage this afternoon would be conducted within the realms of her professional employment—but no doubt at all that her fears had been confirmed. He wanted her physically, but that was the extent of their relationship for him.

As she watched him leave she tried to find some satisfaction in knowing that he would probably be in greater physical discomfort than she was for most of the day. Even so, it was little consolation.

When Elsa came to collect Jasper before Ben's massage she asked Mia if she could speak with her for a moment in her office. After giving Jas a packet of crayons and a coloring book to scribble in, Mia gave her mother her full attention.

"Mom, what gives? This feels like an appointment or something, rather than a mother-daughter chat," Mia said as they settled in two chairs.

"Well, this isn't exactly a social visit."

A trickle of unease ran down Mia's spine. "What do you mean, Mom? You're okay, aren't you? I thought the cardiologist was really pleased with your management and heart health the last time you saw him."

Elsa waved a graceful hand in the air. "Oh, no, don't

worry, darling. It's nothing to do with me physically. More to do with me personally, actually."

Mia stared at her mother. She looked different today. As if she was bursting with news but was working hard to keep it suppressed.

"I'd like to apply for the manager's position here at Parker's Retreat."

"What? Why?"

"Now, I know that I'm probably underqualified for the role and that it's been some time since I was in the paid workforce, but I've realized, with your marriage to Ben, that it's past time I picked myself up and dusted myself off and got on with my life. I've relied on you far too long and it's time you could rely on me again now."

Mia couldn't believe her mother's words and grasped at the only straws she could to try to sway her from this sudden and very unwelcome suggestion.

"Mom, it's a huge undertaking, and what about us? Don't you want to come to Isla Sagrado? Ben has it all arranged. I thought you were happy about that?"

"I'm sure Jasper will settle in quite nicely without me. Besides, the three of you need time to get used to one another as a family, especially if you want to make this marriage of yours work. And *you* do, don't you?"

Elsa gave her daughter a look that told Mia she had already gleaned the truth of her daughter's feelings.

"Mom—" Mia started, ready to protest.

"Look, the last thing you need is your mother hanging around and clogging up your marriage. And please don't try telling me I have no experience in running this place. I have probably more knowledge than you had when you started, plus I have the advantage of being able to pick your brain when I need help. Honestly, you've set things up so well here all it needs is a gentle hand at the tiller and it'll be smooth sailing all the way. We have a great staff, and if the forward bookings are anything to go by, I'll be far too busy to miss you all."

"You don't have to miss us—you should be coming with us, too."

Elsa shook her head. "No, darling, my mind is made up. Even if you don't let me take on the management role here at the hotel I've already decided to stay here—in Queenstown if I can't stay at Parker's Retreat. I…"

To Mia's surprise a faint blush stained her mother's cheeks, but that surprise was nothing compared to the bolt that came from the blue with her mother's next words.

"I may as well come straight out with it. Don and I have become close in the past few months and I would really like to give our friendship a chance to develop. It may come to something, or it may not. And yes, I know he's younger than me but there's something about that man that makes me feel younger, too. I gave up on so much when Reuben died, I'm not going to give up on anything else ever again."

Mia rose from her seat and rounded her desk to give her mother a huge hug, words spilling from her lips automatically, without her being truly aware of what she was saying. She knew she'd said all the right things when the smile broke out on her mother's face, but as Elsa left her office and closed the door behind her Mia felt completely cast adrift. How had she been so oblivious to the changes in her mother's life? Had she been so wrapped up in her work that she'd missed all the signs that her mother was ready to risk a new relationship and reach for happiness again?

As for what Elsa had said about taking over as manager at Parker's Retreat, Mia couldn't tell her mother "no," could she? Not when for the first time in a long time she could see that Elsa was actually looking forward to the future and had a purpose—had someone to support and nurture her. But without Elsa in Mia's corner when they moved to the other side of the world, who would be there for her?

Twelve

"Why doesn't Mommy sleep in her own bed?"

The clear tones of his son's voice roused Ben from a deep slumber. A slumber he'd earned after yet another spectacular night in his wife's arms. It didn't matter how aloof she kept herself during each day, the nights were most definitely their own. The mornings, however, were another matter.

Ben opened his eyes and fixed them on the dark-headed miniature of himself standing at the foot of their bed. Mia was doing a wonderful job of feigning sleep, her fists clenched in the sheets and holding them firmly against her naked body.

"You're awake early, *mi hijo*."

"What's a ee-kho?" Jasper scrunched up his little face in concentration as he twisted his tongue around the unfamiliar word.

"It's the word for you, my son."

"And you're my daddy!" Jasper said with great exuberance as he climbed up on the bed and settled in between his parents.

"Yes, and I'm your daddy."

Ben gathered Jas in a big hug. He knew he'd never get over the incredible sense of pride that swelled within his chest every time he saw his little boy. The knowledge that the accident that had robbed him of the choice of fatherhood had not been the final death knell on his dreams and his promise to his family was at times overwhelming. Ben couldn't wait until *Abuelo* saw Jasper in the flesh.

They'd called the old man on Skype last night. Ben had installed the necessary hardware and software on Elsa's computer, so she and Mia could stay in touch more closely when they left. Of course they'd had to try the system out and *Abuelo* had been surprised beyond belief that he could finally meet his first great-grandchild through the Internet. While *Abuelo*'s bluster over having to learn to master modern technology had been voluble, there was no mistaking the silver track of tears on the old man's face when he'd laid eyes on Jasper for the first time. Alex and Rey had hardly been able to get a look-in, let alone say "hi" to their nephew after that.

Mia had had a brief chance to talk with her friend Rina Woodville, who was engaged to Ben's brother, Rey, and who'd set up Ben's visit to Parker's Retreat, but despite Rina's huge excitement over the fact he and Mia had married and were coming to settle on Isla Sagrado, Ben sensed a deep unhappiness behind Mia's facade.

The knowledge he was personally responsible for that unhappiness had settled like a burr under his skin. He was willing to accept that he'd been hasty in his demands, forcing Mia to accept a marriage and relocation at practically a moment's notice. He'd concentrated for so long on what he would not be able to do that when the proof he'd already succeeded had come into his life, it was all he'd been able to think of.

But his choices and decisions had been far-reaching and he'd failed to fully take Mia's wishes into consideration when he'd made them. Hell, if he was honest with himself, he hadn't even tried to take Mia's wishes into consideration. The truth was a painful thing to face. He owed her everything—from the warm, living, breathing proof of his longevity currently squirming in his arms to the return of his sense of honor and integrity toward his family.

But what of his honor and integrity with respect to Mia? The knowledge that he'd failed her was a bitter truth to swallow and one he needed to face squarely. Face and make amends for.

"Come on, Jas," he whispered to his son, "let's give Mommy a lie-in and we'll go and get dressed and find out what's for breakfast today."

"I'm very hungry," Jasper informed him solemnly.

As Ben rolled from the bed and grabbed some clothes before going through to Jasper's room to help him get dressed, he resolved to find a way to make this up to Mia. She had agreed—granted, under duress—to do as he'd asked. There had to be a way to give her back that sense of identity and pride he sensed she'd felt she'd lost along the way.

An idea occurred to him as he and Jasper entered the dining room of the hotel twenty minutes later. His lips curled in satisfaction and he reached for his mobile phone so he could start to put in action the necessary moves.

In the end, the process of acquiring his surprise for Mia took a couple of days to engineer to completion. Still, Ben was well pleased when things were concluded to his satisfaction. He was even more pleased when he discussed his plans with Elsa and she agreed to take Jasper for the night so he could surprise Mia with a quiet romantic dinner for just the two of them.

After his massage that afternoon, one that actually stuck to massage and not into the activity he usually enticed her into, Ben let her into his plans. Some of them, at least. He swung himself upright on the massage table and pulled Mia in between his legs.

"Wear something special for dinner tonight, okay?"

"Special? What kind of special?" Mia asked with her head cocked to one side.

"The kind of special you can wear in public."

"Oh, I see—that kind of special. Do we have plans for tonight, then?"

"We do." He nodded. "It occurred to me that we've never actually been on a date, so I'm going to do my best to remedy that situation."

"A date? That's a little late now, isn't it?"

"It's never too late, especially when your date is as beautiful and sexy as you."

Ben punctuated his sentence with kisses along Mia's throat and collarbone.

"Are we eating here?" she asked.

"No, I thought we could give the chef the night off and head into Queenstown. Something lakeside. Your mom said she'll have Jas for the night. What do you think?"

Mia smiled and her green eyes lit with genuine joy that matched the smile on her lips.

"That sounds really nice. What time do you want me?"

"Ah, *querida,*" his voice deepened and he rocked her pelvis against his, letting her feel the incontrovertible proof that was there, "I always want you."

Her breathing hitched and her eyes glazed, the pupils growing large and dark. It was another thing they shared. She, too, was as addicted to their lovemaking as he was, and enjoyed it with an abandon she never exhibited in her day-to-day actions. He shifted his hands and gripped her hips, gently easing her away from him.

"Go, while I can still let you go. Have a relaxing soak in the tub and take your time getting ready. It's going to take me a while to be acceptable in polite company myself."

"I could always do something about that for you," she teased, her hands resting on the tops of his thighs, her fingers only inches from his aching flesh.

"Don't tempt me. I'm saving myself for later."

"It promises to be a special night, then." She smiled and for a split second Ben regretted his decision to put her off for now.

"A very special night," he concurred.

He looked at her and knew he'd made the right determination with his surprise. Beneath the generous lover he could see the signs of strain that told of the number of times she slipped from their bed at night to go over figures at the small desk in the main sitting room of their suite. He'd seen her often enough to know that despite the money he'd paid to her for his exclusive use of Parker's Retreat, the hotel and spa were still very much in their earliest stages and as such were financially vulnerable.

Yes, he was absolutely certain about his gift, surprise, whatever you wanted to call it. It was all she'd ever dreamed of and more. The anticipation of being the man to give it to her was so sweet he could almost taste it on his tongue. And he couldn't wait to see her reaction.

Queenstown's lights glittered their reflection on the lake as they approached the main center. They alighted at the wharf and Ben drew Mia's arm through his as they walked toward the restaurant he'd booked for the evening. It was only a short distance but the wind blew a freezing chill straight off the surrounding snowcapped mountains. For a moment Ben felt a deep sense of longing to be home again on Isla Sagrado's sun-baked rock, but he consoled himself that it was only a matter of days now before he had his new family back where they belonged.

The wind whipped Mia's hair across his cheek and he caught a whiff of the scented shampoo she used. The fragrance was so typical of the woman on his arm. Subtle and sweet and yet with a hint of musk that revealed the earthy lover who fulfilled him so completely. Yes, she had given him everything and tonight, in return, he would do the same.

The restaurant he'd booked was up a set of stairs and overlooked the lake with floor-to-ceiling windows. They were shown to a table with a clear view of Marine Parade and the bustling activities there. A resort town, Queenstown was a mecca to skiers and snowboarders alike at this time of year, not to mention those who came simply to drink in the wondrous natural beauty of the area or who preferred to seek their thrills in more extreme sports.

It suddenly shocked Ben to realize that he no longer classified himself in that category. Even immediately after his accident he'd been determined to regain his physical prowess so he could prove to himself he was just as good as before, if not better. He'd already ordered a new model of the car he'd crashed—beating his coast road time being in the forefront of his mind at the time.

But now he knew he'd never attempt that record again, nor would he willingly risk his life in the pursuit of yet another adrenaline rush. He had begun to understand what it must have been like for *Abuelo* to lose his only son and daughter-in-law in the avalanche that had claimed their lives, and how difficult it must have been to continue to raise Ben and his brothers with their penchant for fast cars and even faster women.

He had so much to look forward to with Jasper. He wanted to be there for all the key moments in his son's life—and not run the risk of missing anything chasing some meaningless thrill. And he wanted to be a good example to Jasper. The prospect of his son taking the wheel of an overpowered metal monster and driving it full tilt along any kind of road set his heart in ice.

What an idiot he'd been, tempting fate and railing against the strictures of family. Even more so when he'd turned his back on the very dictates that made the del Castillos who they were. Honor. Truth. Love. He'd never understood them until now. But he had time to make things right. Starting with tonight. With his gift to Mia he could honestly feel as though he'd met all his obligations as a husband and father. It would give them all a fresh, clean start.

Mia loved this restaurant. From the location, the staff, the menu, the wine list—it was everything she enjoyed about dining out. Sure it wasn't the highest of the high class but there was a welcoming sense of comfort in coming here and the massive square fireplace in the centre of the dining floor almost gave it the feel of being in someone's home, rather than in one of Queenstown's many eateries.

Ben was particularly solicitous tonight and she lapped up the attention. In fact, she almost started to believe they were a real couple. One with shared hopes and dreams for the future—right up until the moment he pulled a folded packet of papers from his pocket and laid them on the table between them.

"What's that?" she asked, and wished the words unsaid

the minute she'd uttered them. Some instinct warned her that what would come next was not what she really wanted to know.

"It's my gift to you. I may have gone about our marriage the wrong way by forcing you to agree to my conditions, but I hope this can make it up to you and to Jasper. I want you to know that I will always be there to look after you both and to make your life easier."

Easier? She didn't want him to make her life easier. She wanted him to learn to love her. Why was it that whenever they talked about their marriage or their life together, love was never even mentioned? They were already immensely compatible in the bedroom and they certainly appeared to be on the same wavelength with regard to parenting. She knew they could make a decent go of things if he'd just let down his barriers and let himself love them both as much as they already loved him.

"Don't gifts usually come in wrapping paper with bows?" she asked, trying and failing to inject a note of humor into her voice.

"Not this one, although I could order some champagne if that would make you feel more festive."

Mia shook her head. "No, no more wine for me tonight."

Ben pushed the packet across the table so it sat directly in front of her. "Then perhaps you should open this."

Mia slowly picked up the packet and squeezed the sides, tipping the contents onto the placemat. A sheaf of papers, folded lengthwise, spilled onto the mat. She picked it up and opened them, instantly recognizing the letterhead of the leading law firm in town. She quickly scanned the letter, then, with disbelief, checked the papers behind it.

Like an automaton she folded them again and put them back into the packet.

"Well?" Ben asked, his eyes alight with pleasure.

"It's the bank papers confirming my outstanding loan has been repaid in full," she said woodenly, "and a copy of the deed to Parker's Retreat showing the mortgage has been discharged. Why?"

"Why? I thought you'd be pleased. I told you I'd take care of you and Jasper, and I have. Parker's is yours free and clear now. Isn't that what you wanted?"

Mia swallowed against the solid lump of disappointment that lodged in her throat. What she wanted? Of course it was what she wanted—in time. And on her own terms. She'd been prepared to work for that. She didn't want things handed to her on a platter anymore. She'd finally learned, the hard way, the value of hard work and the sense of accomplishment that accompanied it.

What was it he'd said earlier—that he'd wanted to make her life easier? Didn't he realize that she didn't want an easy life? She'd had an easy life before—a life of extravagance without a thought to the real cost. She thought Ben had noticed that she wasn't that girl anymore. She didn't want "easy." She wanted difficult and challenging and worthwhile, so that at the end of the day, she'd know that she'd *earned* everything she had. Instead, this made her feel as if she'd been bought. Was this just another way for him to keep her under his control?

This wasn't the action of a man who was even contemplating love. It was a stamp of ownership, pure and simple.

Mia laid the packet down on the table and looked up to meet his eyes. She saw confusion reflected there, but nothing else. No hope of pleasing her. No expression of tenderness. And inside, her own hopes suffocated and died.

Ben's brows drew into a straight line, a sure sign of

his displeasure. What had he thought she'd do, she wondered—leap into his arms and thank him effusively for his generosity?

"You aren't pleased," he stated across the table, the rift between them far wider than a couple of feet of polished wood.

"That I'm now indebted to you? No."

He made a sweeping movement with one hand, slicing the air as if he could negate her denial as easily. "You are not indebted to me. This is a gift. My gift to you. I owed you this, if not more."

"You *owed* me? Funny. That'll explain why it doesn't feel like a gift. Ben, did you really think you could buy me and Jasper by buying out my loans?"

"Buy you?"

"Yes, buy me."

"Rest assured I do not consider you *bought*. I had no obligation to give you anything, Mia, but I understand how important your financial security is to you. I thought it would bring you pleasure to know you don't have to struggle anymore. To know that nothing and no one can ever threaten what you've built up." He shrugged. "It seems I was wrong. Either way, what has been done cannot be undone. The place is yours. Do with it what you will."

His dismissive tone brought tears to her eyes. All right, so he hadn't intended his surprise to be another tie of obligation, but it was clear it hadn't truly been meant as a gift. He'd chosen to throw money at the problem rather than making the effort to truly understand how much making a success of Parker's had meant to her. His "gift" showed no understanding of her—or even how much she'd consented to walk away from when she'd agreed to marry him and accompany him to his home. As far as Ben was concerned he'd done his part and that was all she'd ever get from him.

And she'd learned the hard way, money didn't buy you everything. Least of all the one thing she really wanted.

Her husband's love.

Their journey back to the hotel was completed in strained silence.

In their suite Mia missed Jasper's presence with a physical ache, but she would have to put up with waiting to see him in the morning. She went through the motions of getting ready for bed in a state of numbed shock. All of this was really hers. Lock, stock and two smoking barrels. Yet it would never feel hers again. Ben had taken the pride of making it on her own away from her, without even stopping to consider what he'd done. All he'd seen was a way to salve his own conscience.

She slid into the cool sheets on their bed as he went through to the bathroom. He'd dimmed the bedroom lights while she'd readied for bed—setting the scene for seduction, for the coupling that had become their only common ground since their wedding. But tonight she wanted none of it.

She realized that she and she alone was to blame for the situation she was in. She'd allowed Benedict to believe that she was prepared to settle for this and only this in their marriage. It was time she put things straight.

When Ben slipped into the bed behind her and reached to pull her into the curve of his body, she resisted.

"No," she said quietly.

"No?" Ben questioned, his hand sliding over her hip and up to cup her breast.

"I don't want to make love with you."

"Your body makes a liar of you, *querida*," he said, and she could hear the smile on his face.

She put her hand over his and deliberately moved it off her body before rolling over to face him.

"My physical response is one thing, Ben. But my emotional one is something else. You showed me tonight that you don't really know me at all, and when I tried to explain that to you, you simply pushed my feelings aside because they weren't what you wanted to hear. I'm sorry for you, Ben. For me, making love is not something purely for physical release—not anymore. It's supposed to be something special. Something shared by two people in love."

"Our lovemaking is always something special," he insisted.

"It's still just sex, Ben, and it's not enough for me. For some reason you think that if you throw enough money and charm at a situation it'll be okay. But there's more to life than that. *We* could have more than that.

"I'm not going to let you close yourself off from me in every way that truly matters and then compensate for whatever it is that you're putting yourself through by trading off with solving my financial situation and making me climax every night."

"I haven't heard you complain about the climaxes," he said, his voice lethally even, his dark eyes glittering in the semi-light of their room.

"No, I haven't. But they're not enough, Ben."

She rolled over in the bed and presented Ben with her back.

"Good night," she said, her voice muffled in the pillow into which she burrowed her face.

She couldn't let him see the tears that had begun to streak her cheeks, couldn't let him know that even as disappointed as he'd made her feel tonight, she still wanted him with every breath in her body. But she was worth more than that. She was worth his love, and she wasn't going to give up until she had it.

Thirteen

Ben lay still in the darkness. It had been a couple of hours since Mia's breathing had settled in the deep, slow rhythm of sleep. She'd been crying—he knew it and he couldn't do a darn thing about it. Didn't know where to begin.

Her rejection of his gift, of him, had cut far deeper than he'd wanted to admit and certainly deeper than he'd wanted to examine. But since sleep had proven completely elusive, he was forced to think about it and try to work out what exactly had gone wrong.

The evening had started so well. The dinner had been superb, the setting idyllic if a little busy for his tastes. But everything had fallen apart the moment he'd given her the papers. She'd accused him of not knowing her at all—with the implication that he did not care enough to learn about her, as if he was treating her like an expendable commodity. The very thought that she could come to that conclusion was as puzzling as it was infuriating.

He *did* care about her. That was why he had done what he had. To please her. To take care of her problems, the way he had promised himself he would. He had the advantage of money and being able to solve her financial difficulties. Why, as her husband, should he not do so? Her problems were sorted, allowing her to do with Parker's Retreat every single thing she'd ever wanted to do. Wasn't that what she wanted?

She'd given him so much—all he'd wanted was to give her something in return. Maybe she'd simply been taken by surprise. He had no doubt that when Mia had taken some time to consider the ramifications of his gift fully, she'd appreciate it better. Maybe all she needed was some space. Some time to consider what he'd done and why.

Yet as he finally drifted off into slumber a small voice at the back of his mind asked him why he still felt as if something was missing. Something vital and important. Something that lay just outside his grasp.

The morning didn't bring any fresh answers with it except a desire to return home and get his life back on its even keel as soon as possible. He left Mia sleeping, and made the necessary calls. The charter company assured him a plane would be at his disposal at Queenstown Airport in two days' time.

Two days. The thought that he'd be back home, back to normal in such a short period was invigorating. He loved the area here, but he also loved his mountains and valley. The vineyards he'd nursed to full production, the winery where he and his head winemaker explored methods to bring out the best in their grapes to produce award-winning wines year after year. Those were the challenges he looked forward to embracing once more.

Isla Sagrado meant family and tradition to him, but also, it was a place that was his. He'd made it and it was home. Most importantly, he was ready to be back there with Mia and Jasper. No more hiding away. No more facing the future alone.

A sound from the bedroom door stirred him from his reveries. Mia was awake. She came through to the sitting room, tying her robe about her waist and moving with an unconscious grace that sent a surge of longing straight to his groin. No matter what passed between them, their physical connection only grew stronger. It was more than most marriages had.

He decided to take the bull by the horns and let her know of their changed travel plans.

"I've confirmed our departure for Isla Sagrado. We'll be leaving in two days."

"Two days?"

All the color in her cheeks faded, throwing her green eyes into relief against the dark hollows that shadowed them.

"Yes. I was booked here for four weeks. That time is up and I have accomplished so much more than I'd imagined in that time. There's nothing to keep us here any longer, and the sooner you and Jasper settle into your new home the better."

"But I still have so much to do here."

"Mia, I know you were expecting another week with Elsa to complete her training, but there's nothing you can't deal with from Isla Sagrado just a easily. Let her take over now. She's itching to do so, and your being here is holding her back."

Mia flinched as if he'd physically hurt her. Twin spots of color appeared in her cheeks.

"I've made her manager. I'm letting her take over everything. How could I possibly be holding her back?"

He stood up and caught her upper arms before she could wheel away from him.

"*Querida,* I handled things last night clumsily, as I have handled almost everything between us since my arrival. I'm sorry for that, but can you blame me for wanting to take you and Jasper home and show you off to my family?"

"And can you blame me for wanting to make sure my business and my mother are taken care of first? *You're* the one going home, Ben. I'm the one *leaving* the only home I've ever known—and now you're saying I'll be leaving it sooner even than we'd planned."

Benedict sighed, but he refused to be drawn into an argument even though Mia was very obviously spoiling for one. "You are my wife, Jasper is my son. I want you both to become a part of my life, in my home country. Is that so hard to understand?"

Mia shook her head and her eyes emptied of all their fire. "No, it's not hard to understand. It just doesn't make it any easier to bear, that's all."

Mia went through the motions all day, showing her mother the online booking system, referring her to the manuals she'd had set up when the system went live if Elsa had a question—because goodness only knew Mia wouldn't be available to answer them at the drop of a hat once they were gone. It was all well and good for Ben to say she could run her business via the Internet and phone calls, but Isla Sagrado was a good twelve hours behind New Zealand, which made scheduling meetings through Skype or other contact methods problematic.

Jasper had been over the moon when she'd picked him up this morning and told him that they'd be going to Isla Sagrado in only two more sleeps. Of course, he had no concept that going there would mean leaving all this behind, maybe for good.

She wished she had that innocent expectation about the life facing them in Isla Sagrado...but even more than that, she wished she had the simple assurance that Jasper had of being loved by Ben. But it was as if Ben had encased his emotions in ice—determined not to allow himself to feel anything for her except desire. He was holding back from her, and until he could crack apart that glacier that held his heart hostage, their marriage could never truly be happy.

She'd noted a difference in him when he'd first arrived, a difference that had become more marked in the time he'd been here. It was as if he was skimming the surface of everything. Cautious about feeling too much. The only time she believed he was totally up front and honest was when they were in bed together. When, with his body, he didn't hold back on anything.

Maybe that's what she needed to do, she realized. Hoping the words she'd uttered last night could chip away at the barriers shielding his heart was futile. She needed to take positive action to make him face what she was certain was the truth.

She wasn't a quitter and she wasn't going to be a spineless bystander in her marriage either. She loved Benedict del Castillo, and one way or another she would make sure he knew it.

Ben had left a message with her earlier in the day to say that he wouldn't be at the spa for his usual massage, as he was taking Andre into town for a farewell meal and a few drinks. Andre had decided to stay on in New Zealand a little longer and see a bit of the country while he could, so he wouldn't be joining them on their trip to Isla Sagrado. Ben's plans played into her hands nicely. By the time he returned to Parker's Retreat he'd hopefully be feeling mellow and ready for what she had in store for him.

Making her preparations took a little time, but she knew it was worth it when she saw their bedroom transformed with numerous scented candles and the bed prepared for the very special massage she had planned for her husband. Jasper, tired from his second-to-last day at day care, had settled to bed early and she had no doubt he'd sleep the whole night through. All she had to do now was ready herself before Ben returned.

Mia had just finished smoothing her favorite scented body lotion into her legs when she heard the main door to their suite open. She stood up, letting the sheer rose-colored nightgown that was all she'd chosen to wear slide over her body. She put the lotion back on the dresser, her hands trembling with anticipation. Ben entered the room and fixed her with a questioning gaze, his dark brows rising ever so slightly.

"What's this?" he asked, his voice wary.

"You missed your massage today," Mia said, moving forward to take his coat from him before throwing it over the squat Queen Anne chair in the corner. "I thought with the travel we have coming up that you'd be more comfortable if we stuck with your program. But first, a spa bath."

She reached for the buttons on his shirt, undoing each one with painstaking care before pulling his shirttails from his trousers and casting the shirt to the floor. She leaned into him, inhaling softly. The scent of wood smoke—the smell most predominant in the air in town—clung to him and blended with the freshness of his cologne to make an almost unbearably sexy combination.

Taking him by the hand, Mia led him to their bathroom. More candles lit the tiled room, their reflection in the large mirrors on the walls adding to the glow of warmth and intimacy. Her hands made short work of his belt and trousers before guiding him to the bath. Scented bubbles danced on the water's surface. Mia flipped the switch for the jets, and indicated to Ben that he should occupy the body-form-shaped seat so he could gain the most benefit from their therapeutic pulsation.

"Aren't you joining me?" he asked.

Mia shook her head. "I have other plans. Tell me about your evening. Where did you go?"

While Ben told her about the pub meal he and Andre had shared, she poured a glass of red wine and sipped from it before holding the glass to his lips so he could drink from it also—his lips partaking of the ruby liquid from exactly the same spot her own lips had rested upon. He watched her like a hawk, a flush spreading across his cheeks as she licked a tiny droplet of wine from the edge of the glass before offering it back to him.

"What's this about Mia?" he growled. "Last night you didn't want a bar of me."

Mia considered her words carefully. "I was overemotional. I'm sorry. If it's any consolation, refusing you last night punished me as much as you."

"It's no consolation at all. I still cannot understand why you were so upset. So angry."

And that was the problem, she thought. He couldn't conceive of the fact that making her own way here was so important, so vital to her identity and for her own need to make amends for the strain she'd caused her father. But had she been unfair, expecting him to automatically understand? He didn't know what she had been through—and as much as she accused him of being closed off emotionally, she hadn't fully shared herself, either. That would change right now.

"I think, for you to understand that, you'd really have

to walk in my shoes over the past three and a half years. I went from having everything, and working for none of it—taking it all for granted—to having nothing and having to claw it all back."

"Wouldn't most people welcome the prospect of having all their worries solved for them?"

"Most people, yes," she conceded.

"But not you."

"No, not me, because for the first time in my life I actually appreciated how hard I had to work for things and I deeply regret how complacent I'd become over it all. Sure, it wasn't easy, but it redefined me. Made me realize how shallow my life had been before. Having you hand everything back to me on a platter again, well, it just made me feel as if you still saw me as that girl you met the first time. Not the woman I am now."

The woman who loves you. The words echoed in her heart, but she was too afraid to say them aloud.

There was a pause while Ben considered this before he replied. "I think I can understand to a degree. It's probably why my brothers and I have chosen very different paths to expand in our family's business portfolios. We complement one another, but we're each our own master—we do things our own way. That way, we're each able to make our own mark and know that our achievements are uniquely ours."

Ben fell silent and Mia wondered whether she'd said too much, or even too little. She passed Ben the wine goblet and watched as he took another sip before taking it back, then she hit the button that stopped the jets in the spa bath.

"I think that's enough for now," she said and stood to get a large fluffy white towel for him.

Ben stood and she watched the rivulets of water run off his body and into the tub. Once he was out of the bath she moved closer and began to dry him off, taking her time, stroking the thick toweling in firm sweeps across his back and down over his buttocks before drying the backs of his legs. Then she gave her attention to his chest, his abdomen, his groin.

He was fully aroused by the time she was finished, but when he reached for her she gently shook her head.

"Not yet. As I said, I have plans for you. Come over by the bed," she whispered with a smile before pulling away.

She guided him facedown onto the bed and then straddled his legs and reached for the lotion she'd prepared earlier, one infused with heady, exotic scents. She stroked the lotion into his skin in long, flowing movements that started at the base of his spine and worked up his back.

As her hands smoothed over his shoulders, she felt the tension knotted there and doubled her efforts, working into the tissue before lightly skimming away, replacing her hands with butterfly light kisses before returning again with her fingers. Once she was satisfied he was completely relaxed she shifted to the foot of the bed and gave his legs the same attention. As she bent to kiss behind his knees she finally allowed herself to acknowledge the slow, steady burn uncoiling from deep inside her.

With each forward motion her breasts swung against her night gown—fuller, heavier. The sheer silk caressed her nipples with the softness of a lover's touch, but it wasn't enough. She wanted more. She wanted Ben. She forced herself to calm down, to focus on what she wanted for the long term, rather than what she wanted right now.

She rose up onto her knees, shifting her weight fully off him for the moment.

"Roll over, Ben," she instructed, surprised to hear the strain in her voice.

Slowly he turned over, baring his body to her, all of his body. She kept her eyes very firmly on his, knowing how he felt about the scars that crisscrossed his abdomen, understanding on an unspoken level that, more than anything, it was their constant reminder of his mistake that made him hate them so.

Ben's eyes were dark, the blackness of his pupils consuming his irises, the flicker of candlelight reflected in their bottomless depths.

Again Mia straddled his thighs, teasingly avoiding his arousal. She leaned forward to massage his chest, her hands still soft with lotion, and felt his erection buck against her as her nightgown stroked his sensitive skin.

Still she maintained eye contact, although it became more and more of a challenge to her with every movement she made. Avoiding his abdomen completely, she shifted her hands to the top of Ben's thighs, trickling her fingers higher until they coasted along the shape of his hips then behind to his buttocks and back again.

Without letting her gaze waver she lowered herself until her breath shimmered over his swollen shaft. He'd never allowed her this intimacy before. Every time they'd been together he'd been all about her pleasure before taking his own. With his hands and his tongue, he'd wrought the ultimate pleasure upon her. Now she wanted to do the same for him.

Fully expecting a protest, she kissed the tip of him. A bead of moisture appeared and she instinctively darted her tongue out to taste him. Ben groaned at the head of the bed, indistinguishable words spilling from his mouth, his hands fisted in the sheets.

An overwhelming sense of power and control suffused her, together with the knowledge that she was only doing this with the gift of his permission. That he wanted her to be with him, to do this to him, as much as she did herself.

Mia let her lips skim the smoothly swollen head, each time following up with the barest of touches with her tongue. He writhed beneath her, and she took his stretch of control as her signal. She closed her mouth over him, swirling her tongue around him and tasting his essence. She changed her position slightly so she could take him more deeply, driving him nearly wild with the alternate swirling and sucking of her tongue and mouth.

She felt his shaft thicken even more and became aware of her answering moisture pooling between her legs. She ached for him, ached to take him inside her and drive them both to completion. Mia let go of him and arched herself upward, pulling off her nightgown as she did so.

Ben's eyes flew open as she positioned herself above him, felt the hard nub of him at her entrance. She eased her hips forward and back across his sensitive flesh, coating him with her moisture, driving herself mad at the same time.

His hands unfurled in the covers and gripped her hips, halting her teasing. She placed her own hands over his and slowly lowered her body, taking him inside her in a slow, steady glide. She gasped as her body stretched and filled. This was more than sex, more than making love. It was a total unity of body and spirit.

Could he feel it, too? Did his heart swell and contract in time with the movement of their bodies the way hers did?

She braced her hands on his shoulders, felt his hands reach up and cup her breasts, his thumbs abrading their taut peaks, his finger gently kneading the full soft flesh.

Her orgasm took her by surprise, convulsing through her in a streak of lightning, making her body tremble, her inner muscles repeatedly clench and release. Beneath her, Ben thrust his hips upward, a harsh groan rippling from his throat as his body reached its zenith and triggered off yet another burst of pleasure to pulse through her body.

She collapsed, boneless, onto his prone form, her heart thudding in her chest. As aftershocks continued to pulse through her she found the courage to say the words her heart had held hostage.

"I love you, Ben."

Underneath her, she felt his body tense; his hands stilled their gentle stroking. She waited for his response. For the words that would answer her declaration. But only silence hung in the air surrounding them.

Regret pierced her like a frozen arrow. It didn't matter what she did, or said, he would never let her past the barriers he'd built between himself and the world. Mia rolled off him and moved to the edge of the bed, pulling the covers up over her. Ben shifted to lie behind her, his body spooning hers. But the physical warmth that emanated from him couldn't touch the cold, lonely place in her chest where her heart had beaten for him.

Fourteen

Her words were still in his head in the morning as he eased himself from the bed and went into the bathroom to shower.

I love you, Ben.

It had shocked him to realize how much her words had meant to him, and he knew she'd expected something in return. She'd deserved far more than the silence he'd given her. But love? He didn't even think he was capable of love anymore. He certainly didn't deserve it. Not from her. She deserved so much better—deserved a man undamaged by life who could give her every gift of his love.

He'd thought it would be enough to make her world right again, ensure that she and Jasper were provided for. But now he understood why she'd been so offended by his gift earlier. That wasn't what she wanted from him—she wasn't interested in gifts that money could buy. What she wanted was his love. And he wasn't sure he could give it.

I love you, Ben.

The words cascaded over him like the hot water of the shower jets. He let his head rest on the shower wall, allowing the water to flow down his back. Since his crash he'd existed in a state of alternating anger and frustration, both directed very firmly at himself. He'd taken unnecessary risks, and he'd paid the price. But now, it seemed, everyone around him had to pay the price, too, even Mia.

She was a great mother to Jasper and she deserved the chance to have more children if she wanted to. With him she didn't even have that choice. She might say she loved him now, but what of the future? It wasn't as easy as he'd thought it would be all along—simply transplanting her into his world, his life. Now that he understood what drove and motivated her, he wondered how she could continue to love him if he ripped her away from everything she held dear—everything she'd worked so hard for.

She had a purpose here, one he finally understood. He'd scoffed when she'd said she'd changed from the girl he'd first met. But he'd been an arrogant fool. She'd changed far more than she realized. Become a woman worthy of the kind of love and support a proper husband should give her. But he didn't have it in him to be that man, which meant only one thing. He had to let her go. He had to return to Isla Sagrado without her, without Jasper. It was the only way he could live with himself.

And if the curse proved to be true after all—if he was punished for his failure to treat her with the honor, honesty and love that she deserved—well, he could only hope that his respect for his family and his determination to have their wishes honored, even if he'd failed, would be enough to satisfy the governess. He'd finally admitted the truth to himself about his failings, and while he didn't deserve

Mia's love, perhaps the fact she thought him worthy of it would be enough.

But despite all his rationalizations, Ben knew he would be breaking her heart when he left, and that knowledge cut him deep. Still, he was certain she'd be better off without him. And that was the only thing that gave him the strength to make this choice.

He snapped off the shower faucets and stepped out of the stall, drying himself swiftly. The condensation cleared rapidly on the heated bathroom mirrors and he was faced with his own reflection, his eyes riveted on the external evidence of the damage wrought on his body by his own stupidity. He'd robbed himself of the future he'd always believed would be his. He couldn't do the same to Mia.

Ben went silently into the bedroom, quickly dressed and let himself out of the room. He'd tell her of his decision later today, when Jasper was at day care. The preschool was having a farewell party for Jas, but he couldn't stop that. Suffice that Jas would be back there on Monday again, after the weekend. He hoped that it wouldn't confuse the little boy too much, and he reminded himself that children were resilient and adapted to change far more easily than most adults.

As he closed the bedroom door behind him he cast a lingering look over the woman who had given him so very much—pleasure of unspeakable heights, her love, his son—and he knew he was doing the right thing for them all.

Mia stared at Ben in total shock. Her skin felt too tight for her body, her face frozen, her hands clenched into fists.

"You what?"

"You heard me, Mia. I'll be leaving for Isla Sagrado on my own tomorrow. It's for the best."

"For the best? What on earth are you talking about? We're married, husband and wife, we're supposed to be together, aren't we? And what about Jasper? Do you honestly mean to say that after everything you've done to prove he's your son, and in marrying me, that you're going to just walk away from us?"

She heard her pitch rise higher and higher, heard the wobble in her voice that foretold of the tears burning at the back of her eyes, but she could control none of it. All she knew right at this moment was that the man she loved, the father of her son, had told her he was leaving without them.

In that moment all her scruples about leaving New Zealand vanished. What had she been thinking, living her life as if all that mattered was redeeming the past? The past was over and done with, and nothing she did could change that. The only thing that mattered now was finding a life that could make her happy and seizing on to it with everything she had. For her, happiness meant spending the rest of her life with the man she loved. Was the chance of that now gone forever? What had happened to make him change his mind so abruptly?

She'd slept late this morning and so had Jasper, and it'd been a mad dash to get him ready on time for his last day at day care. Once she'd waved him off on the boat with Elsa she'd gone to her office to finalize some paperwork, and that's where Ben had found her half an hour later.

Her life had seemed so normal a few moments ago—now it was spiraling crazily out of control. She stared in disbelief at the man she'd married. The man who'd turned into a total stranger before her very eyes.

"I've made my decision. I'm not changing it, Mia. You should be happy."

"*You've* made *your* decision?" She shook her head in disbelief. "We're married, Ben. You can't just walk away from that."

"We can remain married, until you meet someone else."

His face remained impassive, but she saw a swiftly veiled hint of pain reflected in the depths of his eyes.

"Until I meet someone else," she repeated, her voice flat. "I told you last night that I love you, Ben. I don't want anyone else, and nor does Jasper. He loves his daddy, too. You can't do this to us."

"It's for the best. In time, I'm sure you'll see that."

Ben remained adamant, his arms crossed over his torso, his feet firmly planted shoulder-width apart—holding his metaphorical ground against her, if not his physical one.

"Why? Why are you doing this to us?"

Her voice finally broke and the dam holding back her tears did so, also. They slid, unchecked, down her pale cheeks. Ben's face twisted, and he looked away and took a deep breath. When he spoke his voice was painstakingly controlled.

"I was wrong to treat you as I did—with no consideration for you or your dreams and hopes for the future. I shouldn't have tried to take those opportunities away from you. I have no place in that future. You deserve to achieve everything you set out to do. At least now that can happen."

But you're doing the same thing now! Mia wanted to shout at him, but she knew the words would fall upon deaf ears. He had made up his mind and now he was leaving. If he'd offered her the same opportunity a couple of weeks ago she would have grabbed at it with both hands—but right now she felt as if her life was being torn in two.

"What about your grandfather? What about the curse you told me about?"

"I will explain it all to *Abuelo*. My—" he hesitated a moment and swallowed before continuing "—infertility, everything. He has a great-grandson, I hope that is enough for him to understand that his obsession with the curse was just that, an obsession and not the truth. If not, well, he's an old man and can be forgiven for some irrationality from time to time."

"So that's it, then?" Mia couldn't believe his words. Not after everything they'd gone through to get to this point.

"*Sí*. I will stay in a hotel in Queenstown tonight and be at the airport early tomorrow for my flight. Don is waiting with the boat for me now. My luggage is already on board and I've taken the liberty of having your and Jasper's things moved back into your apartment. I'm sure the sooner you both settle back into your old routine the better for everyone."

Her head whirled. He'd planned that far ahead already? Only yesterday they were going to undertake this journey together, and now he was leaving without them? She struggled for something to say, anything that would hold him here for a moment longer—anything that might give her a chance to make him change his mind.

"Will you at least say goodbye to Jasper before you leave?"

"I think it's best if I don't. He might be upset and he'll adjust faster the sooner I'm not here, I'm sure. There's one favor I would ask of you, though. I will understand if you don't wish to grant it but I beg of you, please bring Jasper to Isla Sagrado for his third birthday. My family has missed his birth and two birthdays already. I will arrange everything for you from my end and I would be grateful if we could all be together for the occasion."

"You could have us there permanently, Ben. We could be leaving with you tomorrow."

"No, I can't do that to you, Mia. I've been a selfish fool. At least allow me this—let me give you your life back, the life you deserve."

Mia's throat closed on the lump of emotion that swelled there, and as Ben turned to go she reached out and grabbed him by the arm.

"So, this is it? Won't you even kiss me goodbye?"

He shook his head and gently uncurled her fingers from his arm.

"Mia, I know how much this is hurting you. I have no wish to prolong your pain for any longer than absolutely necessary. I will let you know when I arrive back on Isla Sagrado. Perhaps you'll let Jasper talk to me online from time to time, so he doesn't forget me completely?"

Mia pushed her fist to her lips, afraid that if she opened her mouth something that sounded completely inhuman would come out. Incapable of words, she nodded, then watched helplessly as Ben walked away. Taking her broken heart with him.

"What do you mean he's gone?" Elsa asked, her voice confused.

"Just that, Mom. He's going back without us. He doesn't want us anymore."

"I'm sure that's not true," her mother said. "He might not know it or even want to admit it, but I'm sure he loves you. Can't you follow him?"

"And what? Face his rejection again? Even I can only take so much, and it's not as if I only have myself to consider."

Mia looked across the room to where Jasper played with

his toys, totally and happily absorbed in his imaginary world.

"Have you told him yet?"

"No, I can't bring myself to, not when I still feel so raw myself. Maybe tomorrow. He'll probably start asking questions by then."

Elsa rose from her seat at the dining table where she and Mia had both merely chased their dinner around their plates. She bent to give her daughter a hug.

"What am I going to do, Mom?" Mia asked, her voice fracturing on the words.

"Take each day as it comes, my darling. It's the only thing you can do."

With her mother's words ringing in her ears, Mia readied Jasper for bed, going through the motions without really paying attention. By the time she slid into the sheets of her own bed, in her own room, she knew that sleep would be the last thing to happen tonight. Her mind replayed that final scene with Ben, over and over, and tears slid unheeded from her eyes, soaking into her pillow.

Morning brought no ease to her sorrow and Mia found herself watching the skies for a glimpse of the private jet that would be taking off any time now and taking Ben back to Isla Sagrado. After giving Jas his breakfast she decided to take him with her over to the hotel, so she could finalize arrangements for a group booking of writers from Australia due to arrive early next week on a retreat. She'd have her full complement of staff back on deck come Monday, and she wanted to be sure everything would be spot on for the group when they arrived.

She was intercepted by Elsa and Don, who suggested they take Jasper to the Queenstown Gardens and lunch in town. While she would have preferred the distraction of his company, Mia agreed. At least it would mean it would be that much longer before he started asking questions about Ben. The prospect of being alone with her thoughts was a daunting one, but in her office she threw herself into the itinerary, complete with spa sessions, for the incoming group.

She'd been working for about an hour when a sound outside her office distracted her. She paid it no mind, knowing that the cleaners were due to give the admin area a bit of a spruce-up this weekend before the hotel resumed its usual operations, and she didn't even lift her head when she heard the knock at her office door.

"Come in," she said absently.

Briefly she wondered who on earth would be bothering her today—her office had already been vacuumed and dusted and her plants watered. She wasn't even supposed to be here, let alone working. She was supposed to be on her way to Isla Sagrado, she reminded herself with a sharp pang of regret.

"Back to work, already?"

Ben's deep voice resonated on the air, making her stop in her work and lift her head in a sharp movement. She couldn't believe her eyes. He stood in front of her—large as life and, despite the hollows under his eyes, twice as gorgeous. She forced herself to take a breath, and then another one, while her hands gripped the edges of her desk. She hardly dared to move in case he'd disappear like an apparition.

"Mia, are you okay?" Ben moved swiftly around the desk and pulled her to her feet. "I'm sorry. I didn't mean to shock you."

"You're back," she stated blankly.

"*Querida*, I couldn't leave."

Words still failed her, but the warmth of his hands holding hers was unbelievably real.

"I've been a complete fool. I thought I could walk away from you, let you have your life back. But I'm so much more selfish than that. I don't want to let you go. I want you and Jasper in my life every day, not just for visits every so often throughout a year, and I'll be damned if I let anyone else have you either."

Mia finally found her voice. "Why did you go? I told you I love you, Ben. How could you leave me, us, like that?"

He closed his eyes for a moment and when he opened them she could see the deep remorse reflected in them.

"I never wanted to cause you more pain. In my arrogance I thought it would be best for us to break cleanly, before you learned to hate me all over again."

"Ben, I've never hated you. I could never—"

"I know that—I understand now. Love isn't like that, is it?" He gave her a rueful smile. "I was afraid to love you. Afraid that one day you'd regret marrying me and wish for more than I offered you. More children, raising them here at Parker's Retreat, your work. I thought it would be an easy thing to walk away and leave you to your world, but I am a weak man, Mia. I want it all. I want you, I want Jasper—I want us to have a life together.

"I didn't want to love you, to open myself up to being vulnerable to you." He shook his head. "How could I have been such an idiot? I thought I was undeserving of your love, that I wasn't strong enough—man enough. But from the moment I left here yesterday I hurt—a pain far worse than I endured after my accident—and it is the kind of hurt that I know I will bear for the rest of my life, unless you can forgive me for being such an idiot, for hurting you so badly."

Mia gripped Ben's hands tightly, afraid to let him go in case they'd somehow lose this precious connection between them. A connection she wanted with all her heart. "Ben, there's nothing to forgive. I love you. I will always love you. I don't care if we can't have any more children. Okay, to be totally honest, and you deserve my total honesty, I am sorry that we can't give Jasper a brother or sister but I can accept that if I have *you*. We have a beautiful, strong and healthy son. He's a gift for us both, all the more precious because he will always be our only child. I don't know if I'll ever fully understand what drove you away from us—I'm just glad you're back."

She reached up and pressed her lips to his, kissing him with both the pent-up love inside her and relief that he had returned. When Ben broke their kiss and leaned his forehead against hers they were both breathing unevenly.

"I've learned a powerful lesson, Mia. I always thought a man's strength was tied into his masculinity. In his prowess as a male of the species and all that it entailed. It's part of what drove me to test myself more every time I tried something—physically, mentally, emotionally. And each time I'd succeed, I'd convince myself I was that much stronger, that much better as a man. Until my accident. It made me accept that when all is said and done, I'm *only* a man. A man with failings—even more so now as a result of that crash.

"We have a creed in our family—'Honor, Truth, Love.' They're the very words the governess cursed us to learn to uphold three hundred years ago and I'm ashamed that not even nearly losing my life made me grasp just how important that ethos, and living it, is. It took nearly losing you to make me appreciate just how important those words are to me, to my life—to *our* life together.

"I love you, Mia. With all that I am, failings and all, I love you. And I promise you, I will honor you all my life, with the truth always between us and with my undying love for you and Jasper."

Mia's heart swelled as she heard the words she'd waited so long to hear from his lips. A tremulous smile spread across her face.

"Does this mean we'll be leaving for Isla Sagrado together now?" she asked, mentally repacking all those things that had been unpacked back in her apartment only yesterday.

"No."

She reeled back from him, stunned at his monosyllabic reply.

"No? What do you mean, no? How can you say you love me in one breath and then say we can't come with you to Isla Sagrado in the next? You can't do that to me, Ben. You can't."

He reached for her and dragged her stiff and unwilling body back into the cradle of his arms.

"I mean that if you'll let me, I want to stay here. With you and Jasper. I can do what I do anywhere in the world, Mia. Goodness knows my vineyard and winery have managed quite nicely without me since my accident and they will continue to do so. But what I can't have anywhere in the world is the knowledge that you're fulfilling the dreams and goals you've set for yourself here. So here is where we belong until you say otherwise.

"I love you and Jasper more than anything in the world. I could no more walk away from you than I could stop breathing. I nearly lost my life once before, Mia, and I didn't believe I could ever feel that scared or that vulnerable again. But I am now. You and Jasper are my life now. Without you both I am nothing, no one. I'm not prepared to risk it all again. I've been forced to face some hard lessons in my life recently and at least I can say I have learned from them. I know now that my strength, such as it is, is not tied up in my achievements or my fertility or how fast I can drive a car. My strength is tied to my love for you and for our son. Will you let me stay with you?"

Mia raised her hands and her fingers traced the defined planes of Ben's features. Features of the man she knew she would love for every day of the rest of her life.

"I will never let you go again, Benedict del Castillo. You're my husband, the father of my son, and the only man I will ever love. I don't care where we live—home will be any place that I share with you."

Joy filled her, replacing the remnants of sorrow, overwhelming the disappointments and the fears she'd borne in the past. And she knew, without a shadow of a doubt, that her future—*their* future—was one they could step toward with a full heart and without hesitation.

Epilogue

Their commitment ceremony in the chapel at the castillo last night had been beautiful—it was a moment Ben knew he'd treasure for the rest of his life. Insisting they were already married, Mia hadn't wanted the pomp involved in a second full wedding here on Isla Sagrado, where they'd brought Jasper and his new family face-to-face for the first time, but she'd acceded to his wish to reaffirm his promises to her with his family as witness.

Seeing the delight on *Abuelo*'s face had made the struggle of the previous months worthwhile. Knowing he'd done his part and finally brought joy to his grandfather's heart, and peace to his soul, was priceless. Having done so was more precious than any gift on earth, and had been more enriching than he'd imagined.

In the chapel, Ben had felt the weight of expectation of nine generations of del Castillos upon him as he'd exchanged vows with Mia in front of their family, in the private ceremony that had held more meaning for them both than the wedding he'd forced upon them both only weeks ago.

And now, walking with Mia and Jasper, together with his brothers and their chosen life partners, on the beach below the castillo, Ben finally felt at peace with his world.

"Rey, I think we should can the big wedding and just have something small in the chapel," Rina said to her fiancé, breaking in to Ben's thoughts.

"Are you sure you want that? You already have everything planned ahead," Reynard responded, bringing her hand to his lips and kissing her knuckles.

"I know, I know. Old habits die hard, but since last night I've been thinking that it would mean more to me if we married at the castillo. Kept it small and intimate and made it sooner. Ben and Mia's ceremony was so beautiful, so *theirs,* you know? I want that for us, too."

"Alex and I had our own private ceremony in the chapel, just the two of us," Loren, Alex's wife, admitted in her gentle voice. "It was very special and uniquely ours. I think you're making a good decision. When all is said and done, it's between the two of you. That's what's most important, yes?"

Out the corner of his eye Ben saw Alex squeeze Loren to his side, silently affirming her words.

Reynard gave his fiancée a loving look that told her she could do whatever she wanted as long as he remained at her side.

"You do what you need to." He smiled. "All I want is this engagement to be over so we can be husband and wife. I can't believe my little brother beat us to the punch."

Ben laughed. "I always was faster than you, Rey. About time you admitted it."

"Never!" Rey teased in return. "But hey, I'm really

happy for you, Ben. A wife *and* a son? I think we can safely say the curse is well and truly lifted, don't you?"

As he and Alex concurred, Ben's heart swelled. He really had it all now.

"Where is Jas?" Mia asked, her voice suddenly strained with a note of anxiety.

Ben cast his eyes up the beach. They were nearing the headland upon which the castillo perched and the beach curved away from them, its rough shores obscured from their view. He couldn't see Jasper anywhere.

"He wouldn't have gone near the water's edge, would he?" Loren asked, a corresponding thread of concern creeping into her words.

"No, he knows better than that. He's grown up around water, but he's not used to waves such as you have here. If a rogue wave has washed up…" Mia's voice trailed off.

In unspoken agreement the three brothers broke into a run, the women close behind, all of them pounding along the sand until they reached the headland.

"There he is," shouted Alex. "He's all right."

Ben didn't halt until he reached Jasper, swooping his precious boy into his arms and holding him close, silently vowing he would never let him out of his sight again.

"You gave me a scare, *mi hijo*. Stay where I can see you next time, okay?"

"Okay, Daddy," Jasper said with a smile that rocketed straight to Ben's heart.

As he settled his son back on the sand and the women caught up, he noticed that Jasper clutched something in one hand.

"What's that you have there?" he asked, holding out his hand.

Jasper uncurled his pudgy fingers, revealing a tangle of heavy gold chain with something large and solid nestled amongst it. Ben's blood ran cold. *Dios!* It was *La Verdad del Corazon*. The Heart's Truth. The necklace the governess had cast from the cliffs so very long ago. He reached out and took the necklace from Jasper's hand, letting it swing in the air in front of him, the massive heart-shaped ruby surprisingly clean and glowing brilliantly in the sunlight.

Both Alex's and Rey's faces were white with shock.

"Is that what I think it is?" Rey asked, his voice little more than a whisper.

"*Sí,*" Alex replied, lost for more words.

Mia knelt in the sand next to Jas.

"Where did you find that, darling?"

"The smiling lady gave it to me," he answered, looking fretfully from one adult to the other, his little face beginning to crumble as he picked up the vibes that strained between them.

Ben squatted next to Mia.

"It's okay, Jas. We're just surprised, that's all. Tell me about the lady. Where did she come from?"

Jasper pointed to the waves crashing on the rocks on the water's edge. "Over there, from the water. Daddy, where's she gone now?"

Ben smiled and hugged Jas to him. "I can't see her, my boy. Maybe she's gone home now, to be at rest."

He slowly straightened and exchanged a look with his brothers. While none of them said a word, each held his woman a little closer. The irrefutable proof that the curse was finally broken lifted an unseen weight from their shoulders, enriching them with the promise of a happy future for them all, forevermore.

On the cliff top high above the beach a woman watched the family below. Finally, a true family in every sense of the word. She lifted both hands to her lips, then threw her arms wide to encompass them in her imaginary embrace before fading away, her face serene and smiling, her soul at peace at last.

* * * * *

MILLS & BOON® Book Club
2 Free Books!

Join the Mills & Boon Book Club

Want to read more **Desire**™ books? We're offering you **2 more** absolutely **FREE!**

We'll also treat you to these fabulous extras:

- 🌹 Books up to 2 months ahead of shops

- 🌹 FREE home delivery

- 🌹 Bonus books with our special rewards scheme

- 🌹 Exclusive offers and much more!

Get your free books now!

Visit us Online

Find out more at
www.millsandboon.co.uk/freebookoffer

SUBS/ONLINE/D

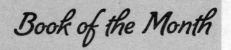

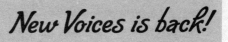

Top Writing Tips from Mills & Boon Editors

Starts 13th September!

We're looking for talented new authors and if you've got a romance bubbling away in your head we want to hear from you! But before you put pen to paper, here are some top tips…

Understand what our readers want: Do your research! Read as many of the current titles as you can and get to know the different series with our guidelines on www.millsandboon.co.uk.

Love your characters: Readers follow their emotional journey to falling in love. Focus on this, not elaborate, weird and wonderful plots.

Make the reader want to walk in your heroine's shoes: She should be believable, someone your reader can identify with. Explore her life, her triumphs, hopes, dreams. She doesn't need to be perfect—just perfect for your hero…she can have flaws just like the rest of us!

The reader should fall in love with your hero! Mr Darcy from *Pride and Prejudice*, Russell Crowe in *Gladiator* or Daniel Craig as James Bond are all gorgeous in different ways. Have your favourite hero in mind when you're writing and get inspired!

Emotional conflict: Just as real-life relationships have ups and downs, so do the heroes and heroines in novels. Conflict between the two main characters generates emotional and sensual tension.

Have your say or enter New Voices at:
www.romanceisnotdead.com

Visit us Online

NEWVOICESTIPS/A

Avoiding the dreaded cliché

Open your story book with a bang—hook your reader in on the first page and show them instantly that this story is unique.

A successful writer can use a conventional theme and twist it to deliver something with real wow factor!

Once you've established the direction of your story, bring in fresh takes and new twists to these traditional storylines.

Here are four things to remember:

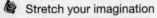 Stretch your imagination

🌹 Stay true to the genre

🌹 It's all about the characters—start with them, not the plot!

🌹 M&B is about creating fantasy out of reality. Surprise us with your characters, stories and ideas!

So whether it's a marriage of convenience story, a secret baby theme, a traumatic past or a blackmail story, make sure you add your own unique sparkle which will make your readers come back for more!

Good luck with your writing!

We look forward to meeting your fabulous heroines and drop-dead gorgeous heroes!

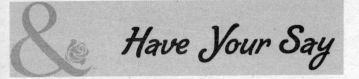

Have Your Say

You've just finished your book. So what did you think?

We'd love to hear your thoughts on our 'Have your say' online panel
www.millsandboon.co.uk/haveyoursay

- 🌹 Easy to use
- 🌹 Short questionnaire
- 🌹 Chance to win Mills & Boon® goodies